The Lost Girl

CAROL DRINKWATER

PENGUIN BOOKS

PENGUIN BOOKS

UK | USA | Canada | Ireland | Australia
India | New Zealand | South Africa

Penguin Books is part of the Penguin Random House group of companies
whose addresses can be found at global.penguinrandomhouse.com

First published by Michael Joseph 2017
Published in Penguin Books 2018

001

Copyright © Carol Drinkwater, 2017

The moral right of the author has been asserted

Set in 12.82/15.06 pt Garamond MT Std
Typeset by Jouve (UK), Milton Keynes
Printed in Great Britain by Clays Ltd, St Ives plc

A CIP catalogue record for this book is available from the British Library

ISBN: 978–0–718–18311–0

www.greenpenguin.co.uk

MIX
Paper from
responsible sources
FSC® C018179

Penguin Random House is committed to a
sustainable future for our business, our readers
and our planet. This book is made from Forest
Stewardship Council® certified paper.

PENGUIN BOOKS

The Lost Girl

Carol Drinkwater is a multi-award-winning actress who is best known for her portrayal of Helen Herriot in the BBC television series *All Creatures Great and Small*. She is also the author of over twenty books, both fiction and non-fiction. Her quartet of memoirs set on her olive farm in the south of France have sold over a million copies worldwide and her solo journey round the Mediterranean in search of the Olive tree's mythical secrets inspired a five-part documentary film series, *The Olive Route*.

Carol lives in the south of France where she is writing her next novel.

In loving memory of Phyllis Drinkwater, my wonderful
mother, best friend and guardian angel.
I miss you so.
1924–2016

Each man in his darkness grapples towards his light

Les Contemplations, Victor Hugo

Prologue

Charles Gilliard was whistling as he strolled the Parisian avenue, heading in an easterly direction. Glancing to and fro, enjoying all that was going on around him on that fine spring morning, he was relishing the day that lay ahead of him to do with as he pleased. He was suffering no headache; he had risen early after sleeping soundly, which was to say relatively peacefully and without his recurrent nightmares. No reason, then, not to be in an optimistic frame of mind. The city was pulsing with life: the boulevards were busy; the chestnuts were coming into bud; a merry-go-round of automobiles was tooting and turning as though the engines themselves were in song. Although he was grateful for what had come out of the war – he had done well for himself during those years of silence, of wartime emptiness and repression – it lifted his spirits to witness the capital's renaissance. Paris reawakening. Peace time. The jazz clubs, the gaiety, the night life. Dancing be-bop at the Caveau de la Huchette over on the Left Bank; drinking with the Americans who had brought a light-heartedness and latitude to the liberated city. The pretty girls, the free and easy lifestyle. Life was becoming *cool*. An excellent description, thought Charlie, who had sweated it out for too long now.

He was marvelling, too, at the continuance of his own good fortune, even beyond those years of occupation. Surely, though, such luck could not continue for ever. His opportunities for making money were slowing down. The black-market possibilities for income had been drying up in his field since the end of the war. In any case, he had long ago grown tired of such a fly-by-night existence. And, more to the point, the money he had stashed away could not be eked out for more than another year or two. It was unwise of him to fritter it away on all-night boogying. He should invest in some fresh clothes, give some serious thought to his future, find gainful employment. The grey suit he was wearing was beginning to look shabby, threadbare about the cuffs. It would not serve him for much longer. Fortunately, he still had access to the apartment he had installed himself in and made his home. Its owner was a woman – that much he had gleaned – a Jewess, Madame Friedlander. Where she had fled to, he had failed to discover. There were no clues, or none that he had found left lying about in the high-ceilinged dusty rooms. Or, most importantly, any information about when she might return to reclaim her home and pick up the threads of her life. Of course, there was always the possibility that she was dead, killed in a raid as she fled the city, or from natural causes, or had been arrested and imprisoned in one of those atrocious camps everyone was reading and talking about. Judging by the photographs hanging on her walls, she was well into middle age. Might there be offspring, relatives with an interest in her estate? He must remain alert, and look to the future.

It had been chance, another stroke of good fortune, that had led Charlie to the Friedlander address in the first place. Early 1943. He had been sipping a late-morning coffee at a *zinc*, a bar in the vicinity close to Trinité Church when he had overheard a trio of old biddies prattling. Grouped together, clustered round one of the small round tables, a forest of elbows tight up against one another, smoking, grouching, deploring the demise of their neighbourhood, missing their fellow citizens who had fled before Hitler and his cronies had marched into their beloved city. During the course of their conversation, Madame Friedlander was mentioned several times as one of the earliest to escape. On the day the Germans were marching towards the capital, as the tanks were approaching but had not yet passed through the city gates, she had disappeared. 'While all our own men were retreating.'

'No one left to look after that beautiful apartment of hers. Sitting empty all this time.'

'The fifteenth of June 1940, it was. I was buying bread. When I stepped back outside the bakery with my baguettes under my arm, a guard had been posted at the door, a gun slung over his shoulders. Frightened the life out of me.' The grey-haired Parisian who had been carrying her sticks of bread was now gesticulating wildly, eyes popping, acting out her surprise at the sight of an armed soldier. 'Yes, I remember it as though it were yesterday. Barely a soul about even before Madame Friedlander hot-footed it with little more than her purse clutched in her hand. Left everything behind her. Scared witless.'

Charlie had shuffled closer.

'Where has she fled to?' one asked of the others, leaning closer, conspiratorially. 'Has anyone heard?'

The women shook their heads.

Charlie had overheard this conversation in March 1943. Madame Friedlander's apartment had been empty for almost three years by that date, if all that he had eavesdropped was accurate.

'I was crossing la Place de l'Opéra. All the shops were boarded up.' Heads nodded as they all recalled the fateful day. 'Not a soul in sight. It was eerie, spooky. There, in the middle of the square, was just one parked car. A Citroën, if my memory serves me, and on its front window was a white card with *À Vendre*, for sale, in big letters. I felt as though the bottom had just dropped out of my world. Everyone scarpering, leaving Paris to the Germans. Three years on and they're still bloody well here.'

'It's the waiting that drives you round the bend. Since the tanks rolled in, those stinking Germans aboard them, our lives have been about waiting. Waiting in line for bread . . .'

'For a half-stale baguette, more like . . .'

'. . . that is costing eight francs . . .'

'Swastikas decorating l'Opéra. How much humiliation must we be forced to endure?'

'We swallow our anger, spit on the streets as they pass by and wait for this war to end, for the Allies to liberate the capital, for those bastards to get their comeuppance.'

'"Work, family, fatherland", my arse.' One old girl banged her fist on the table. Spoons on saucers rattled.

'And for our fellow citizens to return.'

'Or to learn of their fate.'

Sighs all round as the women fell into silence. And then, 'We're living in a semi-inhabited city. No caretakers to look out for the buildings. It feels half dead sometimes, doesn't it?'

Talk of the end of the war had been on the lips of all Parisians during the fifty months of occupation. Every day was counted, ticked off, prayed over. Charlie had been in hiding for more than six months and growing a little desperate when he had overheard that first conversation. He was doing well enough, earning more than sufficient to keep the wolf from the door, saving his francs, squirrelling them away, but living from day to day behind a false identity and with no permanent base.

A fine empty apartment would suit him down to the ground. Fully furnished, no expenses.

After that, he had made it his business to hang about in that particular café, keep his ears and eyes open, engage in conversation those inhabitants who remained, until he had finally pinpointed the precise address of Madame Friedlander's quarters.

The *bâtiment* in question was situated at number nine rue de Lagrange. A handsome example of Hausmannian architecture. His 'landlady' – she who had disappeared, leaving the place empty for him to settle into – was a well-to-do widow, who had been living alone in style, it transpired.

The concierge's widower had also done a runner, although no one could explain for what reason. He wasn't Jewish, a pervert or a gypsy. A Communist, then, or a thief, perhaps. He'd always had the dustbins out on time. Might he have raided a few of the flats, helped himself to what he'd fancied, then buggered off? No one could fathom why or to where he had disappeared. The *bâtiment* needed someone to be responsible for it, pay attention to the comings and goings of strangers, of deliveries, the cleaning of the common parts . . . Charlie soon cottoned on to the fact that no one was keeping a watchful eye. It fell to the remaining occupants to take it in turns to keep the stairways and hallways clean. The lift was out of order and there was no handyman to call on for its repair. The men had gone to war, and no one knew when they'd be back.

Charlie had listened to the endless chatter, calculating the odds.

Who would know of his presence? This was an ideal opportunity. He'd be a fool not to take advantage of it.

And with next to no effort, no damage, arriving by night after a daytime recce, he had ascended by the back stairs, the service entrance situated twenty metres towards the rear of a side alleyway, and slipped inside the building with his one small bag, installing himself through a sashed window in Madame Friedlander's very comfortable fifth-floor home.

A woollen jacket hung from a chair back; black rubber wellingtons with an umbrella poking out of one on the tiled floor inside the front door; a toothpaste tube lacking its cap, browning at the edges. A cursory scout about the rooms gave him the impression that she had just popped out to buy provisions, to meet a companion for an hour's conversation over *un grand crème*, except for

6

the cobwebs, the thick layer of gathering dust and the smell of mothballs and damp that hung, like mildewed sheets, over the rooms. A life abruptly evacuated. And from that day on, time within these walls had stood still, sealed in, left to the insects and natural erosion. He ran his fingers through the powdery particles, and auto-graphed his name across the mahogany dining table. Taking possession. Not Charlie Gilliard, no, the other name. His *real* name. The dead man's name. Robert Lord. 'Lordy' to his mates, to his colleagues in the war, his fellow fighters. 'Our Bob' to his dear old mum. Our Bob, who had been killed in action. An illustrious finale.

His mother must have been broken when she'd received the news, the dreaded envelope with the telegram inside, but she would have found solace, appeasement in her pride. 'So proud of my boy who gave his life for his king and country.' She would have taken consolation from that knowledge, and Charlie took consolation from the thought.

And then, with the sleeve of his newly purchased overcoat, he had brushed away his identity. Gone for ever, floating away with the spores. Robert Lord was no more. He was lifeless on a beach along the coast of Dieppe, growing cold, food for the rats, face burned to a cinder, unrecognizable, unidentifiable. Robert Lord, wireless operator and gunner. His best friend, Peter Lyndon, pilot of their plane, was on that beach too. A heap of body parts. Both men had been twenty-two years old, the pair of them airborne out of Northolt in England to take part in the raid on Dieppe, Operation Jubilee, on 19 August 1942. The largest single-day air-battle of the war, it had proved to be. But it was a catastrophe, a bloodbath swimming in all that was foul. The RAF had lost 106 aircraft, at least thirty-two to flak or accidents. He and Pete had been shot down, nose-diving as though in slow motion out of the sky, wrestling to keep control. The shouting, cursing within the plane still echoed through Robert Lord/Charlie Gilliard's sleepless nights.

An abashedly ill-prepared shambles, during which his fellow crew members had lost their lives. Pete Lyndon had been not only his closest pal, but also his strength. He had kept Lordy sane when he was sure he'd lose his mind. When his courage was failing him, Pete had always bolstered him.

Beyond his mate's death, through searing pain and crazed grief, with his grimy cupped hands, he'd shovelled up bits of the bones, sinews and ragged lumps of his friend, fumbling frenziedly with the fragments of lost life, shaking, sweating, vomiting, blubbing over his pal's charred remains. Tears burning his scorched flesh. All his comrades – good, decent men – had died screaming around him. He was alone, the only one still breathing, still in one piece, weeping for his lost friends, weeping out of fear, shock, terror, weeping because he was so frightened and hated this shitty war and wanted to go home.

Since when was murdering people an honourable Christian act?

Pete had given him mettle, balls, forced him onwards when he'd wavered. Together they were a team, enjoyed a beer in one another's company, talked of the future and their girls, and now Pete was no more.

Like a jigsaw, he'd married the pieces of flesh together, assembling, reassembling all that he could gather up, strewn across the pebbled beach, to recreate some semblance of a human form, but the pieces didn't come together. They'd been blown to smithereens. They could have been the parts of not one but two bodies. Couldn't they? And in that moment, in the rag-picking and harvesting of another's exterior identity, he had decided to shed his own. He'd looked about him at the cliffs, the towers controlled by Germans, the endless machine-gun fire. He'd known then that he couldn't stomach another minute of it. Not without Pete. He had to get out. No more! No more of this filthy, ugly war, of the bowel-emptying terror, the senseless raids. Pete Lyndon's shredded brevet, his identity badge, Robert had snatched up and pocketed as a souvenir of all that remained of a cherished friend. In return he'd left his own, tossing it among the ensanguined stones.

And then he'd fled, scuttling and scrabbling like a crab, beach stones rolling underfoot. A fucking miracle – bloodied, shot up, shivering and pissing with shock and distress – he had scrambled on all fours from the scene, found refuge outside the town of Dieppe and hidden himself for days on end in a foxhole, which he had enlarged with his filthy fingers. Inland of the French coast, he'd stared blindly out, out at the dripping, misty coastline, birds dead and rotting, shot into particles ... burned, smashed trees fallen like broken lampposts, himself howling like a wild beast, until he had almost starved. God knew how – even today his memory was a snarl of disconnected circuits, of falling burnished early-autumn leaves, the thunderous roll of wagon wheels, sounding like guns discharging, the baying of nearby livestock – but he had survived and eventually, after months on the run, he had made it to Paris.

1943. The year after Dieppe, his first full summer on the run, installed in comfort in place of the invisible Madame Friedlander, he had slept by day, worked by night. Stealthy in his comings and goings, rarely crossing paths with any of the other residents. On the infrequent occasions when he did so, no one had questioned his presence, assuming him to be a tradesman, perhaps. A nod was the most he'd exchanged. Every inhabitant had been too taken up with their own concerns, too lost in their interior worlds – rationing, survival, loss, fear, national humiliation – to pay him more than glancing attention.

March 1947. Charlie closed his eyes now as he strode onwards, summoning up the sounds and perfumes of his recent past: the sweetly scented blossoms in the urban parks; stone figures in the squares, the songs of those wartime nights; the comfort of Radio Londres; the heat and sweated bodies of whores, whose faces he tried never to engage with. He had remained indoors all day, every day, hiding his face, his guilt, descending to the streets at twilight. And never had twilight felt so sweet, so enticing. Paris was his. He existed in its shadows, but he danced in the penumbrae. He owned those shaded corners, drank in the darkness as though it were a narcotic. He was king in his own underground world. Of course, he was far from a king, not even a prince or a knight, but striding the deserted boulevards, the chest-nut trees in full spring flower, the birds in full throat, pausing to take in the architecture, the façades of the impressive buildings, the echoing sighs of the vacant city, he had come to an unlikely pact within himself. He would survive. Not as Bomber Robert Lord, of course not, but as the man he was today, answering to the name of Charles Gilliard. Charlie.

Charlie was now twenty-seven. He had been surviv-ing on his wits for almost a fifth of his short life. The Parisian counter-culture had flourished. With the help of a member of the gang he was working with, he had acquired papers: a forged British passport for Charles Gilliard. To earn his keep, buy fresh clothes and make some extra cash on the side – at which he had succeeded with surprising facility – he had worked as a fence. There was no legal work to be had. He would have starved but for a stroke of good fortune. He had insinuated his way into a busy network of petty thieves, felons and con artists, ex-police most of them, who had set up a very profitable business selling illegally confiscated goods, mostly art, jewellery and precious stones. He had received a very modest commission for each article he moved on.

And for a stretch of time, Charlie had been more or less at peace with his situation. Among such company, mobsters and jailbirds, no questions were asked. No one expressed even minimum interest in his story. He became a loner, relishing the emptiness, grateful for the obscurity, the facelessness of the midnight city. The iso-lation helped him come to terms with, or at least cope with, the swell of grief that engulfed him, to comprehend and accept the evolution in his life, the complete change of direction forced upon him by a decision he had taken in a traumatized split second.

He haunted the abandoned city, a metropolis that felt too large for those who inhabited it, the denizens who had remained behind. Anonymity had suited him. Left to his own devices, he had paced the deserted squares at night, sometimes catnapping on benches, possessed by the bruised purple glow emanating from streetlights embalmed in blue paper. He had refused to allow himself to reflect on how he had reached this place, to remind himself that he was a man without a country, with an expunged identity. A shadow among shadows. His footsteps echoed in the empty streets as he grappled to reach reconciliation with the repercussions from all that had befallen him. The smoke from his cigarettes rose into the air. The red buds of scorching light hung heavy with grief, with remorse.

His life had been erased. *He* had erased it.

He was a *deserter*. The very word sickened him.

He was not a bad man, had never in the past been dishonest. He'd nicked a few boiled sweets from the corner shop when he was a gauche and impressionable kid, along with others from the village gang, but that was about the sum of his misdemeanours. He'd been looking at a bright future. He'd had a girl . . . He could no longer summon up her features in any precise detail – even the colour of her eyes was lost to him now. Doris Sprigley. They would have married, Robert and Doris. They would have tied the knot and reared a large family in the Kent countryside close to where they had both been raised. He was fond of children, hated to see any creature harmed, had always wanted kids of his own, a free-spirited, healthy young squad of them. Boys and girls.

Doris Sprigley, a buxom, country beauty, with breasts as round and plump as the apples from his father's orchard: she would have borne his babes one after another with docility and ease. On their last outing together, days, weeks, before his terrifying foray into Dieppe, they'd done away with each other's virginity in his father's modest plantation, the fruiting trees and summer sky witnesses to their fumbling, unrefined love.

'My gift to you, Lordy,' she'd whispered in his ear on that late July evening, 'so you'll be sure to come back to me.'

He had fully intended to return to Doris. To do right by her. To carry on the family traditions of fruit growing and child-rearing.

Doris would have been informed of his death. By whom? Her parents? His mother? He'd played the scene over and over in his head: Doris standing in her parents' tidy, cramped living room, bravely taking it in, handkerchief over her mouth, her breasts heaving with shock.

'We're so sorry for your loss, Doris, but in time you'll find someone else.'

How he would have liked to hold her tight, stroke her cheeks, comfort her, the invisible shadow of him begging her to forget him. 'You'll find a better bloke, Doris, more deserving of your love.'

She would have wept for her gunner boyfriend in the arms of his mother, consoling each other through their tears. And then what? Mourned him a while before tying the knot with one of the other lads in the village? Gently putting the memories of Robert Lord aside, allowing his image to fade, growing sketchier with every passing season until she'd forgotten him altogether, just as he was losing sight of auburn-haired Doris?

In spite of his situation, for a while he had felt a sense of release. His fear was of a very different nature once he'd absconded, and for weeks on end after he'd fled, he had felt no fear at all. Numb, then washed clean of that shuddering, convulsing terror. He couldn't die because he was already dead. He could not be found because who would hunt for the charred remains of a man left lifeless, along with hundreds of others, on a beach?

Today his French was almost fluent although, due to his accent, he could not pass himself off as a Frenchman. Neither would he attempt to, even after almost five years in the country. And he preferred to remain British.

Did he miss Britain, good old Blighty, the clogged, foggy streets of London? Or leafy Kent, the 'Garden of England', where he had been born and raised? The damage caused by the Blitz he had read about in the newspapers. In 1940, on that first long stretch of bombing, his own rural neighbourhood had suffered a hit. Casualties and deaths. Had his street been flattened? Not during that first raid, but later possibly. He'd read of Londoners taking shelter in the stations of the Underground.

Robert's kid sister, Sylvia. How old would she be now? Twenty-four? Had she married? Might there be kids? Nieces and nephews whom 'Charlie' would never know?

Charlie's guts began to tighten. His head swirled and beat. He must always steel himself against such memories, such links to his past. He was not a wicked man, but he could never return. A fact. He had come too far. What were the punishments meted out to deserters? Execution? Life imprisonment? Or was his own guilt and shame the heaviest burden of all?

Britain was lost to him now. In any case, his loved ones would have mourned him, laid him to rest, moved on with their lives. His family and lovely Doris. There was no choice but to leave well alone. Let his bereft mother grieve in peace.

Bury the past. They had their lives. He had to make do with the traded-in version of his.

Charlie smelt coffee. He was passing a café. His step faltered. A moment's indecision before he settled himself at a pavement table. One hand above his shoulder, signalling to the *garçon* for a *double espress'*. He stretched out his legs and lifted his face to take comfort from the rays of early spring sunlight. He drew out some loose change and a packet of Gitanes – he had grown accustomed to the local black tobacco, bitter but satisfying. He lit up unsteadily, inhaling deeply. He had shaken himself, given himself the heebie-jeebies recalling Kent, Doris and his dear old mum.

If they could see him now.

The shame. The reprisal.

He picked a shred of tobacco off the tip of his tongue with the index finger and thumb of his left hand and watched the limping arrival of an old grandfather carrying a stuffed, stitched-together satchel. The elderly fellow – a veteran from the Great War? – shuffled between the tables, selling newspapers, coughing and spluttering, racked by chest problems. Charlie scooped up a one-franc piece and beckoned the under-nourished pensioner, handing him the coin. In return he helped himself to a copy of *Le Monde*. It smelt of fresh print and the promise of an afternoon's entertainment. He'd go to a picture house, wile away the hours . . . Too early for a drink . . . for the jazz clubs.

He needed some solid work, a challenge. It was time to set his thoughts in a new direction. Move on. Leave Paris. But to go where?

During his early days on the run, Charlie had earned a crust by labouring on farms, helping folk with their livestock and crops. He had enjoyed the physical exertion, the outdoor existence, the sweat of hay harvests, collecting corn. It had reminded him of home. The elderly, those farmers who were too old or infirm to go to war, showed him what needed to be done with gestures and sign language. They asked no questions, only too glad of the extra hands because all the young Frenchmen had been called up to fight. Just as long as he wasn't a Kraut, they were grateful for his presence. Many of the housewives welcomed him into their homes with warmth, feeding him as handsomely as they could under the circumstances, treating him with the affection awarded to a son. Boiled eggs from hens in the garden. 'These sell in the capital for ten francs each,' one rather attractive farmer's wife had told him, suggesting that he was privileged, being given a special treat. Two or three of the women, the wives, had tended his wounds, washed his torn flesh, sponged down his shock-riddled body.

Most demanded no explanations, begged nothing in return. On several occasions he was offered a missing soldier's room.

Those women were lonely, aching for their own boys or husbands, starved of company, but Charlie always chose to keep his distance, never allowing himself to be drawn into the family environment, the intimacies, preferring to sleep on straw in barns, knowing that his own emotions were open and sore, running like his wounds, and that before too long he would be moving on. From his first days on the run, Paris had always been his goal.

Aside from that, even though his ability to express himself in French back then had been scratchy, he'd dreaded being drilled with too many questions. Being found out for what he was.

A deserter.

He glanced at the date on the front page of the paper: *mardi*, 27 March 1947. Two years beyond the war. The sun had risen at 06:41 and was due to set at 19:13. The days were getting longer; the war was receding ever further. He turned the pages slowly, glancing at a short article, an analysis of Britain's recent nationalization of the coal industry. Pages turning, moving towards the back to the arts section where he knew to find the cinema listings. A striking photograph of Simone Signoret drew his eye. She had celebrated her birthday a couple of days earlier, he read. She was twenty-six. One year younger than he had turned a little more than a week ago. *The Jolson Story*, he had seen that film. And *It's A Wonderful Life*. That one had made him homesick – Christmas, and all the anniversaries he forced himself never to remember. *Brief Encounter.* No, he'd give that one a miss.

The Best Years of Our Lives. He hadn't seen that picture yet. He rather fancied Teresa Wright and was a staunch fan of William Wyler. He ran his finger down the listings to see where it was playing that afternoon, hoping it would be in colour, recalling that it had picked up some awards at the recent Oscar ceremony.

At that moment, the loud talk of a pair of Yanks caught his attention. He glanced towards the pavement to see a couple of tourists with a raised camera taking snaps willy-nilly as some tourists are prone to do. Quickly, he swung his body away from the street, head down, until they had moved on, then returned to his paper.

He found a cinema in the eleventh *arrondissement*, a healthy walking distance, not far from the impressive Bastille square. It was a cinema he had never frequented before. Downing in one slug the remains of his strong coffee, he threw twenty *centimes* onto the table, checked his watch, folded his newspaper, tucked it into his left-hand jacket pocket and headed off along the street, buoyed by the knowledge that he had a convivial plan for his afternoon. Cavities of time, loneliness: these were the hardest challenges for him to overcome, but he feared to make friends, to allow anyone to draw too close to him: they could never be given access to his real self.

The picture house, when Charlie drew near, resembled something out of a Chinese operetta. A very curious piece of architecture indeed. He was twenty minutes ahead of the scheduled start time for the programme. Drawing open the doors, he stepped inside and was hit by the acrid smell of smoke, as though someone had a fire burning in the foyer. A small blonde in the ticket kiosk noticed his arrival. She seemed distressed. Charlie sniffed, closed his eyes and frowned. He turned about him, seeing flames in his mind's eye. A plane combusting, its Merlin engine sputtering, parts disintegrating, falling out of the sky. The all too familiar terror ran through his veins, tightening his arteries, buzzing in his head, like swarms of angry bees. The flashes, the memories stiffening his spine.

'You're on fire!'

'Peter – Pete, are you hearing me? They're hammering fire at us. Your tail's been hit, burning up. Try to land her.' To the right side of them, another plane had copped it in the fuselage and exploded in flames. A thin white plume of smoke was all that remained as the machine spiralled seawards. And then another. And another.

Pete gripped hard at the controls, muscles taut, as the flames licked their way towards where he was seated, heating his back, disintegrating flesh.

'Something's burning!' Charlie Gilliard's voice broke the silence in the empty cinema lobby. He was fighting for breath, grappling with the memories that never let him be.

'All right, don't get into a state. I dropped my cigarette, singed the carpet. It's nothing to make a fuss about.'

He took a moment, drew himself back to the present, then stumbled towards the kiosk window.

The cashier lifted her eyes, lilac-blue. She pouted at him with lips as sweet and pink as sugar candy. She smiled, but she was teary-eyed. Close up, she was tantalizingly pretty, if a little on the young side. He watched her for a moment while she fiddled with a roll of tickets. He sniffed again. A whiff of petrol, perhaps. He was reliving the nightmare again.

'Mister, do you want to see the film,' she asked, 'or are you from the fire department? I've lost my job in any case. What do you want?'

'*The Best Days of Our Lives.*'

'If you say so. Starts in fifteen minutes. Admission is forty *centimes.*' The blonde tore a ticket off her roll and slid it, with chewed fingers, through to him. 'So far you've got the place to yourself. Enjoy the film.'

Charlie lingered for a moment before picking up his ticket. There was something about the girl. He smiled. She'd lifted his spirits.

Paris, November 2015

A woman in calf-length leather boots strode into view, paused, looked about her. She took another step, hesitant, then continued onwards, her black slacks moulded to her figure, a mane of hair bouncing off her chic leather jacket. Tall, striking to look at, hauling too much luggage, she was making her way along an unfamiliar street in a city that was not her own, pausing as she glanced across to the far side of the boulevard. She was trying to find a bar. A casual, friendly kind of joint to hang out in for a couple of hours, somewhere she could get this load off her back and chill. As she approached a crossroads, she slowed. There was a place right alongside her. Flashing lights from within. A tad garish? No, a TV screen. It looked fine, rather inviting.

Kurtiz Ross pushed at the door with her foot, stepped inside the unfamiliar bar-bistro and glanced about, pausing to choose a table, a concealed corner, not too busy. To her surprise, it was more than half empty. Friday night and no more than half a dozen singles and two couples: sleek, casual Parisians, lolling against pillars or lounging against the zinc surfaces, cradling drinks. From overhead speakers Charles Aznavour was crooning 'La Bohème'. In the centre of the room where the diners, when they arrived, would be served, there were several sets of red plastic banquettes and half a dozen small wooden tables adorned with red and white check tablecloths. Kurtiz was deliberating whether to grab something to eat now or hang on until Oliver turned up after the concert, hopefully in the company of Lizzie.

Lizzie, twenty years old. Lizzie. *Please, God, in the company of Lizzie.*

Kurtiz's stomach was bunched into what felt like a snarl of wires that were twisting and tightening. She needed a drink. First, a drink. This was not going to be easy, even without the tiring day of editing behind her, followed by the journey from London on a crowded Eurostar, a Friday evening taxi from the Gare du Nord, which had delivered her with her overnight and camera bags to Place de la Bastille. From there, somewhere to kill an hour or two.

Before she stepped any further inside, she threw a swift glance upwards, making a mental note of the name of the brasserie flashing in neon outside, L'ARMAGNAC, then down to her watch. Ten to eight. She was too early, way too early. She could have caught a later train or gone to the hotel first. She hadn't been thinking straight – too keen to cross to this side of Paris, to be close to the concert hall. No matter, she was here now, and with time on her hands, so, yes, she might as well grab a quick snack. Once settled, she'd send Oliver a text to let him know she was now in town and where she was. The remainder of her evening would be about waiting . . . waiting, sitting it out, and praying to whoever might be out there listening that she would, by the end of the night, be back in the company of her daughter.

It was on occasions such as this that she wished she smoked. Occasions such as this? Surely to God this was a one-off in anybody's lifetime. Meeting up with your own child again for the first time in more than four years. Four heart-breaking, despairing, dislocated years. Four years and five months almost to the day. Oh, Lizzie, have you any idea of the desolation your absence has caused?

The bistro was warm, fuggy, hearteningly traditional, comforting with a slightly pungent smell of vegetable oil and fried onions. Burgers? Kurtiz shivered, brushing off the day, the winter evening outside, and her rising dread of . . . what? Inadequacy? Disappointment? A no-show?

Everything was hanging on Oliver's hunch.

But what if he had got it wrong? What if Lizzie wasn't at the concert? Or if she was – What if she refuses to come and meet us? What if she's angry with Oliver and tells him, her own dad, to fuck off? Lizzie, little Lizzie, please, please, be there. *Little* Lizzie? She's twenty. Lizzie is a young woman. A young woman and a stranger to her mother. How had this come about? At what point had their daughter made the decision to run away, skip out of their lives? For what length of time had she planned her escape? Had she always been intent on Paris, or was that simply the way it had rolled? Had Kurtiz's absences been to blame? Oliver would have her believe so. Oliver had never stopped pointing the finger at her.

And what did she believe? Was she responsible for her daughter's departure?

Wearied by the same tired questions, fifty-three

months of them, never missing a day, Kurtiz dropped her travel bag and cameras alongside the chair and sat down at one of the small square tables in the middle of the dining area. A wintry Friday night in Paris. She glanced about her. The place was hardly buzzing, but it was early yet. A waiter strolled towards her, casual, in no hurry, but with an amiable smile. It's not true what they say about Parisians, she was thinking as she prepared to order.

'*Bonsoir*. What time do you close, please?'

'One thirty a.m., Madame. Are you alone or expecting guests?'

She hesitated. 'Guests? Yes. We'll be . . .' She was determined to be positive. 'We'll be three, but not until a little later.'

He nodded. 'What can I bring you?'

'*Un whisky, s'il vous plaît, avec une grande carafe d'eau sur le côté, je vous remercie.*'

The flat-screen television, the sound muted, attached to the wall above the bar, drew her attention. As was the custom in all these watering-holes, it was tuned to a sports channel. A football match was getting under way. The players were shaking their bodies, hopping from booted foot to booted foot, limbering up, loosening their well-toned muscles. France, in the blue shirts, was about to play Germany, in white. A scoreboard flagged it in the top right-hand corner of the screen. Currently, pre-match, it read 0–0. Advertising boards encircled the pitch. A band of men decked out in black costumes, some with drum kits hanging from their necks, were readying themselves for the national anthems. The spectators were singing, waving flags, swaying. Expectant audience members, thrilled to be there, men with small boys on their laps, adrenalin surging for this floodlit game.

Kurtiz turned her attention to the street. Football held no real interest for her. In any case, she was too wound up to concentrate. Her whisky arrived. She nodded her thanks and took a satisfying slug, straight. No ice, not even the water. Wow, that hit the spot.

A young couple, early twenties, had pushed open the door and stepped inside, shivering, shaking themselves like dogs. With them came a rush of cold air. The corners of tablecloths rose and fell. Two yellowed and rouged chestnut leaves sailed in and sank gently to the tiled floor. The couple heaved themselves up onto two tall aluminium bar stools. They were talking in English. Kurtiz studied them, mentally composing a picture, a double portrait. Both were good-looking. He ordered a beer and the girl a mineral water. Kurtiz observed them for a moment longer as their body language, even in duffel coats, conveyed deep affection, hunger for one another: eyes locked together, they were unable to keep their hands off each other. The young woman with long, dark pre-Raphaelite hair was pregnant; possibly five months, no more. Kurtiz smiled, remembering her own Lizzie-carrying days and her early life with Oliver. She sighed and turned her gaze elsewhere. Twenty years on, what will be the story for this couple? Will they fare better than her family life had?

She glanced at her watch. Eight fifteen.

The door to the street opened once more, swinging and banging. Another blast of air swirled around her legs. The waiter hurried to the entrance and scooped up the chestnut leaves as a solitary elderly lady wrapped in a voluminous mink coat stepped inside. She had a small dog with her, a Maltese, on a lead. The waiter shook her gloved hand and without hesitation led her to the table alongside Kurtiz. She nodded a *bonsoir* to Kurtiz, shucked off her fur, laid it neatly and with great precision across the empty banquette opposite and settled herself comfortably. Meanwhile, the ivory-haired dog had flopped like a shaggy cushion against its mistress's high-heeled boots. Kurtiz snatched a glance. It was hard not to stare, not to be drawn to the woman. Her grace, her poise, called for attention. She was possibly in her late seventies, early eighties, hard to tell, petite, obviously French, impeccably coiffured, and beautiful. She must have been sensational to look at once upon a time – seamless make-up applied to flawless skin with barely a wrinkle, cheekbones high and as chiselled as the starched wings on detachable collars, beneath pale lilac eyes that were extraordinary not only for their unusual colour but because they were so round and full they might have been jewels, orbs.

Kurtiz had to resist the temptation to pick up one of her two cameras and grab a shot.

Without having received an order, the waiter returned with a jug of water, a long silver spoon, a highball glass with a measure of Ricard *pastis* poured into it and a beaker of ice.

The beauty smiled a *merci* – what a smile, full of generosity, allure, with perfectly aligned teeth – and drew the Ricard towards her, pouring several measures of water into the *apéritif* and afterwards spooning in ice cubes. She peeled away the taupe leather gloves she was still wearing, finger after finger, dropped them to the table, placed them in alignment one alongside the other, and stirred her drink slowly, deliberately, waiting serenely while the liquid clouds began to rise until the entire glass had taken on a milky complexion. All the while her gold bracelets jingled.

She turned her head and flicked a glance to Kurtiz. *'Bonsoir, Madame.'*

Embarrassed to have been caught staring, Kurtiz smiled, then pulled her phone from the pocket of her leather jacket, fidgeting with it, pecking at the message box with the tip of her nail. No new mails. Had Oliver and Lizzie crossed paths yet? Was Lizzie at the concert? Might they be together right this minute? Kurtiz closed her eyes and tried to envisage the conversation. Were they yelling at one another above the chords of rock? Or might Lizzie have caught sight of her father across the rows of seats – were there seats in the concert hall or was it standing room only? – turned her back, pulled up the collar on her jacket, wrapped a scarf around her face, fearful he might recognize her? Might she hurry from the auditorium, making a split-second decision to give the concert a miss?

Deciding not to return, she'd slip out, slip away, making a furtive escape along the boulevard Voltaire, beating a retreat towards a Métro station or turn about her in search of a taxi for fear her father might have followed her.

Or might she stay? Was there a part of her, an ache in her heart, that craved to be reunited with her mum and dad, her broken-hearted estranged parents?

'Oh, Lizzie. Please don't run out on us. Not again.'

'*Pardonnez-moi, Madame*, what did you say?'

'Sorry?'

'I thought you said something. I'm a little hard of hearing, these days. Apologies for that. I have a hearing aid but I hate to stick one of those contraptions in my head. It's pure vanity. A life in the cinema and on the stage. Actresses don't appreciate the harsh realities of growing old.'

Kurtiz twisted her head to her left. Was the old woman speaking to her or muttering to herself? Now her neighbour was gawping at her and frowning. 'You look a little distressed, if you don't mind me saying. Is there something I can do? I'm not trying to be a busybody, you understand.'

Kurtiz attempted a smile. 'I'm fine,' she mumbled, and downed the remainder of her whisky. 'Thank you for asking, *merci*.' She did not want to be drawn into conversation. She was not capable of engaging with another. Not this evening.

'My mind is not what it used to be.' The ageing diva shook her head, with its finely waved white hair. 'Learning lines was never a problem in the old days. Are you in show business, dear?'

Kurtiz replied that she wasn't.

'What line of work, then?'

'Photographer, and I've been . . .' her thoughts flashed to Alex '. . . involved in a few films,' she admitted, still preferring not to be co-opted into this conversation.

'Have you, dear? How very splendid. Hollywood dramas or here in Paris? I have spent my life in the film business. Well, my early life. Later, I returned from the south to perform in the theatre. Many of the great tragic roles, I have interpreted. Several seasons with the Comédie Française. I could have been a star in Hollywood, but . . . but . . .' she sighed and disappeared momentarily into her history '. . . I was a little naive when that opportunity came along, oh, dear me, another lifetime ago.' She waved her hand and the bracelets shimmied. 'In any case, I prefer Paris. I chose home ground, you might say. *Jean-Claude, un autre, s'il vous plaît.* Will you be my guest? Please, do join me. I am obliged to drink alone most of the time, these days. Since my husband died . . . My second husband, that is. My first left this earth many moons ago.'

'I won't, thank you. You're very kind, but I'll stick to the one. I'm meeting my husband and – and daughter later and . . . they've gone to a concert.' Kurtiz glanced at her watch: 8.35 p.m. Time was dragging. The door opened, another couple entered and bumped up tight against one another, shrugging off the cold as they bustled their way to a distant table.

'Ah, L'Opéra. Our new opera house is really very splendid, don't you agree? Quite different from the Palais Garnier, of course. Who is singing at Bastille this evening? Or is it the ballet? Tourists come from all over the world to spectate. I am not an opera fan myself but it has done wonders for this *quartier.*'

'No, not the opera.'

'Jean-Claude, please bring my friend whatever it is she was drinking.'

'*Bien sûr, Madame Courtenay.*'

'I have been coming to this bar, this *petit bistro*, oh, for years now. Such friendly service. They know me well, treat me kindly, as a member of the family. I live a couple of blocks up the street. Many locals frequent this place, including one or two retired stars such as myself.' She winked coquettishly and touched her hair as though posing for a photograph. A smile crossed Kurtiz's lips.

'*Je suis* Marguerite Courtenay, by the way.' She held out her leathery hand, which was mottled with liver spots but gilded with heavy rings above pearly painted nails. The cluster of interconnecting gold bracelets looped her tiny wrist. 'Marguerite Courtenay. It's my stage name.' The actress hesitated, for effect or because she was expecting an effusive recognition of her fame, Kurtiz could not tell.

'Marguerite Courtenay. Oh, there were nights when Paris rose to its feet to applaud me.' She paused, head held high, as though replaying the sweet music of handclapping, the cheers and the acclaim. 'Alas, those days are gone. No one gives a damn about an ageing actress nowadays. Michel Piccoli, he will turn ninety just after Christmas, the old devil. He and his generation go on for ever. There are always roles for the men, whereas we *filles* are more or less forced into retirement. Such an ageist industry, ours. Tell me about your photography, your films.'

Kurtiz ran her fingers through her hair, grown to shoulder length, hennaed a rich chestnut tone, darker, more luxuriant than her natural colour. The waiter placed the whisky, ice and water on the table in front of her. She stared at it. She hadn't yet sent a text to Oliver. The concert must have got under way by now. His phone would be switched off. She glanced up to the television where the athletes were slogging it out, but the score remained nil-nil.

Her neighbour continued to watch her, eyes roving over her profile. 'You seem a little anxious, *ma chère amie*. Troubled. Do you want to talk about it? I'm here to help. I've known heartache and turmoil too.'

Kurtiz pressed two fingers into her eyes, rubbing at them, as though attempting to ward off a threatening headache and to protect herself against her neighbour's interrogation. She had closed off her heart, shut down her emotions four years earlier. Intimacies, even with strangers, panicked and threatened her.

'You're English, aren't you?'

Kurtiz nodded, poured a splash of water into her fresh glass of whisky, dropped in a couple of ice cubes and rattled them.

'I never visited England.'

Cubes clinked against glass. She wished the woman would desist, even though the old soul obviously meant no ill. She was probably simply in need of a natter. Days alone enclosed in her apartment with nothing but memories. Sad.

'Are you staying near here? Filming, perhaps?'

A plate of food was delivered by Jean-Claude to the actress. She winked at the young man flirtatiously and slid the meal an inch or two to her right. 'I'll have a carafe of red. Bordeaux, *s'il vous plaît, comme d'hab*.'

'*Oui, Madame Courtenay*.'

A group of four arrived. Guys intent on the football. They chose a table across the room in a corner with a good view of the screen. 'Nil–nil,' one cried.

'*Allez les bleus,*' boomed another.

'I wish they would remove that bloody screen,' muttered Madame Courtenay, with an unexpected edge. 'These football nights are a curse on one's tranquillity. Even up in my lovely flat on the second floor I can hear the riff-raff yelling in the streets. I believe our president is attending this game tonight, isn't he? It doesn't look as though he's bringing the French team a great deal of luck. No score yet.'

Kurtiz dug into her travel bag and drew out a slender creased paperback. *Love and Summer*, by William Trevor. She was a huge fan of the Irish author and had been intending to read this work for a while. Fascinatingly, its central character was also a photographer so it should offer an added pleasure to the theme. She opened it to the first page, then placed the book, spine down, splayed on the table, one hand resting against the first page. It was getting a little too hectic to concentrate. She'd finish her drink and grab a taxi to her hotel. Why had she not booked somewhere in this *quartier*? It would have been so much less hassle. Was there time to cross Paris and return, ready and calm in a nearby bar, or should she simply sit it out here until the end of the concert? Why had she and Oliver not even managed to agree on a matter as simple as where to hook up at the end of the show?

A gaping lack of communication. Resistance. Embedded anger. An inability to let the other win. Stupid power games.

'My first husband was English. Charlie Gilliard was his name,' confided her neighbour softly. 'He was a gentle creature, a man of the soil. I really was too young to appreciate his goodness, his fine qualities. I was a silly ambitious girl, and by the time I knew a bit about life and what a gift I had in him, he was gone. Too young. Tragic. How curious. I haven't spoken of Charlie, not even mentioned his name, in a long while. Decades, in fact.'

These last remarks, spoken almost to herself, drew Kurtiz's attention, given her entangled existence with Oliver and her own loss of a loved one.

'You are fortunate to have a husband and daughter waiting for you, excited to be meeting up with you later after the opera. Oh, what I wouldn't give to turn back the clock. I have had a rich and varied life, but growing old when one is alone is not for the fainthearted. Somehow, I didn't see it coming. The darkness, the silence of an empty flat. It was not what I had expected. I had painted in my head a very different scenario.'

The carafe of Bordeaux was set on the table in front of her. '*Merci, Jean-Claude.* But I am grateful and . . . delighted to be sitting alongside you in this bistro this evening. *Santé.*'

'My family –' Kurtiz coughed '– my daughter and husband . . . they are not at the opera. They have gone to a rock concert. Well, Oliver's gone to the concert because he's hoping . . . we both are . . .' Kurtiz dried up. It was too complicated, too tortuous a story to pour out the details, to elaborate. In any case, she had no desire to. She should have attended the concert. It was bullying of Oliver to insist he go without her. She had every right to be there. She had paid his fare over, stood him the hotel, bought the ticket. She lowered her head. The headache threatened, the fury, the despair, the loss. A hammer beating against a chisel making headway in her brain. No, he hadn't been a bully. She was too tough on him. There had been logic in his argument.

'If Lizzie sees us both, she'll think it's a plot rather than a coincidence. She'll think we've tracked her down and intend to force her to come home. Under such circumstances, she would never agree to have a drink with us.'

'Oliver, she's twenty. We can't coerce her into coming home, and we have tracked her down. To a degree. Haven't we? God, I hope we have because if this trail leads nowhere . . .'

'She'll think it's back to the old days. The arguments. Your absences. We need to prove to her that everything has changed.'

'Yes, it *has* changed, Oliver, and it's not back to the old days. Our situation has moved on. We cannot fool our daughter or ourselves into believing we're back together. And we –'

'Because you left. *You.* You walked out. When I was at rock bottom, you buggered off, but I'm willing to give our marriage another chance. You can see the efforts I'm making.'

'I didn't – I didn't bugger off. I . . . It's too late, Oliver. We've already given it several second chances.'

And so it had gone on, the escalating spiral of blame and criticism and argument. The impossibility of escape. Except for Lizzie, who had escaped, who had disappeared without a trace, until Alex had serendipitously and quite by chance found her.

Alex . . . It would be such a tonic to have a drink with him before she left Paris. If he was in town . . . But she knew she wouldn't contact him. The pact she had made with herself.

Kurtiz touched the fingers of her left hand to her forehead, massaging the flesh, pressing against the bone, attempting to erase the clamour in her skull. She signalled to the waiter. 'Would you please bring me a sandwich? Any sandwich, it doesn't matter, and a glass of red wine. Oh, and some more water, please.'

'*Désolé, Madame*, we don't serve sandwiches in the evenings. No snacks. Meals only. Do you want to see the menu? Hamburger, perhaps, or a steak to accompany Madame Courtenay?'

Kurtiz shook her head, glanced at her watch: 8.49 p.m. She was doing a quick mental calculation, working out the time the concert might finish. No text from Oliver. Was he with Lizzie right now? Bright-eyed Lizzie, was she happy to see him?

Eight or nine youngsters burst through the door, exuberant, carefree and boisterous.

The actress had been talking. Kurtiz had not heard a word.

'Is that the name of the concert hall, where your husband and daughter are now? It's really the only one within this vicinity.' Marguerite Courtenay frowned, trying to recall. 'No, there's no other. Who is playing there tonight? Not that I would know one rock group from another.'

'Sorry, are you speaking to me?' Kurtiz raised her voice. 'It's getting pretty noisy in here.' Not exactly conducive to conversation.

The actress was talking again. To Kurtiz or herself? Either way, Kurtiz had to strain to catch any word at all.

'It used to be a cinema before it was turned into a concert hall.' The old lady threw back her head and laughed. Her face creased with delight. 'I worked there. Oh, for a very short while. Days, weeks. I don't remember. They sacked me. After the war. It was a cinema . . . ooh, right up until the fifties or sixties, I believe. Until 1969. I met my first husband there. The Englishman. The one I was telling you about. He came to see a film. I was in a terrible fix and he helped me out. Such a sweet person, he was. The perfect gentleman. Who could have known where that would lead? He was always so very generous.'

'Forgive me, but your steak and *frites* are getting cold.'

'I'm not hungry, dear. I never touch the meals they serve me. Even in my younger days I wouldn't have tucked into such a substantial plate. I have spent my life watching my figure, making efforts to take good care of myself. I come here for the company, to enjoy good conversation such as the one we're having now, and a drink or two before bedtime.'

The din in the bistro was notching up decibels. Added to which, canned music was now blasting out of the invisible speakers, violin and piano swing. Stéphane Grappelli? Neo bossa nova? 'How High The Moon'? Impossible to identify it. Toes were tapping. Bodies jigging as their owners talked, yelled, watched the game. One party after another of young folk, breasting the cold night air, pushed through the door, squealing, squawking, hallooing as they recognized mates, colleagues, scrambling and shoving good-naturedly for bar space, calling for beers, shots, bottles of wine. Such fresh young faces rouged by the cold November air, energized by life. Paris gearing up for its weekend.

Might any of these youngsters have come across Lizzie? Ridiculous. It was rather like asking a Londoner if he had met the Queen.

Kurtiz closed her book. She had time to kill and the old woman seemed hell-bent on conversation. She caught only one word out of every three but she might as well indulge her, hear her story. Pass the time. It was not yet nine. A noise rose from a table of men. Still no score. They were berating the screen, fists clenched above their heads – reminiscent of a Russian Communist poster from the past. The young English couple, honeymooners perhaps, were huddled close at a small table by the window, having vacated the bar. Enclosed in a world that excluded all others, they were sharing a plate of *frites* and the *magret avec miel*, feeding chips to one another, laughing, making plans, relishing the prospect of a promising future.

'It was 1946. No, wait, I think it might have been 'forty-seven. Yes, it was March 1947. My, such a distance in time. Over half a century ago. I was eighteen, broke, hungry and just a little desperate. I had arranged a screen test in Nice at the Victorine Studios. Have you ever worked on those lots? It's all wound down now, I hear. They shoot commercials there now. Japanese clients filming sports cars speeding along the Haute Corniche. It's all very scenic but it's not cinema. In my day, it was epic moving pictures. Sound had come in, colour images too. There was no going back to the silent era. It was such a

37

thrilling, innovative time. The beginning of France's Thirty Glorious Years. The film sets were extravagant, costumes opulent, scripts gritty. Some of the greatest films of French cinema were shot at the Victorine, and, without wishing to blow my own trumpet, I played in one or two of them. Cameos, of course, modest roles.'

Kurtiz was already lost, captivated by her companion's post-war world.

'But, first, I had to make my way from Paris to Nice and I didn't have the price of the train, not even in third class. I persuaded Charlie to lend me the few paltry francs for the ticket. He invited himself along for the ride. Without being aware of it at the time, dear sweet Charlie changed the course of my life. He changed his own life too. It is hard to describe to you now, after half a century of peace, the wounds, the damage we were all suffering, the scars we were hiding. Some of us had lost family. Some fled, never to return. We were both on a one-way ticket to freedom.' Head turned upwards, the old woman's lilac eyes lit up, gleaming. She might have been eighteen all over again.

Marguerite and Charlie, Paris, March 1947

The film Charlie Gilliard had sat through had been an ill-considered choice. Its quality could not be faulted. It was the subject matter, the story, that had rattled him. Members of the armed forces returning to the United States after active war service. The warm embrace of families. He needed a stiff drink and fresh air. He paused for a moment in the foyer to steady himself and shrug on his jacket.

'You all right, mister? Want a beaker of water?'

He swung round. The cinema had been completely empty. It was the neat-looking blonde. She was locking the door that led from the ticket booth, slipping the key into the pocket of her mackintosh. A slender creature, she turned to him with an expression of concern. She reminded him of a lighter-haired incarnation of the movie star Loretta Young, with her shoulder-length curls rolled into ringlets – and what about those rather startling purple-blue eyes? Large, round peepers, quite out of proportion to the rest of the features in her delicate, fawn-like face.

'Jeepers Creepers' . . .

He was humming a well-known melody to himself, waiting where he was, appreciating the blonde's hip-swinging gait. The curves and indentations of her young body. A rather sexy body. He lowered his gaze, fearing to expose his vulnerability, his loneliness. 'It's a little stuffy in there,' he lied.

'There's a café down the road. I know the proprietor well. He'll give you a glass of water if you need one. Or a lemonade.'

A lemonade! It was a shot Charlie needed. 'Let me invite you for a drink.' He smiled, experiencing the rare sensation of his face muscles wrinkling with pleasure, knowing he shouldn't get involved, chastising himself silently as she stepped towards him and he inhaled her ferny perfume. He felt his emotions caving in. All of a sudden, and with a certain desperation, he was craving the proximity of her, her female companionship, her long strands of hair against his face. 'I'll buy you a lemonade for your kindness. And take you dancing if you like.'

She was squarely in front of him now, a foot shorter than he was, gazing up at him with concern. He was momentarily confused. The haunting blue lights began to flash again. No, not lights – *stay in the present* – eyes: the girl's beautiful, penetrating eyes.

'I ought to be hurrying back for my tea,' she said. 'I've got to be here on duty again in half an hour. The boss owes me money. Today's my last day. He fired me. The bloody *merde*. And I want my wages.'

'One quick glass, go on. After, I can walk you back here, if that would make you feel safer. Sorry to hear you got the push.'

She hesitated, knocked sideways by his good manners. 'You're very pale. I don't want you throwing up over this carpet and getting me into more trouble. Can you credit it? This moth-eaten, pre-war bit of old rug, and he's made such a song and dance about it! Still, the old grouser can't sack me twice. Come on then, let's go.'

Charlie ordered whisky and water, no ice, and downed it in one slug. She had a cup of tea, which she slurped thirstily, and a double helping of *tarte aux pomme,* which she gobbled down in a matter of mouthfuls. He recalled the gannets over the Kentish coast and chortled silently. Her name, she told him, was Marguerite Anceaume. 'Marguerite with one T,' she insisted. Marguerite was not a Parisian by birth. She hailed from further north. 'My parents have a village store west of Reims. My father bakes bread and croissants while my mother takes charge of the cashbox. Not a bad little business. But . . . but . . . well, I've got dreams,' she confided. 'I'm just waiting to get paid, then I'll be on my way. You don't talk much, do you? Where are you from?' she encouraged, staring at him with her wide, earnest eyes, conscious of his silence.

He hadn't proffered his name, hadn't revealed anything about himself, as was his habit. To the people of the night, to the whores and the pimps, the dancing girls, he'd had no qualms about inventing stories, a distinguished past, but this girl was as fresh as a buttercup. He smiled to himself, then almost wept at the stab of pain in his gut. He was remembering his nan holding a buttercup beneath his chin.

'Are you listening? I've got to go.' She rose to her feet, knotted tight the belt of her drab raincoat and pulled up its collar. Even in her lacklustre clothing she was stylish.

'How old are you?'

'Never ask a lady her age.' She giggled flirtatiously. It had the effect of making her seem even younger, ever more waif-like. He debated in his head whether she might be little more than an adolescent, certainly younger than he had initially estimated. Better to keep his distance, not get involved. He didn't need trouble but, my, she was a pretty, jaunty thing. He wanted to hold her, embrace her.

'Can I see you again?' he heard himself asking, still marvelling at her eyes, the largest eyes he'd ever seen. Big lilac globes planted in such a delicate face. Everything about the make-up of her features was irregular. It shouldn't work and yet it did. She was more than pretty: she was really quite beautiful.

'I don't even know your name.'

He hesitated. 'It's Charles. Most call me Charlie. *Je suis Charlie.*'

'You English, then?'

He nodded. 'Come dancing with me later. We can go to a club, listen to some jazz. Do you know be-bop?'

She furrowed her brow, glancing at a clock set high on the wall above the bar.

'I'd get you home safely. No pranks.'

She was gazing hard at him. It was rare to meet someone with such a gentle approach. She'd never been to a club, never been invited to go dancing. Pity she hadn't met this fellow sooner. All these miserable months alone in Paris.

The way he was looking at her.

She took a deep breath. 'No, no, sorry, I've got to get back. I need my wages so I can pay my digs and collect my stuff. The landlord of the *pension* where I'm staying has snatched my case with all my clothes, keeping hold of it, he says, till he gets his wretched pittance. I'm leaving Paris tomorrow evening.'

'Leaving Paris?' Charlie felt an unexpected tug of loss, of sadness. Unplugged. He was losing her. It wrenched at his throat, like a noose tightening.

She nodded and tossed her head. 'Heading off by train from the Gare de Lyon. I'll be on that overnight fancy blue train to the sunshine tomorrow, Charlie. The French Riviera, imagine it, where all the movie stars take their vacation. I'm going to Nice. I've got work there. Nice meeting you, Charlie. Thanks for the tea and cake.' And with that she was gone, waving as she strutted away to the corpulent bartender behind the counter who was buffing wine glasses with a checked tea towel.

Charlie stared at the closing door. He shivered at the sudden chill in the air and called for another whisky, pulled his newspaper from his pocket and wondered, besides getting drunk, what he would do with the evening that yawned before him. His loneliness gnawed at his heart, turned his stomach into an iron bar. For one brief half-hour, a warmth, a pleasing light had crept into those dark chambers within him and he had felt almost carefree. Perhaps it was time for him to leave Paris too. Ride along with Lilac Eyes. Jeepers creepers, he hadn't felt so attracted to a girl in a long while, not since dear Doris Sprigley.

Towards the first light of dawn, when Charlie returned to his digs at number nine after meandering for hours alongside the Seine, he clocked through the cracks in the shutters that a light was on in *his* flat. He crossed the street. A habitual caution always led him to glance upwards. A front bulb was burning. In the bedroom. Heart knocking, he slipped down the alley by the side of the building and tried to assess the place from where the dustbins were stored, but the building was too high and the yard lacked depth, no matter how he craned and twisted his neck. His few belongings were tucked away in a bag at the back of the mahogany *armoire* in the spare bedroom. No article of his was ever left lying about, a precaution he'd taken from his very first encroachment. He made his way stealthily up the back stairs, the service entrance – which he had habitually used – and approached his front door. His, Madame Friedlander's, was the only apartment on the top floor. The attic space was included with her rental. Had he been so careless as to leave a light on? Surely not. The shutters had remained closed since the genuine occupant had departed and he seldom, if ever, had switched on a light. On the rare occasions when he had been home at night, he had survived by the crepuscular glow of candles.

He pressed his ear against the door, straining for sounds, movement. All was still. Sweat was prickling his forehead. His identity papers were in the jacket he was wearing. Instinctively, his left hand pressed the pocket to confirm this. Had Madame returned at last? If he turned the lock and crept inside would he find her sleeping, at peace in her own heavy wooden bed, content to be surrounded by her possessions? His watch read 4 a.m. Five minutes passed. He had been gone since before noon. A floorboard creaked and his heart took a dive. He should disappear, leave his small bag of belongings and slip away from here. His money, his stashed cash, was buried beneath a floorboard under a rug in the unused box room. It was the sum total of his assets, everything to see him through the next couple of years until he created a new, honest existence for himself. There was no way he could walk away from it. He had gambled imprisonment to earn that handsome wad of francs, accumulating those notes like a miser over the past five years. Coughing from within the apartment caused him to stiffen. What was he to do? If no one knew of the woman's presence in the city . . . Sickness swirled within him. He was no more capable of threatening or distressing her than of . . . what?

Six years ago he had been a decent, loyal young serviceman. Before the war, he wouldn't have lifted his finger to harm a butterfly. Now, he was a man without a past on the run.

The coughing ceased. Heavy footsteps crossed the parquet flooring in the hallway, shuffling their way towards . . . Towards the kitchen. The familiar squeaking rotation of the cold tap with the worn washer he had never fixed for fear of giving away his presence. Water began to splash. If he turned the handle and entered now, right now, might he make it to the spare room across the hallway without her hearing him? The rush of running water, a susurration camouflaging his movements. Could he occupy that space for a short while, lift out his money, his bits and pieces – even his toothbrush was carefully stowed away each time he went out – work in the darkness? He knew the layout of the room sufficiently well. Then, when she was sleeping soundly, he could steal out again. How high the risk? What if she woke, heard him and started screaming?

How much cash remained in his pockets? With his false papers he could check into a nearby *pension*, return in the morning, wait until Madame Friedlander went out, then collect his gear. What were the odds she'd find proof of his presence before he returned to remove everything? He was mildly drunk. His head ached, thick with exhaustion, befuddled by too much whisky and a heart that felt weary. This was not clear thinking. A few hours' sleep, a few hours' delay would make little difference. The odds were he would achieve his goal more swiftly, with less jeopardy. He heard shuffling back along the hallway. She was just a few feet from where he was standing. One oak door was all that separated them.

Charlie stepped back a metre or two, lingering, procrastinating, eyes still fixed tightly on the door – he must reclaim his stashed cash at all costs – then slowly, almost in one springing motion, he swung to the left and descended the stairs.

Beyond the building, daylight was breaking.

Any hotel clerk worth his salt might judge it odd, suspicious, that a man with no luggage and little loose change was checking into a hotel at this hour in the morning. Better to proceed with caution. He would walk to Les Halles where the market traders and stallholders would be busy setting up for their day's merchandising. Plenty of cafés and bars would already be open in that district. He'd get some breakfast while weighing up his options. The city by night, by dawn, was a familiar and healing landscape, a salve to him. He had become an animal of the night, a hunter. Breaking into a trot, he decided upon coffee, thickly buttered sticks of warm bread, a large slab of strong hard cheese and a carafe of rouge at Au Pied de Cochon in rue Coquillière. He needed cigarettes too. Later, when the light returned, he would face the challenge of breaking and entering into his erstwhile domicile to steal back his possessions.

There had still been no word from Oliver. Kurtiz had been listening, with only a fraction of her attention and without interruption while the lilac-eyed diva recounted her story, or the fragments she could remember. Kurtiz watched the old girl sift through her rusty memories, as though drawing towards her boxes of fragile souvenirs, opening the damaged treasures stored in corners, delighted to rediscover her lost past. Until, midstream, she stood up unexpectedly from her table, tugged at her sleeping dog, and wished her new companion a good night.

It shook Kurtiz back to the present. Had she missed something? Had she not been paying sufficient attention? Had she appeared rude, dismissive, uninterested?

'I am so sorry if –'

'You seem to have a great deal on your mind. I wish I could help you. I feel a desire to. Some attraction I cannot define draws me to you.'

Kurtiz apologized once more, profusely, for her lapses of concentration.

'Please, don't worry. I never stay up late.'

It was eighteen minutes past nine. Kurtiz bade the elegant dowager *bonne nuit* and drew her book towards her.

'It was a pleasure talking to you. Our encounter has

unleashed a flood of memories, reminiscences. Most extraordinary. After so many years. I feel as though I have just spent a contented hour or two in the company of my long-lost love.' She spoke effusively, arms gesticulating, hands upturned, wide. For all her warmth and compassion, she still had an air about her of the grand actress on stage.

'Good to meet you, Madame . . .'

'Courtenay. I live on this street, rue de Charonne, at number seventy-one, on the second floor. My name, *Courtenay* . . .' she emphasized it and paused for effect '. . . is on the buzzer outside. If you are passing, please look me up. I am always grateful for a little company. It would be a pleasure. *Bonsoir, Madame*. I sincerely hope whatever is causing you such visible distress is resolved soon.'

Kurtiz nodded her thanks. For one brief second she wanted to reach out to the kindly stranger, delay her departure, beg her to remain, to keep her company on this uncertain vigil. 'It's about my daughter . . .' Unburden her heart. Instead, she kept silent, as she had grown used to doing, and watched as the woman shrugged on her fur coat, chivvied her less than enthusiastic dog and shouldered her way determinedly through the throng of young citizens enjoying their Friday night out. One young man kissed her twice on each cheek as she passed. Madame Courtenay accepted his gesture of admiration with a flutter of eyes and a gloved hand on the youth's shoulder while inching her path onwards into the night.

The bistro was full to bursting now and there was still no score in the football match. Kurtiz picked up her phone and typed out a message. *Oliver, am in rue de Charonne. The bistro's called L'Armagnac. Shall I wait here for you? Is Lizzie with you? PLEASE send news. Thanks. C U later. KZ*

A cry, a wail, a plea for a goal circulated thunderously round the place. Someone was rhythmically pounding the flats of his hands against the bar's surface, slippery with spilled beer. The thumping, like a primeval drumbeat, surged round the room, inciting impatience. The mood no longer felt congenial and relaxed: a degree of raucous agitation was building. Husky male voices admonished the overhead screen for its lack of a score. A glass went spinning to the floor, lager flying horizontally, like flapping translucent wings, causing those close by to jump and squeal, then erupt into inebriated laughter.

Kurtiz shivered. Restless, she glanced upwards: 9.17. Some disturbance appeared to have unsettled the play. The pace of the game was slowing. The footballers were looking from one to another with perplexed expressions. A lean black athlete in blue holding the ball at rest beneath his booted foot was glancing to and fro as though awaiting instructions. Play had drawn almost to a halt. No, all was back on track. The player released the ball, dribbled and kicked it to a team mate. Kurtiz was getting hungry, her stomach growling. She signalled to Jean-Claude to bring her a plate of *charcuterie* and a glass of red. The cold steak and *frites*, untouched by her erstwhile companion, stood forgotten on the neighbouring table. She was tempted to lean over and nick a chip.

A howl, like that of a wolf at night, rose from the bar. She glanced at her watch: 9.21 p.m. The game had been interrupted again. She lifted her reading glasses from the table to take a better look.

A handful of spectators were rising from their seats, jumping over them, gathering up their possessions, carrying their young, descending towards the pitch. Groups of confused people from every direction. The Friday-nighters, the party-goers, surrounding Kurtiz were calling, whistling, jeering. What was happening? Hundreds of people, children too, were congregating at the perimeters of the football pitch, looking about them, confused. Heads were lifted towards giant screens as though awaiting instructions from on high. Parents were hugging their frightened offspring tight against them, protectively, as though something diabolical was about to take place. It reminded Kurtiz of shots she had taken in war zones. Those numbed, stupefied expressions that spoke of shock, loss, death. Victims of desolation.

But this was a friendly football match in Paris. What was going on?

A *mec* at the bar gave a yell to Jean-Claude to switch off the canned music and turn up the sound on the TV. Something was amiss. Kurtiz glanced at her phone. Still no response from Oliver. Should she walk to the theatre and hang about outside? It was November. The day had been mild for the time of year but it would not be getting any warmer as the night closed in. Too nippy for hanging about in the dark. There would surely be an interval soon. Perhaps she could slip in and watch the second half of the show, unseen by Oliver or Lizzie. She would never find them in any case among the fifteen hundred strong concert-goers. It might be fun. How long since she had attended a rock concert? Donkey's years.

A plate of cold cuts landed on the cloth in front of her along with a glass of red. Jean-Claude was harassed and sweating. She nodded thanks and requested her bill, then delayed him to know if he had understood what had come to pass at the Stade de France. 'Has there been an accident?'

He shrugged. 'They might be stopping the match, Madame. Or pausing it for some reason. We are trying to understand. Our President Hollande has been called away from the stadium.' The waiter slid out of sight, obscured by coats, scarves and hands grasping drinks, his attention demanded elsewhere.

Kurtiz glanced to the street. Night had fallen some while back and the city was in the grip of a deep, gloomy blanket of winter. She thought of the old actress shuffling up the street, cradling her loneliness, with only the dog to protect and entertain her. Should she have offered to accompany her, stroll along the street with her? No, it was better to keep her distance. Her own botched life was best not shared.

Her bill arrived on a small white saucer. Along with it came a tiny boiled sweet. She pulled her purse from her bag and from it a twenty-euro note and another of five euros. She picked up a slice of *saucisson*, popped it into her mouth and chewed. She downed the wine in two swift gulps. This place was becoming frenetic. Her head was thumping. It was past nine thirty. She had expected news from Oliver by now. 'Christ,' she muttered, taking on board the possibility that something had gone wrong – no Lizzie - and he had started drinking. She should never have agreed to let him handle this on his own. He was irresponsible, didn't she know that? Wasn't that partially what all this mess was about? Easy. Take it easy. She was getting het up.

The denouement of the night was moving inexorably towards her. And she was apprehensive about its outcome.

She grabbed her bags. She'd get some fresh air, then decide where best to suggest to rendezvous with Oliver – a quieter place. She was feeling restless, uncomfortable in this bar. The crowd pressed against her as she negotiated and jostled a path to the door. Outside, ranks of diners and drinkers were smoking, cradling glasses or bottles, braving the cold for the sake of a cigarette, talking, laughing loudly. She slid through them and halted, poised at the edge of the pavement, looking to right and left. She took a step onto the street. Fresh air. From an overhead apartment, she caught the strains of Miles Davis, 'Sketches of Spain'. Perennial Davis. Left, in the distance, some ten buildings along, she made out the shadowy silhouette of the old woman and her dog approaching another café, animated with a crowded candlelit terrace. The woman stopped and bent low to fuss over or chide her pet. She was a kind soul.

As Kurtiz stood gazing to her left, contemplating her own solitariness and what a shambles this situation with Lizzie was and how the craved-for embrace of Alex was possibly just a few Métro stations away, a black car drew alongside the bistro Madame Courtenay had just been standing in front of, masking both woman and dog as it cruised by almost in slow motion. Then two things happened at once. The car came to a halt and Kurtiz gazed open-mouthed as the muzzle of an assault gun – two guns? – appeared from out of the car's windows. A man, medium height, dressed from head to foot in black, stepped out of the car, cradling a pointed rifle. This was followed, seconds later, by a volley of bullets. Firing at close range with a velocity speed of somewhere in the region of 700 metres a second, the gunslinger was shooting to kill. Kalashnikovs were known to hit targets accurately at a far greater distance than that. Kurtiz had travelled through a sufficient number of hellholes to have witnessed at first hand the capability of those relentless bursts of fire. One out of five bullseyes at 800 metres. The car was stationary, and less than twenty metres from the restaurant. There *were* two guns.

'Holy shit!'

Bullets were perforating windows. Glass was shattering. People were screaming. Bodies were folding, falling. Cartridges were flying repeatedly, round after deafening round, the shallow flat cracks of a Kalashnikov, an AK-47 or AK-12. Behind her, the smokers' chatter had been stunned to a cold silence.

A hush descended all along the street until a newly loaded magazine released further rounds of cartridges, streaking from the barrel. Those deep dark sounds of assault guns. Kurtiz bent forward, an instinct for preservation, readying herself for action, as the bullets whistled, yawed and exploded, penetrating glass, metal, cement, flesh. Behind her, several of the smokers witnessing the carnage had hurled themselves back inside

L'Armagnac, screaming at Jean-Claude to call for the police, for the emergency services, to lock the doors, bring down the metal shutters, create a shelter. Others had darted onto the street, hopping and skipping. Many were jabbering into their smartphones.

'Keep back, for *ferrrrck*'s sake!' someone, a young woman, bellowed drunkenly.

Strident voices. Yelping, clamouring.

Kurtiz began to lope in the direction of the slaughter. She hugged the buildings, bouncing her shoulders off walls as she advanced, keeping herself clear of the line of fire should one of the assailants turn his attention down the street and target his rear. Above her, windows were being unlocked, heads poking out. Three shoulder bags were slapping against her lower back, giving her kidneys a walloping. In a professional capacity, she wouldn't be carrying so much darned stuff. As she ran, still hunched low, she was unbuckling her camera holder with the facility of one who knows what's next. A professional instinct. She pulled out her Leica M9, raised it skilfully to eye level and began to record the scene.

Smoke was rising from somewhere close by. Acridity permeated the shaken neighbourhood. One minute. Two minutes. Three minutes. No mercy, no let-up from the gunshots. These firearms were rigged to launch grenades. She knew that and prayed a grenade would not be the hoodlums' parting shot. The black car was revving its engine. Impatient to be done, or gaining in excitement at the seeping lake of blood and bodies. Exhaust fumes added their poison. The killer swung himself into a back seat and the black saloon screeched its getaway even as its door was closing, leaving mayhem in its wake.

Kurtiz rose to her full height and snapped, then snapped again, its skidding departure from its tail end, recording the make, model – a Seat – and number plate. Then she picked up speed, sprinting in great strides, her breath loud even to her deafened ears until she reached the terrace, candles spluttering, where diners had been eating al fresco. All was silent. No one was moving, no one crying, frozen, muted in shock, as though dead on their feet.

A still life riddled with holes. Ravaged.

'Oh, dear God.' Kurtiz wanted, needed, with a visceral longing, to be hugging Lizzie, her precious girl, squeezing her hard, to feel her young frame safely tight against her own. She wanted to erase all that she was gazing upon, for none of this to be the reality.

Food had spilled in what looked like clouds of vomit onto the wooden floorboards of the terrace. Wine bottles were leaking their contents, like another source of blood. Then, as though a switch had been flipped, a female diner in high heels started to scream and shout. Ear-splitting incomprehensibility. Incessant yells. Her shrill cries, a smoker's rasp, sliced through the shock and paralysis.

Bodies were supine or curled like overblown foetuses on the ground, higgledy-piggledy, some on top of others. Overturned tables, like great wooden shields, fretted by gunfire, hid bleeding, crouching figures who had taken cover there, thinking naively to protect themselves. At a large, round, still upright table, the celebrants were all at once crashing into and against one another as they attempted to lift from beneath their feet others who were no longer members of their party, merely felled, bullet-ridden corpses. Some were calling on their mobiles, begging, pleading for assistance. People began to flood the scene, from other bars, restaurants, from neighbouring blocks. They were hugging one another, weeping or staring without seeing. The seesaw whine of approaching sirens broke into the night like a second impending threat, a second attack, a further act of war.

Kurtiz let her camera drop to her side and lifted her head, tilting it skywards, like a dog sniffing the night's scents. Sirens everywhere, distant and close by, penetrating the darkness. Keening. As though the entire city was emitting a call, an affronted cry, a banshee wail for the still-warm dead. Tears of shock, of horror, spilled down her cheeks. Her entire body was shaking.

Where was the old actress who had been making her way home from the bar? Had the assassins caught her or had she managed to walk on to safety? Kurtiz wiped her face with the back of her hand, sniffed, breathed deeply while casting about her, searching along the road and gutters for the fur coat and an ivory-haired dog.

Marguerite and Charlie, Paris, March 1947

Charles Gilliard was in a triumphant, reckless frame of mind. He would seek out that dainty young slip of a thing from the cinema and buy her a hearty dinner before she left town. She looked like she could use a square meal. Meat, potatoes and a farmer's cheese. A slap-up affair with wine in a bottle, not the usual rough carafes he ordered for himself. A celebration was in order, and he wanted to share his exultation.

Access to Madame Friedlander's apartment had been painless, 'a piece of cake', as they would have said back home. He'd watched the old girl go out of the main entrance with a large woven shopping basket, and he had trailed discreetly behind her for a short distance to confirm that she was making her way to the local market, ensuring that she would be gone for some time, then round the back he'd jogged, up the stairs, two at a time, and he was inside the flat within the turn of a key. Charlie had found two big leather suitcases on the bed in the spare room. Clothes, bed linen, a ticking clock, hairbrushes, washbags, shoes, a stuffed jewellery box: everything was spilling out, erupting all over the lime-green quilt and floor. Her Highness was back for the duration: that was evident. A rare and lucky Jewess in the light of recent history. After Charlie had swiftly gathered together all that was his own, including, most essentially, his precious great bundles of francs, he had loitered a moment longer. '*Merci beaucoup, Madame.* I wish you good fortune and peace,' he had said aloud. 'And a long life.'

He had replaced the spare set of keys he had found in the flat when he had first entered it. Back into the vase they'd dropped, so Madame would never suspect they had been used. And then he had walked away from the comfort he had called his own for the past four years. It was time to move on, although to where he hadn't yet the faintest notion. He needed to secure a plan. What were his options? Back to England? No, that was out of the question. Once recognized and tried for desertion, he'd be imprisoned if not executed. East, towards Germany? No. Krauts were Krauts and he'd seen enough of them, lived in their oppressive shadow for too long. There wasn't much to attract him in a westerly direction. Normandy, apple farms . . . He fancied an apple farm, would relish any farm of his own, land and growth, but just beyond lay the English Channel. Too perilous. South to Lyon then, and on to the Mediterranean coast, perhaps. A warmer climate. Land that had not been occupied by the Germans, or not until very late in the war, so the cities and towns were less in need of emotional refurbishment and the inhabitants might be less jittery. In other words, he'd find a warmer welcome and better work opportunities.

Paris, November 2015

Upstairs in the second floor flat at 71 rue de Charonne, the clock on the mantelpiece read five minutes to ten. Marguerite Courtenay was hanging up her mink in the cupboard by the front door. Somewhere behind her in the sitting room her dog was yapping, moving about in frenzied circles, impatient to go out.

'What's the matter with you, Lola? You've had your walk and your *pipi*. Sssh, now, be a good girl. It's time for bed.'

The retired actress's soothing hum had little effect on the unnerved animal, which, upright on its hind legs, began scratching and clawing at the legs of the furniture.

'What *is* the matter with you?'

Marguerite brushed down her dress, smoothing non-existent creases with the flat of her hand, then primped her wavy white hair. Satisfied, she pushed up her sleeves and made her way through to her modest kitchen to pour water into the Maltese's bowl.

As the tap was running, she grew aware of and confused by oscillations of noise, shouts and cries, the braying of sirens. The uproar was coming from outside. Congregating gangs of footballers or overexcited foreigners? She placed the steel water dish on the floor, ruffled the head of her best friend – 'Calm down now' – and wandered into the sitting room, gathering up a duster she had left on a side table as she passed. Forehead pressed against the window, she saw spinning lights, violet spills unspooling like threads of yarn. Police vehicles? There must have been a fight, although they were rare in this district where every creed and nationality lived alongside one another in peace, close-knit and supportive. Old Paris, tolerant. If there were fights, street brawls and punch-ups, they were usually the result of aggressive misunderstandings between drunken tourists. She pressed her nose to the window, peering hard, rubbed her clouds of breath off the glass with the cloth still in her right hand, and focused her attention across the street. Yes, police and fire service. Pyramids of shattered glass were winking beneath the headlights of the patrol cars. An astonishing assembly of ambulances too. Heavy-booted security men laden with munitions, some wearing visors, patrolled back and forth.

'What in Heaven's name?'

She craned her neck to take in more of the scene. La Belle Équipe seemed to be surrounded.

'What on earth . . . ?'

Bodies were being dragged, bagged and rushed away in ambulances and fire engines. Had a bomb exploded? Was there a fire? Should she take the lift back downstairs and see what she could do to lend a hand? Marguerite felt her old body, thin as a wheat stalk, begin to shudder. She staggered to the television and switched it to the third channel. There she read, at the foot of the images: *Paris sous siège.*

Paris is under attack?

The sirens cried out from the screen, counterpointing those wailing beyond her windows, homing in on the *quartier.*

An image of Hollande flashed up. He had been called out from the football stadium, one of two anchormen was relating. There was a note of real urgency to his commentary. An attack on a restaurant. No figures yet of the numbers injured or possibly dead. A young man with a voguish trace of beard was burbling into a microphone. He was speaking directly from the scene of the attack. The tenth *arrondissement.* In rue Alibert. Not here, not rue de Charonne. Marguerite was confused. On the screen, behind the tense young man, clusters of stationary fire engines, striped yellow and red. Dark-clad police officers with firearms and helmets were striding to and fro.

She shuffled backwards, grappling for a chair. 'Are we at war?' she muttered. If so, with whom? Where would she go? Was there to be a mass evacuation? What could she, a defenceless old lady, do to protect herself? She had known the horrors of war as a girl.

Rue de Charonne, her own street with its façades so familiar, was not mentioned on the television, yet what was going on beyond her own apartment? She hobbled back to the window and pressed her hands to the glass. The devastation below was horrifying and real. People bent double, sobbing, on their knees howling. In pain, in grief. She must go down. She must offer her home as refuge to those who needed solace, alcohol, tea. Had they confused the address? Reporting rue Alibert when in fact the destruction was right here in rue de Charonne?

Back on the screen, a news update.

'We are receiving incoming bulletins that suggest there has also been an incident at the Bataclan concert hall, in the eleventh *arrondissement*, boulevard Voltaire. Unidentified men, three or possibly four, have entered the concert hall by the bar area, it has been reported. It has been described to us as a "hostage situation". A number of accounts are emerging from within the theatre, audience members in hiding, sending messages of distress from their smartphones, calling for assistance. This is a developing story and we will be back to you with news on it as soon as we have more.'

Dear God, the Bataclan. Marguerite had been reminiscing about that building, the horrid old carpet upon which she had inadvertently dropped cigarette ash, only this evening.

But wait . . . Hadn't her companion at L'Armagnac mentioned that her family was attending this evening's concert? Marguerite's mind was growing befuddled. These events were too shocking. She rubbed her hands together, one over the other, rings scratching flesh. Her fingers were becoming numb. A circulatory problem. She must not forget to take her bedtime pill. She was so lax about it.

Yes, she was convinced of it. The woman's daughter and husband were at a rock concert at the Bataclan. She must return downstairs, no question about it. It was her duty to hurry to L'Armagnac, seek out the lady and warn her. Marguerite was crossing the carpet in her stockinged feet, rooting out a pair of shoes from the cupboard. Not her boots – they were fiddly to zip up and took too long. She was all of a fidget, drawing her mink back off its hanger. Where were her keys? She must go down and warn that poor Englishwoman.

What a terrifying business.

Only an hour or two earlier she had been sitting comfortably with a Ricard between her fingers, rings tapping against the cool glass, chatting amiably to the young photographer while recalling her own post-war Bataclan days. All those years back, decades and decades ago, when it had been a picture house, when she had first set eyes on Charlie. How naive she had been. '"In my salad days when I was green in judgement . . ." Oh, yes, and so puffed up with my own importance.' She shook her head at those hazy memories of herself, of the handsomeness of that young Charlie. Charlie, to whom she should have been more loving. She had been too young and damaged to know better, wrapped up in her own self-centred concerns.

She put on her fur, ready to brave the cold for the second time that evening. Better to put aside the past and help those suffering now in the street beneath her. There was nothing to be done about poor, long gone Charlie.

Marguerite and Charlie, Paris, March 1947

Marguerite scanned the steel and glass interior hall of the Gare de Lyon, eyeing people's passage, the preoccupied or harassed faces of travellers, the mass of unknowns who were waiting for trains, for loved ones, departing or arriving. She was faint with hunger, dizzy from lack of sleep, dragged down by defeat. Four strangers had refused her plea for assistance, her request for a franc or two, while others had simply walked on, ignoring her approach with stuck-up expressions as though she were nothing better than a vagrant. Her confidence had taken a belting, more so because she was so tired and hungry.

The place was heaving with others, Europeans speaking foreign languages: Polish, Hungarian, Croatian. These were the 'displaced people' all the newspapers were writing about. Eyes that were glassy and hollow, hanging arms, bony fingers with tattered suitcases. Were they Jews? There were ragged families of them in the rundown *pension* where she had stayed. She had tried hard not to look at them, never to meet their gaze.

She had to find help soon. She needed a square meal but, most importantly, a railway ticket to the south. She would not give up on this. Her open-toed sandals were scuffed, dusty, and the straps were biting into her ankles, swollen after the three-kilometre trek across the eastern streets of Paris. She turned slowly in a circle, her worn beige raincoat hanging limply between her clasped hands, a travel bag containing all her worldly possessions slung over one shoulder. That was all she could claim as her own since she had pawned her watch to feed herself and sold her leather gloves for a paltry few francs to pay for the last of her drama lessons a few weeks earlier. The evening before, that bastard of a landlord had confiscated the suitcase containing all her gorgeous frocks. She silently cursed the manager at the Bataclan picture house for denying her those hard-earned wages and leaving her with nothing. Not a *sou*. Her weary eyes were darting this way and that on the hunt for a potential target when she suddenly became aware that a teenage boy with a soft clean-shaven face was watching her, spying on her.

Half hidden, peering from behind a pillar, he was wearing a bedraggled fawn cap pulled down over his eyes. It made him look gormless. She might have attempted to charm him, fall upon his mercy, but he looked menacing as well as daft. A pick-pocket, perhaps. There were so many of them about. He did not resemble someone she would feel easy to sit with over a *café au lait*. She turned her attentions elsewhere, making certain that the boy's gaze did not meet hers. Was he a thief or might he have the same purpose in mind as she? Begging. He was possibly after money while she required a ticket on the night express to the south. She had dreamed of travelling first class in a fine new hat and high-heeled shoes – she had dreamed so many dreams throughout her adolescent years. Now she would accept a seat even in the recently installed third-class carriage. But how to obtain one without a single miserable *sou* left in her pocket?

Just when she was beginning to think she would be forced to spend another night on a bench out in the open and, if so, miss her rendezvous in Nice, which was drawing ever closer, her attention was caught by a man wearing a black astrakhan coat, black Homburg hat and shoes as polished and shiny as one of those newly minted five-franc coins. He strolled at a leisurely pace – not in a hurry, time on his hands, time to offer a kindly ear to her plight perhaps – as he ascended the stairs to the station restaurant. Maybe she could beg a meal off him. Hot food. Her stomach growled. He pulled out a silver pocket watch, slowed down to read the time, then continued up to the restaurant's doorway. He looked very rich and was unaccompanied. Marguerite was desperate. Why not him? He was a bit wrinkled, puckered skin, but as good a choice as any on this friendless afternoon. Somewhere close by an organ-grinder started to play 'Blue Skies Are Round The Corner'. She flashed a look behind her and caught sight of a scrawny, ring-tail monkey in a scruffy red military-style coat. The creature was collecting coins in a tin cup for its owner, who wore a scarlet shirt and kerchief to match the monkey's costume.

Blue skies are round the corner, indeed! Well, let this be the change in the weather. Heart palpitating, Marguerite began to hum, biting back her nerves, bracing herself as she stepped forward with her most confident stride, ascending the stairs to the posh eating house, delicious aromas wafting her way. A simple act of kindness was what she was after but, dammit, she had not expected a waiter, some Cerberus at the door, to bar her access. He looked her up and down, disapproving of her down-at-heel appearance. '*Oui, Mademoiselle*? What can we do for you?'

Marguerite's heart was racing faster than the thud of galloping horses. She was thinking on her feet, glancing into the golden-domed room with its ornate statuettes and painted ceiling, overwhelmed by its sumptuousness, eyes scanning for the stranger in the black overcoat. Several tables were occupied by large groups – some were families, no doubt, off on their holidays by the sea. All were laughing and quaffing. Such familial ebullience stung her when she was so adrift, so alone in the world, and still grieving her lost brother. In her desperation she was pinning her hopes on the hatted stranger. She spotted him. Thanks to the heavens, he was seated at a solitary table.

'I have been asked to deliver a message to that gentleman over there,' she lied, in her finest accent. She was not an actress for nothing.

'Allow me to do that for you, Mademoiselle.'

'Oh, I am afraid not. It is of a rather personal nature and the news is not as rosy as he might have hoped. It needs to come directly from me, broken to him tactfully. I am sure you will understand, Monsieur.'

The waiter was confused. Uncertain of the protocol, his white face twitched. A bead of sweat popped out on his temple. His role was to keep the riff-raff out, not invite them in. He had a wife and a young child to feed. He didn't need trouble or to lose his job in these struggling times.

'Sir, I am sure you wouldn't want anything untoward to happen to a member of the gentleman's family because he hasn't received vital news and cannot react to it, now, would you? It could be a matter of life and death. How could you live with yourself if you were held responsible –'

'Oh, very well,' the waiter conceded, 'but please be quick about it. This is most irregular.'

Marguerite shuffled across the dining room as fast as her swollen feet would carry her, attempting not to lose all dignity. She sat down at her portly redeemer's table, shot a glance back to the entrance where the black-and-white-clad waiter stood worrying, and set to work.

'*Cher monsieur*,' she began, almost before her companion was aware of her presence.

'*Que diable se passe-t-il?* What the dickens . . . ?' He glanced about him, evidently fearing someone might spot him in the untidy girl's company, attempting a little nervously to keep his surprise in check. His anxiety seemed to temper hers and she snatched the opportunity to take control of the situation. Marguerite gave the stranger a smile of such intensity – her most winning smile – while her lilac eyes begged him for a little consideration, a dollop of human kindness. She saw now that the man opposite her was even older than she had at first surmised, perhaps as much as fifty, and he wore a light coating of powder on his jowly features. His moustache curled at its two extremes and was greased and shiny as though coated in a blue-black boot polish.

Might he be an actor too? Unlikely, if he could afford to dine in the fancy Buffet de la Gare de Lyon. She had no choice but to keep going.

'Do you know anything about cinema, Monsieur?'

Bemused, he shook his head.

'Talking pictures, sir.'

Again he showed not a flicker of interest. This was not the reaction she had anticipated. She had hoped the gentleman might be impressed, overawed at the notion that a future film star was sitting across the table from him. 'But you have been to a picture house in your time?'

'Why this ridiculous quiz? What the devil do you want?'

'Sir, please, don't be impatient with me or raise your voice. The fact is I am on my way to Nice,' she was losing the advantage and quickly continued, 'where I have been invited to perform in a screen test. Odds are I am to play the leading role in a major new film . . .'

At that moment a large round plate of oysters arrived and was placed on the table between them while over the gentleman's other shoulder stood another waiter in an ankle-length, starched white apron. This fellow was bearing a tall glass of chilled beer. Chunks of baguette appeared. Marguerite's stomach began to howl, like a dog chained to a post. An orchestra tuning up. Her head was light and she was overcome with a spinning giddiness. She was clutching her hands tightly in her lap, holding fast to her raincoat for fear she would seize the bread.

The man lifted an oyster between podgy fingers to his pursed lips.

'Please, sir, listen to me, I need help,' she begged.

He slurped the shiny grey mollusc noisily, slurped and sucked until it disappeared, sliding down his gullet. The shell was replaced on the plate. Marguerite feared that her presence, her company at this table, had been upstaged by the food. She had never tasted an oyster but they looked lustrously delicious surrounded by quarters of lemons, all packed on ice. What a repast!

'Sir, may I, please, have a piece of bread?' She did not wait for his response but snatched at the loaf – her hands had a will of their own – stuffed a morsel into her mouth and munched greedily. Midway to his lips, the second oyster hung. If he was not interested in helping her, she would at least have appeased the direst pangs of her hunger.

And then, most unexpectedly, he returned his uneaten shellfish to the table, watched her chewing, almost choking, on the bread and started to laugh. 'Have you come hoping to beg money from me?' The mirth just as instantly disappeared. 'Well, we'll see about that!' He was looking about, shifting and snorting, agitating in his seat. Seeking the management, Marguerite supposed. He would have her kicked out, like a mongrel, a beggar. Or, worse, arrested for theft.

'No, sir, I'm not begging. I want to make you an offer.'

'Oh, dear God!'

'No, no, nothing like that. The price of a ticket on tonight's express train to Nice – any class, sir, I'm not fussed – as a loan. Only a loan. Paid back in full as soon as the role is mine and, as well, a ticket for you, two if you wish, a second for your wife –'

'Wife!'

'Two tickets to the première of my film, which will most certainly screen and be applauded in Paris. What do you say? Please, God, help me. My intentions are honourable. You'll see. I'm a really good actress. I just need a break.' She was gabbling, nineteen to the dozen.

Staff were approaching, bearing down upon her. She would be out on her neck if she didn't think fast.

The waiter from the entrance had appeared at her companion's side. He who had previously obstructed her. 'Is there a problem, sir?' Before another word could be said or any harm done, before the situation grew out of control and she was apprehended, Marguerite was on her feet, snatched up her flimsy travel bag, grappled with grubby fingers for one more chunk of the freshly baked bread and took flight, crumbs trailing, heels clacking against belle-époque tiles, hair flying wild.

Back on the station concourse, out of breath, she found sanctuary on an empty bench and threw herself down, leaning back, legs in the air. Her heart was beating like the pendulum of a long-case clock, similar to the one at her parents' home, and she felt a whizzing in her brain. During the kerfuffle upstairs, she had managed to grab not one but two more thick wedges of baguette and was stuffing them into her mouth, chewing ravenously, almost choking with a desperate appetite. The station clock read twenty past three. It was now Wednesday. Time was running out. If she did not board this evening's Mediterranean-bound blue train, she would not be in Nice for her screen test at the Victorine Studios on Friday.

She sighed, battling tears, which would mess up her mascara. She wasn't very good at begging. But what alternatives were left to her besides returning whence she had come, to her parents' bakery, admitting defeat? But she would never, never do that.

Her brother, Bertrand, had left for the front and never

returned. She'd hated life at home without him. He'd been her best friend and had encouraged her ambition. The sight of him in uniform going off in a lorry had lit a fire within her. How could her parents accept the loss of him with such composure, never a word, never complaining? She'd wanted to run away. So, one afternoon when they were at the mill purchasing bags of flour, she'd slipped out and taken the road to Paris. Sixteen years old, with a head full of dreams of moving pictures, of stardom. Her mother had always derided her, dismissing them as 'castles in the air'.

She would never go back, not until her name was in lights.

In the midst of her recollections, she spotted a sandy-haired young fellow whose face was vaguely familiar. He was giving her the eye, a bit of a come-hither look, grinning, amused by her. She frowned. What the devil was so funny? Did she know him? If so, from where? She turned her attention in another direction, hoping he would go away. What *was* he staring at? She needed to concentrate on finding someone who would lend her some money.

'I could stand you a sandwich and a beer, if you like? Why not join me?'

Charlie was leaning over her, his travel bag on his arm. He had addressed her in impressive French, but something in his accent or his manner suggested that he was a foreigner. Lord, of course! He was the rather engaging customer from the Bataclan picture house, who'd bought her a cup of tea and some cake. The last time she'd eaten, except for the bread. She rubbed at her face and hair hoping she did not look too frightful.

'I am not in need of a sandwich, thank you very much. I have just dined in the very fine station buffet over there.' She looked him in the face and saw that he was a great deal older than she. Twenty-six, or -seven.

'Dined?' He grinned again. 'Do you call filching a stick of baguette "dining"?'

'Such impudence. Are you accusing me of stealing? Be on your way.' Hoity-toity manner, crossing one leg over the other.

'I've been looking for you, keeping an eye open for you.' He spoke with an intensity that turned her attention. 'We met yesterday,' he persisted.

'Yes, I remember. What do you want?'

'You are beautiful.' He sat himself down on Marguerite's bench and gazed at her.

'Please go.' She turned her face away from him and shunted herself further along the wooden seat. 'I can't sit and talk to you now. I'm busy.'

'You appear to be in trouble.'

She bit her lip.

'Where are you going?'

'I told you yesterday, I'm going south.'

'But you haven't boarded any train.'

'Well, neither have you! I'm going to Nice. I'm in the movies. Now go away, please.'

'Would you like a beer?'

'No, thanks.' It was the sandwich she craved. She glanced at the station clock again. Two minutes to four. Three hours were all that remained to purchase herself a ticket and get on board. She must find someone who would buy it for her. She lifted her gaze towards the young man at her side and softened her expression, fluttering her eyelids. 'You're too young to be rich, but perhaps you have a few francs to spare?'

He smiled and shook his head. 'I can afford to eat and I usually have a bed to sleep in.'

'I am not looking for a bed, and don't you go getting fancy ideas!' She swung her body back towards him and looked him full in the face. His grey-green eyes seemed kindly enough, although who could say in this city of chancers? His chin was stubbly, as though he had forgotten to shave. 'What's your name?'

'I told you yesterday – Charlie. And you are Marguerite, yes?'

Marguerite was taken aback that he had remembered. 'That's right. Very well then, thank you, Charlie. I will accept a beer on the condition that you go on your way afterwards because I need to give my urgent attention to a little business matter.'

Charlie led her across the street, where they entered a brasserie. It was packed and noisy, fuggy with smoke. Toulouse-Lautrec posters on the walls. Cheery accordion music drowned the chatter.

'You were at the pictures yesterday, weren't you? So you must enjoy cinema, the silver screen? Unless you're one of those who goes in there to sleep and keep warm.'

'You should be in films, you're so pretty.'

'Oh, do you really think so? Well, I am an actress.'

Their beers arrived. Marguerite emptied hers fast and felt instantly – not quite drunk but woozier, even more lightheaded than before.

'Do you want another?'

She shook her head. She had to keep her wits about her.

'Something to eat? Oysters, what would you say to oysters?' He was laughing.

'Oysters! Ooh, yes. As it happens, I am very fond of oysters.'

Charlie beckoned to the waiter and ordered two plates of a dozen each.

Marguerite studied the young man opposite her who seemed so civilized, so well-bred. She took a deep breath. She couldn't bear to be humiliated, ridiculed again, especially by one so handsome, but who else was left to ask? 'I'm in a spot of trouble. Only temporarily mind.'

He sipped his beer.

'Do you think you could . . . might you be able to lend me the price of a ticket on tonight's express to Nice? I have a job waiting for me there and I can send you back the money next week as soon as I'm paid my first wage.'

He did not reply but seemed to be thinking it over. Hope rose like a new day within her.

'I lost my purse, you see. Well, not lost. It was . . . stolen and –' Her hand was in the dish of bread even before the waiter had placed it on the table. She was eating and talking at the same time, blithely unaware of her coarse manners.

'How old are you?' quizzed Charlie, watching the movement of her full mouth, those rosebud lips. He waited.

'Twenty,' she lied, 'and you?'

The oysters arrived. Marguerite picked up the first from her plate and, following the example of the horrid old man in the astrakhan coat – what a queer one he was – she slurped and sucked as hard as she could, almost choking on the slippery mollusc as it slid down her throat. 'Ooh, goodness me. Very salty, but delicious.' Her eyes were watering. 'I do *so* love oysters, don't you? Might I have another beer?'

They ate their oysters happily, although Marguerite was growing anxious. Charlie hadn't given her an answer yet. She scanned the room for a clock. 'I mustn't miss my train. What do you say for the ticket? My watch was stolen along with my purse or I would have left it with you as a guarantee, so to speak.' She blushed beneath his penetrating gaze.

'Why don't I buy two tickets?'

'But I am not coming back!'

'Two singles. I could travel with you.'

'To Nice?'

'Why not?'

She was mulling it over, stuffing her face with food, gulping more beer, governed by the hands of time marching onwards. 'You can't hang around with me, you understand that, don't you? I've a job waiting for me. At the Victorine Studios. No doubt you've heard of it. It's the Hollywood of the South of France.' Her voice seemed to rise an octave as she pronounced the word 'Hollywood', as though she were singing. Singing its praises, singing her dreams.

Charlie was silent, considering his choices. He was indeed attracted to the crazy, half-starved feral with her bright lilac-blue eyes. And what had he got to lose? It would be judicious to leave Paris, sooner rather than later, prudent to move on, and in the company of a woman was even smarter. 'I have friends who live near

Nice. Usually I spend a few weeks of my summer vacationing with them but what with the war and all . . .' Charlie blagued, crossing his fingers beneath the table as he did so.

Marguerite fixed him with an incredulous gaze. 'You have friends near Nice? Whereabouts?' She didn't know a soul in the south. Might this be a bed, a place to store her belongings until she was settled?

'Cannes. In fact, I had been mulling over their invitation.'

The idea of this Englishman tagging along did not appeal to Marguerite Anceaume, even if he was ever so debonair, but what other possibilities were available to her? None. She was out of alternatives. Her two previous screen tests, both of which had been at the Studios de Billancourt outside Paris, had not been successes. Neither director had spotted her evident talents, in spite of the acting classes she had worked hard to pay for. She had been too nervous, too unsure of herself. Consequently, her comportment in front of the camera had been stilted; the words spoken had sounded laborious, without fluidity.

'You lack the quintessential ingredient, the magic, the charisma required for stardom.' The damning words; the director's summing up of her test.

Flabbergasted, she'd listened to his comment, staring numbly as he'd turned his back on her and strode away. She'd bitten back the rejection. Steeled herself. What did he know? Who'd ever heard of him? She couldn't even remember his stupid name. In Nice she would do better. She knew the ropes now, understood more precisely what was expected of her. She had hung around outside several film sets at Épinay-sur-Seine, watching other actresses at work, peeping from the sidelines in the hope of being contracted for a cameo, but nothing except several walk-on parts had come of it. Her paltry savings had been consumed. Her cashier's job at the cinema had not worked out . . . The fact was, she was in a right pickle. Her future did not lie in Paris. In Nice it would be rosier. It had to be, and she was more practised now. She was almost a professional.

But she would be nothing if she didn't get to the south. René Clément was to direct a picture there soon. Merle Oberon had been hired as an extra at those very same studios before the war and see to what heights she had risen. Once Marguerite reached Nice, everything would change. Opportunity would shake her hand and beckon her onwards.

'It would be a pity for you not to say hello to your friends, and if you really could lend me the price of that ticket . . . What do you say? A loan, mind you, I wouldn't dream of not paying you back. Cross my heart on it.' Marguerite smiled warmly at Charlie and he melted at the delicacy of her features, the sad simplicity of her clothes, her bitten nails and air of desperation. A state he was all too familiar with.

'You finish your meal and I'll go and buy the tickets.'

'No, wait!'

He stopped in his tracks.

'I'm coming with you.' She dared not let this opportunity out of her sight. Charlie, this handsome freckle-faced Englishman who spoke surprisingly good French with a delicious accent, was to be the gateway to her future.

*

The train standing on platform four was awaiting departure to the south. Directly after the Second World War, the carriages of the blue train, officially named Le Train Bleu in 1949, were a lot less fancy than they had been during the golden years of the twenties and early thirties when, in first class only, it had ferried the rich and famous up and down the country. Certainly, where Marguerite was settled in a third-class carriage, it was all a bit shabby, no frills, rather basic, not that she was complaining. She was over the moon to be on board with a bona fide ticket, firmly tucked up in her seat, hat off, raincoat folded, bag slipped neatly beneath her soiled swollen feet, bound for the Côte d'Azur.

But where was Charlie? Had he decided at the last minute against accompanying her on this grand journey? She hoped not. He seemed like a decent man and he knew the south. Perhaps he'd take pity on her and offer her lodging with him and his friends. And then she caught sight of him through the grimy window, running, laden, arriving with his case and other parcels, out of breath. And her heart lifted.

'I thought you weren't coming back,' she cried, unexpectedly relieved.

'I gave you your ticket. What were you worrying about?'

'But what took you so long?' Her stomach had been in a knot. She had not understood how much she hoped he would return. When had she last been in the company of someone who treated her with respect? Life in the capital had been grim. Suddenly, Charlie's proximity was a ray of sunshine.

'I went to find an evening newspaper and I bought us some sandwiches and a few beers. Look, I have plenty of provisions. We won't starve.'

She wanted to ask him more about his friends and their villa, but decided against it. She was getting carried away. She mustn't count on him or she would open herself up to further rejection, to being hurt again. Better, once they arrived, to give Charlie the slip. She couldn't allow him to hinder her career, to become entangled in her life. She had to think of herself, only herself, and her future. However, if he should offer her a room, just for a few nights . . . She yawned. Her feet were throbbing and she was worn out.

'Take my coat, why don't you? Use it as a pillow.'

She lifted her head drowsily while Charlie slipped the coat between the seat and her curls. She was exhausted but her tribulations, her gruelling days of hunger and anonymity, would soon be behind her. Nothing but a distant memory. Fame and acclaim awaited her.

The train was pulling out. Finally, at last, Marguerite Anceaume was on her way, climbing the pathway to stardom. She watched the rooftops and sooty chimney stacks of Paris disappear behind her, then closed her eyes to sleep for a while, secure in the company of the nice young man.

Marguerite was sitting in her mink and outdoor shoes, fixated by the images being screened on France 3, an *édition spéciale*. It was informing the nation that residents of Saint-Denis, a suburb on the outskirts of Paris, were being evacuated. Not all residents but those inhabiting streets abutting the Stade de France, the football stadium where the nation's team, Les Bleus, had been playing a friendly game against Germany. Many of the spectators from the match were still on the pitch, eyes trained upwards to the floodlit sky, as though anticipating visitors from outer space, ears tuned to the loudspeakers, awaiting instructions. Three suicide bombers had blown themselves up outside the stadium, killing one person, as yet unidentified.

Among the kerfuffle and the distressing news, and the dog's incessant, restless yapping, Marguerite's hearing took time to tune into the fact that her doorbell was buzzing. Short strident bursts. Urgent.

'Who could it be at this hour?' she asked aloud, clutching at the chair's embroidered covers. The police or fire brigade? They will attempt to evacuate me, but I have nowhere to go. The doorbell's non-stop burring sent the dog into a hysterical fit of desperate growling.

'Stop it, *arrêt maintenant*, Lola,' Marguerite snapped irritably. 'Let me think.'

Its tail cocked in the air, the Maltese began whining, unsettled by the tone of its mistress's command.

Marguerite's hands were trembling. She couldn't lift herself from the seat.

Why can't they leave me here? I would rather die in my own home than be shunted about by strangers. Homeless again.

She was affronted by noise. It was becoming insufferable. Paris under fire, under siege, yet still no mention of the horrors below in her own street. It was unthinkable. A nightmare of the worst kind. Others could take comfort in loved ones but to whom would she turn, and where to go? Eventually, if for no other reason than to put a stop to the commotion, she struggled to the door and pressed the intercom.

'*Oui?*' Her voice was croaky.

'Madame Courtenay?' An unidentified female enquiring.

'This is Madame Courtenay. Who are you?'

'It's Kurtiz Ross.'

'Who?'

'We sat alongside one another at L'Armagnac this evening.'

'Oh, yes, my dear, so we did. I was concerned about you.' And a frown crossed her aged features. 'Are you all right? Are you hurt? Come up. Why don't you come up?'

'There has been an attack.'

'Yes, I kn-know.' An attack, but where? Downstairs or elsewhere? She was quite unsure what information she had gleaned. But none of it was good. 'I was going to take the lift down and look for you. I was putting on my shoes. Or do you want to come up? I'm on the second floor.'

'*Merci, Madame.* I won't, thank you. People need help here. I wanted to reassure myself that you are safe. Have a good night and forgive me if I woke you.'

'Woke me? Goodness, no. I was on my way down. I was coming to look for you. To tell you –'

'Sleep well, Madame. Apologies once again for waking you.'

'Hello? Hello?' The intercom was silent. There was no one there.

Below, at street level, lights were flashing, pin-balling, spinning in every direction. A caravan of vehicles had slowed to a standstill, doors flung open. Orderlies, paramedics, nurses with transfusion units climbed in and out of ambulances. Burly men loaded with vests of ammunition paced to and fro. A ladder was propped against a wall, giving access to nowhere. People stood alone or in groups. The mood was subdued, intent, single-minded, outraged. Within an hour, everything had altered. The city had changed its face, turned it towards the darkness. It was numbed by the Armageddon that had taken it by the throat. It was ignorant of the facts, the many pieces that had not yet fully fallen into place.

Kurtiz spun about her, snapped a few shots. She listened to the city. This was war. She recognized it, the sick-sweet odour of death. And her daughter, her estranged husband were out there somewhere in the fray.

Kurtiz, Jerusalem, July 2011

Kurtiz was woken by the phone bursting into life. She opened one eye. Overhead, the creak of the aged fan was spinning in uncertain circles. From beyond the small open window, beyond her cramped first-floor room, with its jumble of dark hardwood furniture, and multi-pigmented carpets hanging from the walls, joyous laughter exploded in the gardens below. Music was playing, Palestinian instrumental music, like the soft clop of horses on cobblestones. She left the phone to ring. Her eyelids closed heavily, drowsily, without returning to sleep. It was bound to have been Alex. Her body stretched instinctively at her mental pictures of him. She glanced at her wristwatch before her arm flopped back against the flimsy bedding. It was ten past eight. She should get up, grab some dinner, put in a couple of hours' work editing the photographs she had downloaded that afternoon. Send Oliver and Lizzie a message, then get some real sleep. She, along with the crew, would be heading off into the mountains before first light.

A light tapping on the door dragged her from the bed. She grabbed a shirt and wound it round her breasts and midriff. 'Who is it?' She spoke softly into the wood, fingers locked round the smooth brass handle.

'Are you working or sleeping?'

'Showering.'

'I'll see you in the bar in twenty minutes.'

Kurtiz sighed. Alex had a habit of ordering rather than inviting her. Machismo manners, so outdated. But he was a damn fine filmmaker, and he knew it and used it, and she admired and respected him. And loved him. Maybe.

This was their fifth professional outing together in eighteen months and the work was proving to be exhilarating, challenging: a breakthrough for Kurtiz. It had lifted her out of the rut of traditional photography – mundane celebrity portraits and interior-design magazine shoots – to the international arena of war and conflict. It had also caused a deepening in the fissure of her sadly crumbling marriage. She sighed.

Kurtiz had met Alex Peters quite by chance at the Groucho Club in London's Soho two years earlier. She had been in the lounge waiting for Oliver. As had been his habit for some time, Oliver was running late. She had been perched on a stool, camera bags at her feet, jacket slung carelessly across them, idly checking her phone messages while flipping through the pages of the *Guardian* and sipping a gin and tonic. A double. It had been a tiring day: a portraiture of an actor, whose new film, a comedy, was due out in a couple of weeks, and his father, a profile-relationship piece for the *Sunday Times*. The old man had been a gentleman; the actor nervy, awkward, embarrassingly lecherous. She was skilled at handling insecure actors: she was married to one.

She was exhausted, not from the creative input into her day but by the futility of so many of the commissions her agent assigned her, and she was looking to shift the direction of her career, if she could only track out a new path. Changing directions was never easy and she had been badgering her agent to find her something more challenging.

She and Oliver had agreed that morning to meet up at the Groucho, then go to see *State of Play* at the Curzon. She was hoping to persuade him to skip the film and just grab dinner.

Alex had settled himself on the empty stool alongside her, the one she had mentally allocated to Oliver. There were several others unoccupied further to the corner of the bar, any of which the unknown male might have chosen. She was tapping out a text to her agent – *Selection of portraits on way to editor in the morning. We shot some decent stuff* – when she glanced up at the stranger and smiled.

'You waiting for someone?' He was American, African-American, with a wide open face and smooth, clear skin. Dark skin, black hair cropped close to his head, neatly but casually dressed. Mid-forties. Lean, fit, but not muscle-bound.

'My husband,' she returned, 'but, please, go ahead. He's running behind schedule, quote, unquote. Always is.' She returned her attention to the newsprint. A flick of the eye told her that Oliver was now more than thirty minutes late and she was glad she hadn't dropped into the cinema to buy the tickets while walking along Shaftesbury Avenue. The programme was due to begin in seven minutes. 'I seem to spend half my life waiting.' Was she bemoaning this fact to herself or encouraging conversation?

'It's the nature of the work. Seen on the screen, film

86

looks like it's all action. However, you and I know the hours involved, the hanging about, the endeavour, all for that one thrilling shot.'

A quizzical crease crossed her forehead. She had been talking about her life with Oliver.

'Your camera bags on the floor.'

'Oh, I see.'

'I'm Alex Peters, by the way. May I request of our fine bartender Dominik, here, to refill your glass? Dominik!'

Kurtiz was about to refuse, then changed her mind. Why not? 'And, Dominik, when you've served the drinks, please can you call through and ask them to hold a table for Mrs Ross.'

'Staying here?' Alex's question when the drinks arrived. She shook her head. Alex was, as it happened. 'Always do, when in London.' As it also turned out, Oliver didn't show. Or he was running so late, his text informed her, that Kurtiz typed back a response not to bother. She'd see him later at the house.

Serendipity?

She and Alex took the table she'd booked, ordered two more drinks and settled to conversation. He had been born and raised in Boston, a documentary filmmaker who had worked his way through the system from public radio to public-service TV and later had crossed over to films, working for a short while in commercial cinema, which he had not greatly enjoyed. Now he had set up his own company as an independent. 'So, that's me, to date.'

She liked this man and was vaguely aware of his award-winning work. He was assured, opinionated even, charming. They talked movies; they talked photography.

At his request, she showed him a selection of shots still filed on one of her cameras, the Canon 5D, and confessed that she was looking for different opportunities.

'Impressive.' He nodded. 'You been working as a photographer for long?'

'Fifteen years.'

They moved on to the subject of working in war zones, the risks, and then to the rise of citizen journalism. Alex Peters was erudite, greatly travelled – knew the Middle East like the back of his hand. She admitted she had never visited any of those countries.

'The furthest east I've ventured from Europe is Turkey.' She refrained from adding that it had been a family beach holiday in a packed-with-British-tourists zone with Oliver and Lizzie when their daughter was eight or nine. The one subject both she and Alex skirted around was that of families and marriage. She had noted the slender gold band on his wedding finger. Discreet. He mentioned Boston and his life back in the States only in passing; nothing to hint at the domestic situation. They shared a bottle of Saint-Estèphe. He knew his wines too. Talked some more about the film he was in the process of raising funds for and she never noticed the time passing. When she turned her head, the restaurant had emptied. Theirs was the last occupied table. The staff were hovering by the kitchen doors.

'Time to go.'

'Nightcap?'

'No, thanks.' She shifted her body, making moves to rise from the chair. He invited her to his room. She was surprised, quietly flattered, but shook her head, thanked him for his company and the meal.

'Pity.' He smiled. He was flying out the next day.

'To?' She ignored the sink of disappointment in her stomach.

'Paris, Beirut, and from there back to Boston. I'll catch you next time I'm in town, shall I?'

She nodded, hauled her camera bags over her shoulder and shook his hand. 'Thanks for the evening. It was fun.'

Three days later she received a call from her agent. 'The name Alex Peters mean anything to you?' Kurtiz held her breath. 'He's looking for a stills photographer for his next feature. It's shooting in Lebanon. I thanked him, explained it wasn't your cup of tea, but I have to put all offers to you and he was rather insistent. Now I've run it past you, I'll suggest Jack. It's right up his street.'

'Sorry, Gina. The job's mine.'

'It's not your expertise, Kurtiz, and it's three weeks away from home. I thought you never did that?'

Kurtiz hesitated. She didn't. She and Oliver had made a pact: until Lizzie had turned eighteen Kurtiz would not accept any assignments that meant more than two nights away from their London base. She closed her eyes, held tight to the phone. Oliver hadn't scored a decent acting job in over a year, nothing more than a cough and a spit and some relatively well-paid voiceovers. She wanted this opportunity. She craved it emotionally, artistically, and it just might be the commission that would shift the direction of her career. And then there was Alex Peters.

'Gina, can you email me through the details of Peters's offer and I'll get straight back to you?'

'Will do. And the *Mail on Sunday* have come through with a three-day shoot on a costume drama, location

Yorkshire. It's yours if you can get there this coming Thursday. Another last-minute booking, drives me crazy. I accepted it.'

The next time Kurtiz set eyes on Alex Peters was six weeks later when she stepped off the plane in Beirut and strode through Customs out into the heat where he was leaning against a four-wheel drive, arms crossed, waiting for her.

'We'll start gently,' he promised, while steering a path through the fraught city in a fridge of a vehicle blasted with air-conditioning. 'No danger zones until you know the ropes. First, I want you to meet my crew, Darryl and Tim. Just the three of us. They're both tough, reliable and experienced in the field, and then there's me. You're in safe hands. Welcome aboard.'

Two years on, Kurtiz headed downstairs. Outside in the East Jerusalem garden bar and restaurant, a stone oven had been lit. Its flames danced and crackled in the hot Middle Eastern darkness. The abiding stink of diesel from the bus station across the street almost overwhelmed the more agreeable aromas of fried chicken and sumac, and the heady smoke from the narghiles, but Kurtiz had grown used to the cocktail and did not dislike it. It conjured up for her a sense of liberation, of independence, of working in the field.

'You need to be on your mettle. No mistakes. These are high-risk territories, war zones.' Alex had warned her.

The challenge she had hoped for.

Each table was hooped with a circular glow from a lit

candle. The place was filling up, as it did every evening. The vibe was exuberant, spirited. This was one of the most popular hangouts in the eastern section of the city. Old Palestine. Arabs, Jews, Westerners congregated here without animosity. Intellectuals talked cinema, journalism, and mostly kept clear of the war. One of the waiters, Mustafa, waved to Kurtiz. His other arm was held aloft, bearing a circular beaten-copper platter stacked with gaudily coloured mocktails for the Muslims, doubles on the rocks for the Israelis and foreigners, and shots of thick sweet coffee in polychromatic glasses for all.

'*Masaa el kheer*, Miss Kurtiz.'

'And good evening to you, Mustafa.'

She spotted Alex alone at a far table alongside the breakfast room, scribbling in one of the notebooks he always carried with him, and wove her way through furniture, guests and water-pipes to reach him.

'I don't know why you don't join us at the American Colony. It's quieter. We can talk more agreeably.'

During their first outing together in Lebanon, Alex had booked her into the hotel where he'd been staying and, not unexpectedly, had made a pass at her, which Kurtiz had sidestepped and he had accepted with grace. From that moment, they had steered a professional relationship, but the attraction had endured.

'The room rate is three times higher than I'm paying here. Besides, I like this place. It's friendly and vibrant, Alex. I get more for my per diems and it keeps you at arm's length.'

He raised a brow, but his eyes were smiling, taking in the woman standing across the table from him.

91

She pulled out the chair opposite and sat down, placing her camera bag between them. Alex glanced at it and picked up his drink. He admired the fact that she never let those damn cameras out of her sight. The flame from the candle between them danced an elongated shadow across his face and lit her complexion to amber. 'Whisky. You want one?'

She nodded. 'I have work to do, so just the one.'

'You're too diligent.' His sarcasm was one of his least attractive qualities. If she didn't deliver he would send her home, whatever his personal sentiments towards her. He had made that clear many months and several locations back.

The music had stopped. There was a polite trickle of clapping, like wind scudding along paving stones. The musicians sat cradling instruments, sipping fizzy drinks, smoking, holding their cigarettes between thumb and index finger, observing the comings and goings of the clientele.

Alex had lifted his hand to attract the waiter's attention. When he had it, he raised two fingers to suggest two drinks, both whiskies, doubles, the digits nimbly enacting the order.

He turned his attention to Kurtiz, her long sandy hair drawn up untidily with a couple of tortoiseshell clips. 'It suits you.'

'What?'

'Your hair up like that, off your face, emphasizes your bone structure, your skin tones.'

Kurtiz made no response. She had been deliberating about whether to snip it all off, change style, colour, a new Kurtiz, a new start.

'How are the images?'

'I have some good stuff from this morning,' she said, glancing behind her to where the musicians were strumming chords, progressing towards another melody, running hands over strings and drums.

'The unending struggle for Jerusalem. Abbas is preparing a formal request for full UN membership. It will cause stress and anger here. There will be waves of reprisals all across the West Bank. Once this episode is in the can I want us to go to Tripoli. Libya's fomenting. Will you come?'

'Lizzie breaks up from school this week, and I have a flight out on Saturday. Alex, we discussed this.'

'Take three days, four if you need to, mollify your family, then meet me in Libya next Thursday. We can get your visa organized while you're in London.'

'Don't you ever go home, Alex? I promised Lizzie some quality time, a family holiday before she begins the big haul to A levels.'

'With that drunken husband of yours?'

'That's out of order and I resent such a remark.'

He lifted a hand, offering up the soft pink palm towards her, placatory, conciliatory. 'Stay on with us. Take your holiday after Libya. Come with us, Kurtiz. I need you. The *New York Times* are interested in a spread for the weekend magazine. I sent through some stills and they're excited by your work.'

She dropped her gaze. He was persuasive, commanding. It was all too easy at this distance to say yes to him, to keep travelling, to stay away from home, from the recriminations and all that had gone wrong between her and

Oliver. At this distance, *here* had become the reality, not London. Nothing but the work, the film and Alex. But she would tell him later when they had reached Hebron. 'No, Alex, sorry. I'm going home. Lizzie comes first.'

One of the duo of *oud* players, a striking Palestinian with a hooked nose and black agate eyes, was now embarking on a complex solo. He caught her interest, bowed his head and smiled. A wide open smile with startlingly uneven, tobacco-stained teeth. Kurtiz grinned and, after a second's hesitation, returned her attention to Alex, her colleague in the field. Her employer, mentor and the man she was wrestling with herself not to fall into bed with, not to fall in love with.

Why are you resisting? How can it hurt Oliver, Kurtiz? You are far from home and your marriage is over. It riled her when Alex spoke the truth to her so frankly and without emotion, assessing her predicament with more clarity than she did.

Their drinks arrived. Mustafa, one of a gaggle of sons and cousins of the proprietor of this down-at-heel yet enchanting hotel, with its pretensions to 'boutique' status, beamed at her as he placed the glasses before them. A mischievous and delightfully childlike expression. A generously heaped bowl of shelled pistachios and an oval plate of sliced crudités – cucumber, carrots, celery interspersed with black olives from Nablus – were set before them. Alex dug into the bowl of nuts. From the palm of his curled hand, with his fingertips he popped them one after another without pause into his mouth.

'Early breakfast again, Miss Kurtiz?'

'Too early for you, Mustafa, don't worry. We'll grab something on the road. *Shukran.*'

'Where you filming tomorrow?'

'North West Bank. Beyond Nablus towards Jenin.'

The waiter bowed and reversed backwards with his unloaded tray.

'You shouldn't answer every damn question.'

'We're hardly the Secret Service, Alex. Or the CIA in your case.'

'I suggest we set off around four. The American Colony will give us coffee and croissants at any hour if you want to come by there first . . .' Alex's remark hung in the air. The unspoken *or stay over there with me tonight* needed no words.

She ignored it. She always did, even if it stung her to do so. 'You can pick me up here when you're ready. Send me a text five minutes beforehand. I'll be on the steps outside Reception, waiting.' She lifted her glass and slugged the whisky back in one. It swam and burned beyond her tongue as it coursed down her oesophagus. 'Thanks for the nightcap.'

'Kurtiz?'

She paused. Their eyes met. He screwed his mouth tight, scanning her face, searching for the breach he had as yet failed to penetrate. 'If you need anything, you know where I am.'

'Night, Alex.'

As Kurtiz proceeded alongside the band, the black-eyed performer watched her. His concentration, his inner self, was with his strings, his nimble dark fingers, but his eyes admired her loose-limbed northern European beauty.

Back in her room, she threw herself and the camera

bag onto the bed. Its springs creaked as she landed, and she inched her laptop off the side table where it had been charging. There was a mail from Oliver — *What time does your flight arrive on Saturday?* Curt. And there was *nada* from Lizzie. Not a word. Sixteen years old, disgruntled and 'deeply pissed off' with Mum. With Mum and Dad and their incessant inability to see eye to eye. Fair enough, sweet Lizzie. Kurtiz felt that all too familiar stab of parental guilt. *I should be there at home with you, supporting you through to your A levels, chivvying and bear-hugging you through your teenage crises, an ear to the confusions and angsts, a shoulder to cry on when the first heartbreak occurs. Are you even seeing anyone? Yes, I should be home.*

That was certainly Oliver's opinion. But back when Lizzie had been a bawling child, it had been she who had remained at home, renouncing her studies — oh, she was too tired to ride that ferris wheel in her head again. She had a life, a burgeoning career now, and she was the only one of the pair bringing home a regular salary.

To Oliver she typed: *One of those hellish flights that takes off before midnight and gets me in about three or four in the morning. The dawn patrol. I should be home before breakfast on Sunday. Hope all well? KZ*

She hammered off a quick note to her daughter: *Hey, lovely Lizzie, welcome to the summer holidays. How's life? Send Mum in the desert a word.*

Love you, see you Sunday. Brunch somewhere delicious? Looking forward to it. Mum xxx

Paris, November 2015

Not one atom in Kurtiz's entire being had alerted her to the fact that the sentiments and intentions typed in that late-night email to Lizzie, her Jerusalem missive, would never come to pass, that the Sunday brunch she had proposed to her daughter would never take place. Her maternal instinct, premonition, dark foreboding, name it whatever you will, had evidently been switched off, along with her phone. Long-distance vibes, the presentiment that all was not well? Not operating. Aside from regular teenage dilemmas, in the doldrums about her weight, her body image, school results, it had not crossed Kurtiz's mind that Lizzie was undergoing a monumental shift, a crisis of a proportion so dramatic it had caused to her behave in the way she had. Kurtiz had been elsewhere, seduced by her personal and professional preoccupations.

For that negligence she had never forgiven herself.

And Oliver had never let her off the hook, never allowed her to forget it.

'You took away our daughter's sense of security,' was Oliver's allegation. 'By not being here, you, not me, *you* splintered this family.'

Alex had not been the trigger. He had never been a

part of that scenario, her London life. After the loss of Lizzie, she quit working with him, broke off communication with him, even though it pained her and perhaps she needed his wisdom more back then than ever before. She had moved into a small pad of her own, a generous-sized studio nestled in a back-street in Covent Garden, leaving Oliver to sweat it out alone in their family home.

Another lack of percipience on her part?

Kurtiz was as pale as egg white when Marguerite picked her way across from one pavement's edge to the other. The surface beneath her feet was treacherous, slippery with runnels of burgundy blood, spurting water nozzles. Heaped in a desultory pile, like shifting sand, Kurtiz's bags were on an outdoor café table. Only the camera hung from her neck. Her face was damp, caked with perspiration, rigid with shock, her trousers besmirched with dust and the blood of strangers she had helped lift. Her breath exhaled as clouds.

'Apologies for the disturbance. I wanted to know you were safe,' she murmured, as Marguerite drew near. 'I saw you walking home along the street, passing by the bar, and then the next moment, this. You were lucky.' She gestured with her head, heavy as a boulder, towards the shot-up restaurant. 'There are several dead. No one's quite sure how many. The police have been interviewing everyone here, attempting to build a clearer picture, doing what they know to do. I got some coverage on camera. The number plate . . .' She was babbling, babbling for the sake of it, mentally recording the information for journalistic purposes, as Alex had taught her: *Make a note of everything you see. No matter how irrelevant the detail, it could make the difference of life or death to some poor victim.*

How many poor victims here?

An ache deep within her for Alex took her by the throat. She forced the ghost of him to one side. Not now. Tonight, soon, very soon, if all went according to Oliver's predictions, she would be holding Lizzie tight . . . She would beg her forgiveness . . . Were there words enough to express her broken heart?

White SAMU de Paris vans were screeching to a halt or departing. A merry-go-round, the musical chairs of emergency services. Her head was heavy, yet light with spinning illuminations. She staggered backwards.

'I think you need a whisky. Let me get you one.'

Somewhere in the background, on a TV screen within a bar, empty because everyone was outside on the street or had fled the scene, a chorus had broken into 'La Marseillaise'. In the neighbouring *arrondissement*, spectators at the football stadium were finally being evacuated in an orderly fashion. The anthem was picked up by one or two present in rue de Charonne. One or two were humming softly, humming for sanity, singing and weeping. Soldiers were approaching. Marching boots, rifles, helmets, fatigues. Newspapers, takeaway cartons were blowing down the street. The temperature was dropping.

Kurtiz shook her head. 'No, no, *merci*, Marguerite, no whisky.' She needed to rendezvous with Oliver or make her way to the Bataclan. This monstrous devastation would not have reached his ears yet. Or had it? The interval must have come and gone at the concert hall. Surely he would have switched his phone on during the break, checked to see that she had arrived in Paris. She had still had no feedback from him. Why not? If he had even glanced at his messages, he would know where she was by now. And he would know that the street had been hit ... Wait ...

She glanced up and down the road. No film crews. No reporters. She frowned, swung about her to confirm the fact. Why not? Had this decimation failed to draw the attention of the media? Was every journalist and TV station at the Stade de France?

'There appears to be a hostage situation at the Bataclan concert hall,' she heard a voice shout. Her heart lurched. Dear God, *no*. NO. Her innards tightened, bunching to a ball.

'The Bataclan? Did somebody say the Bataclan? Where did you hear this?' She spun about, yelling to no one in particular, to everyone present.

'There's a TV screen playing in the bar. The theatre's been infiltrated. Three or four men in black forced their way in, carrying weapons. They've taken every spectator as hostage.'

'Jesus Christ! Lizzie!'

'A handful have escaped.'

The radios carried by security and police burst into life all around her, broke into overtime. Messages being transmitted across Paris.

'Christ, oh, fucking – I have to go.' She was hauling her bags off the table. Packing away her camera, swinging about her. 'I need a taxi.'

'The city's started a lock-down, Madame. Streets cordoned off. The Métro's been closed already, most certainly the stations around here, and you won't find a taxi.'

She glanced at her watch. Just past 11.10 p.m. It was a twenty-, twenty-five-minute hike. She should have left this street more than half an hour ago, but how could she have walked away, turning her back on the dead and wounded?

'They're reporting fusillades at the Bataclan. Possible deaths.'

Kurtiz swung in a circle. *Lizzie*. The bags slapped hard against her body. Which way to go?

'I'll take you,' chipped in Marguerite.

Kurtiz was confused. 'What?'

'I have a car in the parking under that block of flats on the right. I don't drive it all that frequently. One has no need to in Paris, but it's reliable and I still remember how.' She smiled. 'Come up with me. I'll fetch my purse and the keys.'

'You won't get through,' a bystander warned, his voice almost inaudible beneath the roar of motors, the screech of sirens.

Radios were hissing, patrol cars wailing. People standing, insensible, waiting, gazing blindly at tablets and smartphones, scrolling internet sites, coughing, talking or silenced. 'Three attacks,' someone muttered.

She couldn't simply stay here and do nothing, Kurtiz thought. Voices were shouting information. Relaying in a numbed and robotic fashion their city's crisis situation to anyone listening.

'They've closed off the roads round the theatre.'

'I'll drive you as far as I can until we're blocked and you can walk the rest of the way.'

'Let's go.'

Settled in the ancient car – a powder-blue tank of a Mercedes with leather upholstery, a model from the seventies, Kurtiz guessed, which reeked of mould and high-octane gasoline – they set off on the short journey. At every street, a roadblock. Marguerite reversed, switched direction, turned the car on a sixpence, a *centime*, even though it pre-dated power-assisted steering. She was determined, zigzagging back and forth, intimate with the streets. Still, they barely drew an inch closer to their destination.

Kurtiz had just witnessed cold-blooded murder. Armed men with at least two Kalashnikovs. Was a gun being pointed at Lizzie right now, at Oliver? What were they up against?

What are we up against here? Always one of Alex's first questions when they infiltrated dangerous territories. He had to measure the odds before he made tactical decisions, weighing up his crew's safety. Innocent lives at stake.

Oh, Alex, you would know what we're up against here. Should she call him?

'This is impossible. We're getting nowhere,' she wailed aloud. 'I have to get through.' She banged her fists against the dashboard. 'I have to talk to Lizzie. I have to tell her . . .'

Don't panic. First rule, keep your head.

'Is this radio functioning?'

They were limping forward a metre at a time, crawling slower than a pedestrian's pace.

Kurtiz began twirling a dial, then pressing and prodding at it. She broke her nail with the force. Static crackled into life – a woman's voice – then died away. Bursts of interference hissed at her, like a sleeping cat disturbed and on the defensive. She pulled out her iPhone, scrolling for an update, news. Hostages? Confirmed.

'Hostages at the Bataclan.'

'How many? Any deaths?' Marguerite was leaning forward, peering through the windscreen, dwarfed by the Mercedes.

Kurtiz directed Safari to Twitter. 'Jesus!'

Tweets were flashing up, photos being posted, hundreds, from all across the city. Other eateries, bars, had been hit. 'Three attacks,' she was reading. Nothing reported in the eleventh. Other nightlife spots in the tenth. At the Bataclan: 'CARNAGE' were the seven letters that chilled her blood.

'They're shooting people. Concert-goers. They have them locked inside the theatre. Some have escaped. I have to get out. Stop the car, please, let me out.' They were moving at a snail's pace. Marguerite attempted to pull over. Kurtiz couldn't wait. She was scrabbling her possessions together, readying to leap.

'Leave your bags with me,' the old woman advised. 'I'll keep them safe for you at my flat.'

Kurtiz abandoned everything – passport, purse, everything – except the camera and her phone, and she began to run, stumbling, gathering herself back to her feet, pelting forward.

'I'm at number seventy-one, remember. I'll be waiting for you,' called the actress.

Kurtiz neither heard nor responded. Heart pounding, punching against her ribcage. Feet torpedoing faster than she ever remembered such speed before. Saliva congealed like metal in her mouth. A stitch clawed at her side. A dull thudding in her temples. It squeezed a tight belt around her head. She ran through the boundaries of exhaustion, adrenalin and fear cranking up, jackhammering her limits, crashing through her speed barriers. Her booted feet battered the pavements. A rhythmic war beat. Cold air slapped her cheeks. Tears sprang from her eyes. 'Lizzie!' A lioness's roar into the night. 'Oliver! Lizzie! Be safe. Be safe.'

A savage, she hared the length of boulevard Voltaire, thrusting her body onwards.

If she could get there. If she could only . . . She *must* get there. She must reach the site before it was too late. She must find Lizzie, explain to her, apologize, beg her forgiveness. Before it was too late . . .

Alex and Kurtiz travelled together, riding in the same vehicle. The hire car was booked in both names; both driving licences had been cleared. It was a precaution Alex always insisted upon. In case of an emergency, he had explained. 'In case one of us gets injured, or kidnapped.' Equally, his minimal crew of two travelled in another 4x4, which transported the principal cinematography camera, separate sound mikes, recorder, mixer and two monitors. Alex kept the other camera with him. If one was seized, there was always a reserve. Material was downloaded onto a hard drive and a second back-up was copied before anyone got to eat dinner each evening. Whenever possible, the rushes, the unedited shot material, were uploaded to cyberspace via WeTransfer and sent to Alex's editorial dock back home in Boston, where his post-production manager and editor went to work on a rough cut, following instructions Alex sent to them by email. He preferred to work with the same crew and if, for an unanticipated reason, one was not available, it did not please him. His demand on the loyalty and commitment of his team was unrelenting, unforgiving.

Kurtiz, as stills photographer, was the only female on board. She had a great deal to learn about working in zones where conflict was a daily reality and she was hungry for the education. Alex taught her everything he knew, taught her to look out for herself, taught her new approaches to her lens, when to shoot pictures and when not. Encouraged her to use a hefty sum of her earnings to invest in better camera equipment, hence the Leica and the Fuji. 'You'll earn the investment back in image sales.' He had also linked her up with the London office of Getty Images, one of the most active agencies in the business, featuring some of the greatest photographers of their generation. She was in good hands, selling worldwide now and slowly building a modest but international reputation for herself. She was more than grateful to Alex and determined that she wouldn't blow this unique opportunity by sleeping with him.

It could only end in tears.

Alex had no qualms about using her sex, her femaleness, her open nature, her charm, to gain access to homes, families, to women, to record their personal and frequently intimate stories, and to those who did not trust Westerners but were more likely to hedge their bets, unburden their hearts and share their experiences and truths with an unknown female than a man. 'Over here, though,' he joshed, 'it helps that I'm black. They have more confidence in me than in a white American.'

When she was home in the UK and not working with Alex, the job offers she was receiving were from TV stations and some of the high-quality periodicals, such as *Time*, *Le Point*. She had a great deal to be grateful to him for.

Falling in love with him would be foolish.

*

Their early-morning run up through the West Bank was calculated to take them no more than a couple of hours. After collecting Kurtiz at her hotel, Alex doubled back on himself, passing the American Colony before crossing Meinertzhagen junction. They were leaving the city. Moving north, they would be negotiating road works, cement blocks, earth mounds, and crossing bridges. Dawn was breaking as they sped by the walls of the ancient city of Jerusalem with its biblical gate names, where only the Muslim bagel sellers were visible on the streets, backs bent, hauling their laden carts.

Palestinian men, pinioned and bumped tight together in a long queue that tailed back for more than half a kilometre, were waiting submissively to be cleared through the Qalandia checkpoint, queuing to gain entry to the capital for their day's employment. It was cold, no sun yet to warm the embittered land. They shuffled forward in their slow march, steps foreshortened by the mass of human bodies pressing in on them, heads and faces muffled in black-and-white or red-and-white *keffiyehs*. Others, the younger ones, had pulled their cheap jackets up around their heads to keep at bay the dust and chill wind. In the iris light, they looked like herds of bobbing seals. Pillars of cigarette smoke rose towards the awakening sky. Beyond the witching hour – when the day has not yet unpeeled itself from the throes of night but is slowly developing its own tone – the heavens were changing hue. Orange and reds were breaking open.

Few of the Palestinian men glanced in the direction of Alex's 4x4 as he and Kurtiz inched slowly by, heading in the opposite direction. Rarely were he and she pulled over by one of the IDF crews, the Israeli Defence Force, laden with combat gear, although Alex's black skin occasionally provoked a passport check.

'American? Welcome to Israel, man. What's your trade?'

'I buy fruit,' he'd lie boldly.

'Cool, man, we have great fruit farms here in Israel. Enjoy your day.'

Alex had warned Kurtiz to make no protests, don't argue with the soldiers – allow them to be right, then move on out of their radar – and never take photographs at the checkpoints. 'Don't even lift your camera into view.'

If discovered, they risked the confiscation of not only the cameras: any exhaustive car search would relieve them of all their material. Cameras, memory cards and anything else the IDF soldiers, barely more than teenagers, judged worthy of requisitioning.

Once out on the open highway, which progressed through villages shaded by fruiting mulberry trees and farmland where olive groves abounded to left and right, they took a break for coffee. Alex continued at the wheel because Kurtiz was now free to take landscape, scenic or human-interest photographs. As they proceeded along the highway, they passed through Palestinian villages. Dark eyes glanced warily in their direction. They made a detour into a settlement town, enclosed within barbed-wire fences, with security gates and patrol. Kurtiz grabbed a few discreet, not well-aligned pictures and Alex sped them back out. A cultural desert, judged Kurtiz. Alex made no comment. Too wise, long in the tooth, to waste his breath.

They had a prearranged rendezvous at a gas station two exits further along where Darryl and Tim were awaiting them. Alex usually took the precaution not to travel in convoy but at an exit eight kilometres further they were cutting off the Israeli-built highway 60. Israelis knew it as 'Way of the Patriarchs' because it passed through 'Judea' and 'Samaria'. From there, they'd be climbing into ancient Palestinian agricultural territories. Many of these farmlands had been encircled by settlements of red-roofed houses and little else.

The two black hire cars, both caked with grit and sand from two weeks on the road, wound their way through villages bordered by ancient olive groves, or newly planted orchards, with runnels and tributaries hewn out of the red earth to ease the irrigation process. They stopped at occasional traffic lights and spotted barefoot kids playing in the street, piggybacking, jumping and hopping through squares marked with chalk, or dribbling scuffed old footballs. No electronic gadgets or PlayStations here. Outside the villages they encountered goatherds or shepherds on mule-back, heads wrapped in the ubiquitous *keffiyehs* to protect against the dust. Sometimes the herders were children, again barefoot or in rubber shoes made of discarded tyres. These youths were moving with their stock from one feeding ground to another, climbing further upland, to summer pasturing. As the beasts crossed the fields, the heavy oblong, folded-iron bells hanging from their necks clanged and reverberated. Rural music.

To the right, as the sun rose and the morning broke with explosions of golden light, the views across the hills and valleys, the fruiting almond and olive groves, to the mighty Jordan valley and river and beyond into Jordan itself, were, as Alex had promised, nothing short of sensational. Or, as Lizzie might have described it: 'Amazeballs, Mum.'

Kurtiz smiled quietly at the mental image of her daughter. She was so looking forward to seeing Lizzie soon. Just a few days now. How she wished she could share this precious alchemy of light, time and geography with the teenage girl who always accompanied her in her heart. How to explain to Lizzie what all this meant to her.

They reached their destination around lunchtime. Close to five hundred metres above Mediterranean Sea level.

The Palestinian village they were to film was situated halfway up a hillside and looked out over an extended valley that might have been an ancient hippodrome or a vast modern stadium for rock concerts and sporting events, so flat and expansive was it. Alex parked in the valley in the shade of a lofty rock-face and a lone spreading tree, which he identified as a *Pistacia palaestina* or terebinth.

'There are many references to this plant in the Old Testament. It's a stunner when in flower with its shots of vibrant red. Come early winter, Upper Galilee looks as though it's on fire with the spread of these flowering beauties. I'll take you there one day when we're doing nothing. Their wine is mighty fine too, although little in the region compares with the volcanically reared reds up on war-won Golan Heights, some of it planted by members of the Rothschild family.'

Kurtiz stepped out and stretched her legs, stamping her booted feet against the desiccated earth, trying not to dwell on the improbable odds of her and Alex ever enjoying carefree days together in Upper Galilee. Or any vineyard anywhere, come to think of it.

'I'll rig our tents over there later.' Tim pointed to a shaded patch so concealed it looked unlikely the sun would ever penetrate it.

The valley was embraced by an amphitheatre of limestone hills. On the apex of each ran a flat scree surface, which had been stationed with caravans and shacks, rusted, half-twisted temporary accommodation. Kurtiz had witnessed similar sights elsewhere. It was the first stage of land grab before the construction of a settlement. What was new to her were the watchtowers and the floodlights. Several metres high, the towers had been rigged up at strategic points on the peaks of the horseshoe of hills. All were trained directly on the small Palestinian village.

Two Americans, a retired couple with broad Midwest accents, and one precisely spoken Englishwoman descended a hill path leading from the village, to greet the arrival of the film crew.

'We're very glad to see you here,' said the male American. All three were voluntary workers for a human-rights organization, run by the Anglican Church, whose headquarters were based in Switzerland.

Darryl and Tim were unloading and preparing to set up the cameras, working in the patch with shade from the terebinth, alongside what was to be their campsite. Alex was preparing for interviews, firing questions at the Americans about the identities and backgrounds of various residents within the village, jotting down dates of infractions, trespassing. He had already instructed Kurtiz on the run-up from Jerusalem to shoot 'daily-life material'. He reiterated it now. 'And make sure to get some good portraits of these aid workers.'

'Our role here,' the British woman explained to Kurtiz, 'is to act as witnesses. We're not allowed to get involved. Under no circumstances. We must remain neutral. It's not always easy. We cannot allow ourselves to be emotionally swayed.'

'The lights from the watchtowers stay on all night?'

'All night.'

While the men disappeared to look for locations and to meet potential film subjects, Kurtiz went for a stroll, taking nature shots as she moved to and fro, close-ups of lizards, rock formations, red and green pomegranates, skins like leather, on stunted spiny trees. In the distance she could see terraced terrains. They had been planted centuries earlier with trees, predominantly olives. The terracing protected against land erosion and aided irrigation.

The village had been carved out of the rock, centuries, millennia earlier. It was remote, nothing besides the settlement trucks within view in any direction. Even the silence had an echo to it, like a ringing in the ear. The landscape felt ancient, stratified, embedded with history and strife. Its beauty was an idyll, if you could handle the remoteness, the solitariness.

One of the two female volunteers, the Englishwoman, whose name was Beth, approached Kurtiz and took up pace alongside her with a smile. They walked in silence, relishing the moment, ingesting the expansive scenery, ancient Holy Land, while, eyes aloft, they followed the wheeling trajectory of a pair of buzzards.

'Crested honey buzzards,' confirmed Beth. 'In spring,' she continued, moving her arm in a circle to her right, 'that swathe of flatland over there is golden with wheat. A staple food for these villagers.'

Beth was a retired magistrate in her sixties with straight, iron-grey hair that hung to beneath her ears in clumps, like a set of knives and forks. The thick strands were kept off her face with a shiny cream slide. Her complexion was smooth, slightly furred, like peach skin. To Kurtiz's eye, she fitted the description of 'British and a good sort'. A pressed poplin blouse, of a blue paler than an English summer sky, was tucked into the waistband of a knee-length cotton skirt sewn with capacious pockets. Here, she rested her hands. On her feet were purple Birkenstocks. She had been visiting the West Bank for at least a decade, she said, and had taught herself from tapes and practice to speak more than passable Arabic. Palestine, she claimed, was her spiritual home. 'It has a way of drawing you in, enchanting you. Palestine never fails to work its magic and its suffering breaks my heart.'

Kurtiz wondered whether Beth had any family. Whatever, she was filled with admiration for the woman, for each of these volunteers who spent up to three months at a time within remote communities such as this one. Afterwards, they awaited relocation elsewhere within the West Bank, to villages or hamlets, no matter how tiny or how few the inhabitants, who were facing similar threats.

Once installed, there was nowhere to go, no television or internet available, no telephone. Once here, they were here. Kurtiz tapped in her code to unlock her phone. She had no signal. No one had. They, and she, were entirely cut off. If she had known she would have forewarned Oliver and Lizzie. She slipped the phone back into her bag. A redundant item until they returned to Jerusalem.

'It's a little nerve-racking at first but you get used to it. I read a lot. I help the women in the fields and I contemplate the heavens, when the sky is not bleached out by those hateful floodlights. But no matter what those settlers do, they will never drive these villagers off their lands.'

Beth invited Kurtiz to the house she shared with the retired American couple up in the Palestinian village. The climb was steeper, more arduous, rockier than Kurtiz had anticipated. Tossed among the briary bushes that bordered the path there were hillocks of litter: plastic water bottles, broken chairs, wind-torn rags of clothing, the remains of a gas stove and threadbare tyres. There was no such service as refuse collection.

As they entered the property, crossing a stone stoop, cool air enveloped them. The furnishings were minimal, the atmosphere austere. A stack of books lay on the floor. A camera, a Canon EOS, lower end of the range, hung by its strap from a flat-headed nail driven into the wall. Three pairs of boots, one much larger than the others, were lined up in a neat row behind the door. The room smelt musty and in places its limestone walls were puckered and crumbly where subterranean mountain water had seeped through, causing great swabs of damp. Kurtiz took a couple of shots of the interior, a close-up of the boots, then the two Englishwomen made themselves comfortable in the communal living area, while Beth boiled water, poured from a bucket. 'There is no mains water here,' she explained. 'We fetch it from a spring.

The Palestinian women collect and carry it from the natural springs on a daily basis. Up and down the hillsides.'

The water was boiled in a solid black kettle on a free-standing two-ringed gas stove. They sat on hard wooden stools and drank mint tea. Kurtiz's choice between that and cardamom coffee.

Beyond the bare walls and the curtain-less windows there were chalky hills, still, arid, dotted with thorny bushes and gnarled trees, whose canopies had been pushed sideways by the wind.

After their refreshments, they strolled about the tiny village where they encountered dozens of scrawny cats that flashed into the shadows at their footfall. The Palestinian residents, women only, were huddled in groups of four and five on doorsteps; most appeared to be octogenarians. They were the occupants of the stone houses hewn and chiselled from the mountainside. Each house, with its wonky, colourfully painted wooden doors, pressed tight against the next, as though containing one extended family. Beth translated Kurtiz's questions and the responses from the whisker-faced, black-clad women. While the inhabitants talked and cackled and drooled, darting their twisted fingers for emphasis in the air, Kurtiz snapped dozens of photographs and they laughed and nudged one another, like coy schoolgirls. Two old women with amber skin, corrugated faces and barely a tooth between them claimed to be over a hundred although they were not quite certain how far over they were. They and a handful of children were the village housekeepers, the cooks, the cleaners, the laundry team, operating with the most basic equipment: straw brushes, water and open fires. The men were toiling in their groves, orchards, vegetable and wheat fields and would not be back till sunset. In total, fewer than seventy Palestinians, born and raised there, resided in this outermost station; caretakers of the surrounding lands, which had been in their families since before written records began.

The caravans, shacks and watchtowers had been on site, expanding ominously, inexorably over the past eight years.

By the time Kurtiz made her way back to base camp, it was after four. The light was softening, the heat dissipating; a few trees moved in what passed for a breeze in this arid territory. Feeling mildly apprehensive, she tried her phone again, hoping to reach Lizzie, but there was still no signal. None of her team was in evidence. They were gathering material in the outlying lands, she supposed, or perhaps discreetly recording the encircling settlements, the concrete watchtowers. She opened the hire car and was rooting through her luggage in search of her washbag, wondering whether she should have asked Beth for a canister of water or where she might locate a source, when a child's alarmed cry broke into the afternoon calm. She ditched everything on the passenger seat save for her Leica M, which she looped over her head, and ran back in the direction she had just come from.

Four burly men, with pointed sticks, were grouped together at the foot of the winding pathway that led from the valley up towards the village. They appeared to be harassing a black-haired boy of eight or nine. Without warning one of them whipped at the child's left thigh. He let out a yell. Another whacked the other leg. And so they continued. One slap or dig following fast upon another. The boy was jumping, dancing, shrieking, trying to block their passage or to negotiate a route round them. Beth appeared, running down the dusty path from the centre of the village. She stopped short when she saw the intruders.

Kurtiz raised her camera and began to record the scene. One of the men caught sight of her and swung towards her, shaking his arm, long arms like a chimpanzee's, brandishing his stick, back and forth, as though poking jerkily at a fire. She ducked her head, fearing he would jab her eye. He was swearing at her in a language she could not understand. He drew closer as she stepped backwards, almost stumbling over a bush directly behind her. As the assailant, in his big flat shoes, stalked like an emu towards her, looming over her, attempting to snatch at the strap of her camera, one of his companions called to him, terse garbled instructions. The only word she thought she could make out was 'American'. The man in front of her, bearded, six foot plus, bushy eyebrows, with those loose-hanging simian arms, held his ground. His face was a swarm of spittle and bad skin. He locked his gaze on her. It was a threat, a scowl, an arrow of hatred fired directly at her. His companions, fellow trespassers, called a third time before he drew back with a growl and sloped away.

Kurtiz was shaking. She feared he had been intent on swiping her camera, with its recorded evidence of the men's attack. Where was the injured boy? Was he safe? Beth was escorting him back up to the village, soothing him. His thin cotton trousers were ripped ragged and his upper legs were striped with bloodied weals.

Paris, November 2015

Eventually, finally, as Kurtiz was flagging, caving in, her muscles cursing her with razor-edged shooting pains, the Chinese Theatre loomed into view. It stood to the left side of the wide avenue beyond a barrage of vehicles with illuminated strobe bars: warning lights and beacons of green, violet, blue or white, flashing, pulsing, rotating. Colours spooling outwards like ribbons about a maypole, or an al-fresco disco display.

As she veered left towards the old concert hall, she heard the echo of what sounded like fireworks. Special effects? No. Gunshots. Repeated, flat as rubber. Assault rifles. More of what she had already witnessed during the Charonne massacre a few hours earlier and what now seemed to her a lifetime ago. She picked up speed and slammed full frontal into a uniformed police officer, who grabbed her by the shoulders, swung her body in a circular motion and steadied her, hauling her to a standstill.

'Whoa, lady, lady . . .' He was trying to calm her.

'Let me go!' she yelled. Tears began to spurt again, acid burning her up. She was attempting to pull herself free.

'You can't go any further, Madame,' he warned, without aggression.

'My husband's in there, my daughter too! Let me go,' she raged, yanking herself away from his bulk of flesh.

He held fast. 'Others also have family inside, Madame.'

'No, please, you don't understand. I have to explain –'

'You must wait here. We're doing everything we can. You don't have the authority to go closer.'

Kurtiz squinted through sweat dripping in runnels from her soaked hair. Silhouettes crystallized, grew clear, like a focus pull, into her line of vision. A small crowd was waiting. Some strung together. Others, apart, alone. Large groups here and there. Lone individuals, whose contorted body language depicted pain or distress.

Her damp frame went limp, began to sink, implode. 'Is it true that there are dead in there?'

As though in answer, screams broke out. Bloodcurdling screams. Figures were running, escaping, leaping. A door burst open. Salvation through a fire exit. One female hanging from an upstairs window, arms extended, rigid, fingertips clawing, clinging to a sill, swinging like a monkey. Beyond, within the belly of the building, deep-throated bangs. Bang, bang, bang. Voices screaming, 'No! No!' Hands pressed over bulging eyes. Arms wrapped around torsos.

And coming from the interior another ejaculation of relentless firing. Another dead or wounded. Cartridges ricocheting.

LIZZIE!

Kurtiz ripped herself free from the policeman's thick arm that had bolted her against him and ran to where the music-lovers, mostly young, under thirty, were fleeing for their lives, scrambling beneath a red and white flapping cordon line, skipping past two other officers. 'Lizzie! *Lizzie!*' Her voice was strangled, hoarse, like fingernails scratching blackboard. She cleared her throat and foghorned her daughter's name once more. Others were bawling a variety of others. A female, who was drugged or shocked or both, groaned, 'I'm here, I'm Lizzie,' with no more power than a stunned bird.

Kurtiz bulldozed her way to the young woman lying on her stomach on the ground. She hunkered down at the girl's side, gently lifting her shoulder to get a good look at the face. Disappointment like a diving bell. It was another Lizzie. Nonetheless, some mother's daughter. Kurtiz settled beside her. The girl was bleeding, or blood had splattered the length of her arm and the left side of her cheek. Mascara seeped down her beige-skinned face in arabesque swirls. 'Hello, Lizzie, I'm going to get you some help,' she promised the teenager. 'Wait here, I'll be back. Can you hear me? I'm getting help for you, Lizzie.'

At that moment a member of one of the aid teams appeared, followed by another, a woman from the emergency services. Both bent low alongside the barely more than adolescent Lizzie. Kurtiz stumbled backwards. The girl was lifted onto a stretcher.

'Is she your daughter?' A petite female in white with a mask over her mouth enquired. Kurtiz shook her head.

'Any idea who she is?'

Again Kurtiz answered with a negative. 'Lizzie. That's all I know.'

'Thanks.'

As the young woman bearing her daughter's name

was conveyed away to an ambulance, Kurtiz wove through the swelling numbers, repeating her call over and over. Then she called out for Oliver. To neither name was there a response.

Shapes lay huddled on the paving stones, in the alley of Saint-Pierre Amelot. There, an open door from beyond which concert attendees were scrabbling, fleeing for their lives. The crack of gunshots died down. Stopped. Silence. Only yelping, yelling could be heard.

'What's going on in there?' she begged of someone, only just resisting the urge to shake the remaining life out of the benumbed creature.

'Murder. They're killing everyone. "Get down on the ground," they shouted at us. "Face the floor. Death is behind you."'

'How many have they killed? How many? Oh, God. I'm going in.'

'Don't be fucking stupid.' A hand grabbed her and threw her backwards, sending her slamming against a wall. Her head cracked, rang, swam.

Loved ones were calling to loved ones in vain – and then the executions started again. One. Two. Orderly. Three. Systematic. Picking the victims off. Four. Five. A trained, professional firing squad.

She hurled herself through the pandemonium of living and wounded, cross-legged or collapsed on the ground: terrorized people.

Doré's *The Massacre of the Innocents*.

Heads in laps, heads thrown backwards, eyes closed or open, staring, dead-eyed, fish-eyed. Locked in a nightmare. The music echoing, no longer heavy metal rock.

Bullets flying past their ears. Lead streaking through the air. Spent cartridges bouncing off their bodies. Was Oliver lying face down on the ground, screams, gunfire erupting all about him? Was he shielding Lizzie? Was she also a hostage in the old theatre, held at gunpoint, or had she managed to escape?

'LIZZIE! LIZZIE! LIZZIE, *forgive me . . .*'

Before the night shoot, which Alex had decreed would
be filmed hand-held and Kurtiz was not to be involved,
they ate with the residents and volunteers in one of the
village houses. Built into the rock, it was surprisingly
large, rambling, but devoid of furniture, save for a few
cane and wood chairs. The cooking was achieved outside on an open fire by a small team of women squatting
on the ground. Grilled lamb and a great steaming aluminium pan of couscous. They sipped fizzy soft drinks
of bright orange and mud-brown hues, which were
loosely related, the labels promised, to orange and cola.
Kurtiz would have killed for a whisky. She was still
shaken by the afternoon's ugly confrontation. The talk
was of the recent slaughter of a small flock of Palestinian
sheep. A punishment, Alex explained to her, for a Palestinian, not from this village but from somewhere closer
to Nablus, who had entered the settlers' camp by night
and fired rounds from a gun aimlessly. No one had been
hurt, but it was logged as an act of terrorism.

'Sometimes, they don't do their cause any favours by
shooting off rockets, using arms recklessly, but they are
a people in resistance. They are frustrated, deprived and
in pain, and sometimes they make unwise decisions and

it costs them. Such ill-advised responses give the crazy extremists out there grounds for killing. We'll be out of here tomorrow,' was Alex's comfort to her later.

Kurtiz went to her tent soon after they had eaten. Alex told her to get some sleep and not dwell on the cruelty she'd witnessed. She would have dearly liked to touch base with home, with Lizzie, whose voice she was aching to hear. Under normal circumstances – if any of this work was normal – she would have forewarned her husband and daughter that she would be out of range for a time. That way, no one grew concerned. Too late for the regret.

Eventually, she must have fallen asleep, dozed off while reading by torchlight. Through the thin white skin of the tent, the floodlights poured their unremitting light down upon the village. An ever-watchful malevolent eye.

How do these people suffer this night after night? she asked herself. This torture.

Half of her had an ear alert, listening for her colleagues' return. She wasn't afraid, but she wasn't entirely at ease either. She feared snakes as much as the threat of violence. Beth had offered her a bed in her room but Kurtiz felt it was her duty to remain with her team, to be waiting and available where they could find her, if necessary.

It was the shot that shocked her into full wakefulness. Its metal bounce echoed round the curvature of hills, seeming almost to sing. Sharp, high-pitched. She threw off her sleeping bag and pulled on her boots, fingers jiggling clumsily with laces. She was already dressed in a T-shirt and trousers. She snatched up a denim jacket, punched her arms into it, and the smaller of her cameras, the Fuji pro2, she stuffed agitatedly into the right pocket of her chinos. Ready to go, she smacked at the tent flap and faced the night.

In the hot white light, the figures drew instantly into her line of vision: a lens image coming into focus. Men on the hillside, silhouettes beneath a wide sky. A flank of them abreast. Purposeful in their approach, like a sequence from a classic western. Two were hatted, two carrying rifles. All were descending not by the paths and the winding donkey tracks but directly down the face of the hill – the scrubland, the uncultivated dust, rock and earth. Digging their booted feet into the ground beneath them, sinking as they came closer, growing larger, more threatening. Earth and stones were dislodged and dispersed, rolling downwards, thudding like a landslide against the flat valley surface in front of her. There was something chilling about the earth moving in this way. Bestrewn. Getting out of harm's way. Kurtiz counted four, no, five men. Big men. One shorter. Three were bearded. She hung back by the entrance to the tent, gripping its cotton fabric, inhaling its mothball scent. She would be in full view due to the lights that flooded this natural arena. She glanced towards the other three tents. Were the men occupying them or were they still out somewhere, working? Close by, she prayed.

She stood at a distance, full on to the men. Their descent brought them within range. The hillside sloped in her direction. Faces grew more defined, identifiable, but she was uncertain what she should do. Should she raise the Fuji, focus, grab the image? If so, they might know about it and it would enrage them. Where were they going? Not to the village, it seemed. To whom should she give a warning? Should she scream, raise an alarm? Had no one else heard the shot? Had it been a shot? Or had she dreamed it? She glanced upwards to the heart of the village. The American couple were outside their accommodation in their nightclothes, arms wrapped tight about their torsos. Some of the local men were out on the ridge too. No one was bearing arms besides the approaching quintet, one of whom had a pitchfork resting on his shoulder, like a soldier standing to attention. Two had chainsaws. They had dropped to ground level now and were no more than thirty metres from where Kurtiz was standing. She shivered, recognizing among them her pockmarked challenger from earlier in the afternoon.

The entire scene, illuminated with such intensity, was taking on a surreal aspect. It was trance-like, and it was menacing. This, in itself, might have been a film. The moment before something abominable happens. An act that is irreversible.

No, her mind was running along apocryphal scenarios. She must find Alex, alert him, warn him. The armed men, one with a turkey-wattled neck, glanced in her direction but did not appear to register her presence. Was she invisible? He, from her point of view, was larger than life. His eyes were smouldering, on fire. Volcanic spit. They were not climbing to the village. They were advancing towards the nearby fields. They would be passing almost directly by where she was standing. Instinctively she pressed herself back a step or two inside the tent until they had marched by. She tilted her head upwards to the village square, if one could describe a scruffy patch of beaten earth as a square. A small crowd had gathered. Men, women and children. And all three of the overseas volunteers now.

What was happening? Did they know?

The intruders had moved on, and were approaching the outskirts of a recently planted olive grove. Their intent was clear to her. They were bent on destroying the trees, chopping or, rather, chainsawing them down. Just as they had slaughtered the sheep, deftly by night. Kurtiz knew that, in the West Bank, to destroy the olive groves, wipe out the livelihoods of the resident farmers, was a political act. Over the past two weeks she had witnessed the results of such vandalism but she had not been present for its execution.

She had to find Alex. Surely to God the crew were not sleeping. She hurried across the scrubland to his tent. 'Alex. Alex!' Her call was low but urgent. No reply. She pushed at the flap. The tent was empty, which would mean the two others would also be vacant. Both cars were in place. They couldn't have gone far, not with all the equipment. They needed to be *here*.

She heard the stut-stuttering of a chainsaw firing up, as it diced into the silence of the night, followed instantly by a second machine. A crude symphony of destruction. The whip and whack, air whooshing, as wooden sticks beat against living branches. Disregarding their own safety, unarmed men, farmers, were running to protect their groves. The Palestinians were shouting, calling. Kurtiz had hared back to the tent for her Leica. She was working with both cameras at the same time. Shooting everything. Feet crunching, ankles twisting on unseen stones, regaining her balance, stooping and dipping in and out of cover towards the groves, which were beyond the range of the floodlights and illuminated only by a last-quarter moon and stars. Trees were falling, thudding, dark shapes bouncing and rolling. Men were weeping; women halfway up the hill in the village were wailing like ambulance sirens.

From another direction, Alex came running. He was slower than usual, bearing the weight of the larger of the two movie cameras. His crew were no distance behind him. The destructors, vigilantes, were incensed by the arrival of cameras. Like wild bulls they came at the foreigners wielding sticks and pitchforks. A scene from a medieval revolt. Trees were whirring in a dance of death to the pale earth. A small boy; at first Kurtiz thought it was the child whose legs had been thwacked earlier in the day, but it was another, older, thirteen perhaps, resembling him, a brother, cousin, relative or perhaps not. This one was ramming a path, using his elbows, through a forest of knees, thighs, limbs, beating his way to the front of the madding crowd. Working at an eye level lower than everyone else's, he was not immediately spotted as he lunged forward, grappling the legs of one of the bearded bear men. He hammered with closed fists at the man, knocking him off balance. The fellow reeled backwards, feet kicking upwards, as though in a jig, and then the boy, still clinging to his prey, bit into the man's thigh. A curse rose above the other cries. One of his comrades pulled his gun, an M16 assault rifle, and fired two shots into the air while another beat the boy on the back with a stick, a third with a gun butt, whipping and beating, beating and whipping. The boy crumpled, curling like a flayed hedgehog.

Kurtiz let go her cameras. One swung from her neck; the Fuji she stuffed back into her pocket. She was on her knees at the boy's buttocks. His back was bleeding. He seemed to be unconscious. A thud caught her on the shoulder. The pain momentarily disjointed her. She ignored it. A brawl had broken out around her. Gunshots. Everybody spilled, dispersed. The boy lay still. The vigilantes fled. She was lifting the young Palestinian, dragging him. 'Someone help me, please.' She should probably leave him be.

Alex was at her side, leaning down over her. 'Let me,' he said, bending. He scooped the boy into his arms, attempting not to press against the flesh on the child's back, and conveyed him towards the village. His crew stepped in to take charge of the equipment. Kurtiz followed Alex, stumbling, unbalanced. Her head was whizzing, her ears ringing from the shots, the shock; her shoulder was wounded. Her teeth were chattering, her nose running.

The boy died within hours. Before daylight he had drawn his last breath, his mother at his side. He was the older brother of the boy whose legs had been lacerated. Kurtiz, who had been boiling water, soaking rags and bits of shredded, bloodied cloth in a plastic bowl to bathe him, slumped to the floor in the living room of the family's stone house. Another stone house sparsely furnished. She pressed her head, which had the weight of a cannonball, against the cool wall. The floodlights from the watchtowers were still emblazoned. The boy had died in full glaring light. No privacy for his final exhalation.

Ironically, moments later, the lights snapped out. Darkness fell in an instant, or a quasi-darkness because the first glow of the rising sun was making its way skywards. An aubergine-violet light crept up beyond the window as the mother of the two boys sank to her knees and sobbed. It was an ugly rasping, a guttural, visceral moan. There was no grace or dignity about her. A spewing of rage and pain. Kurtiz dragged herself to her feet, walked to the woman and pressed a hand hard upon her shoulder, stroked her untidy hair. The woman shook her head and brushed her away, then clung to her violently before turning her face to rest it against her dead son. Kurtiz, as she left the house, vaguely wondered where the father was. Outside, she paused on the step to ingest the first moments of dawn, breathe the daybreak coolness. Then, slowly, she trod the dust path, returning in the gloaming to her tent.

She had no idea what had happened to the small crew she had arrived there with.

She and Alex returned to Jerusalem later that day. The flesh along her collarbone was bruised, patches of purple appearing, but no bones had been fractured. They exchanged barely a word on the journey back. They were no longer in convoy. The other jeep had set off a couple of hours earlier. Alex had insisted the women up in the village dress Kurtiz's shoulder wound before they hit the road. Their next location was Hebron, down in the south. It was two days till her plane would take her out of here. Hebron, then home. She wondered how anyone had the stamina, the guts, for this calling.

Back in her hotel room she stood under the shower until the water ran cold. Warm water flowing over her, into her mouth, her nostrils, choking her, soothing her, mingling with her tears. When she was done she lay in a towel on the bed, wet. Too enervated to dry herself. Her cameras, her memory cards, her telephone lay in her bags, forgotten. Of little importance. She needed to rid her soul of the violence, of the beating to death of an innocent child.

When she woke, she heard a tapping on the door. She was freezing, damp, sticky. Hair bedraggled, skew-whiff from lying on it wet. The tapping increased in force. She had no idea what time or even what day it was.

'Who is it?'

'Alex. Let me in.'

She rolled off the bed and grabbed something, a bed-cover, a shirt, and hauled it over the wet towel. The key was in the lock ready to be turned. His dark face was creased, full of concern.

'Shit! Have I missed the call? Crew waiting for me?'

'Let me in,' he said, and gently nudged at the door. She did not resist him. Instead, she shuffled awkwardly into the cramped room with barely space to move around the bed and sank backwards on to the quilt. He closed the door with his foot. 'I've been up here four times,' he said. 'I was getting worried.'

She shrugged. 'I was sleeping. What happened back there . . .'

'Was unconscionable. Yes. And you look awful.' He sat down beside her and she instinctively shifted herself towards the foot of the bed, out of range.

'Alex. I'm not coming to Hebron. I've thought it through carefully and I am not coming.' Her voice was low, strangled. 'I'll wait here or take the bus to Tel Aviv for my plane on Saturday. I want to go home.'

'You will come.'

She dropped her gaze and shook her head.

'You've been witness to your first death. The first murder. I'm very sorry for you that it was a child. Always tougher. This is a war, Kurtiz. An internationally undeclared war, but that is what is happening here and it's what we are making films about. Man's inhumanity to man. To redress the balance, find the stories that will open up another perspective to the lies and the cover-ups that are perpetrated out there in the wider world. To see this through is *your job*, Kurtiz. You took it on. You hungered for it. And now you're committed to it and I'm counting on you. Get dressed. I'll buy you a large drink, and when you're ready, we'll have dinner. I'll see you downstairs in fifteen minutes.'

She shook her bent head but there was no force in her disagreement.

'And before dinner I'm moving you to the American Colony where I can keep an eye on you. You are a member of my team and I have a responsibility. Get dressed. Come and have a drink.'

They dined with Tim and Darryl. Alex judged that companionship was the best panacea for all four of them.

'No one takes pleasure in witnessing such brutality, no matter whose side the victim is from.' She took comfort from Darryl's words. Even these guys who were habituated, having worked in war zones all across Africa, the Middle and Far East, were subdued, smoking cigarette after cigarette and drinking shot after shot.

She sat alongside Alex at the round table, aware for the first time that the men were bonded to one another by hellish experiences. They drank heavily, all of them, but they were accustomed to it. Whisky for them, wine for her. Her innards were wrung out. None of them had slept the night before and they would be making another early start for Hebron in the morning. She would accompany them, not only because Alex had insisted but because it was her job and she had promised herself to be a trouper.

And once this West Bank trip was over she would go home and spend special summer days with her daughter, her precious child. They'd go shopping, take the bus to the Heath, swim in the open-air pool, eat long lunches together, buy chocolate and vanilla ice cream, toss aside all-calorie counting, talk about Lizzie's teenage issues. Yes, she was going to relish every moment, make the most of being a normal mother in the company of her lovely blossoming girl. It briefly crossed her mind during dinner that she didn't have her phone, hadn't switched it on since the signal had been disrupted, lost up in the West Bank hills yesterday. She'd ring home, she told herself, when she returned to her room. Dinner arrived; they ate, discussed. The evening moved on. Slowly, the events of the previous night were assigned to a rarely visited place inside her, which she had mentally labelled 'work experience'. Still the ache remained, the rawness. Raw on the inside as well as the shoulder, as though someone had stuck a brush down her throat and scrubbed.

She begged off the second round of nightcaps and bade them 'Sleep well.' Alex offered to accompany her, which she refused but he insisted. He had her key, had taken it from Reception when they had checked her in. He walked her to her room. Above them, taking up an entire floor, were the offices and suites of peace envoy Tony Blair. Little peace here, she remarked silently. Kurtiz's new room was set at the far end of a gently curving corridor.

Alex unlocked the door – room 206 – and hung back while she entered. Then he followed her in. She'd known he would. She wanted him to. She had always wanted him to. He closed the door and took her powerfully by the shoulders, careful to avoid the bruise, folding her body into his, wrapping himself around her. His dark, muscular body enveloped her. His lips nudging beneath her light hair to find the pale flesh of her curved neck. He danced her in spins to the bed, which, with her fatigue and the alcohol she had consumed, left her giddy. With its white cover, it was a capacious double, unlike the iron skeleton in her box room at the East Jerusalem.

Without further ado and with proficiency, he peeled away her clothes as though they were paper. Deliberate movements with both of his hands, as though removing the outer layers of an exotic fruit, leaving her body exposed and naked. And then he undressed himself, hurriedly, letting garment after garment fall. Kurtiz hadn't made love in a while, hadn't had sex in a while. Her life with Oliver was too acrimonious for sex, for physical proximity. She had exiled him to the spare room, which she was sure Lizzie had known and was brooding about. She was possibly even angry . . .

Lizzie! She still hadn't called home.

'What time is it? Alex, stop, I need . . .' She lifted herself onto her elbows, scrabbling fingers against the pristine sheets, attempting to shift and inch herself from the bed, from the arms of this man. Alex eased her back to a supine position and lowered himself to her, against her, his firm flesh against hers. She inhaled his verveine cologne and felt the solidity of him, the rock of his desire shifting, awakening the muscles within her. The call home could wait. Lizzie would be at the end of the phone tomorrow. And they'd have a fun time together on Sunday. This moment belonged to Kurtiz. Only her. She let go, spread herself wide, breaking every inch of herself open for the man she had desired and resisted for too long, the lover whom she knew already was a part of her.

When she woke, she was alone. A scribbled note on hotel paper in his handwriting read: *6 a.m. in the lobby. Don't be late.*

She glanced at the digital bedside clock. It read 5:50 in accusatory red figures. She shot out of bed and into the shower, crying out as the pain in her collarbone wrenched at her, soaping the tenderness in her groin.

The men were waiting, seated in the lobby when she appeared, hair wet, out of the lift at 6:04.

'You're late,' commented Alex. 'Let's go.' Was he using such a crisp tone because he had so recently left her bed and did not want his colleagues to sense that some balance within the quartet had shifted? Whatever the explanation, his manner took Kurtiz aback.

On the journey south they rode for a while in silence. He slipped a hand from the wheel and touched her knee. 'I'll get you coffee as soon as we can make a stop,' he murmured. She switched on her phone. Seven a.m. in the West Bank, Eastern European summer time, meant five a.m. in London. Friday morning. Lizzie and Oliver would still be in bed. Way too early to call. She found three phone messages. All from Oliver. She hit the phone to listen to the most recent.

'KZ, where the fuck are you? Why are you not picking up the phone? Are you receiving these messages? I have sent you two emails. Call me. I'm out of my mind with worry and I need you here.'

Had Oliver started drinking again? His voice sounded steady. Since when had he shown such concern over her absences? Except to make her culpable for being away in the first place. She calculated backwards. She had sent emails to both Oliver and Lizzie on . . . When had she last written? Tuesday?

She hit the button to listen to the first of the three messages.

'Kurtiz, it's Oliver. Wednesday morning. I haven't seen Lizzie since yesterday. She's not picking up on her mobile. Did she message you about where she might have stayed overnight?'

'*What? No!*'

Alex glanced in her direction. Kurtiz ignored him, barely registering his interaction. She scrolled her emails to see whether there was anything from Lizzie. Nothing. She returned to the phone icon to play the second message.

'Kurtiz, any reason why you didn't reply to my message? It's now Wednesday afternoon and Lizzie still hasn't come home — home, Kurtiz, remember it? — since Tuesday. Yesterday. I am going to call the police. Pick up the damn phone.'

When Kurtiz eventually managed to get through to Oliver, Lizzie had been missing for three nights.

'Have you telephoned the police?'

'I called them on Wednesday about four in the afternoon. I left you messages, dammit! They asked how long she'd been gone. "It's too soon," was their response.'

'And then? Have you called them since, taken a photograph into the station?' She covered her phone with her hand and leaned towards Alex. 'I have to leave,' she told him. 'Now.'

Oliver was talking again. His words were slow as though he could not recall the sequence of events. 'They said it was most unlikely I had any cause for concern. However, if Lizzie hadn't returned by Wednesday night, I was to make contact with them again.'

'And did you, Oliver?' She felt her impatience rising, panic sharpening.

Oliver had waited in all day for his daughter's return. That same evening he had called again.

'The matter is in the hands of the police,' he reiterated. 'Lizzie's room was searched. They turned it upside down, looking for possible explanations, clues as to her whereabouts.'

'And have they found anything, got any leads?'

'She's on the missing-persons list.'

Her guts seemed to fall away as her heart began to race, as terror stepped centre stage.

'When can you be here?'

'I'm on my way. Listen, Oliver . . . Oliver?' He had cut her off.

Alex swung the car round and sped her west along the central highway to Tel Aviv airport.

The terminal was a bazaar. Queues of travellers backed up to the outer doors, shouting to one another, complaining loudly. Kurtiz and Alex squeezed and shoved a passage to the British Airways desk. Changing her ticket required a reissue. Alex took control. Eventually Kurtiz was given an economy cancellation on that evening's overnight to Heathrow. He took her for a coffee and stayed at her side until she cleared Immigration.

She wanted to be alone, on her way, to erase the last few days. Oliver's accusation: 'Where the fuck have you been?'

Was *she* responsible for Lizzie's departure?

'Listen,' said Alex, taking her hand. 'She'll probably have returned by the time you land. If not, take what you need to get this handled, bring her home and then I want you back with me. Do you hear me?'

Kurtiz swung her gaze away from him, concentrating on the crowded terminal, Jewish families heaving over-sized cases and trunks onto the check-in scales, officious

Customs officers disgorging trunks before clearing them. The worn faces, the tearful farewells, the staggering loads of baggage. The guilt she felt weighed heavier and was threatening to overwhelm her. *What was she doing here?*

'I'll be in touch when I arrive. Thanks for your help.' She pushed her drained coffee cup to one side, rose, hauled her cameras and hand luggage on to her undamaged shoulder and walked the distance to Passport Control, aware of the sound of her every step against the marble floor. She felt Alex's eyes boring into her back. The man who, just a few hours earlier, had been in her bed; her first infidelity to Oliver. She was probably in love with Alex, yes, she was, but she would not allow herself to think about it. She didn't turn her head, didn't look round. She slid her passport back from the officer, gave him a curt nod and kept going.

When she unlocked the front door ten hours later, Oliver was alone, unshaven, looking half-starved and unwashed. He had been sleeping in the chair in the sitting room, keeping watch for his daughter's return. She probably looked equally scruffy, equally freaked.

'What happened?' were her first words to him, as she threw her house keys onto the table and felt the empty, mausoleum mood of the house. It was eight in the morning, Saturday. She felt as though she hadn't slept in a week.

'You should have been here. We needed you.' His voice was a low whine. What had happened to the young dreamboat she had fallen in love with two decades earlier? So full of promise. Where had he gone?

She crossed to him and pecked him on the head, gently stroking his hair with the flat of her hand. He exuded stale body odours, those of a man who has stopped caring for himself, and it was clear to her that he had been drinking. He had abandoned the wagon. Now was not the moment to chastise him for it.

'I'm going to have a shower and hunt about in Lizzie's room. Is there anything you want to tell me, anything she said, that I need to know?'

Oliver made no comment. His shoulders hung heavily over his extended gut. 'Kurtiz?' He said no more, incapable of summoning up the sentence.

Kurtiz waited. She was desperate to get to Lizzie's room. 'Have you eaten? You look . . . Shall I heat some coffee?'

'We're out of coffee and milk.'

She sighed, swallowing unspoken recriminations, and left him in his chair, hurrying up the stairs in search of her daughter.

Paris, November 2015

Kurtiz stood in the diminishing cold, stamping her booted feet against the ground, arms wrapped round her midriff, fists beating her torso in an attempt to keep warm. Her breath exhaled in clouds, as she stared about her. Victims were being wrapped in gold-foil space blankets as thermal protection, shivering, shaking, convulsing. Ambulance, fire brigade and paramedics were trolleying injured bodies, some with oxygen tanks, and heaving them one after another into red ambulances. Blood had laid its fingers on everyone, smeared its autograph. Blood marked the cross for Death to follow. While, silently, unremarked, unmoved, desiccated leaves from the mighty plane trees on the far side of the boulevard were falling to the ground, gathering in the gutters. A leaf for every victim? For every shot fired? Winter was here. The trees would soon be bare, stark, denuded. Winter. Her companion. It had taken up residence inside her heart, closed her down, on that Saturday morning more than four years earlier.

Kurtiz, London, July 2011

When Kurtiz opened the door to her teenage daughter's bedroom she was greeted by a state of disarray and a stale, sweetish aroma. What was it? It hung in the air, unidentified. Clothes were strewn everywhere, bags emptied and tossed on the floor. It looked as though Lizzie had been frantically searching for something and in haste or frustration had chucked aside each unsuccessful attempt. Or was this the result of police intervention?

Hovering a foot or two inside, back pressed against the open door, Kurtiz's eyes darted in every direction. The mess in the room suggested a burglary. Would the police leave a site like this or had this been her daughter's state of mind? Kurtiz backed out without touching anything and hurried to Lizzie's bathroom. The door was closed, not locked. She tapped on the wood.

'Lizzie? Lizzie, are you in there?' Of course she wasn't. She had no idea why she was knocking. As though this foolishness might spin back the clock to the evening before her flight to Tel Aviv almost three weeks earlier.

She pushed the door open to find the room in stillness. A leaking tube of toothpaste left carelessly on the washbasin, its cap forgotten elsewhere. A loofah lying dry on the windowsill. Shower curtain half in, half out of the bath. She breathed in the scent of Chanel No 5. Lizzie had been filching her eau-de-toilette again. Dolling herself up. Might it be for the attentions of a new boyfriend? Kurtiz crossed to the mirrored cupboard above the basin. Within, she found a half-empty bottle of paracetamol, tweezers and a small blue plastic container shaped like a clam shell. Kurtiz gripped the basin and steadied herself. She knew what that contained. Hand raised unsteadily, she lifted it out of the cupboard and opened it. Its base was sprinkled with talc but it was otherwise empty.

She swung about her and savagely yelled her daughter's name back along the corridor. A sick sense of fear engulfed her. Had Lizzie been wearing the diaphragm when she left the house? What mood had she been in? Upbeat, afraid, troubled?

The evening before Kurtiz had left for Jerusalem – she had brushed the incident aside until this moment, dismissed it – she and Lizzie had bickered. Not a blazing row but picky niggling at each other. She had laid into Lizzie for some misdemeanour, her lethargy – plates left dirty in the sink or something equally trite. Lizzie, uncharacteristically, had not stormed off in a temper, taking refuge in her bedroom with a resounding thud of the door. No, she had hovered at the door of the box room Kurtiz had transformed into her study. 'Don't go, Mum,' she'd said. 'Please, don't.'

Kurtiz, still mildly miffed with her daughter, had replied simply, 'Don't be silly. I'll be back before you know it.'

'You don't give a fuck about us, do you? It's all about you and your sodding work.'

Kurtiz had lifted her head from her computer and fixed her gaze on her daughter. 'Don't you ever talk to me like that again.'

Lizzie had slunk away, hurt by her mother's response.

Kurtiz had missed the sounding bell, the distress signal. Her precious girl's *cri de coeur*? If she had listened, would Lizzie still be here? She had been too caught up in the logistics of her own upcoming journey, the packing that lay ahead and the quiet joy at the prospect of being in Alex's company again.

Had the girl been suffering with a private injury, a grief or insecurity that she had held back from her parents? A teenage malaise kept hidden. Was there a boy who had become the subject of her affections, replacing her mum as number-one date? He for whom she had been fitted with the diaphragm? Gone were the days when Lizzie had confided her secrets, whispered and giggled in her mother's ear, held her hand as they walked along the high street, talking about school and friends, counting calories, diet fads, clothes, pop stars she fancied – 'He's crackerjack, Mum'; 'He's fit' – and the rock concerts her dad loved to take her to. Never boyfriends or personal relationships. Kurtiz had still been a virgin at sixteen. Evidently not Lizzie. Should she discuss this with Oliver?

If she had simply left home, wouldn't Kurtiz have heard from her? *Don't worry about me, Mum. I'm doing fine. I've met someone.* Where might she have gone?

Had she been kidnapped, lured away by a malevolent contact who intended nothing better than rape and murder?

Kurtiz spun back to her daughter's room and stepped inside, kicking her way through the piles of clothes, books, DVDs, the personal gallimaufry. In the centre of the space she turned about in a circle, giddying herself, scanning from left to right. The walls were papered with posters. Rock legends. Jesse Hughes, Josh Homme; Them Crooked Vultures; the late Jeff Buckley, whose voice and good looks made Lizzie swoon, she claimed, with girlish giggles. Some of the display pinned to the walls had been purchased at concerts her father had taken her to, stoking his daughter's passion for rock and blues. Was there a big concert, or a music festival taking place anywhere in the UK about now that she might have sloped off to? Isle of Wight, Glastonbury? Oliver would surely know. Was there information about Lizzie's disappearance that Oliver was keeping to himself? Had he argued with his daughter, hurled drunken words at her, which had driven her away? Or had Lizzie been trying to convey a deeper, more desperate concern?

Don't go, Mum.

It was 11:57 p.m. Marguerite was standing in her sitting room, her feet snug in furry slippers, hands clenched together and pressed against her chin, too troubled to be seated, staring at the television screen hoping to hear news from within the Bataclan. Had that poor young woman reached the theatre safely? Had she been united with her family? What a distressed soul she seemed.

François Hollande was mouthing words with precision, standing erect, rigid between swept-back burgundy curtains against a grey pillared backdrop. He was addressing the camera, making a speech to *les citoyens*. His expression was grave, skin parched. Once or twice he paused and almost imperceptibly bit the right side of his lower lip. He was declaring a state of national emergency. The borders were to be closed. Public transport had been shut down. 'We must perceive the atrocities that have been perpetrated this evening as acts of war against our nation.' *C'est une acte de guerre.* He spoke the words emphatically. Syllables as weapons. Heavy rolling of consonants like a guillotine falling.

'Go back to your homes and, *s'il vous plaît*, be prudent. Stay indoors.'

But what of the young woman? Marguerite begged

the empty room. Had she got through? She glanced towards the hallway where Kurtiz's bags lay neatly stacked on the floor. Will she remember where I am? Should I try to find her?

Go back to your homes and stay indoors.

It was almost midnight. She had not been up so late in years. She must try to rest. But what if she fell asleep and the young woman came knocking, ringing her bell, and she didn't hear her? No, more sensible to brew coffee, stay awake. Beyond her, on the television screen, fleets of Red Cross vehicles were drawing up alongside other vehicles with spinning lights, banked in crocodile lines, making a flashing tail that stretched from the Bataclan to La République. Elsewhere in the background of the grainy night-time images on screen, members of the armed forces were building a barricade with dustbins.

Thirty confirmed mortalities was the figure released by the national press office, stated the anchorman gravely. 'The Bataclan remains a hostage situation. It is calculated that some twelve hundred people are still captured within, held at gunpoint, with shots being fired unremittingly.'

Marguerite slumped into a chair. What could she do? Her eyelids were heavy. Her heart and poor worn-out body so dog-tired. 'They should have taken me,' she muttered. 'Not the young. Not some woman's lovely daughter.'

Marguerite and Charlie, La Côte d'Azur, March 1947

Marguerite stirred. Someone was gently shaking her, stroking her knee. 'We've reached the coast, Marseille.'

'What?'

'You slept through the night.'

'We are not moving.'

'We're in Marseille. The train has stopped for a crew change, I believe. I thought you might like to look out of the window and watch the sea as we travel east towards Italy. It seems to be a beautiful coastline.'

Alongside him on the seat Charlie had a wrapped paper package containing the sandwiches, and a dog-eared open copy of *Animal Farm*, spine turned upwards. He must be a gentleman if he reads books, she thought, as she yawned, stretching her arms and legs. Glancing at her reflection in the window, she saw that her hair was a rumpled mess. She rubbed at it furiously with her fingers.

'Hungry?'

She nodded, and he passed over the greaseproof package. How much further? she wanted to know.

'There will be quite a few stops from now on, so that makes it longer. But we'll be in Nice this afternoon.'

It was Thursday morning. Her screen test was the following day. She needed to wash her hair, spruce herself up, and iron her one remaining frock. It had been squashed in her bag for several days and creased so easily. If she didn't iron it, she would look drab and unattractive. Ill-presented – that would never do.

'Are you going directly to your friends?' she asked him.

'Maybe.'

'Are they far from Nice?'

'Two stops before.' He coughed, picked up his book and closed it. He was going to have to come clean with this young woman before the day was out.

'Two stops before' had unsettled Marguerite. She had been hoping the friends lived close to Nice. She had nowhere to stay. Everything depended on the success of the following day's test or she would be stranded, but until then she *was* stranded. Even if she were immensely fortunate and found employment as a barmaid today, they wouldn't pay her directly. She would have to wait for her wages. She must try for a live-in situation somewhere along the coast. Chambermaid in a hotel, perhaps. Nanny to a wealthy family. The wealthier, the better. Or might Charlie advance her a few more francs? How prosperous was he? She didn't want to push him too far. And she'd need to pay him back. Quite possibly his friends were comfortably off and wouldn't mind offering her a bed for a few nights, and the company might distract her from her escalating nerves.

They fell silent, munching on their baguettes, chewy, slightly stale, but welcome all the same.

The train had left the port city and was on the move again, curling, creaking, chugging round the coast. The sun was climbing high above the horizon as they inched along beside the sea, turquoise at the water's edge. Marguerite had never seen the sea before. The cliffs and rocks were baked with heat and shone rust and purple. Disappointingly, there were few boats now that they had left the great harbour behind them. Even at this early hour, she could feel the power of the sun bleeding through the window, warming her tired skin. This was more like it. Without warning, surprising even herself, she leaped to her feet and began to sing 'La Mer' . . . 'Do you know this song, Charlie? It's my favourite . . . "The sea, dancing along the shores . . . We're at the sea, the sea . . ."' she improvised.

She was turning in circles, arms outstretched, dancing with herself, delighting in her youth, radiating happiness and the opportunities awaiting her. 'Oh, Charlie, we're at the sea. We've reached the seaside. The sea,' she was crooning again, 'I'm at the sea . . .'

Her voice was scintillating, sweet, full of grace. She sang like ribbons of silver scudding through wheat fields in the wind. Charlie chewed his sandwich; his eyes lingering on her, smiling with delight. He liked her. She didn't threaten him; she had no interest in quizzing him or snooping into his story. This crazed girl improvising music, dancing on an imagined shore. Her small thin body waving and bending exaggeratedly. Now she was laughing almost drunkenly, head tossed backwards, glowing, unmindful of her true beauty, her inner beauty, her untapped sexuality.

'What say we both leave the train in Cannes, Marguerite?'

Cannes, where the new film festival had been inaugurated the previous year. She could quote the date –

20 September – having drooled over newspaper photographs of the ceremony, kept cuttings of the stars disembarking the liners from America, waving to the cameras, to the resort city, the French movie industry, the unconquered territory. Even so, she shook her head, mouth full. He knew what her objection was.

'Listen, tomorrow I'll accompany you to Nice to the Victorine Studios, if you like. Unless you have other plans for tonight, that is?' Charlie winked at her, which took her aback.

She felt her cheeks and neck grow hot, a flush rising pink as candy floss. 'No plans,' she replied softly.

From the railway station at Cannes, they walked with their luggage to the illustrious promenade known as La Croisette in the early-afternoon sunshine. Palm trees and tropical shrubs bordered the wide sea-breezed boulevard. Its full length on the inland side seemed to be constructed with impressive hotels painted white, like freshly starched linen. Tourists motored by in open-top cars exuding a carefree air. They passed a shop, Rémy's Chemisier. It faced directly towards the water and was stocked with elegant handmade shirts. Striped, silk, fine Egyptian cotton. Outside, gleaming in the sunlight, was parked an open-top Bentley, the colour of sucked toffee.

'It's another world,' breathed Marguerite, solemnly. 'Wondrous and so glamorous.' A world she lusted to be a part of. Strolling onwards, awe spinning them in circles, they came to a standstill outside the Carlton Hotel; their heads craned in amazement, as they exclaimed at its grandeur, its sophistication. Marguerite closed her eyes and the spectacle of women in backless floor-length frocks swam into view, strappy high heels of satin, spinning, swaying by starlight on the terrace. An orchestra flanked by potted palms, seducing the guests with easy-going swing rhythms.

Although they were both tired, Charlie took her by the hand and led her alongside a stretch of beach where clusters of people were seated beneath striped parasols to keep the sun off their heads. Others were swimming in the sea, calling to companions, rising like seals as the water danced off their suntanned limbs, or playing ball games at the foam's edge. It was the beginning of the holiday season, he explained to her. The overexcited, high-pitched yells of children wading into the sea brought Marguerite to a halt. She held her face skywards.

Charlie watched her, thrilling to the grace of her movements, her long lashes when she closed her eyes. She seemed to be a flower opening, a bud unfolding, before his eyes.

Marguerite moved her head back and forth lethargically, basking in the sun's rays caressing her skin. There was a mood of joy, mirth, of ebullience about this seaside town that eased her tensions, soothed her emotional scars. She was determined to stay in the present. The past was gone. The war was over. Now mattered, and tomorrow. 'Where are your friends? I'd like to meet them, may I?' she asked him suddenly.

'No friends.' He grinned. 'Like you, these are my first footsteps along the Riviera. So, we have to find ourselves somewhere to sleep.'

'No friends!'

'But you have given me a reason to be here.' He laughed. 'It was high time to leave Paris in any case.'

She looked up at him, alarmed, then studied him, appraising him. He seemed to know the world, know what he was about. He was a classic English gentleman. Not that she had met any before, but she had recently seen Trevor Howard in *Brief Encounter* and been dazzled by his penetrating gaze and respectful manners.

Was she angry with Charlie for the lie he'd told her before they boarded the train?

'You have beautiful eyes.' He smiled. 'A film star's eyes.'

'It's what I dream of, Charlie. It's all I want. Nothing else.'

No, she wasn't angry. In fact, she rather liked him. Aside from Bertrand, no one before had ever shown her such consideration. Perhaps she could persuade him to teach her the rudiments of English? The Americans in Hollywood spoke English, didn't they?

My, but she had fallen on good luck with Charlie! He had booked her a room of her own at the *pension* and paid for it. It was a modest but clean refuge they had found in a narrow street set back from the station. What was more, she would be able to iron her crushed frock. She had asked the desk clerk, who had shown her to her tiny *chambre* up in the eaves and he had politely assured her that it was certainly not a problem. In fact, the house-keeping would be done for her. She was here, finally here, in the south, just a bus ride from Nice. A little tired and dishevelled, but she didn't care. Not tonight. All boded well for her screen test the following morning. Luck was smiling down on her. She could be confident at last.

'*La mer* . . .' She hummed softly as she hung up her raincoat in the *armoire*, skipped a step or two, unpacked her scruffy little bag, carefully unfolding her few remaining possessions onto the iron-framed single bed. Life was improving by the minute. All she needed was to triumph at the studios.

Paris, November 2015

By close to 2 a.m. on Saturday morning the killings were over. The incessant spit of gunshots had been gagged. Although for some this was just the beginning of a different kind of nightmare. Those who had survived the onslaught, who were not dead, seriously injured or traumatized, were liberated from the concert hall, free to make their unsteady way to another part of the city, anywhere else, for refuge, comfort, the healing power of loved ones. The perpetrators of this hell, the terrorists, were dead. Three jihadi males, clothed in black, had blown themselves up after triggering suicide vests when the RAID, an elite law-enforcement team, the task force of the French national police, had eventually gained access to the venue and intervened.

Kurtiz remained outside in the grey street with its charcoal sky. She was shivering in diminishing temperatures. Shivering from fear and shock. A wind was whipping up. Blood and vomit graffitied the paving stones, and the rank odour of sulphur, accompanied by the sweeter, cloying scent of blood, hung in the air. Hints of faeces, too. A physical reality of terror.

'You can smell fear. It's pungent, no doubt about it,' Alex had once said to her.

The interior of the concert hall was out of bounds to all but the special services and medical workers. Their task now was to unravel the carnage, gather up the bodies strewn about the floor. Locate any whose hearts were still beating and transport them without delay to one of the city's hospitals. The dead required preparation before the gurneys could wheel them out.

There was no Lizzie. So far, no Lizzie. Kurtiz had looked into the face of every injured female she could get close to. She had badgered officers and care staff to scan their lists, which were scant of confirmed information. Oliver had been tracked down.

A woman logging the names of victims whose identity cards were on their person yelled his name. Kurtiz elbowed her way through waiting crowds. 'Yes, here,' she called. 'Here!'

Identity papers. British passport. Age forty-seven.

'Yes, that's him. How is he?' She was hopping alongside the gurney. 'Was he on his own?'

Condition: critical.

Two bullets had ripped through his coeliac – or solar – plexus; bullets fired from a Kalashnikov AK-47 assault rifle.

Kurtiz gazed upon his unconscious, blood-stained body, his face ragged and pale as alabaster as they transported him across the street.

Shot twice, he was marked down for intensive care.

'Which hospital, *s'il vous plaît*? May I come with you?'

'*Désolé, Madame.*'

'Is my daughter on your list? Lizzie Ross? Was she at her father's side?'

'Madame, please keep back.'

'Which hospital is my husband being treated at?'

The paramedics were requesting she liaise with the hospital for further updates on Oliver's condition. 'Step away, make space for the services to do their jobs.'

'Yes, but which hospital?'

'*Malheureusement, Madame*, we have no directive yet as to where he's being taken.'

She watched impotently as they loaded him into an ambulance along with two other victims. Metal doors closed hard; the driver pulled away.

Should she try to follow or wait for Lizzie? She was so tired it was as though someone had slugged her, beaten and coshed her. Clubbed her into insensibility. Coordination of thought felt impossible. She didn't know where to turn, who to turn to, where to go. She needed sleep, coffee, guidance, every kind of sustenance, but more than anything she needed reassurance that Lizzie was alive and that they would be together soon.

Every hospital in Paris was operating at full tilt. Plan Blanc, one of the aid workers informed her, had been *déclenché*. Kurtiz had never heard of Plan Blanc. The White Plan? Alex, if he were here, would know of it. How she craved his solidity and wisdom right now.

A woman whom Kurtiz quite literally stumbled over, crouched on the pavement, drinking beer from a can, rolling a cigarette, waiting for news, 'like all of us here', told her that Paris was a graveyard of decimated bodies and victims. Many had not yet been identified. Six targets had been established, six locations, all within the eastern suburbs of the city.

The smell of tobacco drifted to her, warm and reassuring. Kurtiz begged a cigarette. She didn't smoke, hadn't rolled a ciggie since she'd been a student. Her fingers were clumsy, cold and numb, but she took comfort, consolation from the company of another whose anguish must equal hers. They hunkered on their haunches side by side, puffing silently.

'Who are you waiting for?'

'My son, Michel. He's sixteen. We live off Richard Lenoir, just round the corner. I've been here since quarter past ten. As soon as I heard the news, I came running. You?'

'My daughter.' The nicotine caused her head to spin. She coughed and heaved.

The woman offered her a slug of beer. Kurtiz was grateful for any liquid.

'No sign of Michel yet. He must be among those pinned to the floor inside. A young girl who'd been hiding under the stage and managed to escape through a fire exit while those bastards were reloading their guns told me the assassins had ordered everyone to get down on the floor. Anyone who moved, they shot. I pray to God Michel's still breathing.'

Kurtiz closed her eyes, barring the possibility.

'He saved for weeks to buy this ticket.'

Was Lizzie somewhere on the floor, perhaps clinging to Michel, or was she in a mortuary? Kurtiz dragged on the roll-up. Just a girl whom no one could put a name to, who'd gone to a concert.

She scrambled to her feet, thanked her companion for the smoke and began to walk along the lines of bodies, the rows laid on the ground outside the concert hall, praying not to identify Lizzie, praying that, after all her hopes of being reunited with her precious girl that evening, she had, for whatever providential reason, decided at the last moment not to attend.

Or might she have been among the few who escaped early? Had she caught sight of her dad and fled at the outset?

No, Kurtiz could not entertain this last scenario. If Lizzie knew that her father had been present at the Eagles of Death Metal concert, even if she guessed that he was there on a quest to find her, if she knew that her flight had saved her life, she would be questioning the fate of her father. She would come forward. She would want to know his fate. Wouldn't she?

And soon his identity, his condition, would be public, one on a list of more than a hundred of those gunned down, more than eighty fatally, during this night of hell. No matter Lizzie's circumstances, no matter where she was or what anger she might still harbour towards her mother, for her father's sake, her beloved dad, she'd make herself known. Wouldn't she?

Kurtiz bent to the floor and picked up a CD. The jacket pictured a close-up of a female's backside in tight jeans, and two fingers, the pinky and index, extended. The *Death by Sexy* album. Blues or garage rock, Kurtiz wasn't sure which. Oliver had taken Lizzie to that concert at the Brixton Academy in June, a couple of years back. The group had gone directly to the number-one slot on the list of fourteen-year-old Lizzie's Favourite Rock Bands. From there on, Eagles of Death Metal had become a bond between father and daughter. She was crazy about the ginger-haired singer-songwriter, Josh Homme. 'Almost as old as Dad,' she'd teased, 'but fit.' The posters of him were still pinned to her bedroom wall. One with Homme playing his Maton BB1200, dated 2007. Homme was also a contributor to the Arctic Monkeys' albums, another fave of Lizzie's.

No matter the dissent between Kurtiz and Oliver, he had never been less than caring and attentive to his daughter. He idolized her.

What exactly Kurtiz was looking for, she couldn't have said. A clue obviously. Her mind was running in circles. Where was Lizzie's mobile phone? On the bedside table? No. At her work desk? Also negative. So, she must have taken it with her. Had Oliver tried calling her? Could it be traced by its in-built GPS? Had the police been given her phone number?

Why did the knot, tight as a brick, in her stomach, and the palpitations of her heart, signal to Kurtiz that this was no jaunt for a few days to a concert, to Glastonbury or the coast with a carload of juveniles playing truant? Her sixteen-year-old daughter had not simply decamped for a long weekend to hang out with hipper, happier companions than her forever wrangling parents. Something intangible, an invisible absence, *a deadness in the room*, sounded an alarm. Lizzie had gone.

Kurtiz sank to her knees and began to scrabble and dig for the umpteenth time, excavating the chaos that was Lizzie's existence, throwing up scarves, underwear, trainers, socks, CDs, scratched and lacking jackets, coloured biros. She was rooting for clues, for a scribbled note, an address book, her daughter's iPad, laptop. Anything that offered an indication, a spoor to follow. A message. A message on her own phone? She scrambled to her feet and scooted from the room in search of her handbag on the hall table. Inside was her phone. She stabbed at the screen, awakening it. No messages. She fast-dialled the local police station and was connected to DI Blackwell.

'We have explained to your husband that a fair percentage of teenagers do this sort of thing from time to time and they are back within a few hours. Worst case, as with your daughter, a few days. Unless you have a particular reason, exceptional circumstances, to believe that she might have run away?'

'No, of course not.'

'Or that she was in touch with someone, via the internet perhaps, whom you would not have approved of?'

Kurtiz closed her eyes, picturing the empty diaphragm case upstairs.

'You mean a man she might have met online?'

'That will almost certainly not be the case, Mrs Ross. She's from a happy family. Your husband's a successful high-profile face. We are simply investigating all options.'

Dear God, no. She slapped off the phone, shoved it into her jeans pocket and scaled the stairs two at a time.

She needed to keep her head, be systematic, think clearly. She entered the master bedroom, the room where for some time now she had been sleeping without Oliver, and methodically she checked everywhere, cupboards, drawers, wardrobe, pockets, scouring for a note. A secret message left for her eyes only, perhaps? *Here's why I begged you not to go, Mum . . .*

It was easier in here. She could breathe; the room had an order to it. Even so, she found nothing.

If Lizzie had disappeared with friends, who would she have gone with? What day was it? Saturday. Who might she be with? Angela Fox? Lizzie's best friend. She should call Angela. She tugged her phone from her jeans and stabbed at it, waking up the screen, scrolling in search of Jenny Fox, Angela's mother. Hadn't Lizzie mentioned that Angela's parents had separated and were going through a divorce? It was the reason she'd given for spending a fair amount of time over at the Fox house, 'offering moral support to Angie'. Lizzie stayed the night there more frequently than Kurtiz felt comfortable about but Oliver saw no reason to be concerned. Lizzie's pal was going through a bad time and they ought to give Lizzie space for that, he'd said.

Kurtiz was still scrolling back and forth, searching for a number. The Fox landline or Angela's mobile. She was sure she had both listed. Finally, she found what she was looking for. And then it was ringing.

'Hello?' A female voice.

'Angie?'

'Yeah?'

'Angela, it's Kurtiz Ross, Lizzie's mum.'

'Oh.' The girl coughed. 'Hi, Mrs Ross, erm, Kurtiz.'

She hesitated. 'Angela, I'm sure someone has already been in touch with you and asked this, but . . . is Lizzie with you?'

'No, she's not.'

Pause.

'She's not at home . . .'

'Yeah, I heard. Sorry about that.'

'Did she mention to you any plans she might have had for this first week of the holidays?'

'I haven't seen her in a while. Except at school. I already told the police. Sorry.'

'Haven't seen her in a while? How long is "a while"?' Pause. 'Angela? Angie, are you still there?'

'Not for a couple of months.'

A couple of months?

Had the girls fallen out? Lizzie hadn't mentioned any rupture. Kurtiz was trying to recall when Lizzie had last asked for permission to spend the night with her best friend. Hadn't it been the weekend before she had left for Jerusalem?

There had been a concert, or a club outing that had necessitated staying over at Angela's place.

'Aren't you both still in the same class?' When had Kurtiz stopped paying attention to her daughter's schedule?

'School broke up for the summer this week.'

'Yes, I know, but . . . Angie, is there anything you can tell me that might –'

'Sorry, Kurtiz, I've no idea where Lizzie's got to. I've got to go now.'

They were silent in the living room, she standing, Oliver still sitting as though he no longer possessed the ability to lift himself upright. They were looking at each other, resisting blame, trying to put the difficulties, long brewing within their marriage, to one side, to focus on the reality that was staring at them. The one soul they would both have given up their lives for; the link that had bonded them for close to two decades in spite of everything. Lizzie. Little Lizzie.

Everyone starts out with a dream of how they think it will turn out. Kurtiz's had been in this house, this home, with Lizzie and Oliver. She had sacrificed her own early ambitions for that dream. And now she was staring at rubble.

'I just spoke to Angie . . . Was there a disagreement, a bust-up between her and Lizzie?'

They were looking at one another as though in the heart of the other lay the answer, the end of the puzzle.

Where was Lizzie? What glimmer of hope remained that she would be found, that she was safe?

'Where were you, Kurtiz? Why didn't you return my calls? I've been going mad.'

She glanced at the empty wine bottle on the floor by the chair leg.

'And, yes, before you start, please don't start, don't fucking start, because, yes, I've had a drink or two.' Oliver's hands were now covering his face. He was weeping, his back heaving, coughing, a smoker's hacking, spluttering, crying, like a child.

Was this what had driven Lizzie away? The sight of her father weakened by alcohol? Kurtiz stifled the rush of impatience, the frustration that threatened to explode within her. Instead, she crossed the room, dipped to her knees and laid a hand on his lifted arm, holding it firmly but not aggressively. 'Oliver, okay, fine or not fine, you've had a drink. That's over now and I am here. Listen, hush. Please, hush. What counts is finding Lizzie, getting her back with us again. We've got to stand together, Oliver, and find Lizzie.'

But they never did find Lizzie.

The media had a field day. TV actor's daughter . . . Mother away from home, working with an all-male crew . . . Photos of Oliver in his heyday and now surprise-snapped as he sloped out of the house, dressed in old jeans and a pyjama top, face raddled, a devastated man. The paparazzi camped at their gate. It seemed to go on ad infinitum, until it stopped. One day they were gone. They were gone, but there was still no Lizzie.

Paris, November 2015

The wind was gaining force. Iron shutters were rattling lividly, rattling like her nerves. Kurtiz was standing in the street, a street she had never walked along before tonight, in a city she knew well and of which she had many happy memories. This was Paris, not a war zone, or it had not been until tonight. Paris, where she had hoped to find Lizzie. To heal the rift. To beg her forgiveness. To start to understand.

The woman who had been waiting for her son had disappeared. Her boy had been located. Shocked, but unhurt. The streets were emptying. The night was biting. How many bodies remained inside the concert hall? Should she hang on until the last, the very last, corpse had been retrieved and brought out? Or should she find Oliver and go to him? Whatever their differences, she should be at his side. He had done his best. But even the power of his love had not brought their Lizzie back. His gamble had been misguided. There was no Lizzie.

Then a thought struck her. Many of the victims both living and dead had checked their coats and bags into the Bataclan's cloakroom. Their identity cards were not with them. Others had fled. leaving their belongings with passports and papers behind them. It was causing pandemonium for the identification process.

Might there be a coat, belongings, some trace of Lizzie's presence locked in among the pyramids of winter wear, the possessions of fifteen hundred people? Kurtiz hurtled back across the street, barely avoiding a speeding motorbike, which screeched to a halt, ploughing her way through the handfuls of mourners, the weeping figures, the new arrivals who had stopped to lay flowers, to light a candle, say a prayer. She beat her fists against the Bataclan's door. A gendarme on duty outside came to her aid.

'Madame, I think I've warned you already tonight, more than once if I'm not mistaken, that the door is locked and you cannot gain entry.'

'I have to get in.'

'No, Madame.'

'My daughter's coat,' she was sobbing. 'A leather jacket quite possibly. She loves leather. In the cloakroom.'

'The place has been cordoned off. Only forensic and security have right of access now, Madame. You must respect this.'

'It might be a way for me to know,' she wept. 'If I could just go through to see . . .'

'Out of bounds.'

'How many bodies are still in there?'

He scratched at his face, uncertain, loath to reject her, to cause her more anguish. 'You must be patient. There are others, many, in the same situation.'

'Please.' The many meant nothing to Kurtiz. Selfishly, it was only her one that counted.

'Telephone the helpline. Here.' He pulled a ragged slip of paper from one of his pockets. On it was a series of digits written large with a ballpoint pen. She glanced at them. 'Ring them, register your search. They will help you.'

She accepted the scrap of paper.

'Do you have someone to accompany you, access to transport? You should get some sleep.'

She shook her head.

'Wait here,' he soothed. 'I'll be back directly.'

Sirens were still hee-hawing in every direction across the eastern section of the assailed capital, more distant now, most of them, as though the batteries were winding down after so many hours, so many trajectories back and forth. She closed her eyes, her forehead against the locked door she was barred from entering where a torn poster flapped, danced and scuffed her cheek. She took a backwards step from the old vaudeville hall. Yes, she should get some sleep, but where? The hotel across the city she had booked a million years ago and never checked into? She couldn't even recall its name. Or she should find Oliver? But she had nothing with her, no purse, no identity papers, no change of clothes, no washbag. Only her Leica. She couldn't think where she had disposed of everything. There was a hole in her memory. At the café where her evening had begun? She pressed her spine against a stone wall, unloading her weight. A wall with black and yellow graffiti drawn in bold strokes across it. There were few vehicles about now. Intermittent violet spinning beacons.

Two corpses, oversized by layers of covering, appeared

in front of her. They were being wheeled out of the theatre. Four uniformed figures ran towards them, stepping backwards in hefty boots, guiding the gurneys to a pair of trucks parked across the street. The inanimate shapes were lifted for loading and slid gently into the vehicles to be driven to hospitals or overcrowded city morgues. Bodies covered with white blankets resembling horizontal ghosts. Either of those corpses might be her daughter's.

'Wait,' she cried, voice hoarse. 'Wait.' The quartet who had stepped back from the ambulance turned.

A police officer, two, hurried towards her.

She begged frenziedly to be let through to approach the medics, to peel off the blankets, to reveal the faces, to confirm identities, but she was driven back. 'You must remain behind the cordons. There are no exceptions. Respect for the dead, please.'

All her effort for no reward.

Earlier, she had managed to insinuate a path through a temporary, rigged-up medical camp where many wounded had lain in the street while they were injected, syringed, massaged. She had confirmed that none was her daughter. She wished she hadn't looked at the dead faces, bruised, the hollowed-out expressions contorted with fear. Eyes closed now. Rigid and drained of animation. The images might pursue her for all time.

Pursue her for all time . . . Just as Lizzie's words had echoed from the pages since the day she had found the remnants of a notebook crumpled and rolled beneath her sheets. A draft letter addressed to someone? Or random thoughts? She had no idea . . . *If Mum had been here, none of this would ever have happened . . . I can't wait to see you . . . Lx* The sentiment had been followed by pages of wild, tormented scribbles, and the remnants of torn sheets of paper.

Kurtiz had begun the process of putting the room back together. Each day a few hours . . . hours spent in Lizzie's company, her private world. On that particular day, to strip Lizzie's bed, inhaling, stroking the cotton pillowcases in search of the girl. It was where she had found the remnants of the destroyed notebook, weeks after her daughter's disappearance. She'd perched on Lizzie's desk to read it, handwritten in blue ink, her fists clenched about the pages, trembling. Was it something she should give to the police, confide in Oliver? She couldn't. She'd intended to. Every day she'd promised herself, but she was too ashamed. Eventually she'd ripped out that one page, kept it, folded it into a stamp-sized wedge and slipped into her wallet. It was still there.

Her bags were with the old lady, she recalled all of a sudden. The actress. She had left them in her car. She must retrieve them. She had no money for a taxi. There were no taxis, no public transport. She was obliged to walk the length of the boulevard Voltaire in the direction of Bastille, to make her way back to rue de Charonne. She took tentative steps, one foot in front of the other. Her back was screaming from the weight of the three bags she had been hauling about with her earlier.

She pulled out her phone, tapped the Twitter icon. Her fingers were so numb she could barely spell out the letters and figures. *My daughter Lizzie Ross was at the Bataclan tonight. Possibly with her father, Oliver Ross, who has been hospitalized. If anyone has any news of their whereabouts, please DM me.* Damn. She was thirty-four characters over. She divided the plea into two and tweeted both parts.

The phone responded with a notification in a white square: 'Low battery. 10% power remaining.'

Had the message got through?

She was staggering along the street, drunk with exhaustion. The sky above her, ash grey.

Someone, a stranger, returned her tweet with a hash-tagged message.

#porteouverte. 'Open door. Contact us if you need somewhere to sleep. We are in 11th *arrond.* Are you nearby?'

Another came through. *#porteouverte.* 'How can we help you? Bed? Ride to hospital? We speak English.'

The phone was buzzing now with responses, dozens of offers of assistance. Paris to the rescue. She flopped down at the pavement's edge to scan the kindnesses. Might there even be a tweet from Lizzie? Should she accept one of these invitations before the power on her phone blanked out or should she continue on to rue de Charonne?

And then to her astonishment a message flashed up from Alex. Her heart skipped a beat, a catch in her breath, as though she were inhaling through a rusty pipe, but before she could open the text, the screen on her iPhone went dark. The phone was dead; her charger was in her luggage. She slapped at the screen, bullying it. Nothing. That decided her. Back to rue de Charonne. This was the destination she would make for with a shot of renewed energy.

A few steps further, she stumbled, tripped over a

loose paving stone, lost her footing and found herself back on the ground. Her first instinct was for her camera bag. Its strap had twisted and the camera was balancing on her back but not damaged. She remained slumped there in an eerie pre-dawn light, hands and arms grazed, head thumping from the blow she'd suffered when someone had hurled her against a wall. She was not seriously hurt, no ankles twisted, no bones broken; she was simply dead beat and within her was a pain, a dread that was gathering in momentum as though someone had struck a match to a fuse and the flame was slowly, ineluctably burning its way to the bomb.

Would Oliver survive? There had been a time, those joyous early years, when she had loved him so. Oliver, with his film-star good looks and his hazel-eyed charm. She had never stopped caring for him, had she? All the way through, even during the rough patches. She'd been there for him. Whatever Lizzie had believed, she had loved them both.

Kurtiz, London, June 1994

It was nearing the end of Kurtiz Fellows's first year at
drama school. London was sweltering. She was looking
forward to some time out in the Kent countryside at her
parents' home. But, before the term ended, three weeks
of showcases had been scheduled for the final-year students' graduation. The task of the first-year students,
including Kurtiz, was to assist in the backstage mainte-
nance of the shows. Three plays: each to be performed
in front of an invited audience for four nights. This gave
those who were soon to be seeking work as young actors
the opportunity to display their talents to directors and
agencies, both theatrical and casting.

Oliver Ross had been awarded the leading role of
Stanley in *A Streetcar Named Desire*. From the moment
Kurtiz had first set eyes on him, she had been smitten,
dreaming up romantic encounters, which she knew
would never come to pass. He was tall, Byronically
handsome, while she was new to London and green as a
cabbage.

The drama school was situated in a rundown Victorian church in north London. Kurtiz cycled there from
her room in Gospel Oak. On several mornings that
summer she spotted Oliver sitting under an oak tree in

the front yard, speaking lines of dialogue from his script with an American accent while gesticulating nobly.

Kurtiz never doubted that he would make a magnificent, charismatic Stanley. As she watched, padlocking her bike to the school fence, he appeared to her so marvellous and self-assured.

A handwritten list went up, pinned to the cork noticeboard in the lobby. Kurtiz stared at it. She had been allocated the task of 'dresser to Mr Ross and Mr Dennis'. Terry Dennis, another third year, had been cast as Mitch, the secondary male role in *Streetcar*.

'Lucky you,' squealed several of her classmates.

'I'd rather be undressing Mr Ross,' sniggered another.

Kurtiz was not sure what dressing Mr Ross and Mr Dennis involved but, whatever it was, butterflies were taking flight in her stomach and they refused to settle. She dared not let her imagination run away with her.

Several days later, she spotted Oliver in one of the rehearsal rooms, his chocolaty voice bouncing off the empty spaces. She was about to creep in and introduce herself as his dresser when she saw, standing close to him, the petite student who was to play Blanche DuBois, his leading lady. Kurtiz held back, ogling them through the door's gap, her lips pressed tight against the wooden frame. They were working through the text, as though it were a choreographed ballet. Pausing, going back over certain lines, scribbling notes in their well-thumbed copies of the play. Kurtiz, green with envy, observed how the confident Sally Treaves glided her hands over Oliver's body – was she acting or flirting? How he turned about her, stalking, taunting her: a bullfighter in the ring. 'One day he'll be a star,' Kurtiz muttered to herself. 'No woman will be able to resist him.'

The day of the dress rehearsal for *Streetcar* arrived. Plump and practical Jennifer Greenly, also a first-year student, had been allocated the position of wardrobe mistress.

'Here's Oliver's costume. He'll need his shirt ironed during the interval. And this is for Terry. Once he's dressed, he's done. It's Oliver who'll require the attention. He needs to look sexy and alluring. Well, he does anyway, of course, but we can't have him wearing a poorly ironed shirt now, can we? Oh, lucky *you*, Kurtiz.'

Kurtiz accepted the neatly pressed articles of clothing laid across her outstretched arms and nodded. She was too nervous to speak.

The men's dressing room was compact, barely larger than a cell, off what had once been the church apse. As she approached, a couple of her classmates were placing rows of chairs in the nave. There was an almost palpable mood of excitement, even among these juniors.

'Elia Kazan's coming,' someone shouted.

'Rubbish!'

'Yes, he's in London casting his next film.'

Kurtiz proceeded through the old church and knocked on the dressing-room door. She was not expecting the two actors to be in the theatre at that early hour but Oliver was present, seated at a table in front of a mirror. He was unpacking his belongings, carefully placing objects on a towel on the table: comb, brush, skin creams, script. She instinctively began to back out, muttering apologies.

'Come in.' He smiled, rising to greet her. What a smile. It could have melted the cobwebs off the high ceilings.

She tiptoed in, placed the costumes on coat-hangers, hung them from a mobile clothes rail and spun softly on her trainers to leave. 'Don't go,' he said. His voice sounded a little croaky, and now that she looked him full in the face, those hazelnut eyes gave out a look of terror. 'You all right? Can I get you anything?'

'I'm shit scared,' he confessed. 'If this is how I feel this morning, what will it be like tomorrow night?'

'You'll be amazing,' she said, and then, without thinking, 'You were born to play the role. Elia Kazan's coming, did you hear?'

Oliver guffawed. 'Yes, along with Tennessee Williams.'

'He's not!' Kurtiz's mind was blown.

'Tennessee Williams died over a decade ago. No one except my mum and dad, Terry and Sally's mums and dads and my brother Ben will be out there. Don't listen to the chatter. They're talking foolish dreams.'

Kurtiz felt like a half-wit, taken in by the gossip. She wanted out of there before she made herself look even more naive.

'What's your name?'

'K-Kurtiz Fellows,' she stammered.

He frowned.

'My mum's favourite album was *Move on Up*. Curtis Mayfield, remember him? Mum did, at least, have the kindness to spell mine with a K and a Z, so that it was clear I had not been mistaken for a boy. An African-American one at that.'

Oliver was watching her intently. A smile was breaking across his lips. 'No one could mistake you for a boy, KZ.'

She lowered her gaze, blushing. 'I'd better let you get on with your preparations.'

From that day on, Oliver's nickname for her had been KZ, and it had stuck.

After the first night's performance, while she was gathering up his sweat-stained T-shirt and socks, Oliver invited her to the pub. 'Are you joining us for a drink, KZ?'

She made her excuses. 'Better not, I've got to wash these.'

He was gazing at her reflection in the mirror while wiping off his make-up. 'You're very meticulous, aren't you?'

She shrugged shyly.

'Thanks for all your help this evening.'

She shrugged again, tongue-tied.

'So, what do you reckon? Fifteen minutes to wash a shirt and a pair of socks and hang them to dry? Come on, you deserve a drink. Sorry I can't wait for you but my family was in to see the show. Get the Fairy Liquid frothing, then come and join us. Meet my boring big brother. Promise?'

She nodded.

The Horse and Carriage was heaving. Most of the customers were third-year students, their mates and adoring families. Kurtiz pushed open the door and came face to face with a mass of animated life. A swift glance to left and right, as she nudged her way in the general direction of the bar, doubtful as to whether she would be able to locate Oliver, told her that no one famous was in attendance, least of all any film directors. Oliver, all six foot two of him, caught sight of her before she saw him. He elbowed a path towards her, calling her name, and was instantly swallowed by females: wives, mothers, sisters, casting directors. He lifted his arms above his head and called, 'Make way.' The throng of drinkers divided like a holy sea. Oliver locked Kurtiz by the wrist and guided her towards the bar where his brother Ben, shorter and plumper, was waving a fiver to and fro, shouting, his voice drowned by a hundred conversations all around them. Others, too, were attempting to get the barman's attention. Or Oliver's, Kurtiz noted.

Oliver insisted Ben buy every round of drinks, of which there were many. 'He's working, we're not.' The performance had gone well, no hitches, and the mood in the fuggy lounge was lively and theatrical. The world and his wife, mostly the wives, surrounded Oliver, complimenting him on his 'moving', 'charismatic' and 'sensual' interpretation of the role. Oliver lapped up the attention. Ben, meanwhile, was attempting to chat up Kurtiz. 'He's kept you a well-guarded secret,' he shouted in her ear, spittle flying, above the jabbering and cooing.

'No secret to keep,' she muttered, watching every female and gay man in the place press themselves up against Oliver Ross, fawning over him, while he did nothing to deter them.

It was five minutes to midnight when the indulgent landlord rang the bell for last orders.

'One for the road and then bed, eh, Kurtiz? Us actors need our beauty sleep and all that.' Oliver pronounced 'actors' exaggeratedly and with pride. No longer a student, but a fully-fledged performer.

The entire play, every complex emotion, had to be re-enacted the following evening and then for another two nights.

'That's show business.'

'Any agents in?' she asked him, when the crowds had thinned. The attention he had been enjoying had, thankfully, diminished and they could make conversation without giving themselves sore throats.

None had been spotted. But it had gone well. 'There will be tomorrow.' Oliver's mood was jubilant. He took her hand. 'Your support was much appreciated, KZ,' he crooned.

They were outside, standing alone beneath a lamp-post. Everybody else had miraculously melted away. Even drooling Ben had waved his farewells and driven off in a gleaming royal blue Morgan. It was warm, agreeably so, with a clear sky. Kurtiz attempted to stare at the stars, squinted, staggered: her head was spinning. She took a long, deep breath, expanding her ribs as she had been taught to do in voice classes, and inhaled the fresh night air; a welcome relief after the day's heat, the crush of bodies, the cigarettes and the mood of noisy exuberance.

The star of the school slung a leather satchel over his shoulder – a script poked out of it – and raked his fingers through his dark hair. She noticed beneath the streetlights that he was still wearing the residue of his stage make-up. A line of black mascara highlighted his hazel eyes. They were flecked with yellow, like the body of a bee.

'You coming home with me, KZ?' He posed the question so casually, as if it didn't matter a hoot to him whether she did or didn't, as if he were in no doubt that her answer would be an affirmative.

'I've got my bike,' she replied shyly.

Oliver burst out laughing. 'Any chance of a lift?'

She unlocked and wheeled out her bike from the college's forecourt onto the pavement while Oliver stood watching her. He was stretching his arms, yawning. They climbed aboard, he on the seat, she perched on his thigh, and wove an unsteady path up the street with its gentle gradient. By the time they had turned right onto Haverstock Hill, he was gripping her round the waist with his right arm while steering with his left. 'It's not far,' he called into her ear.

She felt the thrill of him so close, the vibration, timbre of his voice. 'I hope we don't get stopped for drunk-driving.' She giggled, elated, not the slightest bit concerned that they could indeed be pulled over.

They parked her transport in the weed-infested front garden of a large stucco-fronted Victorian house in Belsize Park. Kurtiz, full of nerves for what lay ahead and a little clumsy due to the booze, fumbled with the key, before padlocking the spoke of a wheel to a sinking fence. Then she mastered the three stone steps to where Oliver was waiting at the front door.

'Sssh.' He pressed a finger against his lips. 'My two flatmates will definitely have hit the sack and will not be

happy to be woken in the middle of the night by inebriated actors, given they both have proper jobs to crawl
out of bed for.'

He led her along a corridor, where another bike was
parked, into a capacious high-ceilinged, ground-floor
apartment, then into a bay-windowed room at the rear of
the house, which overlooked an overgrown yet elegant
garden. The floor was strewn with CDs, books and videos. The bed was a double, hurriedly made. The room
smelt faintly of joss sticks, amber or patchouli, or possibly hash. She had never smoked pot so couldn't be sure.

She placed her bag on a chair and nervously pulled off
her cardigan. He lit two candles, scooped a CD off the
floor and slipped it into the player. 'David Bowie.' He
smiled. *Real Cool World*. 'The face of seduction is you,
Miss Fellows,' he whispered, as he wrapped himself
around her and lowered her to the bed. 'My, but you're
beautiful, KZ. I've been looking forward to this ever
since you stepped into my dressing room. The exquisite
sight of your curvaceous body naked, bathed in moon-
light. Please, fair maiden, don't deny me.'

They made love till dawn, till the birds began to sing
through the semi-open sash windows. At which point,
as a rose-pink sun crept in through the curtainless panes
of glass, and doors along the corridor began to open and
close, they hunkered down beneath a sheet – too hot for
the duvet – and drifted off to sleep, sated, their damp
bodies carelessly entangled, their sweat mingled, scent-
ing one another. They had barely shared a word since he
had first kissed her, so hungry were they for one another.

*

The bedside clock read ten past eleven. Kurtiz threw back the sheet and sat upright on the edge of the mattress, breathing in the aroma of coffee. She rose and strolled to the window. Her body was damp and loose-limbed. It was a glorious summer morning. A morning like no other, blossoms abounding, soaking up the heat, bees and butterflies flitting from one flower head to another. It was a morning when you wanted to shout, to halloo his name Shakespearian-style, with your arms wide open, because you were young and alive and because you had spent the night – yes, *spent the night* – with Oliver Ross. She began to hum to the music playing softly behind her. A female chanteuse, exhaling the blues like cigarette smoke, whose voice Kurtiz did not recognize.

'I'm in the kitchen,' she heard, 'making coffee. Real percolated coffee, not the instant powdered rubbish my plebby flatmates drink.'

She looked about for her clothes. There was only one chair in Oliver's room and that was piled untidily with what might have been his entire wardrobe.

He appeared at the doorway, two mugs in his hands. 'I've guessed white, no sugar, correct?' He winked. She nodded and returned shyly to perch on the mattress, discreetly pulling a corner of sheet about her, to drink her coffee while he disappeared to shower. When he had gone, Kurtiz actually pinched herself. On the lower, fleshy part of her left thigh. It turned red and began to sting. Ouch. *But this was real.* Her, here, on Oliver's bed.

She knew it couldn't last, that she had probably been foolish to sleep with him on what was not even a first date, but it had been delicious. The sex had been lusty and exciting, and she didn't care. She bloody well didn't care. She would cherish this night for ever, and not tell a soul about it.

When Oliver strode back into his room, hair dripping onto his muscular shoulders, wearing nothing but a lemon-coloured towel hooked around his waist, feathers of dark body hair on his flat abdomen, she nearly dropped her mug.

'There's plenty of hot water, and Rory and Jonathan have already left for work – jobs in the City, don't you know – so you don't have to worry about flaunting yourself in the buff. I'm here to enjoy every turn of your torso, but – alas, alack – I've got director's notes at two so I suggest we have a spot of lunch, if you fancy it?'

'Six o'clock,' she muttered. Her voice sounded as though she were speaking through a damp flannel.

'Six o'clock what?'

'My call to set up for your show.'

'Perfect.' His back was to her. The towel had fallen to the floor as he slid open a drawer, drew out and then stepped into white underpants. She was staring at his legs, his naked buttocks. God, he was beyond gorgeous.

He turned round as he leaned to the chair, rummaged for a shirt, caught her watching him and grinned. 'Bathroom's second door on the left,' he said. 'I put out a clean towel for you.'

She rose, picked up her bag, feeling self-conscious that she was naked in front of him and rather ludicrously hugging a shoulder bag. Utterly stupid to be shy, given what they had been doing for the past six hours. She was grateful that she always carried a toothbrush with her while thinking that she'd have to nip back to her place before the show to pick up some clean underwear.

He stopped her in her path, put his arms on her shoulders and clasped his hands behind her neck. 'You're beautiful, KZ, and, wow, you're great in the sack and there's nothing I'd like better than to whisk you back to bed, but I'd better conserve some energy for the show later. I hope you agree?'

She nodded.

'So, when you're dressed I'll stand you a ploughman's and a beer at the Richard Steele on Haverstock Hill. How does that sound?'

On the strength of his performance as Stanley Kowalski, Oliver was offered a six-month contract for a season starting in September at the newly refurbished Birmingham Repertory Theatre. It meant that he was away from London throughout the week, arriving home to Belsize Park late, after curtain down on the Saturday-evening show, pelting down the M1 in a battered and not very comfortable fourth-hand Mini, bought specially for the purpose. Kurtiz was always there at his rented accommodation, waiting to greet him, a bottle of chilled wine at the ready. Sex on the carpet in front of the gas fire or sometimes they managed to make it to the bed.

Sunday, they lazed about. She cooked lunch and he slept for most of the afternoon, or learned his lines for the next play in rehearsal, while Kurtiz prepared for her upcoming week at drama school. She was into her second year, gaining in confidence, totally inspired by the work.

During the week, while Oliver was in Birmingham, Kurtiz returned to her dull room in Gospel Oak. Life without him was unexciting but she was determined to live fully during his absences. Because this couldn't last, could it? It was just too good to be true.

Most evenings, she waited on tables in a local bistro up in Belsize Park village. The tips wcrc pretty generous and she frequently shared them with Oliver for his petrol home. His weekly salary was pitiful and he was paying for digs and food in Birmingham.

Kurtiz had offered to fund his London living costs as well as her own, but it was a struggle and he insisted that he continue to pay. 'Move in with me,' he pronounced, one Sunday, after breakfast in bed. 'Since I'm away for six months, it's more practical if you're here. Then we won't be forced to give the room up. It makes financial sense.'

Kurtiz willingly agreed.

Rory and Jonathan, baking a cake in the kitchen, cheered; they were perfectly thrilled with the arrangement. 'We never liked the idea that Oliver was a gooseberry in his own home,' teased Rory.

Since Oliver had left college, Kurtiz didn't feel so awkward about her classmates' discovery of their relationship. Even so, she preferred to keep her personal life private. There was plenty of whispering and nudging in the rehearsal rooms and a self-doubt within her heard that she didn't deserve him and everyone bar Oliver could see that; sooner or later he'd meet someone else and Kurtiz Fellows would be history.

*

Oliver was playing in pantomime, *Jack and the Beanstalk*. It involved performing two shows every day – matinees and evenings during the holiday season plus another matinee on Sundays. Sundays, when the theatre was packed to the rafters with grannies and aunts and screaming excited youngsters, unwrapping sweets and ice creams and crunching popcorn underfoot. Mums loudly berated their unruly offspring while dads grabbed the opportunity to kip, snoring loudly. Thirteen performances a week – it left Oliver hoarse and ragged. Because he couldn't get away, Kurtiz took the train to spend Christmas in his digs: one room at the top of a widow's semi-detached house in the suburbs. Their first Christmas together. They were both strapped for cash so presents were minimal. She chose for him a silver-plated Cross ballpoint pen, which she had wanted engraved with his name, but she couldn't afford the extra. Oliver bought her *Grace*, a Jeff Buckley CD, a singer she confessed to never having heard before, and black lace underwear.

And then, in early January, her period did not arrive.

Back in London, she bought a home pregnancy testing kit, locked herself in the bathroom, which reeked of Rory's Eau Savage, and sat on the closed loo seat, hands clasped tightly, praying. She stared incredulously at the pink dot on the test stick. This was impossible. It was erroneous. Wrong. She was on the Pill. How had this happened?

She was having a baby. She was having Oliver's baby.

Had she missed a pill? After a late night? Overworked? Too much wine? She counted back the days, the dates to early November. A child conceived while Kurtiz was at drama school and Oliver was starting out in repertory theatre. A weekend conception when he was home? She always waited up for him, for his little car to pull up outside. Running down the outdoor steps to greet him.

When had she been so careless?

Alone in January, tramping through rain and sleet to get to drama school, trying to avoid catching cold, with little money for extra food or heating, she worried herself senseless over the revelation. With sleepless nights, listless days, lacking in concentration and vitality, her studies were suffering. How would Oliver take it when she eventually broke the news to him? *Would* she break the news to him? Would Rory and Jonathan turf her out? Would Oliver turf her out? In her mind, there was never any question about whether she would have the baby. The alternative was unthinkable, but what if she, a student of twenty-one, was obliged to face such a momentous life-changing experience all on her own?

And what would her parents say?

She feared Oliver would run a mile when she divulged the fact to him. The prospect of facing him, of losing him, caused her even more sleepless nights.

How would they manage? She waited weeks – three Sundays – before confiding in him. Oliver had sensed that she was troubled but she fobbed off his questions with excuses of tiredness, college concerns.

It was the weekend before St Valentine's, which fell on a Tuesday that year, when she finally came clean. He listened silently to her stuttering words, barely coherent phrases, his arm wrapped round her shoulders, a frown of puzzlement on his face. Yes, he'd sussed that something was nagging at her, but never in his wildest dreams had he guessed at *this* possibility.

'How far gone are you?' he asked her quietly.

'Three months, a bit more, I think. It was sometime last November.'

'And you're not mistaken?'

She shook her head, strangled with emotion. He was going to suggest she get rid of it. She closed her eyes, unable to look him in the face. Was this the inevitable break-up? The loss of him she had so dreaded?

'Christ,' he murmured, and rose to grab a beer. 'Want one?'

Kurtiz shook her head.

'You're sure?'

She nodded.

'A real living, pumping-heart baby, with legs and arms and other bits?'

'I hope so.'

He swigged the beer, crossed to the window and stared outside at the dreary afternoon. London in the rain. Raindrops dripping off unformed leaves, bare trunks and branches darkened by the damp. 'Blimey, that makes me a soon-to-be-father.'

'Yep.'

'Lousy timing, KZ, you must agree?'

Yes, the timing was lousy. Neither of them was jumping up and down with joy. It was too momentous, too damn scary, too grown-up.

'I'll soon be home,' he encouraged. 'We can talk about

it more when I'm back. We'll plan for the future when this contract's over, okay?' He swung back to her.

She didn't say anything.

'I'd better start nagging my agent. Get the old boy to concentrate on TV roles. We're going to need some serious cash. I'll be feeding three of us.'

Kurtiz nodded, both drained and relieved that it was out in the open. The baby was theirs now, not some guilty secret held tight against her breast. She had misjudged Oliver.

As he piled back into his Mini before dawn on the Monday morning, shivering, kissing her goodbye, he mumbled in her ear, 'Don't worry, we'll sort it. I'll think of something.'

She waved him off in her nightie and overcoat with the collar up, but the second he was out of sight her doubts re-emerged. Would he change his mind and dump her? Or if his loyalty proved unswerving, *if* they stayed together, how would they cope?

Paris, November 2015

A car pulled up at the kerb. Kurtiz was in the gutter, vomiting, coughing and spewing, the taste in her mouth bitter. The passenger door opened. A booted foot stepped out onto the pavement inches from her shivering, hunched body. 'Are you hurt? Here, take it easy.'

Arms lifted her. She was too weak to stand. Her legs were buckling beneath her. The person, a male, was negotiating her towards the car. Someone, another male, stepped out from the driver's seat, ran round to unlock a rear door.

'Water,' she dribbled. 'Do you have any water?'

'She's in shock.'

A bottle of water was handed to her, but she hadn't the strength to grasp it. The man with his arm round her held it to her lips and fed her, one sip at a time. 'Where are you from? Were you in the concert hall?'

She shook her head.

'We'll take you to a hospital. You need treatment.'

'No.' She attempted to wrestle herself free. 'I have to find my husband. My daughter. If you could give me a lift . . .'

In early March when Oliver's Birmingham engage-
ment had run its course, he returned to London, intent
on securing the next job. With a career that had
started off so well, he was not prepared for the months
of trudging from one casting session to another. The
fierce competition. Rejection after rejection. He responded badly. His ego and ambition took a battering,
while svelte Kurtiz was beginning to fill out. A daily
reminder that a third person was soon to burst into their
lives.

This was insane. They were not ready for such responsibility. As it was, they were struggling to meet
their rental and cover the bills. Oliver was on the
dole, and he hated it, cursed it as demeaning. Being
an actor was one thing but being an out-of-work
actor was altogether another state of affairs. She began
to realize the heights of his pride, his ego. They bickered. For different reasons they both grew downhearted.
Even so, Oliver never once suggested that she move
out or give up the child. His loyalty reassured and heart-
ened her.

And she loved him.

Yet neither had ever expressed such a sentiment to

the other. They hadn't got around to Love. This pregnancy had come too soon.

Kurtiz skipped her morning classes to attend her six-month check-up at the clinic in Hampstead. She walked all the way up the hill. It was a bright, fresh late April day and the wind brought ruddiness to her cheeks. During this, her second ultrasound, the foetus was identified as female.

'See here, it's a little girl. She's on the small side but all the bits and pieces are right where they should be.' The obstetrician smiled. A kindly dark-haired Indian lady, thirty-something, in a red and gold sari.

Kurtiz's attention was glued to the screen, an artwork of grey and charcoal. In the midst of which was a curled sleeping form, like a wingless translucent bee. Could that person, the little *girl*, hear her? Did she have ears and eyes yet? Was the tiny, semi-formed child aware that she was being photographed, that beings were peering into her secret safe space, appraising her? 'It's awesome. I wish I could take a photograph.'

'We can give you a printout.'

'Is she . . . comfortable? Not lonely?'

The obstetrician smiled. 'Yes, I'd say so, and I doubt she's lonely.' The woman glanced at Kurtiz's left hand. No ring. 'Do you have someone to share this with?'

'My baby's father.' Kurtiz nodded, inner pride bubbling.

'Good. It's usually better when you are a couple. Not always, of course, but if he's supportive . . .'

'Very.'

'. . . then you have nothing to worry about.'

She strolled out of the clinic as though walking on air, conscious that with every step she must take care. A baby girl with all her limbs and bits in the right places. It was hard to take in. This was no acting role. She was going to give birth. Kurtiz Fellows was going to be a mother to a curve-shaped daughter. Oliver's child. They would need a name, a cot. By July, they would be three sleeping in Oliver's room. Would Rory and Jonathan complain if the baby cried at night? They must have noticed her condition, though neither had commented. Should she look for other accommodation? A larger space. How would they afford it?

Later that week, without a word to anyone, Kurtiz took a tough and painful decision: she quit drama school to find full-time employment. And it was time to break the news to her parents. She wrote them a letter and then, before posting it, she tossed it into the bin and telephoned instead.

Her mother answered. 'It's an age since we've seen you. Granny's been asking after you.'

'Mum, there's . . .' She would have found it easier to speak to her dad or even her dear old nan, who always took her side.

'What? I need to get your father to the phone. Michael!'

The silence was a time bomb.

'Kurtiz, are you still there?'

'Yes, Mum.'

'Your father's on the extension.'

'Hi, Dad.'

'Hello, baby.'

'Let me repeat what you have just told me within your father's hearing. You've left college, and you're *pregnant*!'

'Yes, Mum.'

'Is that why you didn't come home for Christmas? You knew I'd spot it.'

'Oh, sweetheart,' sighed her father.

'Kurtiz, how could you? After all we've been through to get you there? We are very not pleased. What does the child's father say to this?'

'He's happy.'

'Well, we're not. What can you do? You're not qualified for anything. And you're certainly not ready for motherhood. Your father's very concerned, Kurtiz, aren't you, Michael?' The less-than-encouraging voice of her mother. Her father said no more, but she felt his heartache, his disappointment, and it cut her deep, but she had a minuscule wingless bee-like being inside her and now *she* came first.

'Buzz, buzz,' she whispered, as she put the phone down and rubbed her hands across her extending belly.

To quell her parents' disquiet – she did not want to alienate them – Kurtiz took a train to Kent to spend a few days in her childhood home. Her grandmother, who lived in the same village, was, as she had always been, super-supportive and understanding.

'You'll manage, girl,' she said, 'because you're a bright young thing and I'm proud of you. It won't be easy, mind. I was a single mother – tougher back in my day – but if you've a nice young fellow to see you through that'll make all the difference.' She clipped open her tattered bag and handed Kurtiz fifty pounds in notes. 'Buy the baby some fancy clothes and bring her down to meet her great-grandma as soon as you can.' She winked as Kurtiz hugged her tight.

Their daughter, all five pounds four ounces of Eliza Ross, a gurgling perfect princess with a fluffy soft head of pale gingery curls, was born on 4 July 1995.

Independence Day.

Precious little Eliza with gleaming eyes, that later turned flecked and hazel just like her father's, proved herself a talisman for Oliver. A mere ten days after she was born, Oliver landed a plum TV role as a detective in a long-running series, a police drama, *The Fleet*. A year's contract with a clause for renewal if the character worked well and the audience warmed to him. 'And it's decently paid, my lovely ladies. We will not starve, not for a year or two, at any rate.'

Exhausted though she was, Oliver dragged Kurtiz along with tiny Lizzie, a ten-week babe in arms, to the Groucho Club where he was now a fully paid-up member and where the new parents drank champagne, got ever so slightly sozzled, took a taxi home instead of the tube and made love with their baby sleeping soundly in her own new cot just a few feet to their side, until three in the morning, when she bawled and screamed to be breastfed.

Oliver's 'smouldering good looks' proved popular with both the media and the viewers, particularly the female audiences, and for a short while his face beamed out from the front covers of magazines such as *Woman's*

Own. Four months after his face had hit the small screen, he signed for a second year. His role was written up, offering him more screen time, meatier scenes and a better contract fee. Kurtiz couldn't have been prouder, and those autumn days were blissful. London was enjoying an Indian summer. After Oliver had left for the BBC rehearsal rooms and Kurtiz had finished laundering mountains of nappies, which, when hung to dry, made their room reek like a goat farm, she would push the pram to Hampstead Heath or Primrose Hill and sit reading magazines, frequently articles about her baby's father.

Oliver was voted 'Heartthrob of the Month' by *Cosmopolitan* and, for a heady few years, he was a household name. It seemed he could do no wrong. The BBC plucked him from the original cop show and gave him the leading role of Edward Rochester in a serialization of *Jane Eyre*. He confirmed the network's faith in him by winning an award and topping a viewers' poll for most eligible bachelor.

It was Kurtiz's mother who mentioned it. 'He's a *bachelor*, darling, a rising star, and you are a mother. Has he never mentioned marriage to you? I was brought up by a single parent, as you know, and it was jolly well not easy.'

'Mum, I'm not a single parent. Oliver is my partner. We are just not married, that's all.'

'*Partner*. I know what your father thinks about that. And what about *your* career?'

The offers were flooding in for Oliver, 'the bad guy with puppy-dog eyes', as one magazine dubbed him, and he signed his next, very lucrative contract with a competing network. He was a wild success in the role of a heartbroken doctor, and the ratings soared. He switched agents, ditched the sad chap who smoked a pipe and had only one assistant, who had taken him on directly from drama school, and moved to a smarter, more sophisticated agency in Soho, with links to LA.

'Isn't that a little callous?'

'Finger on the pulse, KZ.' Oliver winked when she expressed her concern for the poor solo agent, who had been toiling devotedly to build Oliver's profile and career.

In those early days Oliver seemed to be lunching almost on a weekly basis with Samantha, his new agent, and he began to talk of movies. The big screen. Hollywood. He took up running on Hampstead Heath, joined a gym, discovered Pilates.

Meanwhile, Kurtiz stayed at home to care for Eliza. She was smitten with her tiny girl, obsessed with the growing process – fingers, teething, tumbling, babbling incomprehensible words, and shrieking: 'She has the lung capacity of a navvy,' remarked Oliver, one sleepless night – content in her all-encompassing world, but she also knew that soon she would have to find something else to occupy her, before she turned into a domestic bore. Also, she feared her mother's warning: that Oliver would lose interest in her, that he would judge her dull. Or was that her mother's fear – an only child reared without a father – feeding into her?

While Oliver lunched at the Ivy or skipped about town to interviews and screen tests, Kurtiz began silently to worry that all the success might turn his head, that an off-screen romance might blossom with an actress or a make-up lady, or even Sam, his agent, that he would find his real-life companion unattractive. Yet her fears continued to prove unfounded. Oliver excelled in the role of besotted dad, as well as that of kind, enthusiastic partner. They were eventually married in the Camden Town register office on a Tuesday afternoon. Rory and Jonathan were their witnesses. Eliza, almost a year old by then, with an upright crest of sandy hair that would have made any punk proud, was beginning to walk, crawl, fall, and gurgle sounds of happiness and curiosity. She was in attendance in the pram Kurtiz had purchased from the Oxfam shop in Kentish Town Road.

Two weeks previously, she and Oliver had put down the deposit, paid for out of his television earnings, on a three-bedroomed house in Tufnell Park. They moved in mid-June, taking with them the few basics they had squirrelled together over the time they had cohabited in his furnished room in Belsize Park. Once they took possession they ran excitedly from space to space, up the stairs and back down again, staring at stained walls, a dying electric cooker, a bath that wept rust. It was clear they lacked pretty much everything – not even the mattress in Belsize Park had belonged to Oliver – but they had a healthy baby and a volcanic level of energy and love. On his first free day from filming, she and Oliver took the bus to Tottenham Court Road and bought themselves a king-sized double bed from Heal's and a bottle of champagne from Oddbins. With those two purchases they had blown the last of their funds. Both their bank accounts now sat at zero.

They went home, drank the bubbles and christened the bed.

Kurtiz chided herself for her lack of faith in Oliver. From their first night together she had believed their relationship was doomed. Yet here they were, four years down the line, a happily married couple with a child, her husband a TV star. It was time to start accepting her good fortune and build herself a career of her own.

She never allowed herself to admit it aloud, and certainly not to Oliver, but she missed acting desperately, even though she had never been employed as a professional actress. She revelled in the buzz, the nerves and uncertainties, when they paid off, which she lived vicariously through Oliver. She took him through his lines in the kitchen after she'd cleared up the dishes from dinner, had fed Eliza and put her to bed. He would talk through his character choices; she offered her opinions and felt her own adrenalin rising. It was only after he'd left for the studio, edgy on shooting days, and she was at home scribbling shopping lists, getting Eliza ready for play school, that the emptiness seized her.

She had everything most women dreamed of – especially Oliver – yet she felt a lack of purpose and drive, and berated herself for not allowing motherhood to be sufficient. Oliver wanted another child, he talked of a son, but it didn't happen. Kurtiz wondered privately whether her body was not playing ball because somewhere within her she needed to get out and find her own place in the big world. But where?

Paris, November 2015

Marguerite had fallen asleep in her chair, feet curled up beneath her, like a small hibernating mammal. The television was still transmitting, mostly replays now and a few first witnesses to the shocking events of earlier in the evening. The sound had been muted. Her exhaustion was causing her old limbs to paralyse, numbed by pins and needles, and her head was swimming, but she could not, would not, go to bed. If she lay down in the other room she would sleep, and if she slept, she would not hear the doorbell. The woman would return at some point. Where was she? What did she have with her? Marguerite knew that the massacres were over. The death toll, the TV reporters continued to claim, remained at thirty with possibly more to be confirmed. The screen jumped between the same three locations as it had hours earlier. It seemed like weeks she had been on watch duty here.

She would think back over her past. For years she hadn't recalled those early days. Not all of them good. No, indeed not. There was a photograph in one of the drawers somewhere. The only photo she possessed of her and Charlie. Their wedding day. She should dig it out.

Marguerite and Charlie, La Côte d'Azur, 1947

The grounds of the Victorine Studios were even more extensive than Marguerite had envisaged. As she and Charlie made their approach on foot from the *gare* in Nice, having taken the train along the coast, a soft-top automobile, all cream and gleaming chrome, sped by them through the high-arched gates and along a winding driveway lined with palms and film-set lots. Behind the hatted chauffeur sat a middle-aged man in sunglasses. Marguerite did not recognize him, but surely he was somebody important. A producer, for certain. Or Fred Orain, big chief of the entire studios. She made a mental note to look out for his office, to introduce herself, let it be known that she was available for all suitable roles. She and Charlie gave their names at the gate and the keeper pointed them to the sound stage and offices where the screen tests were being held.

They strode up the asphalt ascent. The heat embraced and clung to Marguerite's clothes. She pulled at the boat neck of her frock to create a flow of air while glancing about in wonder. To right and left, teams of men were at work. Men with bulging leather tool-belts were screwing and drilling scenery flats. Spiked and dovetailed together, they created a seamless plywood façade of a French village street where doors opened to nowhere other than another stretch of tumbleweed lot. Further along, in a distant expanse, a shooting was in progress, camera swinging high on a crane. A man in a white cap with a megaphone was bellowing directions. Elsewhere, another movie was in preparation: the belly of a great wooden submarine was under construction. Might this be the film she was testing for? A few sleek silver Westwood Coronado trailers were parked in the shade of a small stand of umbrella pines. Alongside them, a table dressed with a starched white cloth, laid with refreshments, was watched over by a waiter in white gloves.

Marguerite's innards were flipping. *I am where I was born to be.* A silent mantra as she inhaled not the Provençal nature abundant with its natural perfumes, but the scents puffed from fashionable eau-de-toilette atomizers, hair lacquer, creams and powders.

Was anyone famous relaxing there, learning their lines while a lesser mortal doused them with cologne? Madeleine Renaud perhaps, or Danielle Darrieux, Michèle Morgan?

Marguerite's stomach continued to lurch and dip. She paused to pat at her dress, ironed and neat. She had applied scarlet lipstick and two fingerprints of rouge to her cheeks and prayed she looked sufficiently grown-up and feminine.

'Getting nervous?' Charlie asked.

'Of course not.' She tossed her hair off her shoulder with a flick of the wrist.

Through into the reception area of a wooden building where she gave her name, enunciating it carefully.

She was requested to join the line. Unnoticed before, a queue of girls were waiting apprehensively for their screen tests. The young painted hopefuls eyed one another suspiciously. All were pretty, well-groomed and maquillaged to perfection. Marguerite had not expected this. In her fantasies, she had been the sole contender for this opportunity, and once this step had been accomplished, her stardom was assured. A young man in shirt sleeves and with floppy dark hair handed her several pages of typed script and told her to memorize them. He would be back for her within the hour. Her nerves began to uncoil: her lips were dry and growing numb as she silently mouthed the dialogue. Charlie had wandered off somewhere outside in the sunshine to take a look around, he'd said, hands in trouser pockets, kicking his heels, whistling. He had wished her luck and brushed her cheek with a kiss as light as the touch of a moth's wing, then held her gaze one moment longer, steadying her. 'Jeepers, you look swell,' he had reassured her. 'You'll bowl them over.'

She must not fail. A name was called, and from the head of the line a brunette with a wasp waist in a sleek green and white outfit with a confident stride was led away. Marguerite glanced down at her own, far less swanky beige dress, cursing the Parisian landlord who had kept her clothes. She rubbed at her knees, then settled to the three-page scene and tried her damnedest not to feel so het up.

The sound stage was cavernous, echoing, empty of activity and dramatically cooler than the waiting area where she had spent the best part of two hours. High, high above her, banks of lights, in darkness now, were trained downwards to the spot where Marguerite was positioned. She craned her head, then looked about her. This space was a story waiting to be brought to life. It was *her* future. A trio of men stood grouped together in quiet conversation. One, the cameraman, was leaning close to his impressive camera, his arm almost cradling it.

'This is Marguerite,' announced the floppy-haired second assistant who had escorted her to her destiny. The men turned their attention towards her, eyes roaming over her. The most senior of them, a man in his forties with tanned skin and elegant, off-white linen slacks, loped the few steps towards her, smiling with teeth that glistened like snowballs. 'Marguerite, *bonjour*. Have you had a moment to look over the lines?'

She nodded, quite unable to speak.

'Good, good, follow me, please, and I will show you to your mark. Oh, I am Julien, by the way. Assistant to Maurice who will be directing this dark domestic drama.'

Marguerite followed Julien, meek as a lamb. She could feel her legs trembling and her stomach rocking in a seasick way. She wished now that she had followed Charlie's advice and eaten the croissant he'd bought her for breakfast, even just a mouthful. Julien was instructing her to position herself in the centre of a large cross marked on the floor with yellow gaffer tape. 'I will read the lines of Henri who is the husband in the piece,' he was explaining as, hands on her upper arms, he physically manoeuvred her centimetres in one direction, then another, all the while looking back over his shoulder to the camera pointing in her direction.

The cameraman was silent, concentrating on his lens. '*Très bien*. Pretty kid.' He whistled.

'Now, Marguerite, when you say your lines, try not to look down at the page all the time. Look up, but not into the camera. Concentrate your attention on me, direct eye contact with me. I will be standing right of camera. Okay, got it? Just imagine that I am Henri, your husband, and it is to me you are talking.'

Marguerite nodded, tongue dry, swelling like a lobster in her mouth.

'Ready to roll, honey?'

She nodded again. The trembling was rising from her knees to her thighs and upwards through her entire body. The shivering was taking hold of her as though she had been plugged into something electrical. She was terrified. All her dreams were fading, all power from her dissipating. She must not fail.

Julien shuffled backwards and pulled a few pages of tatty script from out of his back pocket. She gazed at him as instructed.

'Lights!' he yelled. Suddenly, the space was flooded with a hot white light. 'Sound!'

The third man in the trio returned the cry with 'Rolling!'

And then the cameraman spoke, 'Camera rolling.'

'And . . . action!'

Nothing happened. Marguerite listened to the low buzz of electricity, of the camera equipment operating. The swampy artificial heat radiating from the lights caused her skin to become sticky, her limbs clammy.

Perspiration was gathering at the back of her knees. Her lightweight frock was clinging to her spine, which felt like a rod of iron. She supposed she was being filmed but Julien wasn't speaking. She glanced in panic at the sheet of paper clutched between her sweating fingers. To confirm. Yes, his was the first line.

'We're not using a clapperboard or synch slate, honey, so before we begin the scene, look directly into the camera and speak your name clearly, please.'

'M-my name?'

'*S'il vous plaît, Mademoiselle.*'

'M-Marguerite . . .' she faltered. What name to choose? Not her own, obviously. It was time to change. A screen name with an international ring to it. In the past, in her imagination, she had conjured up so many, and now her mind had gone blank.

'We're rolling, Marguerite.'

'Marguerite C-C-Courtenay.'

'That's fine, Marguerite, thank you. Now look away from the camera and start to cry, honey. Can you do that? Give us some tears. Think of something sad, something that might break your heart and then let us have it.'

Enough had been said. Marguerite recalled her brother, recalled that day of separation. A wartime memory she never allowed herself to dwell on and a sob that might have cracked her in two broke out of her, splintering the silence in the hallowed make-believe space.

'Terrific, sweetheart,' encouraged Julien. Then in a deeper, more affected voice he enunciated the first of Henri's lines. 'I'm leaving here, leaving, do you hear me? Getting the hell out.'

Marguerite glanced at her page. 'Please,' she sobbed softly, 'don't leave.' Gaining force, gaining in confidence as the character's predicament seeped into her, she began to cry out, yelling theatrically, 'Don't go. I couldn't bear it. Henri, don't you know how I love you? I cannot, will not, live without you.'

'Swell, sweetheart, keep going. There's no need to shout. More delicate. Subtle. This is not theatre. Let the emotion, the tears, do the acting for you,' returned Julien, back to assistant director, no longer husband. 'And don't keep waving your arms about, honey.'

'Can you stop that kid flapping the script? It sounds like a storm over here,' called the sound technician.

From then, almost the entire scene was hers, a soliloquy of longing and heartbreak to a man packing his case. Marguerite, trying only infrequently to consult the written script, just kept talking, making some of it up but offering the gist. Before she knew it, Julien was yelling, 'Cut,' and it was all over. She was exhausted, drained. Her rigid body went floppy.

'Thanks, honey. That was terrific. As you leave, ask Paul to send the next girl in, will you, please?'

Charlie was outside in the warm sunshine, leaning against a wooden ladder, one leg crooked up behind him. He was chewing a blade of grass and reading his book. When he saw her, he waved and sauntered towards her, smiling broadly.

A giant palm tree made out of fabric hung limply from a crane above them. Another was now upright on the ground and was being bolted to the spot.

'None of these trees are real.' He laughed. 'Sculpted from wood and fabric. How about that, when they're cultivated so easily down here? I'm guessing it's quicker to chop one down and use the wood to carve another than wait for it to grow.' He shook his head and slapped the trunk of the massive prop, contemplating its extraordinariness. 'How about that?' he repeated. 'How did you get on?'

She gnawed at a fingernail, attempting to conceal her disappointment.

'Well, did you sign your contract?'

'They are seeing dozens of girls,' she admitted. 'I asked them when I could expect to hear and Paul, the junior assistant, said they'd be in touch.'

Charlie and Marguerite stood face to face, looking at one another. Both too unsophisticated to brush off the rejection lightly.

'Lunch?' he offered jauntily.

She lowered her head. 'Not hungry, thanks.'

'You've got to eat.'

'Marguerite Courtenay!' shouted Paul, from the direction of the sound stage. 'You're wanted back on the set!'

'Oh, my!'

'Marguerite Courtenay?' quizzed Charlie.

'A new name for a new life,' she confessed.

'Really?' He grinned and winked. He knew something about that.

Their eyes met and she smiled at him. An unspoken *merci* for understanding, for being there. 'I have to go.'

'I'll wait,' he called after her.

*

The role offered to Marguerite consisted of one brief scene of fourteen lines. It was not the leading part she had tested for: that had been awarded elsewhere. But it was a beginning, her first step into the world of cinema and, although disappointed, she was also thrilled and excited in equal measure.

She carried away the script and sat with it on her lap on the train; her prize; her victory. She stared out at the Riviera beaches, the winking blue water overlooked by luxury villas, confident now that one day such a lifestyle would be hers. Yes, it was all coming together.

She had been given a date three weeks hence for her shooting. Three perfect spring weeks before Marguerite was due back to the studios. There would be a costume fitting to attend and a make-up test, but otherwise her time was her own. The salary offered for the few days the contract covered would be barely sufficient to keep her. She would need to find substitute employment, a roof over her head. Charlie had shelled out for the crumbling *pension* on the outskirts of Cannes. She owed him, and she wanted to be able to reimburse him. He was too kind-natured to be cheated. And, in spite of herself, she was beginning to really like him, to enjoy his company. With him at her side, this big day had been less nerve-racking. He had inspired confidence. Even so, she knew she would have to give him the push at some point soon.

'I need to find work,' she announced gravely.

He frowned, then smiled. 'You just got yourself work.'

'To pay you what I owe.'

'Fine by me.'

They went job-hunting at a shabby agency in Cannes

offering domestic staff to wealthy vacationers and ex-pats. They had no difficulty at all in finding themselves a live-in situation looking after an affluent widow of seasoned years. They had been billed as a young, healthy, employable bilingual couple. Personal assistant and assistant chauffeur. Marguerite was anxious not to tie herself down, not to promote them as a 'couple'. Charlie had been good to her but she was not allowing herself to be drawn into anything that might hinder her career or give him false ideas.

He suggested they take the position, remain together 'at least until your filming has been completed and you have a clearer picture of what your future holds'. As far as he was concerned, he had no plans, and being in Marguerite's company suited him down to the ground. Marguerite considered, then agreed. It would be for just a few weeks until she'd settled her debt and the roles came pouring in.

Paris, November 2015

It was the buzzer that roused Marguerite from her fog of exhaustion and memories. She glanced up at the clock on the wall. Almost 4 a.m. It could only be the English-woman, whose name, at this moment, she could not recall. Under normal circumstances she would be too suspicious to answer the door at such an hour but these were abnormal, terrifying times.

Her legs were stiff as she staggered unsteadily to the hall where she pressed the intercom. 'Hello?'

'It's Kurtiz.'

'Oh, good. I've been waiting for you. Take the lift to the second floor.'

'Lady! Lady!' One of the two police officers who had given Kurtiz a lift to the rue de Charonne was calling her, running towards her. She turned her head.

'You forgot this.'

He was proffering her camera bag. Her precious cameras. Never since she had owned her first Powershot had she let them out of her sight. She noticed as she pulled her camera onto her shoulder that the glass on her watch face was splintered. It must have happened when she'd fallen earlier. '*Merci.*'

'I hope you find your husband and daughter, Madame. We pray they have pulled through this tragic night. *Bonne nuit.*'

Kurtiz's grandmother died unexpectedly. A stroke, which took her within days. 'Mercifully,' wept her mother. 'She would have hated to be in a chair, handicapped, reliant upon us, fussed over. It would have made her miserable and grumpy.'

Still, the unexpectedness of it shocked them all. Mortality spread its threatening shadow. Kurtiz took the train with five-year-old Eliza, now fondly known as Lizzie, to spend a few days with her grieving mother.

'Is there anything of Nan's you want?'

Kurtiz shook her head. 'A small memento would be nice, something you aren't intending to keep.'

'Would you like her wristwatch?'

'Yeah, that'd be lovely, thanks.'

'And . . . I know you and Ollie aren't broke —'

'Please don't call him Ollie — he hates it.'

'Well, he's not here to hear me. What I was saying was that I know he's doing frightfully well and all that and we're both very proud of him, but what about you? Your father and I have been worrying that you've given up everything for him and lovely little Eliza. You have no life of your own, Kurtiz.'

'My choice. Mum.'

'I know, darling, but you must consider your own future.'

Her mother's words hit a nerve which she was not ready to own up to. 'I'm happy, Mum. Don't start picking holes where there's nothing to find.'

'Women drool over him. All my middle-aged friends, even dear old Nan. He won't be impervious to it for ever, darling. When did you last go to the hairdresser, buy a frock, get yourself dolled up, pay attention to yourself?'

'Mum, for God's sake!'

Her mother held up her hands in front of her chest in a defensive gesture, then pulled her chequebook from a kitchen drawer and rummaged for a pen. 'I want you to spend this on yourself. Buy something extravagant, whatever you fancy. Your father wants me to do this. And don't put it aside for later, for a rainy day. Michael has willed a small sum to pay towards Eliza's education or whatever needs might arise in the future. This is for *you*, Kurtiz. We want you to spoil yourself. You don't even have to tell Oliver we've given it to you.'

Her mother signed her autograph with a flourish and handed Kurtiz the cheque.

Twenty thousand pounds.

Kurtiz stared at it, nonplussed. 'Mum, I can't take this. It's far too generous. It's . . . it's yours.' She pushed the slip of paper gently back across the table.

'Kurtiz, I was there watching, a small child, while my mother – God rest her soul – struggled to bring me up alone. No father to bring home a wage. Nothing but a photo of a dead soldier, a war hero. Dead at twenty-two. She lived on that memory all her life, fed off it, sucked at it. And she died having had no life, no real love besides that of a ghost. I want you to take this, keep it for yourself. You never know what might happen.'

'Oliver is not a ghost. I know it was tough for you and I'm sorry for you and so sorry about Nan – I'll miss her horribly – but Lizzie has a father. We're a family and a happy one. This is very generous but unnecessary.'

'The film business is a fickle friend. Be a good girl and do as I tell you. We want the best for you, Kurtiz.'

Back in London, seated at the wooden table in the kitchen, Kurtiz found the cheque secreted in one of the inside pockets of her shoulder bag. Her mother had folded it within a sheet of her eggshell-blue stationery. She unfolded the note, marvelling at her mother's extravagantly scrawled handwriting.

Dearest Kurtiz,

Don't be stubborn. I insist you take this. Think of yourself, please. I want that for you, and so does your father. Spend it and enjoy it. Come and see me again soon and bring Eliza. She is a delightful little girl. You are doing so well with her.

Love Mum x

It was a greater sum of money than Kurtiz had ever possessed. In fact, she had never even come close to such a figure. She found it a little terrifying and knew she should put it against their mortgage. After all, the house was in both their names and Oliver had paid more than the lion's share of everything. Was it fair of her to refuse it when she and Oliver could make good use of it? She left the cheque lying on the table and, while Lizzie was at school, busied herself with mundane chores, wishing that she, like Oliver, was filming.

Oliver was recording the narration for a documentary, a nature film for the BBC. Not really his cup of tea, but the money was good and it filled a slot between two TV jobs. He was working in studios on Old Compton Street. Afterwards, he and Kurtiz had planned to go to the theatre. They had been given two complimentary tickets to the Gielgud in Shaftesbury Avenue. One of his pals had just opened in *Brief Encounter*.

On her way to meet him for a quick drink before curtain up, Kurtiz strolled by a camera shop in Wardour Street. She was early and paused, drawn to its window display of top-of-the-range still and movie cameras. Her mind was elsewhere, thinking about her mother and the loss of her nan, but before she knew it she was inside the shop. The interior smelt of linseed oil. She strolled the deep aisles, not really conscious of what she was looking for until she found herself standing before a presentation of digital camcorders.

A young salesman was at her arm. 'This is the XL1 Canon. Do you know its features?'

She shook her head.

'The broadcast quality is very fine. It was carried on the space shuttle as the NASA official digital camcorder,' the salesman said. 'Are you looking for professional purposes, or home videos? If professional, I can show you something very special. New to the market with an excellent depth of image.'

'I'm just browsing.'

'But you are interested in movie cameras?'

Was she? And then she had a light-bulb moment. She had no real notion about working with cameras, but she loved cinema. She had always been drawn to images, to photography. With the gift from her parents she could afford any of these, and even if all she did was put together albums or short films of Lizzie growing up, how bad would that be? It would keep her occupied, give her an artistic challenge before she drove herself insane filling washing machines and emptying hoover bags. An album of photographs as a present for her grieving mother. Why not? She had been given the opportunity to make this happen. 'I'll be back tomorrow.'

Later that evening, after Oliver had gone to bed a little the worse for too much wine over their late supper, she pulled the cheque out of its envelope. First thing the following morning, after she had dropped Lizzie off at school she deposited it at the bank.

Kurtiz returned to the camera shop and purchased a top-of-the-range stills camera, a Canon Powershot G1; an extravagance that both thrilled and terrified her. It was a neat, potent possibility. She was not even sure that she would master its technology, was all fingers and thumbs, so taking advice from one of the salesmen, she enrolled in a camera-operating course in central London. When that was achieved three months later, with Oliver's blessing and a howl of surprise, she applied for the director's course at one of the London film and television schools. On the strength of her stills photography she was accepted. From the cash that remained, she kept back two thousand for herself and paid the rest against their mortgage.

Did she intend to try to create a career out of this? In the interim, she was filling her time with building a library of stills. She enjoyed the stills work more than the moving pictures and thought she might get herself an apprenticeship with a portrait studio or fashion work. Nothing came of either. Her best achievement was the Lizzie Photo Album, a Christmas present for her mother, who was, not surprisingly, thrilled to bits and determined to see Kurtiz expand the opportunities further.

Oliver's television career was growing quiet. His face was over-exposed, claimed Sam, his agent, who, according to Oliver in one of his many rants, seemed more excited by younger clients.

'You need a more up-to-date look,' Sam advised him. 'Let's try you in another market. Younger character actors, rather than leading roles.'

Financially things were becoming tight. Neither Oliver nor Kurtiz had a regular income. So, she offered to take the portrait shots of Oliver for casting sessions and *Spotlight*, the actors' directory. The photographs well defined a 'new look'. They were grittier, less airbrushed. Sam, delighted, called on Kurtiz to shoot several other clients, which made Oliver irrationally bad-tempered. Kurtiz just laughed at his foolish jealousy.

On his many free days, instead of going to the gym he hung around in the pub on the corner of the street. Or he'd head off into town and stay out to the small hours before rolling home drunk. He became irascible, and on one occasion he missed a casting session because his agent couldn't reach him. From her portraiture earnings Kurtiz bought him a Nokia 3310. The first mobile phone either of them had owned.

Still the rows escalated and grew more fraught as their debts dug deeper.

Once Kurtiz had seen Lizzie off to school, she spent her mornings firing off emails, then trudging the West End agencies depositing samples of her work, until she managed to secure herself an agent. From then on, opportunities began to open up for her.

During the three months Kurtiz had been signed with her new agent, Oliver had still not landed the dreamed-of film role, not even a short stint in the theatre. Their mortgage payments were six months in arrears and the bank was less than reasonable. Sleepless nights and days of bickering and accusations had ensued. A few royalty cheques popped through the letterbox. Their arrival was a godsend. Still, it was on the strength of those envelopes that Oliver had justified his status as 'an actor still capable of earning his own living'.

'Why don't you get a temporary job?'

'I'm an actor.'

'Yes, well, so was I till I gave it up.'

'But *I* didn't give it up, KZ, and that's the difference.'

'I can't get through. The line is constantly engaged.' Kurtiz replaced the receiver on its cradle in Marguerite's living room. She was rubbing at her damp hair with a borrowed towel, refreshed by the shower she had taken, grateful for the kindnesses this stranger was offering her. She stepped towards the TV screen and turned the sound up.

'Five times the usual rota of staff are working flat out. Everyone with medical training has been called in to assist. The hospitals are charged beyond capacity.' Cut to a shot of ambulances drawing up outside a hospital. 'Doctors are in short supply. All beds occupied. Every operating theatre is ablaze with light and emergency teams, fighting to save lives. The stock of blood in all hospitals is low. Blood is being flown in from other cities. Military reinforcements are arriving from various ports throughout France. And the wounded are still arriving. Bodies are still being recovered.'

The screen showed queues of people in every direction. Bodies being transferred on trolleys rolled speedily through the sliding doors of A and E, bottles of emergency blood held aloft by medics running alongside wounded patients. Was Oliver in one of those operating theatres right now? Once she'd had some tea, recharged her phone, she'd get going, make her way – somehow – from one hospital to the next.

'The Métro has been closed and will remain so throughout the day. All public events, sports meetings, school outings, demonstrations, have been cancelled. The country is on red alert,' Marguerite called through from the kitchen.

Kurtiz was on her haunches now in the hall, rummaging through her bag in search of her phone charger, tossing clothes onto a growing pile at her side. Once located, she pushed it into the wall with an adaptor from three-pin to two. The screen lit up briefly to display the zigzag icon that assured her it was charging. She dug down into her bag again in search of paracetamol. The flat gave off a keen smell of herbs, eucalyptus and mothballs, and it was exacerbating the dull ache in her head. She could hear the clink of spoons against china in the kitchen. Two things: she had to determine which hospital was treating Oliver – was his condition deteriorating? How long did she have? – and if there had been a response from Lizzie to her tweet. And – yes, okay, three things – the message from Alex. Was he in Paris?

Marguerite called, 'Once we have ascertained which hospital is caring for your husband, I'll drive you there.'

'Thank you, you've already been very generous. I'll just grab all this lot and be on my way.'

'To where?'

Good question.

'Kurtiz, there is no other method of transport. I've told you, the networks have been shut down. The earliest any will start up again will be tomorrow.' Marguerite was now arranging the cups and teapot on a tray. 'Do you take milk?'

'Yes, I do, very English, I know.' She smiled gratefully at the actress who, even at this hour and after a night of dozing in a chair, presented herself with barely a hair out of place and clothes uncrumpled. But how tiny she seemed in her slippered feet, so vulnerable without her jewellery and mink to bolster her. Kurtiz estimated that she must be well over eighty. On how many previous occasions would this plucky old bird have stayed up all night?

'And what of your daughter? No news?'

Kurtiz shook her head. The lump in her throat was tantamount to a wedged bullet. 'I can't even be sure she attended the concert. I'll have to wait till Oliver regains consciousness to know for sure . . . Or if her body . . .' The air drained out of her, deflating her.

Marguerite frowned, puzzled. 'I had understood they were attending the performance together?'

'It's complicated.'

Marguerite waited but no further information was forthcoming. Her unexpected guest was a difficult nut. Emotionally bruised, was her assessment, just as she had once been. 'Sit down. Try to relax. Let's call the number you were given. They flashed it on the screen. I jotted it down somewhere . . .'

'I tried it less than five minutes ago.'

'Well, we'll try it again.' The old woman looked up from pouring the tea and smiled the smile that lit up her handsome lived-in face. 'I'll dial it.' As she rose from the pot and cups on the round coffee-table, she paused.

'These circumstances couldn't be more ghastly, more horrifying, but I'm glad they have brought us together. I feel connected to you as though we've been friends for a long time.'

Kurtiz bit her lip.

'I'd like to help you. If you feel the need to unburden yourself . . .'

Kurtiz folded the damp towel and shifted awkwardly in her chair.

'Oh, you broke your watch?'

'When I fell.' She'd get it repaired. 'It belonged to my grandmother.' She thought of her dear old nan, who would have been about the same age as Marguerite, if she were alive. She still missed her. 'You're very kind. I really appreciate it. Thank you.'

'I am exceedingly pleased to be able to offer you some assistance, and more than relieved that you are not out there on the streets, trying to unravel this mess on your own. There, now, shout me out the number as I dial it.'

Which was what Kurtiz did. The line was still engaged. Eventually, after several attempts, Marguerite was requested by a recorded voice to press one for the option to hold or put the receiver down and try again later. 'We'll hold,' she said, with a bullish air. 'And we'll keep on holding till they answer. Drink your tea. And then you can tell me all about your daughter.' Kurtiz glanced down at her cup. 'And your husband. What does he do?'

'He's an actor.'

'No!' The old woman clapped her hands with animated glee, almost letting the receiver fall. 'Hello? Hello?

Oh, yes, *bonjour* . . . Yes, indeed, thank you. We are trying to locate an Englishman who was wounded during the Bataclan raid yesterday evening . . . His name?' She swung her body towards Kurtiz.

'Oliver Ross.'

'R-O-S-S. Yes, that's right.' A glance back to Kurtiz. 'I don't recognize his name. Should I have heard of him? Does he work in the English theatre, or – Yes, hello?'

Kurtiz sipped her tea, relishing its burning sensation as it slipped down her throat, which was as dry as sandpaper. The bitter aftertaste of sickness was washed away by the over-sweet liquid. She watched the woman opposite her, studying her, while wondering how much of the truth of her own life she was willing or capable of disclosing. She had kept her remorse locked away for so long. Then a glance towards the hall reminded her: how long before her phone was sufficiently charged for her to be able to collect her messages? Might Lizzie have seen her tweet? If so, would she make contact?

'They will call back as soon as they locate him. Now, please try to rest a little. Together, we'll get through this God-awful night.'

'You were telling me about your husband earlier. I'd like to hear some more.'

Marguerite broke into a smile. 'You mean Charlie? Dear Charlie.'

Marguerite and Charlie, La Côte d'Azur, 1947

Le Rêve, the villa belonging to Lady Celia Jeffries, was a secluded property set in its own spacious grounds on a promontory east of Cannes, hidden from the winding coastal road. To reach it, Marguerite and Charlie took the train to Antibes and then, an extravagance, a taxi-cab. It followed a labyrinthine route round a *cap*, which led eventually onto a stony track. As they rode into the grounds, the car was flanked by cypresses and palms, at the feet of which were clusters of flowering thread-leaved irises. Banks of purple-blue. Like cosmic-sized pupils. Each uplifting its gaze to a deep-blue heaven.

'A thousand pairs of Marguerite's eyes growing by the sea,' remarked Charlie.

Fashioned in the belle-époque style, the house faced directly out towards the Mediterranean and Italy; a south-easterly aspect. To Marguerite and Charlie's unsophisticated perspective, it was a mansion of grandiose dimensions standing three storeys high. It was wide too, like a giant lump of white sugar, with dark green shutters flipped open at every upstairs window. They climbed curved stone steps and Charlie pulled on a heavy bell chain.

A plump maid in uniform with a cap perched carelessly atop her hair opened the door and greeted them formally, disdainfully. Lady Jeffries was making her afternoon telephone calls and would not be available to meet them until 'the cocktail hour', they were informed. Her orders were for the new staff to settle themselves in.

Warily, they stepped inside. Everywhere smelt fresh, clean, of mint and lavender. The hallways and corridors were bathed in tiptoes of sunlight where it had crept in through cracks in the closed shutters. Displays of striking flowers flowed out of tall crystal vases. Marguerite was shown to *her* room, which was modest but boasted two tall windows that dropped to the floor. It faced out across a sweep of pine and palm canopies towards the emerald water. One pair of the French windows opened onto a tiny balcony. She stepped outside into a world of calm and still-ness. Beneath her, buried from sight by fronds, someone was watering plants and whistling. She heard the soft bark-ing of a dog and a man's voice talking in caressing tones to the creature. A light breeze floated up from the blue-green-drenched sea. Lemon, olive and pine trees mingled with the scent of roses wafting through the midday air.

'This is magical,' she cooed, but no less than she had dreamed of. A perfumed land where film stars resided. She stretched out her arms, embracing her new exist-ence. 'And I will too.'

Lady Jeffries was a socialist, she confided, over a glass of Campari and tonic later on, a great fan of Léon Blum – 'A fine politician and recent but short-lived President of the Temporary Republic. A Jew of sound mind and courage who in 1936 passed a bill that gave paid holidays to the French working classes. Two weeks a year. I adhere to that policy and you will both be given two afternoons off every week plus every Sunday and one Saturday in three to do exactly as you please.'

Charlie was allocated the job of sous-chauffeur, keeping the two cars cleaned and in good running order, while Marguerite was offered light secretarial work. Neither had any experience in either of these roles. Charlie knew a thing or two about plane engines, although he sure as hell did not own up to it.

In the evenings, Marguerite and Charlie wiled away after-dinner hours together. She was hungry to know the English for everything. And she was a smart, keen pupil. On their free days, fired by the spirit of adventure, the pair took bus rides inland into the scented hills towards the city of Grasse. Palms and lemon trees adorned the coastal strips before the swift ascent to silvery olive groves, vineyards, mountainsides of lavender, jasmine and rose gardens. Beyond, in the distance, the blue outline of the lower Alps stretched into Italy. All around them was natural beauty: the coast to the south, the Alps to north and east. Italy was east and the Var, a famed wine-growing region, stretched out of sight to the west.

Charlie expressed a desire to settle somewhere there. 'This'll do,' he repeated over and over, gazing about with a stupefied wonder. 'Has life anything better to offer than this, Marguerite? Magnificent, eh? I'll put down roots here. This'll do the trick.'

Marguerite found her new friend's satisfaction curious. She had no thoughts of settling anywhere. Her brief stint in front of the camera had gone well and she had been promised another test with a director of great renown, whose identity had not yet been revealed to her. That someone would be in touch had been all the assurance she could winkle out of the first assistant.

She was growing fond of Charlie, the best friend she'd ever had, but was determined not to fall in love with him. He, though, was smitten. Marguerite's iris eyes and too-skinny frame – she half-starved herself for 'her art and stardom' – plagued his sleeping hours, so intense had his longing grown for this creature who was barely more than a girl.

Marguerite's daily chores involved assisting Lady Jeffries in her study: filing papers in cabinets, writing addresses on envelopes, making up lists for the kitchen staff, ordering books, preparing pamphlets, taking dictation and, at the end of her shift, riding a bicycle to the *bureau de poste* in Antibes with a bag of letters all destined for England or the United States. Lady Jeffries had dedicated her life's work to the suffrage movement, the rights of and education for the working classes. France had awarded the vote to women later than most, in 1944, just before the end of the war. 'You must use your vote, Marguerite. Women have died for your right to have it.'

But Marguerite dismissed such nonsense. Fame was her driving force. She had never before heard talk of politics or women's rights, except on the wireless.

The modest wages she received from Lady Jeffries enabled her to settle her debt with Charlie. He was reluctant to accept it but she had insisted, even badgered him, 'to keep matters clear and even between us'. She had invested in a new frock, booked a visit to a hairdresser – her first ever because at home her mother had trimmed her hair and in Paris she had managed it herself – made a purchase of a small bottle of Revlon nail varnish to paint her fingernails as ruby-red as Rita Hayworth's, a face cream so that she might take better care of her skin, and a bottle of cheap and nasty perfume, which Lady Jeffries requested she dispense with immediately: 'I cannot work alongside someone who exudes a body odour so cloying.'

In return, the dowager offered the girl an unopened flacon of Guerlain's L'Heure Bleue eau de parfum. Marguerite was spellbound by the gift. The bottle had been fashioned by Baccarat and came in a dapper box, sealed with a pink tassel. She carried it carefully to her room and vowed only to use it, one tiny precious drop at a time, for film business.

Her every free waking moment was dedicated to her career; she invested every spare *centime* in the purchase of magazines, which she lined up on a shelf to pore over in bed: *Ciné, Cinémonde, L'Écran Français, Modes de Paris* and, the most treasured of all, the new post-war fashion magazine, *Elle*. How Marguerite Anceaume drooled over the silk jersey pleated dresses with swing skirts, and Christian Dior's ground-breaking New Look, with cinched waists and skirts lifted to reveal calves. She read avidly about the accentuation of bosoms. Long hours in front of her mirror examining her own skinny frame and pea-sized breasts did not fill her with confidence. She studied reverently the depiction of the film stars' universe, their constellations – Lana Turner, Ginger Rogers, Marlene Dietrich, Loretta Young, Danielle Darrieux – the details of their intimate lives and loves, secret tips, hairstyles, shoes. It became a university of Marguerite's own making, building experience and the foundations for her upcoming screen test with the big-shot director.

She talked of little else, breathy paragraphs of gleaned glamour statistics, while Charlie, reflective at her side, was thinking of moving on, investing his hard-earned illicit francs, still carried about with him in a hidden bag, in a plot of land. A smallholding of his own. He fancied the idea of growing sweet-scented flowers close to one of those Grassois villages they had visited on the bus, drawing upon his own farming experience. He was not comfortable on Lady Jeffries' estate, or strolling the sea-side villages thereabouts. The war was behind them. Tourists were returning. And he never felt entirely at ease. He worried about the arrival of English guests for the summer. The odds that someone from his own past might turn up was remote in the extreme, but he couldn't afford to take any chances. He was a man on the run and Lady Jeffries was too well connected. Unnervingly, she also asked a heap of questions. Curious in the extreme, the old dear was, though he believed it came from goodwill and a genuine interest in the world and people around her.

His cover was rock solid, he was confident of that, but what if the British government made it their busi-ness to hunt down deserters, hand out leaflets with faces printed on them? On all occasions he avoided having his photo taken, which amused Marguerite no end because there was nothing she delighted in more. There were nights when the fear, the shame, nearly drove him out of his skin. Should he have gone further afield? To a plantation in Africa? There were daily sailings from Marseille to the top of Africa, the French colonies. It was not too late. He could still make his way by train back along the coast and buy a one-way passage, sailing out of the great port. It would be more prudent to disappear from Europe altogether – and his money might go further in Africa. Nothing in the world stopped him. Except . . . except Marguerite. Foolish of him but he couldn't bring himself to leave her, to abandon her to her own gullible ambitions. How would she fare? What were her chances of success in so risky, so ephemeral a business as the film industry?

The promised rendezvous with the illustrious director seemed never to materialize. Day after day, Marguerite hovered in the hallway, staring hard at Lady Jeffries' beastly silent telephone, and each day she grew more disheartened and more desperate. Had the studios forgotten her?

Charlie hated to see her so wound up, so racked with disappointment. If he could only make her forget all this pie-in-the-sky nonsense . . .

On her free afternoons, Marguerite no longer felt inclined to accompany Charlie into the hinterland, to the fertile lands of sloping vineyards, olive groves and yellow-blossomed broom hills, to wander aimlessly about meadows, climbing through orange groves and plots of land covered with nothing more interesting than stone pines, grass and wild flowers. Each field, to her eye, seemed identical to the last, aside from it being smaller or larger, flatter or more inclined. She judged him dull to take such an interest in horticultural matters.

Instead, she rode the bus to Nice, retracing her steps to the Victorine Studios, batting her big lilac eyes at the gatekeeper, joshing with him, gaining entry to the compounds without an appointment whenever she wished. Once within the magical territory, she mooched about the lots, contriving to meet people, put herself in the path of famous directors, and flirted with crew members in the hope they might pass on the unannounced comings and goings of the famous. The reality was that she spent hours sitting on walls, kicking her legs, watching others who paid her little attention as they hurried to and fro about their business.

René Clément was at work at the Victorine on an epic picture, a gritty film noir, *Les Maudits* – The Damned. The sound stages were bustling with activity. Cameras were being wheeled from one location to the next; make-up artists, heads bent close over ermine brushes, sponges and Max Factor pancake, gossiped about who was sleeping with whom. Each started at the call of their name. Red lights flashed, green lights flashed. Recording! But there was nothing in this movie for Marguerite. She slipped inside one of the studios and peeped at the innards of one section of the make-believe submarine. Everywhere smelt of freshly sawn wood, of turpentine and paint. There, she caught sight of assistant director Julien in intimate conversation with Jean Cocteau. *'Bonjour, Julien, c'est moi.'*

He could not recall her until she nudged his memory. 'Right, right, you're the *gamine* who played the scene in Maurice's picture. I saw the rough cut and you look pretty good. Keep in touch,' he called blithely, as he hurried on his way, locking his arm in Cocteau's.

She watched them disappear into the great shadowed warehouse of illusions, cringing and cross at being described as the 'kid', *la gamine*. When would they take her seriously?

Before returning to Le Rêve, she walked into town, browsed the Nice open-air market down near the port and spent her few francs on false eyelashes, plastic bracelets, hair slides and sometimes lemonade.

On each of these unfruitful afternoons, she took the bus or train back to Antibes in the growing heat, downhearted, flicking through her latest issue of *L'Écran Français* for which she had just handed over twenty *francs anciens*, dreaming, or clutching at and fiddling with her paper bag of gaudy trinkets.

Eventually, the long-awaited contact from the studios came through. Marguerite, alone in the entrance hall with its black-and-white-chequered marble floor and vases of tropical flowers, grasped the receiver with the prickly fingers of her right hand. Her touch smudged sweat prints on the polished black Bakelite.

'Hello?' With her spare hand she was winding the braided handset cord around her fingers as though it were her hair.

Her test was scheduled for one week hence. The director, Leo Katsidis, was mid-passage from the States, having set sail from New York. He was planning to attend the second Cannes Film Festival, which was due to run from 12 to 25 September. He was billed to present his latest movie, *Rebound*, based on a modern American murder story. Leo Katsidis. She mouthed his name with the reverence her mother gave to her own hero, Pope Pius XII.

Marguerite had seen and admired Katsidis' first picture, *The Seamy Streets of Brooklyn*. He was big news, she bragged to Charlie that evening, as they sat drinking chilled beers from tall glasses down at the waterfront in Juan-les-Pins.

'This is the break I have been dreaming of, Charlie. I'll be packing and on my way before you know it.'

The Greek-American, she was informed, had been sent the screened audition she had recorded when she first arrived in the south, as well as rushes from a few of the takes in Maurice's film. Katsidis had been impressed by what he had seen and had requested of the studio, in his absence, to 'give the girl a screen test for the supporting female role' in his upcoming picture. If he liked what she delivered, he would meet with her and try her out in front of a camera again. The second audition, he would direct himself. '*If* what he sees pleases him. Oh, Charlie, this is it. No more horrid secretarial work, and no more hanging about the studios in the vain hope someone will say hello, that some junior director's assistant will recognize me. "Marguerite Courtenay" will soon be writ in big, bold letters and flashing lights. All over France, Charlie, and before long, winging its way across America too.' Arms waving in exaggerated circles to describe the extent of her notoriety, she almost knocked her glass over. She was walking on clouds, puffed up and pleased with herself. 'I'm going to blow every *centime* I earn this week on a fancy new frock. The stripy one I told you about at the market in Nice.'

Charlie sipped his beer, stared out at the fancy yachts ploughing through the water and felt a sinking dread for the disappointment she was bound to suffer. He was bursting to ask her to marry him, but he knew she'd guffaw in his face.

At that moment a man bearing a camera strolled by. A seaside photographer in a coloured hat. He lifted the lens to snap their picture. Charlie, catching sight of him, buried his face in Marguerite's shoulder, tilting her backwards off her chair. Her beer glass went over and the sticky liquid spilt. Marguerite jumped to her feet, worrying about her outfit. 'Charlie!'

The photographer slid away awkwardly.

'What's up with you?'

Charlie wiped the table with his handkerchief. 'Sorry, I . . .' This had been a warning. He must not forget the risks. He must set his mind to his own plans. Move on, find himself a remote spot and build a new life before someone came hunting for him.

As the days progressed, Marguerite had little time for Charlie, who had found a decent patch of land near the hamlet of Plascassier, seven kilometres from Grasse. He was intending to put in an offer and invited Marguerite to visit it with him. He wanted her to be excited by it, but Marguerite's mind was elsewhere. 'You chose that quickly, Charlie,' was her only comment.

During the hours she spent locked away with Lady Jeffries in her library, time dragged. Lady Jeffries was firing off letters to English newspapers concerning the unsettled situation in Mandate Palestine and the recent murder by Zionists of two British army sergeants found hanged and booby-trapped in a eucalyptus grove near the city of Netanya. A backlash back home in Britain was gaining in force against the Jewish refugees, anger fuelled over these brutal acts.

'We must not allow the Irgun or any militia group to gain the upper hand: no one should tolerate these shocking atrocities. Nonetheless, the Jewish people have suffered profoundly and Britain must support rather than ostracize or condemn them. Many have come to Britain as asylum seekers. It is our duty to protect them, not threaten them. Marguerite, we must voice our concern. I'll dictate a letter. Dig out my files for *The Times* and the Foreign Secretary, please. If the British pull out of Palestine, as they will, I fear for a Middle Eastern war, and who knows where that will end?'

Marguerite was struggling with such meddling politics. She didn't know who these people were that Lady Jeffries was trying to save. Her mind was elsewhere, until she was stringently chided: 'Everyone here is cheering for you, dear child, but you cannot drop everything else around you. You are neat, smart and efficient, and you are doing admirably with the book-keeping, learning fast, but I require your full concentration, please, or I will be obliged to replace you.'

Marguerite bit her lip. She needed employment until her film career took off. Still, she had outgrown these living arrangements, this situation. Even Charlie, who was her pal but had been acting strangely, was hell-bent on moving on.

Her restlessness, her air of rebellion, escalated when she received a message to say that her second Victorine test had been positively received. The American director, Katsidis, had requested an interview with her during the week following his arrival on the coast. She scooted outside into the palm-fronded summer garden where only the cicadas gave voice. There, she squealed and jumped with delight. It was time to take flight, and she intended to rise up like a butterfly, soar like a balloon. She'd cut the string and sail into the skies, across oceans, scudding above the clouds, the war memories, never to bump back to earth.

The assistant escorted her through an open door, then announced her name: "Marguerite Courtenay, sir.'

Marguerite was trembling from head to foot as she stepped into a large room with a wide picture window that looked out over one of the exterior film lots. The room reeked of stale cigar smoke. She was back at the Victorine where her first encounter with the up-and-coming god of modern American cinema, Leo Katsidis, was about to take place. An overhead fan turned slowly and did nothing to alleviate the stagnant air.

Katsidis was seated behind a desk, one leg folded over the other thigh. He was a small, muscular man with a crooked nose ... flinty, penetrating eyes, heavy peat-brown brows and a crop of lustrous dark wavy hair. There was an aura about him of one who knew who he was and feared the opinion of nobody. He surveyed her entrance while swivelling from side to side in his chair.

She hovered at the edge of the carpet in a quandary, awaiting instructions. The door behind her closed discreetly.

'Sit down.' He gesticulated at a leather chair on the far side of the desk. The desk was empty but for an ashtray spilling over with the butts of cigars and cigarettes, a large blotter and a tall half-filled tumbler. It was as vast as a brown lake.

'What's your name?'

She was perplexed. He must know who she was. Someone had just announced her. She enunciated it anyway, and he replied that he liked the way she looked on camera.

'So have I got the part?' she squeaked.

He lifted a thickset hand, staying her excitement. 'In spite of the fresh image you present, there's too much goddam acting. If we're to work together I'll need you to lay yourself bare, hear me?'

She nodded effusively. It couldn't involve more than another screen test, surely. Her blood throbbed and pulsed with the almost tangible taste of success. She could barely stay in the chair, she was so excited.

'I will require you to let yourself go.'

Marguerite listened intently while clasping her damp hands tightly in the lap of her skirt, which she had purchased only a few days earlier. Its newness itched her thighs. She fluttered her eyes, attempting a smile, Ginger Rogers allure, hoping to win over the short stocky man, flirt with him, break through to him.

'You have to trust in me.'

She was confused by the American's words and his apparent lack of response to her charms. 'But you are pleased with the test?' she persisted, flustered.

He waved his hand and fingers agitatedly as though he were swatting away an irritating gnat. 'Sure. You've got a great body, fine bone structure. You look good on camera, but I want something else. Get up. Move about the room. Go on, do as I say,' he barked. He wore the sleeves of his pale lemon crisply ironed open-neck shirt rolled to just beneath his elbows. She noticed an expensive gold watch with leather strap wrapped round an arm that was a riot of dark hair. He was virile, a man who was winning, who demanded the best from life, and these observations made her rather afraid of him. She rose tentatively from the chair and paced, measured dainty steps, towards the wall, swung as though skipping and back again.

'You see what I mean? You're *acting* walking. Just be yourself. I want to see your body move as it does naturally when no one is watching you. When you're alone, unobserved. I want to see a private moment, as though I'm spying on you, you get what I mean?'

Marguerite was at a loss. She stared at the floor, studying her meticulously painted toenails.

'Come here.'

She hovered, her scuffed, cloddish white sandals glued to the rug on the wooden floor.

'I'm giving you a direction, goddammit.' He slammed his hand against the desk. 'This is how we make pictures. I give directions. You take them. Move towards me.'

Her body was taut, sensing some undefined danger.

He lifted up a few pages of script held together with a paper clip. Then tossed them across the table. 'Cinema is about sex. Acting is about seduction. *Seduction*, you hear me? Anna Magnani, she's no obvious beauty, but she dominates the screen. She's all woman. Earthy. Voluptuous. Charismatic. You understand me?'

Marguerite nodded, although she wasn't sure where this was leading. Wherever it was going, she was cowed by the tone of it.

'How old are you?'

'Twenty.' It tripped off her tongue, her well-practised lie. What difference did it make if she was just eighteen? Twenty had a ring to it, mature. The threshold of womanhood, not a grubby teenager who had skipped off from home, missing her brother, shirking family responsibilities.

'You're just a whippersnapper,' he snarled. 'Passion, Marguerite, that's what this about. If you want me to take you to Hollywood, I need it from you. You want me to take you to Hollywood, don't you? You'd do anything for this break, right?'

'I c-can do it, Mr Katsidis,' she muttered. 'I really feel this role. '

He smirked. 'Study the script. Maybe I'll test you Monday.'

'I feel the passion, honest I do.' She beat her fist against her breast.

'Get lost, I'm busy.'

On the train back to Antibes, slumped in a corner, the calm sea beyond the window, pale-skinned tourists bobbing within it, Marguerite wept silently. A bitter pain was spreading like heartburn within her, cold tears stripping her carefully applied face powder. Three travellers watched her, rocking in their seats, doing nothing. She had behaved like a frightened grasshopper, humiliated herself, exposed her innocence, her ignorance. Her comportment had suggested nothing worldly about her. She was miserable. Her nose was running. How could she portray the emotions of a grown woman when she was just a stupid virgin?

Charlie was in the garden when she struggled up the drive, wilting and frazzled with the heat, the dust and her own perplexed defeat. The straps of her sandals were cutting into her swollen pink feet. She hadn't seen much of her friend for days and wondered now whether her lack of attention might have made him lose interest in her. He was polishing Lady Jeffries' open-top, Robin-Hood-green Riley Kestrel. He nodded when he caught sight of her in the wing mirror but he didn't slacken his pace.

When they had first arrived here, several months back, he would have slung his rags to the ground, beamed a great broad grin at her and given her his full, wide-armed attention, but not today.

'Hello, Charlie. *Bonjour.*'

'Been at the studios?' he asked, but to her ear the remark rang more like a reproach than an interested query.

She burned to confide in him about Katsidis' behaviour but broaching the subject would be tricky. 'Yep, big Hollywood director.' She waved her arms in the sunshine, acting carefree, then instinctively let them slap against her thighs before raising one hand to grip her throat. 'It's a fabulous opportunity. A very . . .' She trailed off, drained of all energy to play-act, recalling the stultifying minutes in Katsidis' office. She closed her eyes and let her head roll sideways. 'It's a very passionate role.'

Charlie had his back to her, bent low over the *carrosserie*, the bodywork, which was gleaming, blinking in the sun with great enamel saucers of light. His naked arms and shoulders were striped with black grease. She recalled Katsidis' lower arms and the watch.

'That car still looks pretty dirty,' she joked, but Charlie wasn't looking at her. 'I've got the afternoon off, rest of the day free,' she trilled. 'Wondered what you're up to.'

No response. He *was* angry.

'We could take a picnic somewhere.'

'What do you need, Marguerite?' he butted in, rubbing his nose with his greasy fingers, not bothering to give her as much as a cursory glance.

'Company,' she whispered tremulously. 'Sorry if I've been a bit . . . you know . . . thoughtless. This role, it –'

'Means a great deal to you. Yes, we know. We all know it, Marguerite. The whole household is aware of it, suffering your moods, airs and graces, your food fads, different diets every day. And after this role, so will the next one, and so it goes.'

'Please don't –'

The gardener's pointer barked somewhere beyond the garages, drowning her sentence.

Charlie tossed his soiled rag onto the gravel. He swung on his haunches to face her, to give her a piece of his mind – his hair, almost the colour of pine resin, shone damp and amber from exertion and heat – but he stopped short when he saw the desolation in her face. The quivering lips, the smudged mascara, the pallid cheeks. He rose to his feet and loped towards her. 'Hey, what happened? You didn't get the part?'

She nodded, then shook her head.

'You got it or you didn't?'

'We're rehearsing,' she mumbled.

'Still rehearsing? Well, that's positive, isn't it?'

'Americans. They're . . . they're tougher. Seem to want more insurance, you know. Director needs to be more persuaded of my . . . ability, my inner . . . before he makes a final commitment for Hollywood. I have to go back on Monday.'

'Hollywood, eh? You'll be fine.' Charlie turned on his heels to continue his chores when Marguerite touched him, holding him gently by the elbow, face up against his profile, but careful not to let her new cotton skirt get stained with oil. 'If you're free later, how about we go for a drive? We could take a spin in this beauty, eh? One day I'll own one of them.' She caught the flash of scepticism that crossed his face. 'Oh, Charlie, I'm just kidding. Let's take a bus somewhere, you and me, go for a jaunt. Hey, I'd like to see the plot you've found. Let's do that. All those vine- and flower-clad hills you've been describing.'

'I thought you said you had no time.'

'Of course I have. I want to picture where you'll be when you leave here, when we go our separate ways. I can think of you there when . . . when I'm in Hollywood. Katsidis says if I get this right, he'll be taking me.'

The man crouching winced.

'Charlie?'

'What is it?'

'You don't want me to know where you'll be?'

'I haven't signed all the papers yet. It might not work out.'

'But we could take a look. Wiggle our toes in those grasses where your dreams will grow. Please, let's, Charlie . . .'

'I'll be free in an hour or so,' he conceded.

'Perfect. I'll get my glad rags off, wash off the stickiness and throw on some slacks. It's like standing in a greenhouse out here. See you out front at two. How does that sound?'

'Fine.' You always get your own way, don't you, Marguerite? He sighed but he didn't voice his regret because he couldn't resist her, couldn't resist her ebullience, her shiny optimism. Instead, he watched the reflection of her retreating figure, her splendid hips, distorted in the car's polished wheel hub. 'Hey,' he called after her, 'why don't I get us some cold drinks from the kitchen on our way out?'

'You're a pal, Charlie.'

It was a fertile valley with views sliding all the way south to a distant V-shaped crack of turquoise sea, an empty scoop in the folds of hills not yet planted, save for an old fig tree and several contorted almonds possessing few leaves. On the far side of the valley, the hill dotted with pines and local oak rose up again until it reached a flat surface, a crest, which Marguerite supposed was the road that circled the land. The inclines surrounding where the pair of them were standing were wild with thyme, savory, juniper and boxwood. There was not a hamlet or farmstead, not even a shack to be seen. Nothing but nature, where wild grasses had shot up, tall and burly.

Charlie had been reading up on the landscape, the Mediterranean vegetation, and was calling out the names of each plant for Marguerite's benefit.

'If you look carefully, squint hard and focus, you can see that on the far side of the valley, where the land rises up again, there are the outlines of ancient stone terraces, *restanques*, the locals call them. They're overgrown and tumbledown in places, but I'll rebuild and reinstate them.'

'All of this will be yours?' she crooned incredulously. 'It's a bit of paradise, eh?'

Charlie was opening two bottles of beer. He passed one to the girl at his side. She tipped it to her lips and swallowed. After the climb, the tepid, bitter liquid slipped smoothly down her throat. She was deliberating about when she could broach the subject of her meeting at the studios earlier. Would Charlie be able to advise her? He was a man, after all. He'd know about . . . such things. She glanced about her, absorbing the stillness. A site to make anyone forget their troubles. 'It's sure peaceful here, isn't it, Charlie?'

No one'll come calling, he was thinking. 'And there's good money to be made in these hills,' he announced, wiping a moustache of foam from his upper lip. He was proudly surveying the acres, *his* acres, as though he were a miner and the first to discover gold in the hills. 'We're at an altitude of three hundred metres above sea level. It's nicely tucked away, private, few passers-by, and it's prime growing country for jasmine and roses. *Rosa centi-folia*. And the petals of both blossoms sell for a good price in these parts. Harvested with care, picked by hand by those who have the skills, we – erm, I mean me . . . I'll be able to sell everything on. All the other producers round here are retailing their flowers to the perfume companies in Grasse.'

Marguerite listened to Charlie eulogizing; his ardour for this scrubland made him glow. She was brushing at the bib of her blouse, trying to keep the wind from messing up her clothes and hair. She wished she could love somewhere the way he did, wished she could get so excited about plants and a green valley. Was that what Katsidis meant by 'passion'? She had to extend her experience, and develop *passion*. And she had to do it before Monday.

She observed Charlie bursting with enthusiasm for the flowers. Jasmines, he fancied in particular. Chanel No 5, he cited. 'I bet you'd kill for a bottle of that perfume, eh, Marguerite? One day, with these fields patterned with pink May roses and jasmine, I might be able to afford to buy you a flask.'

'Where'd you learn to love the land, Charlie? It certainly makes you full of zest.'

He responded that it was in his blood. He'd learned the basic skills from his father, who'd been an apple farmer in Kent. He let it slip, cock-a-hoop that Marguerite was taking an interest. The words spilling out from his memories, the beer lubricating his tongue. His guard dropped. 'I used to love the autumns when I was a kid, those days when we carted the wooden ladders out into the orchards to pick the fruit, two of us working each tree. Heads poking up to the heavens through the gnarled old branches, leaves flicking against our cheeks, a clear sky above us, trying to keep the late-season wasps from fighting with us over the fruit. I'd be nattering away nineteen to the dozen to my father . . . After, we'd lug the loaded buckets into the barn, ready to press the apples, even my small sister, Syl–' He stopped short, bowed his head and kicked the stony earth with the toe of his boot. He was tussling with ghosts she could not see and would never become acquainted with.

His silence drew Marguerite's attention back to the present, tuning her into the reminiscences of the man standing close by her. He appeared to be so ordinary, so buoyed by enthusiasm, and then she read the expression in his eyes. The pain there. 'Hey, what's wrong, Charlie?'

He shook his head from side to side, and for one crazy moment she thought he might be crying. 'Charlie?' She took a step towards him and lifted her hand. An impulse to stroke his cheek, to draw his focus in line with hers. Instead she tugged at his sleeve as a dog might do to a troubled master. 'Hey, Charlie, tell me about your flowers and your plants. I'm here listening. I am, I promise.'

Without further ado he wrapped an arm around her and drew her tight against him, pressed his moist face into the nape of her neck and began to sob. Her thoughts flashed back to Katsidis, his horrid manner earlier that morning.

'Don't you feel anything at all for me?'

'*Mais bien sûr*, I do, Charlie. You're the best friend I ever had.' She was inching herself out of his grasp, wriggling to get some air, to extricate herself from the intensity of his emotion. A gust of wind blew through them, lifting the back of her blouse. She tugged at it with a frenzy, tucking it back beneath the waistband of her trousers.

'Kiss me,' he begged. 'Kiss me.'

Such ardour came as a bolt out of the blue. She giggled awkwardly. She had never seen Charlie expose this side of himself. He was English and stable, not excitable like her or peculiar and heavy-breathing like Katsidis. She leaned forward hesitantly, stretched upwards on tiptoe and pecked at his clean-shaven cheek, lifting her hand to make contact with his flesh, which smelt of carbolic soap, to press the palm against the right side of his face. As she did so, his head tilted towards her hand and was surrendered into her grasp.

He felt the warmth of her young flesh and was at peace, but longed for more.

She watched him. His eyes were swimming with such a well of hurt, of anguish. 'Are you ill?' she asked him. 'Shall we sit on the grass for a bit and look at your land, or do you want us to start walking back towards the bus stop?'

Without waiting for his response, Marguerite pulled away from him and threw herself backwards onto the ground, laughing as she fell, kicking her slender legs into the air, play-acting. High above them, an eagle soared. 'Where will you live?' she asked him, attempting to dissipate the mood. 'Show me the spot from here. Describe how your house will look.'

He remained upright, appearing not to have heard her, lost in a place she had never visited and would never be familiar with. It occurred to her then that they were acquainted with such tiny fractions of each other. They never talked of their pasts, of where they had come from, of what their stories were. It had become an unspoken agreement between them, a pact. Still, she tried to picture him in his father's apple orchards, just a kid, lean and sandy-haired, lugging wooden wheelbarrows of fruit. A world before war. Did he have brothers or sisters? Yes, he had just mentioned a sister, hadn't he? Had he said her name? She had never talked of her own brother, her beloved Bertrand, who had gone to fight and never come back. Their souvenirs from childhood they had both kept locked within them and each held tight their key.

'Where's Kent?' she asked. 'Is it near the sea? I love being here by the sea, don't you, Charlie? All that distance ahead of you to the horizon.' She patted the ground beside her, fingers rippling through the long grass and the spattering of yellow and pink flowers, beckoning to him.

Slowly he dropped to his haunches and settled himself close, colliding against her shoulder, causing the fall of her curls to brush her blouse. The gingery hairs on his arms glistened like golden feathers in the sunlight. She dismissed a fleeting memory of a goldcrest spotted in a wood with Bertrand when she was small. She noticed Charlie's freckles for the first time and how his skin was roasted pink in the heat before it turned brown. Light brown, not a deep Mediterranean baking. Not olive like Katsidis. Charlie's skin was younger, more pliant, kinder to the touch, not threatening. Being in Charlie's company was not oppressive. He always made her feel less troubled.

He was her brother now. He must be somewhere not far off Bertrand's age. She furrowed her brow, curious as to why her companion had never gone home to the apples and his family. He had never before uttered a sentence about England. Had a girl broken his heart? Might Bertrand be sitting in a field somewhere with a sweetheart and all the while she and her mother had thought him dead and gone? She should write to her mother, let her know she was safe.

She lay back in the long grass, which smelt so sweet, so pure, almost of honeysuckle. A bee approached, a fat furry thing with black legs and stripes, hovering near her nose, buzzing low and loud. She waved it away from her face. 'I don't want to get stung.' She giggled nervously.

'Don't hit at it. You'll hurt it. Let it be. It'll fly away quietly in its own time. The bee means you no harm.'

The mighty brown bird circling overhead had disappeared too and the sky was wide and empty, watching them, amused by their secrets and the dark futures they could not yet foresee. Marguerite closed her eyes and saw coloured circles in the blurred light. The afternoon was silent save for the humming of insects. She heard a cart's wheels turning slowly in the far distance, the bray of a donkey, but there was no one in sight, just the two of them and the perfumes emanating from the hills around them. Strangers. Strangers who had been looking out for one another. She was debating about whether now was the moment to confide in Charlie about her meeting with Katsidis, but she feared he might accuse her of having, in some imperceptible way, done wrong, behaved in a manner that had been inappropriate and had provoked Katsidis' talk of sex. Had she behaved like a tart, a whore? A whore. That was what her mother might have accused her of. Her heart was troubled and she had so little time to resolve her dilemma. 'Is London in Kent, Charlie?' She delivered the question as casually as she could without opening her eyes, without wanting to interrogate him, feeling the warmth of the sun on her face and for one fleeting moment not caring about the possible reddening of her skin or her screen test. Just being here alone on this hillside with her friend hushed her concerns.

Charlie made no answer. She could have been talking to the sky. Did he believe in God, this man at her side? Was he a Catholic? He had never visited a church during the months since she had met him but neither had she. Yet, as a child, she and her mother were always at the local *église*, always present in the same pews for the Sunday-morning service. Praying, weeping for Bertrand's safe return.

'I had a brother. He was older than me.' Her voice was soft and hoarse. 'We think he was killed in the war. "Missing" was what the letter said. Did you fight, Charlie?' She opened her eyes. The Englishman was lying beside her, back flat against the stony wild-flowered earth, staring at the heavens, watching a cloud scud by. She rolled towards him, lifted herself onto her elbows and studied his face from above. He looked so serious. 'Did you, Charlie?'

'What?'

'Fight in the war? Is that why you're in France?'

He spun his gaze towards the nature, concentrating on the hill to his left, thinking about the best spot to plant a few trees for shade and build his house. Just a simple home that he had silently dreamed he might share with Marguerite. He swung his attention back to her, those lilac eyes crawling all over him, examining him.

'Yes,' he said, 'I fought.' She waited, wanting more. 'My mates were killed. I was seriously injured, head messed up, unable to return to duty. Leave it now.'

'Killed where? Here in France?'

'Drop it, please.'

She lifted up his shirt, gently easing the cotton away from his body, exposing his flat, tanned torso. 'Do you have scars?' she teased, but her heart was beating fast. She felt something shift within her, an emotion she had never known before. A yielding, desire.

He watched her, in shadow against the backdrop of the sun, rays like a halo encircling her blonde head. Those agile, almost feverish features of hers piercing and puzzling as she slipped the soft, warm palm of her hand against his flesh. He let out a release of air and she began to stroke her hand back and forth. He felt his own hunger awaken and blaze within him and he raised an arm to draw her tight against him, inhaling the scent of her – 'Oh, Marguerite' – before he kicked his legs and rolled them both over so that she lay on her back.

'Ouch!' She felt a stab of thorn in her shoulder blade. A flash of uncertainty registered. She studied the man on top of her. He was handsome, this stranger from another land.

'Your first time?' he whispered, as he felt her body go rigid in spite of her determination to see this through.

She nodded. 'But I want to do it, really I do.'

'Sure?' He scoured her features for an assent.

'I really like you, Charlie. Please, let's do it.' It was a rasped command. Too late now to divulge the morning's encounter with Katsidis, she squeezed tight her eyes. Better to get it over with. Better to do it with Charlie, her best friend, than anyone else. She wanted to be a woman who knew the secrets, craved it now, not a girl who was ignorant of passion, who was afraid when a man drew close, who didn't know what this sex business was all about. She wanted to be able to look Katsidis in the face – equal to equal – not brave this territory of longing and passion from the wrong side of the fence, looking in from beyond a closed gate. She would learn to be 'earthy'. She would train herself.

Charlie kissed her on the mouth and she closed her eyes, kissing him back as she had seen it done in the pictures, wiggling her head about. Then the brush of his tongue caused a rush of tingling to wash through her. She felt the expanse of his body looming over her and his proximity pleased her, thrilled her. Was this passion?

Charlie was unbuttoning her trousers and tugging them away. His hand was fidgeting with her underpants, fingers delving. It stung a bit, felt ticklish, but not horrible. He let out a moan when he slid a finger into her, which caused her to open her eyes again and study him but she as quickly shut out the image of him, fearing the desire expressed in his features. As he moved his hand, she began to experience a sensation she hadn't known before: a melting of limbs, a moistness seeping out from within her. Without any prompting she spread her legs, felt herself go a little a faint, weak like a rag, a relaxation unfamiliar to her until he pulled aside her knickers and positioned himself, thick, hard, against her. She cried out into the soft air, the blue sky, with no one to hear as he entered her, groaning, and began to rock against her, pushing her into the hard earth. Blades of grass pressed like razors against her cheek.

It was a sacrifice given up for her art. But it was done, over with, and she was liberated. A fully-fledged woman, and it had been quite all right.

On the bus back towards the coast, they barely spoke but for perfunctory, essential exchanges about bus tickets. Marguerite's trousers were stained green on the backside and down one leg from the herbs she had lain on and the pressure of this man, and she feared there may have been a few drops of blood but she hadn't been able to look, not in front of Charlie. She was sure that everybody on the bus knew what had caused the stains on her clothes and was well aware of what the pair had been up to. She recalled her mother's chiding tones when she and Bertrand had returned to their little house, muddied and unkempt, leaves in their clothes and hair from afternoons of climbing trees, wading in the river, horse-playing about the countryside.

She felt such a tangle of emotions and did not know how to handle them, how to manage all that was erupting within her. Was she falling in love? No, that couldn't happen. Perhaps she shouldn't have chosen Charlie for her experiment. Her initiation into passion. Perhaps she should have found someone who meant nothing to her. But, then, it wouldn't be passion . . . or would it? She was so bewildered, and yet a bit of her felt warm and safe. Charlie, by contrast, was more light-hearted than she had ever known him. Humming softly, nudging against her upper arm as the bus rocked and rolled down the hills towards the summer coast. *La mer.* He crooned the first lines of her favourite song, grinning at her. He had attempted at several moments to hold her hand but she had swiftly withdrawn it.

'We could go to the pictures tonight, if you fancy it? Let's see what's playing in Cannes or Nice.'

'I've got work to do later. Big test soon,' she replied. 'I can't be wasting any more time.'

'Wasting time? But I thought –'

'Well, don't think. Please, Charlie, let's not get romantic,' she snapped.

She would resist any further flesh contact with him, for the present at any rate and quite possibly for ever. Passion, or sex at least, was a rough untidy business, she decided. It caused confusion, was best left aside and not dwelt upon, but at least she knew what it was all about now, and Katsidis would not dismiss her as a pipsqueak. She was a mature woman as of this very afternoon, an equal to all of them, and in a few days she would show Katsidis what she was made of, the woman she was, the passion with which she could imbue any scene, and he would applaud her and she would be sailing to America to a new life. Stardom. Charlie was a good, kind man, but simple. He had dreams, too, of course he did, but they were modest ones. Of flowers on hillsides. Copses and shacks. Hers were limitless. Boundless. They traversed continents.

On the Sunday, their mutual day off, Charlie invited Marguerite to revisit 'his' plot with him. She agreed because she wanted to make amends, to soften the unkindness she had dealt him, and because she was so agitated about the following day that she needed to keep herself occupied.

'I've signed the *promesse de vente* for it,' he told her proudly. She wondered how he'd earned the money. Were his family rich from their apples? Did they send him francs in an envelope? She'd never seen him receive a letter. Ever. 'I want to walk the boundaries,' he explained. 'See exactly what I'll be getting before I pay the final visit to the *notaire*'s office in Cabris, sign the papers and hand over the cash.'

After they left the bus, it was a fair hike in the heat to the outskirts of his territory. He was carrying a scruffy hand-drawn map, which he kept touching with his finger, gliding it from one spot to the next. They had brought a picnic, which they'd made for themselves in the kitchen at Lady Jeffries'. Still, they had got off the bus in Grasse, several stops earlier, to buy some fresh baguette and some beer and cigarettes for Charlie at a *tabac*. The church bells were ringing in the town. They drowned the warbling of the turtle doves. She enjoyed the squares, taking time to watch the locals on their day off, many dressed in Provençal costume with white frills, strolling beneath the wide umbrella pines. It was a world away from the war years here, cooler than at the coast, and Marguerite felt more comfortable in this higher-altitude climate. As they began their walk out into the open countryside, the air was perfumed with jasmine. It was a heady, exciting scent. She was glad to be having this outing.

'They will begin the harvest next weekend, the first in August,' Charlie told her. 'I've signed up to lend a hand. Saturdays and Sundays, all day.'

'What about your work for Lady Jeffries?'

'I'll be leaving there shortly,' he returned softly. 'I spoke about it to her ladyship yesterday, explained that I'm moving on to begin my own life. She agreed that it is the best choice for me. I think she knows that . . .' he mumbled inaudibly, and his words faded away as he footballed a stone from under his boot.

The fields were white with the unfolding stellular blossoms of the jasmine, as though a blizzard had passed that way. Acres and acres of tiny stars. Charlie paused to breathe in the scent and to dream of his own future there. 'My land will produce the same,' he said. 'I intend to specialize in jasmine.'

Marguerite didn't know whether he was talking to himself or to her. Her mind was on more selfish matters. She regretted her heartless dismissal of him the other evening, and she wanted him to know it, but she could not utter the words to broach their physical act of the other day. And what was she going to do without Charlie? It had never occurred to her that he might be the first to depart. She had taken it for granted that he would be there for her, to support and encourage her, until she had taken those first essential steps on the ladder of fame. She had also taken it for granted that when she left for America, as she was sure she would, and possibly very soon with Katsidis, the final separation between her and Charlie would be a natural step for both to take. It would be painless for them. But what if she could not live without Charlie? What if she pined for him? She was fond of him and getting fonder but she had never taken a good look at what he meant to her deep down. And now she was losing him.

'A penny for them,' he said to her, hiking the strap of his shoulder bag, which contained their cheeses and meats and a bottle of local red wine.

'Do you know when you'll go?'

He shook his head. 'As soon as the documents have been completed.'

'Where will you live till you build your house?'

'I'll work up here for one of the flower producers, learn the trade. Growing from seed, bedding in young plants, pruning, pest control, harvesting. He'll give me board and I'll prepare my own land in the evenings and at weekends. I'll erect a shack, a temporary abode, live there until I have the business up and running, then build myself a modest house. My needs are not great.'

He had given this a great deal of thought, without ever discussing it in detail with her, his closest friend. She was crestfallen, a little miserable. 'I'll miss you, Charlie.'

He threw back his head as though laughing but there was a burning in his eyes, almost of anger. 'The film festival is in six weeks. Two weeks later, it will be over. Your famous man will be sailing back to America and, as you have made clear to us all, you'll be going with him.'

'He hasn't exactly promised me a passage yet.'

'But he will.' Charlie turned away from the wall at the edge of the field where the stones were warm from the heat of the morning sun and, hands in pockets, began to trudge the length of the dusty lane. Marguerite held back, watching his shirted silhouette, pondering how life would be without him. Facing the future alone. She sure as hell hoped she wasn't falling in love.

The sun was shining on this first anniversary day. A kind of mockery for all the days that had been counted, survived through. Kurtiz was driving over to Hampstead to pick up a book she had ordered from Daunt's. It was Saturday on Heath Street, and crowds were milling up and down the pavements and massed outside the hillside cafés. She had forgotten how busy the village became at weekends. She rarely drove this way now, hating to pass the Royal Free Hospital where Lizzie had been born. People holding glasses were spilling out of the pubs, engaged in chatter and laughter. A day of leisure. She was in a queue of cars, stopping, starting, attempting to find somewhere to park. Glancing from one side of the street to the other, hoping for a space, for another car to signal its departure.

It was then that the two girls, arm in arm, backs to her, caught her attention. One glanced in her direction, beckoning and laughing. It was Angela Fox. A third adolescent joined the pair. So dumbstruck was Kurtiz that she almost drove into the rear of the preceding car. Someone hooted violently. She lowered the window. Yes, it was Angela. Definitely. With Lizzie. *Oh, my God. LIZZIE.* And a third: a black-haired teenager was approaching.

Was it Lizzie? She couldn't be sure — she had to pull over.

Kurtiz slewed to the left, jammed on the brakes, exasperated by the lack of opportunities to dump the wretched car. Damn it! 'Angie!' she yelled. 'Lizzie!' She switched off the engine, fumbled for her keys. The door opening caused another to swerve. Cars hooted. Drivers and pedestrians cursed her lack of caution. She sprinted across the street.

The girls were waving to someone inside one of the coffee bars. No tables free outside. Backs to her, they hadn't spotted her. She pushed her way towards them. Jenny Fox, blonde, svelte, expensively presented, was seated at a table for four. She was signalling to her daughter and friends. Kurtiz lunged forward and grabbed Angela and Lizzie by the shoulders. 'Lizzie!'

Angela and her friends swung about, frowning. Vexation on their faces for the violent hand.

'Oh, hi, Kurtiz.'

Kurtiz looked from one to the other. Angela's two companions were strangers to her. One, light-haired, almost sandy-toned. The other darker. She stared from one to the other. How Angela had grown, developed over a year. She was wearing make-up. Quite pretty. Not like Lizzie . . . But this wasn't Lizzie. Not Lizzie. At such close range, the teenage girl didn't even vaguely resemble her daughter. How could she have . . . 'Sorry . . . I . . .'

The girls stared awkwardly, a little fearfully. Wide-eyed, not daring to move.

'You okay, Kurtiz? You look a bit . . . Mum's over there, if you'd like to say hello.'

'I . . . I . . .'

Jenny, at her table, smartphone to her ear, was glaring, open-mouthed.

'Would you like a cup of coffee, Mrs Ross?' one of the girls suggested.

She shook her head, gave a brief wave. More a lifting of the arm. 'I . . . I j-just wanted to say hello. How's – how's school?'

Angela nodded. She swung a glance back to her mother, who was now rising from the table and approaching.

'Nice to see you,' mouthed Kurtiz. 'I'd better . . .' and she stumbled back into the glaring sun, the crowded street, head bent, tears blinding her.

Unexpectedly, a hand reached gently for her upper arm. 'Kurtiz?'

She lifted her head.

'Do you want a drink? The girls are fine on their own. We could pop across to the pub . . . I've been meaning to call.'

'Jenny. No, I'm . . . badly parked. I'll get a ticket . . . towed away . . . I – I just . . .'

Jenny studied her with roving, pitying eyes. 'Look, I'm sorry about Oliver . . .' she began.

'What about him?'

'Oliver and . . .' A frown crossed Jenny's features. She appeared to be examining Kurtiz, with surprise or puzzlement. 'I haven't seen him in a while, you know that, don't you? Not since before Lizzie disa–'

'Disappeared? Yes, we . . . It was her birthday last week. She's seventeen.'

Jenny dropped her gaze. She patted at her slacks,

desiring a cigarette. Her bag was on the table in the café. 'Are you all right? I mean . . . Jesus, I truly hope you and Oliver are finding a way through all this. I wanted to call, to offer to . . . I don't know . . . help, do something, but . . . I am so very sorry, you know, for everything.' Jenny leaned forward and gave her an awkward hug, then disappeared back into the dark well of the coffee bar. When Kurtiz turned to the street, a clamp was on her wheel and a pick-up truck was readying for the tow.

Marguerite and Charlie, La Côte d'Azur, 1947

Marguerite sat in the reception area, scratching her knees with her chewed fingernails. She had painted her toenails and it pleased her to gaze at the small beads of scarlet that looked fine through the open-toed canvas sandals for which she had paid three francs at the Cannes market two days earlier. Her hair was curled and looked quite fancy, her face perfectly made up, lips red and bow-shaped, eyes ringed with kohl. Her chemise was cut low; it hugged her skinny frame, exposing the outline of her rosebud breasts. On the afternoon they had made love, Charlie had told her that her breasts were like 'rosebuds'. May roses, the most perfect of all blossoms. She liked that. She mustn't think about Charlie and his leaving, not now.

She had arrived at the studios early in an optimistic frame of mind, determined that Katsidis would test her, but when she gave her name at Reception she was informed that he wasn't available. She glanced at the clock on the wall. It was now the best part of an hour since she'd arrived. The uncertainty was unnerving her, and she had a hunch that the receptionist, who was either plugging in calls to executives or filing her nails, was rather enjoying watching her twist and squirm as each minute passed.

'He is coming, isn't he?'

'He's watching rushes from a screen test. He'll be here and I'm sure he'll see you.'

Rushes from a screen test! Another girl for the same role? Marguerite pulled out her compact and dabbed powder on her nose. She must keep calm, cool. She was a woman now; he'd spot the difference.

'Help yourself to one of the magazines on the coffee-table. There's an interview with Elizabeth Taylor in that one. Yes, that one there.'

The door swung open. Katsidis thrust his head round it and looked directly at Marguerite, who had just picked up the magazine. 'Come on in, what are you waiting for?'

She rose tremulously, dropped the magazine back onto the coffee-table and walked towards him, head held high to counter her trembling.

'Shut the door behind you,' he snapped, as she inched inside the office. This was a different room from her last visit. This one had a sofa, comfortable armchairs and a table but no desk.

He was scratching at his skull, his back to her, rotating his shoulder as though he had been vigorously exercising. He turned in one move to look at her. She had shut the door and stood waiting for further instructions. Katsidis was appraising her, eyes all over her, like a man about to buy cattle. 'Turn around,' he said.

Marguerite obeyed him, spinning in a semi-circle.

'And back again. That blouse suits you. Cherry red. Good choice, striking colour, hugs your figure.' He pointed to the sofa. 'Make yourself comfortable.' She felt her body tighten and a cold sweat crawled over her. Her hands were clammy. She dithered, preferring one of the chairs.

'Sit down, I said. Do you have the script? Do you know the scene? The new one I gave you last time?' She nodded. 'You learned it word for word?' Again she nodded. 'Lost your voice?'

He sat next to her, swinging himself into the space, stretching his arms the length of the sofa's back, while she pressed herself up against the armrest.

'What did you do yesterday?' he asked, watching her. Eyes glistening, beady, excavating for some hidden trigger within her.

'I . . . we . . . I went to the country.'

'*We?* You have a boyfriend?' He was smiling now, smirking almost, as though the very idea was derisory.

'Yes, I do actually,' she returned, head up, chin out. 'He's very nice. A real gentleman.'

'A gentleman, huh?' Katsidis rocked back his head and laughed loudly. 'And what does your gentleman say about all this?'

'All what?'

'You, his sweetheart, wanting to leave him and come to Hollywood and make pictures.'

Where was this leading? 'He wants what's best for me,' she lied, 'for me to fulfil my dreams.' She tossed back her blonde curls with a coquettish flick of her hand.

Katsidis guffawed, rambunctiously, irreverently, his perfect teeth exposed. 'Bullshit. What man wants to know that a line of directors and producers are going to ball his bird?'

Marguerite was dumbstruck. On the losing end again. And she had been determined to show her mettle. She took a deep breath and lifted her eyes, playing sweet, impish. 'Shall I read the scene for you, Mr Katsidis?'

He watched her. 'I thought you said you'd learned it.'
'I have.'

'Then you don't need the script. Come here.' He took her arm and dragged her towards him.

'Ouch.' She felt her skirt crinkle up beneath her, revealing her firm shiny thighs.

'Come on, come here. Don't be so coy.' He was leaning over her. Close range, his frame forward over hers, forcing her backwards, jammed into the corner. 'What did you and your handsome gentleman do yesterday in the country?'

She was fighting now, fighting for her dignity, struggling to break free of him. He was humiliating her. Hollywood big-shot making nothing of her. Her heart was thudding against her ribcage, her pulse galloping. She fully intended to win this round. She let out a cry, like a miniature roar, to signal to him that she refused this belittling of her. She wouldn't have it. 'I'm a woman. Stop treating me like a child,' she blurted out at him.

But he was not fazed. 'Think of what you and he did, kid, and start speaking the lines. Let me hear what you felt for your boy yesterday as you speak the lines. I want that hunger.'

She attempted again to wriggle free of him but his grip was iron fast, pinching into her. He wasn't letting go. He inched closer. 'Speak the lines, honey. Think of your beau. How old is he? Is he sexy? Does he excite you? Sure, he excites you. Let me have the lines.'

She hated him, this hairy man whose breath smelt of onions and cigars. With every fibre of her being she hated him. Still, she attempted the dialogue. A scene of longing, of lost love. Almost a soliloquy.

Katsidis lifted himself up, affording breathing distance between them. He cupped his two hands, fingers joined to make a square as though creating the lens of a camera. Through his fingers he peered at her. A hawk's shining gaze.

'Turn your eyes towards me,' he said softly. 'Speak that line again, yes, yes. Look at me, move towards me. I am the camera. Play to me. You've got great eyes, kid. Lilac eyes, how about that? Think of your sweetheart and how good he does it to you.'

Her back was drenched with sweat, her cherry cotton top gluing itself to her spine and tickling, prickling her. Her neck ached from holding her head upwards towards the man who was perched with one knee on the upholstery and the other leg outstretched on the floor. He dropped his created lens and began to speak the lines of the male in the scene. He was actor now, not director, as Julien had been in her first screen test here. She knew how this went. She began to relax. Just a little.

'Keep it soft,' he said, director again. 'That's great, kid.' She was encouraged. He was moving towards her, partially crawling along the sofa, nudging her shoulder backwards so that she found herself semi-supine and he looming above her. And then he was on top of her. She panicked, attempting to push him away. His limbs were made of steel. His hand was on her leg. Sliding towards her soft inner thigh. 'You like this?'

'No – stop. Please, stop.' She wanted this role. Were they acting? Was this how he intended to shoot the script?

He was bullying in tone, yet soft, coaxing. Willing her

onwards. 'Come on, kid, let go, don't be tight. Show me what you can do.'

What did he expect of her? 'Stop now,' she begged. 'I want to stop!'

This man was so much uglier than Charlie. She remembered the noises, the groans Charlie had made, and she was revolted at the thought that Katsidis, who was now handling her with rough gestures, might do the same.

'Let me go,' she yelled, beating her fists against his shoulders.

'Now that's passion,' panted Katsidis. 'Good girl.'

'Get off me!' she shrieked. He slammed a hand over her mouth. Her eyes watering, wide with panic, were focused on his watch, second-hand moving, pressing into her cheek. Her lipstick had smudged and was now smeared across his thumb.

'Open your legs.'

''Et go. 'Et go.' Words swallowed, contorted. She wriggled, resisted, drilled a fist against his collarbone, attempted to bite the palm of his hand, horrid, salty, gristly flesh, while his knee kicked and bullied her left leg. He was prising her legs apart. 'Keep saying the lines.'

She couldn't speak, couldn't open her mouth; she thought she might choke. He was tearing off her pants, dragging them expertly downwards, thrusting her legs wide open. She was pinioned as he propelled himself inside her. She raged against him, convulsing, mute, distorted screams. He was groaning, humping her. Now she was fighting the impulse to throw up. Waves of nausea rose to her throat. She was attempting to pull herself free, writhing and twisting, like a trapped catch. Her back was being hammered against the arm of the sofa. The spinal pain shot through the base of her neck to her head. Back and forth against the velveteen arm of the sofa. She thought he would split her apart. And then it was over. Mercifully swift. And he was standing and buttoning his pressed slacks. 'You did good, kid. Now get outta here.'

She couldn't move.

'Come on, kid.' He threw her knickers at her, which she stuffed shamefacedly into her pocket. She hauled herself up, head spinning, dazed, bruised, adjusting her creased clothes. He strode to the door, waiting, shuffling his brogue shoes impatiently.

She paused an instant. As he turned the door handle, she opened her mouth to speak.

'Come on, kid. I got things to do. I'll talk it over with the producers. You'll hear from us.'

And with that she was out in the hot sun.

That evening at Le Rêve, Marguerite excused herself from the communal supper downstairs, an evening ritual with all the occupants of the house, insisted upon by Lady Jeffries. Begging a headache, she remained alone, upstairs, door locked, walling herself into her room.

After dinner, Charlie came knocking. She was surprised. He had never been near her within the boundaries of the house before. 'Open up.' He tapped lightly.

She was lying on her bed, knees to her chest.

'Marguerite.'

She eased herself off the bed, bruised, and turned the key, releasing the door a few inches.

'Hello.' He smiled broadly. 'May I come in?'

'What do you want?' She was reluctant to offer him access to her secret, her private humiliation. Would he be repelled if he knew the debasement she had suffered?

'Can I . . . May I come in, please?'

Cautiously, gingerly, she drew back the door, clutching tight to the handle as he passed on ahead of her into the room, brushing lightly against her.

The air hung heavy with scent. It smelt like Marguerite. Of sweet irises, like her big blossom eyes. There was a radio playing softly in the background, dance music. The attic room was surprisingly untidy. A small dressing-table standing alongside the French windows was cluttered with tubes, flacons of make-up, a little bottle of *L'Heure Bleue* eau de parfum and a white lace handkerchief streaked with lipstick, or was it blood? So busy was he clocking her surroundings that he didn't notice her puffy eyes or that she had been crying. There was a photograph of a young man, unframed, lying face upwards on her pillow. It was ragged as though it had been travelling a while. Charlie, compelled to examine it, crossed the stone floor and gathered it up. The man, boy, was sixteen or seventeen in scruffy country clothes and working boots, with laces loosely fastened. His hair was blond, like Marguerite's, coarsely cut. Was this her brother? Did the face, the features resemble Marguerite's? Or might it be a beau who meant something special to her? Charlie flipped it over to see whether any words had been written there. The reverse side was blank. How many years of her short life he had not known her. It mattered to him, with a deep-seated sense of alarm, to confirm that it was her brother.

'What's his name?' he demanded, then cursed himself for sounding more possessive than he'd intended.

Marguerite had popped her head out of the door to be sure that none of the other staff had seen Charlie entering her room. They would tittle-tattle about her, judge her loose. The other girls, the two plump kitchen maids and the horrid cork-nosed cook, all three of them, yammering. On Sunday mornings, they always walked side by side, three abreast in their best starched clothes, to Mass, huddled tight, humming hymns or fervently gossiping. When she and Charlie had first arrived, they had invited her along with them to the first few holy days, to make the priest's acquaintance, but she had declined the invitation and soon they stopped including her. She closed the door quietly and swung about to catch Charlie holding her brother's photograph. 'Give me that,' she snapped as she hurried to snatch it from him.

'Sorry. I should've let it be. How did you get on today?'

'What do you want?' she demanded, switching off the wireless and then, as an afterthought, turning the knob back on again because the music might serve to drown their voices should any mischief-maker be eavesdropping.

'To be with you, spend a little while together, talking, cuddling.' He bridged the inches that separated them and stroked her hair with the palm of his left hand. It was damp. After her return from the studios, from her hateful encounter with Katsidis, she had scrubbed herself thoroughly, head to toe, shampooed her hair, soaped her private parts, anointed herself extravagantly with her prized perfume.

'You washed your hair. It smells nice,' he purred. Both hands now were caressing her head.

She shrugged him off. 'Stop it, Charlie. I don't want you to touch me.'

He was hurt, startled. Hadn't they recently made love? Hadn't she given herself to him willingly? Why was she always so changeable?

'You'll make the curls drop,' she added, more softly.

Hadn't she given him her most precious gift? He recalled the words of his first love, Doris Sprigley, crooned so sweetly in his ears as they had moved together in rhythmic motion beneath his family's apple trees: *My gift to you, Lordy.*

Marguerite had given him the same. With less enthusiasm, no doubt, but her precious self nonetheless, and he would stand by her. He was not going away. He would honour and love her. He would not let her down as he had dear Doris. He loved Marguerite in spite of her stick-like frame and her all-consuming ambition. Those eyes, so agitated, perturbed. He had fallen in love with those lavender eyes, and he wanted to care for her, protect her. To give her a decent life. He could make money from the flower business, he felt sure of it. He would settle here, try to blot out England and the past, make a life on the hills with this crazy young girl.

Marguerite had bowed her head. Without looking up at him, she slowly placed the precious photograph on the dressing-table. 'It's my brother,' she whispered hoarsely. 'The one who went to war and never came back. Broke my mother's heart. I was just sitting here looking at it, remembering him, wishing I could talk to him again.'

Charlie felt the fish hook catch him in the stomach. Imagining his own mother's broken heart. Doris's broken heart . . . 'I won't disappear on you,' he mumbled, attempting to take her, the small, wan, determined creature who possessed such contradictory passions and opinions, in his arms. How could such a minuscule frame encompass such complexity? She shrugged him off and lifted her face. He frowned. She was crying, great barking sobs, like a seal. He was at a loss to understand her. 'I hope you don't regret . . .' he stammered.

She shook her head but her expression was bleak. 'No,' she said. 'But I don't want it to happen again and I would prefer it if you don't come knocking at my door again, expecting something.'

'No,' he retaliated. 'I don't expect . . . anything. I thought we could sit together, get to know one another . . . Enjoy some free time in one another's company just like we've been doing. Growing closer.'

'Charlie, I'm going to America. I've got plans. K-Katsidis has said . . . says . . . he's – he's taking me. He has to now. *He has to choose me.*'

'Of course he will . . .'

'So you mustn't go getting any fancy ideas about us. What you and I did was . . .' She sighed, a long weary exhalation. *Would* Katsidis take her to Hollywood? Hadn't she proved to him and the producers that she was a woman, that she could convey passion? Even if he had left her feeling grubby and sluttish and shameful. She was so confused, and worn out by the questions circling her beaten brain.

'Was what?'

She gave it consideration. 'An experiment.'

He couldn't believe his ears. 'An experiment? Don't

you care for me? I love you, you surely know that. See how we look out for each other. You said it was paradise up there in the hills –'

'But I don't love you, Charlie.'

He let out a foghorn moan.

'I mean, I do love you, of course I love you, Charlie. I love you as much as I could love anybody. You've been the best thing that's happened to me and you do look out for me like no one ever has, but I've got plans and they don't include you.' She saw the agony twist his face, embedding itself in his grey-green eyes. 'I'm sorry, but that's how it is.' She hated herself for hurting him like this because she did genuinely care for him but better to be blunt now than later when matters had gone too far. 'Charlie, what we did the other afternoon was . . .' *A world away from what happened to me today* was the phrase that sprang immediately to mind.

'An experiment,' he repeated. He swung his arms impotently. They crossed over one another like a giant pair of scissors.

'Well, no, that wasn't what I meant to say.' She wanted him to go, leave her room. Her sacred space where she might unravel the bedlam in her head. This physical business was too complicated to engage in. 'I meant that it was a thank-you, my thank-you to you for being so . . . so . . .' She was treading cautiously, floundering.

'What?'

'Like my wonderful brother . . .'

'Brother?' He released a hollow laugh. Tears sprang into his eyes.

'Charlie, don't say it like that, as though I was insulting

you. I loved Bertrand more than anyone else in the world. It's a compliment.'

'I see.' He made no move to leave, though her gestures, her fidgety manner, picking up a lipstick, a brush from the dressing-table, running her fingers agitatedly through its bristles, tossing it down again, suggested that she wanted him gone. He wanted to be angry with her, to make her realize that he was offering her a good life. He would work hard for them, build a business from the land. He had plans. They could have children. He loved children. He missed family life. He missed the security of sharing with others around him. He wanted to grab that back, but it had to be here in France. Never again England, however much he mourned the Kent countryside. And he wanted all this to be with Marguerite. The scrawny, unsophisticated girl who had crept inside him, begging for shelter, and driven him mad with longing. Did he want her so much because she was so disregarding of him? No. He didn't want to be her brother. He wanted to be her sidekick, her husband, and he wanted her to want him and yearn for him with the same hunger, the craving that kept him tossing and turning at night. She inhabited his dreams and taunted his insomnia.

'We don't really know each other. We're just travelling together, looking out for one another for a while along the road.'

'Jesus, you sound like you're speaking from a script . . . One of your bloody films. Marguerite . . .'

'Leave me alone, and don't come knocking here again,' she hissed, not daring to raise her voice for fear the nosy

God-fearing trio in the adjoining rooms might be listening, ears to the wall. 'I want you to go now, please.'

'Marguerite . . .'

'It's time to go our separate ways, Charlie.'

He leaned backwards against the door, speechless, then attempted to cajole her, wrap his arms about her, but she pushed him off and did not lift her eyes to him again. 'We both knew that this time would come. You are moving on. So don't be sad, Charlie.' She crossed to the radio and turned the music up two notches. Benny Goodman. It drowned the sound of the closing door.

She took a deep breath. Her heart felt as though it was splintering. She needed to do her exercises, keep fit, stand on her head so that the blood flowed through her and took good care of her flawless complexion. She needed to cream her skin, go over her scene again for the hundred and fiftieth time, ready for the producers' call, because they would call soon, wouldn't they? Yes, they would. So she must get some beauty sleep. No tears. She had read in a magazine that all the most glamorous film stars are in bed before ten. They didn't cry themselves to sleep, didn't break their dopey, soppy hearts over saying goodbye to a really special friend when it was necessary. They didn't go falling in love with that friend. No, they made the decision that was best for both of them. Just as she was doing.

Early morning, Paris, 14 November 2015

Kurtiz listened in stupefied silence. Marguerite had survived, made a good long life for herself, but how had
Lizzie fared in a world that had grown cruel and murder-
ous? Kurtiz had been so fortunate with Oliver. The young
Oliver. Oliver who was now somewhere in this city fighting for his life. She got up, shook her legs, pressed a palm
into the base of her spine and crossed to the telephone.

'Might we call that emergency number again? They
may have found him and be just too busy to let us know.'

Might Lizzie be with Oliver, sitting at his bedside?

She was punching out the digits. It was engaged. Half
of Paris must be trying to get through. How many lives,
like hers, were hanging by threads tonight in this city?
She replaced the receiver with a sigh.

She wanted to come clean, confide in Marguerite, confess that she had lost her daughter: Lizzie had run from
them while she herself had been absent. But she wasn't able
to form the words. To own up to the fact that she hadn't
been there for her daughter. She had let Lizzie down.

'I had driven Charlie away, while my girlishly naive
dreams of Hollywood had been nipped in the bud, trampled upon. The next time I set eyes on Katsidis was at the

Cannes Film Festival. I was in the crowd watching, jostled and pushed. I had travelled across on the train from Antibes. He was stepping out of a gleaming black car, in attendance for a screening of his film, *Rebound*, and was surrounded by personnel, security in uniform, journalists, pressed in by admirers. An actress was on his arm. Jane Wyatt, I guess it must have been, but I didn't recognize her. She looked different in real life, not so tall, less striking. Or, perhaps, my jealousy was the judge.

'My heart ached so, I thought it would explode. I wanted to be that actress, there among the paparazzi, lapping up the attention, and yet the sight of that man, that hateful individual, tore my emotions to shreds.

'As he stepped close by me, I hollered out his name above the din of voices, above the excitement, still naively believing that once he set eyes on me again he would remember that I was the girl for his part, that he owed this to me. He heard his name, swung in my direction. Our eyes locked – he saw me, he recognized me, I have no doubt about that. He never said a word. He ignored me. Cut me dead. I wanted the ground to swallow me. I couldn't push my way fast enough through that throng of people. Humiliation burned like fire against my skin.

'Needless to say, I wasn't offered the role. Only a child as inexperienced and foolish as I was back then could have believed he was ever going to give it to me. I carried the shame of that encounter with him at the studios for years. And, what is worse, I blamed myself. His transgression, his rape, and I blamed myself. I renounced all dreams of becoming an actress, or perhaps it would be more accurate to say that I put them aside.'

Kurtiz, London, December 2012

The carriage where Kurtiz was seated on the Northern
Line rattling south towards Leicester Square was
empty, save for a cluster of youths shouting among
themselves, singing, squabbling drunkenly. Christmas
high spirits. She was staring at her reflection in the window opposite. It was late, very late. She should have
been in bed. Instead she was making her way back into
the city, having only a couple of hours earlier ridden this
same line north to Tufnell Park. Now, to check into a
hotel in Covent Garden. A booking she'd made online
an hour earlier. Her camera equipment and an overnight
bag were at her side. This week, when her workload
calmed, she'd search for an apartment, a studio, a solitary base. She had an early start ahead of her tomorrow.
This was the last plan she might have envisaged for the
finale to her day. Until a phone call from a journalist late
in the afternoon had driven up her guard.

'Mrs Ross?'

'Yes?'

'*Daily Express* here.'

Her heart skipped a beat. 'What is it?' Was there news
of Lizzie? Every time her phone rang, a number she
didn't recognize, a crawling dread rose within her.

'Does the name Jenny Fox mean anything to you?'

Pause.

'Is she a friend of yours and your husband's?'

Kurtiz was puzzled, and for a moment she could not place the name. Angela's mother. Lizzie's friend's mother. 'What about her?'

'Any idea when your husband last saw her?'

She listened to the shifting rhythm of her breath, the pumping of her heart. 'What's this about, please?'

'We were wondering whether you would be willing to comment on your husband's relationship with Mrs Fox.'

'I don't know what you're talking about.'

It was close to eight when she'd returned to Tufnell Park, shouldering her way past a small cluster of reporters congregating by the gate. Not again. She and Oliver had suffered sufficiently from their intrusions. 'Mrs Ross! Mrs Ross!'

She turned her key in the lock, ignoring the yelled questions from the press, and found Oliver collapsed in a chair covered with blood. Her heart lurched. The fear that sprang to mind was that he had attempted suicide. Was this related to the call she had received? To the scandalmongers outside?

'Oliver! Oliver!'

Oliver had cut his hand. An accident caused by an unsteady grasp and a sharp kitchen knife. She cleaned and bandaged him up. Then, over strong cups of tea, she asked him about the telephone call.

In return she had received abuse. And blame, and excuses. 'None of it would have happened if you had been here. None of it.'

So it was true.

'Was that why Lizzie and Angela stopped seeing one another?'

The house phone began to ring. 'Hello?'

'Mrs Ross? Toby Packham here, *Daily Mail*.'

Without a word, she replaced the receiver.

'Did Lizzie know, Oliver? Did she find out?'

'And what about you? Where were you when I tried to contact you? Not just once. Days off the radar.'

The evening had threatened to spiral into a full-blown slanging match, leading nowhere, solving nothing, until she had decided to pack a bag and go.

'Leaving me, abandoning me, deserting the sinking ship.' He had flung the lot at her as she tossed some clean clothes into a holdall. She knew he'd be useless on his own, but one of them had to keep their head above water, and she couldn't manage it with Oliver in this state at her side. Should she make contact with the Foxes?

'It's over, KZ. It was a brief . . . It was nothing. She was company. If you'd been here . . .'

'Did Lizzie find out?'

He shook his head, hands clasped in his lap. Head bowed.

'Did she?'

'I don't know. She needed you, Kurtiz. We both did.'

Oliver refusing help, refusing to accept his alcohol dependency, refusing to shoulder any of the responsibility.

It was snowing in Leicester Square. The place was littered with fast-food debris. It stank of overcooked hot dogs. In the doorways lay bodies, hunched against the diminishing temperatures. Someone begged a fag. She handed him a fiver. He focused on it as though she'd given him the moon. 'Merry Christmas, you're a doll.'

A few light flakes fell on her face and she let them melt against her tears. She longed for Alex, but she would not make contact with him. She didn't even know where in the world he was. Like Lizzie, out of reach. She took a step towards Covent Garden. Somehow she had to see this through on her own. Christmas was coming. The second without Lizzie. She couldn't stomach the prospect.

She'd care for Oliver. She wouldn't abandon him. Attempt to balm his wounds? Of course she would. But from a distance. She was better off alone.

Marguerite and Charlie, Late September 1947, La Côte d'Azur

Hoping not to bump into anyone who might recognize her, Marguerite hastened through Lady Jeffries' lush gardens. Cutting along the winding paths, catching the whisper of watering pipes, she passed through the rusted iron gate that led down to the cove and scrambled to the rocky coastal footway growing wild with tall Mediterranean tussock grass, sedge and sea oats. Overhead, a clear sheet of satin sky. Blue, cloudless and shining. Beneath, the deserted horseshoe beach enclosed by great boulders of limestone through which pushed shoots of vigorous rock flowers.

Recalling hours of clowning on this beach with Charlie, she watched the sandpipers and shearwaters feeding daintily at the water's foamy edge as she picked her solitary way along the narrow, winding track to the market in Antibes. Her work for the day had been completed and the afternoon stretched before her to do with as she pleased. It was the end of September. The light was softer; the shadows slid along the pavements and mingled with the early fallen leaves. The summer tourists had departed; the film festival was over and Riviera life was settling to a contented lull before the winter influx of foreigners descended. For the *agriculteurs*, their wine harvests had been brought in; now there were the olive groves to tend. Back at Le Rêve, Lady Jeffries was in the final preparations for a grand tour of the United States: a series of lectures on social reforms in post-war Europe, which would take her through all the major cities from east to west. Her engagements would keep her away until the following spring. She had suggested that Marguerite might like to accompany her as assistant. Marguerite had understood what an opportunity this could be and weeks earlier she would have jumped at it – to set foot on American soil, to take a train all across that vast and magical land to Hollywood and try her luck there – but her trust and optimism had been trampled on. Her self-esteem was in rags. When she recalled Katsidis' expensive brown leather brogues crossing to the door to show her out, she felt herself under them.

She had stopped visiting the Victorine Studios: she was too ashamed to show her face there, fearful that the permanent crews and in-house staff would have heard about the incident between the foolish 'whippersnapper' and the Hollywood director. Surely the telephonist beyond the door had heard the commotion and seen the state of her clothes when she had left.

But the hardest fact for Marguerite to come to terms with was that Charlie had followed through on his promise. He had quit his post at Le Rêve and set off in search of his new goals somewhere in Grasse. She had no address for him. From the day he had taken off, he'd made no further contact. She had watched him go. Lady Jeffries, the gardeners and kitchen staff had waved him off from the steps but she had stayed in the hall, stomach bunched. As he had descended the stairs with his few belongings on his back, he had paused. For a brief moment their eyes had locked. Then, dreading tears or any expression of vulnerability, she had stepped away and he had continued on outside.

As far as Marguerite was aware he had purchased his four precious hectares and would soon begin the construction of his small stone house. She wondered which hillside he had settled on. The truth of the matter was she had lost him, destroyed their friendship, broken it off. She had heard not a squeak from him since the rupture.

Why had she sent him away? She was ashamed: her body was debased, unclean; no one could love her now, and she was incapable of giving herself to anyone.

Since that day, Marguerite had spent all her free hours in her room and had barely noticed the change in the seasons: the browning of the purple bougainvillaea petals, the swelling fruits, the lessening of the searing heat. Aside from her time committed to secretarial work for Lady Jeffries, she did nothing. Her energies and enthusiasms had been crushed. Her drive and confidence rusting away inside her. Her nineteenth birthday came and went and she had mentioned it to no one. Even her mother had not sent good wishes because she had no idea where her daughter was. Marguerite's thoughts turned to her parents' modest country home outside Reims, with its permanent smells of yeast and baking bread, her own little room where she had learned to read and write and had passed innocent hours drawing. Craving the shelter of their uncritical affection, she had settled to a letter.

Dearest Maman,

Forgive my silence. I have been furiously busy working as an actress. I am in films, the cinema, which is why you have not heard from me in a while, and I am sincerely sorry for not sending you my address. I had only intended to stay at this house for a short time but the months have rolled on . . . I think of our Bertrand every day and keep his picture by my bed and I wonder has there been any news of him? I still pray for a miracle, that he might one day arrive at your door. I have been thinking of you too, Maman, frequently, and if film commitments allow me, I would dearly like to come home for a visit. I could try to be there for Christmas, and then . . .

And then?

The reality was, where else was she to go? What had taken place between her and Katsidis tormented her, inhabited her nightmares. She blamed herself. The worst of it was there was no friend to whom she could unburden her locked heart, no one to offer her a kindly ear and help her wash away her shame. She had let him go.

She was in Antibes to post her letter to her mother – the first she had written in too long – but she had eaten no breakfast and was feeling woozy from lack of nourishment and the expenditure of energy along the pathway, so she paused to buy herself a few candied fruits. She hovered, like a wasp near a honey pot, over a market stall decked with bright, sticky glacé fruits: golden gooey apricots, pear quarters the colour of ripening moons and, her favourite, dark treacly orange peel.

Alongside these were stacked slabs of nougat. Thick chewy wedges, solid as bricks. She ought to hurry and make her choice: she hadn't reached the post office yet and it would soon be closing for lunch. She was clutching an aluminium two-franc piece in her fist.

'*Bonjour, Mademoiselle.* Are you desiring a slice of *pan nogat*?'

Marguerite liked that the stallholder, in his brown canvas apron wrapped over an extended belly, had called the confection by its Occitan or Provençal name. She dithered. 'Perhaps.' Fifty *centimes* worth of white nougat, flecked with almond slices. It was tempting, but if she bought a cut she would only be able to swallow a mouthful or two. Then it would go to waste, jettisoned on her bedside table, softening slowly, expanding its shape like a runny cheese, encouraging armies of big black ants to come picking. She ate so little – never meals, only sweets – and she had grown thinner; her perfect skin was dotted with pimples. An expiring stick insect, was how Lady Jeffries described her.

A hand touched her shoulder blade; she jumped and swung round. It was Charlie.

'Charlie! Oh, Charlie, Charlie, what a surprise!' The sweets were forgotten as she rose on tiptoe and threw her arms around his neck. The burden of isolation evaporated in the autumn sunshine.

'I've scoured the market looking for you.' For a brief moment neither let go. His warmth beat against her until she edged herself backwards and they stood in front of one another in silence.

'You got a minute?'

She nodded.

'Come with me.' He led her by the hand. 'I've a surprise to show you.' They were negotiating a path through baskets and shoppers. 'There! Take a look!'

Charlie had bought himself a vehicle, a U23 truck. 'All these trucks were converted for civil and agricultural purposes after France surrendered in June 1940.' He was proud as Punch. 'Fancy, eh?' He waited for her approval as she toured its bodywork, squealing oohs and aahs, all the while hiding her sheer delight at the sight of him. 'It's just a hand-me-down, mind. Three previous owners.' He scratched at his hair, clearly overjoyed that she was impressed. 'But it's in good working order and it'll do me proud.' He had repainted its army colours to render it the same dark green hue as Lady Jeffries' far more exclusive Riley. 'I can take you for a spin, if you wouldn't be ashamed to be seen in this old bus with me.'

'How could I be ashamed to be seen with you, Charlie?'

His spirits rose. Had she missed him, as he had craved for her? 'It'll suit me down to the ground for the harvests.'

She swung back to face him. They almost collided. 'What brings you down here to the coast?' Swiftly, she turned her attention back to the car's bodywork, fearing news of a woman.

'I drove down to pick up a couple of spare parts for this fine girl and dropped in to say hello at Lady J's.' He coughed. 'She suggested I might find you here. But perhaps you have plenty to do. Is your film director friend still about? What's the latest on the role?' He fired off questions, following her as she examined his truck, almost stepping on her beach-sandy heels, unable to curb his jabbering, so elated was he to be in her company again – how he had pined for her, agonized over her absence, but how desperate she was looking. Bones all spiky, thin as a broomstick and tiny as the apple sawflies his father had cursed. Lady Jeffries had described her physical condition perfectly, without exaggeration, in her letter to Charlie. The letter that, in truth, had brought him there in search of her. Lady Jeffries had written:

Since you left, dear Charlie, she seems to have sunk into a decline. Can I prevail on you to come and pay her a visit? She certainly needs cheering up. I have failed to get through to her and she has given me no family of hers to contact . . . and now with my departure imminent, I am growing concerned for her future welfare . . .

'Katsidis? Oh, he sailed last week after the festival ceremonies. He'll be in touch when he reaches California,' Marguerite bluffed, but the lie twisted in her under-nourished gut and stopped her.

They had come to a standstill by the passenger door. Marguerite curled her fingers slowly round the chrome handle, feeling the sun's warmth on the shiny metal; she was holding on for dear life. Charlie's reappearance was a blessing, but she knew she must keep her distance. The depth to which her guilt and humiliation had dragged her was a burden she must carry alone.

'I saw his photograph in the newspaper. The actress

he was with, she looked a lot like you. No wonder he's taken with you.' Charlie grinned. He was trying to be encouraging. He could see for himself that she was broken-hearted and beyond disappointed. Those big jittery eyes were staring out at the world around her with distrust, as though someone had just fired a shot. Charlie could only hazard a guess at what was eating at her, making her so blue. He put it down to the loss of the film part.

They sat outside the Café Felix, set back from the quays of the old port, which they could glimpse through an arched passageway built into the ramparts. Rows of boats moored in the harbour basin were bobbing and spinning like a raft of young ducks. They ate ice cream, licking and slurping, the first solid food she'd swallowed all day. The plane trees were losing their leaves. They drifted and circled to the cobblestones at their feet. Marguerite threw surreptitious glances at Charlie as he licked his ice and looked about him. He always seemed restless in crowds. But he was so robust, so fit. His soft sandy complexion had been baked to a dark biscuit tone. His freckles were more pronounced, like tossed handfuls of brown sugar granules, and he was stronger, more muscular than she remembered him. His teeth were whiter against his sunburned face and his smile easy and radiant. The coast, his new life, had blessed him while she had faded, grown emaciated, mortified. Her skin was a lacklustre beige and she had given up on her exercises and nail varnishes. Even her shoulder-length hair hung drably, a little greasy.

It hurt Charlie to observe the changes a few weeks had wrought in her. He would cosset her, cherish and shield her, if she would only give him the opportunity. 'I want you to come and see my plot,' he said, rising to his feet, kicking at a hitch in the leg of his dungarees.

'Next week, maybe.' She shrugged.

'Now.' He offered his hand.

She hesitated.

'Come on, let's go. We don't want to be traipsing about the fields in the dark.'

Marguerite ditched the remains of her melting ice cream on the table, licked her fingers and rubbed at her skirt, worrying at the creases so she didn't have to accept his hand. She stroked her face, fingers cold from the ice, feeling dampness from the perspiration worked up on her earlier walk. She had forgotten to post her letter, which lay nestled in her bag.

The truck was an impressive contraption and made her laugh with its big yellow headlights and its two rear-view mirrors extending from its body on curved silver stalks. 'You are quite the part now, Charlie, in your blue overalls. A true Provençal farmer,' she teased, and he was uplifted to see even a glimpse of light-heartedness cross her features.

'Let's go.'

The engine sputtered into life, and they chugged their way inland, a zigzagging ascent, rolling along the lanes, mountain paths and passes towards the perfume city of Grasse, then downhill again for four or five kilometres to the flat, sweet-scented plains of Plascassier. It was a perfect end-of-summer afternoon. Wind whistled in through the open windows and messed up her hair, but she didn't care. What did it matter? The vineyards were empty of fruit and their leaves were crisping, turning russet. Few were working in the fields. Those who were there transported voluminous bundles, armfuls of green or red netting to lay at the feet of their centuries-old olive trees. Grey and brown donkeys stood in the shade, bales of netting stacked across their backs. Occasionally, Charlie put his hand out of the window and pressed his fingers against the black rubber horn, as large as a plump ripe pear, and sounded its gravelled hoot. Toot-toot. Toot-toot. The farmers in their black berets lifted their curved backs, shoved away their damp hair to get a better look at who was making such a racket, then recognized the young Englishman, chortled and waved.

'You know them all,' she commented, envious of his kinship with the community. She knew not a soul outside Le Rêve.

'We lend each other a hand, taking it in turns to bring in the fruit. The flowers will be another matter. Next year, when mine are planted up and begin to blossom, I'll hire a team, a small one to begin with, of course. Possibly from Italy.'

She frowned. 'Why from Italy?'

'They're experienced pickers and their labour costs are reasonable. It's a seasonal occupation for them and they've been coming here for generations. Some of the men were posted to this Alpes-Maritimes region during the war, until Italy surrendered, of course. They were here on behalf of the Germans to superintend Nice and its hinterland after they won the Battle of the Alps. This was a free zone, you see. The Italians were never vigorous in rounding up Jews, even when ordered to do so. Life down here under their jurisdiction was reasonably easy-going. Many of the region's agriculturalists, local farmers, count them as neighbours, fellow land workers like any other. They trust the Italians and the Italians know this work intimately. They come in trucks, travelling across the passes. It can be a dangerous journey.'

She marvelled at how intimate he had grown, and so swiftly, with the history and the nature surrounding him.

They passed through a village, more a hamlet. Marguerite didn't know its name, hadn't seen the sign – it had come and gone so quickly. Close by the church, men and women were playing *pétanque* beneath the shade of several fig trees heavy with dark, oozing fruit. Again Charlie toot-tooted and the small gathering of villagers raised their shirted arms, lifted their straw hats and yelled his name effusively. He was clearly popular.

'You've found a home for yourself here,' she remarked, turning aside from the scent of the *figuiers*, which she found a little oppressive; bitter, like the *pipi* of a tomcat.

'Lady J is leaving, I hear? Off to America.'

'How did you know?'

Charlie was anxious that Marguerite shouldn't discover that the Englishwoman had written to him, confiding her disquiet regarding Marguerite's wellbeing. 'Er, she told me when I popped in to say hello.'

Marguerite dropped her gaze to her lap.

'She asked you to go with her?'

Marguerite nodded, head still lowered. 'But I shan't

go.' The departure of her soon-to-be-ex-employer reminded her of the letter in her bag.

'Why not? I thought America was your goal.'

'I have to think about my career, Charlie,' she bragged emptily, in pain to confess the truth, to open up her heart to someone, someone dear to her who might show comfort and listen. 'If we pass a postbox, please stop.'

'It'll have to be on the return journey. We're here now.' He slowed the Citroën to a standstill beside a long stone wall bordering a field, and pulled hard on the handbrake, then switched off the engine. They were in the countryside, the middle of nowhere. Marguerite glanced beyond the window as she rolled the glass up.

'No need to bother locking anything. Let this clean fresh air stream through, let the perfumes in. No one will pinch this old jalopy.' Charlie laughed broadly, opening his door and swinging himself out, hitting the dusty lane with a thud. Birds swooped and dived. A chorus of song.

'The swallows are gathering. They'll be heading south to Africa soon. Summer's closing.'

The idea seemed to please him as he strode in his sturdy boots, stretching his long limbs after all the double-declutching gear work. Marguerite remained in her seat, watching him. He would never have found this spot if he hadn't bought me a train ticket, she thought wistfully. It had worked out for him but not for her. Had she done something wrong? Had she behaved in an inappropriate manner with Katsidis, flirting with him, egging him on without even knowing it? She closed her eyes. A tear threatened. She shoved the door hard with her shoulder and jumped out. Brown grit rose up from the road and settled in the open toes of her sandals.

Charlie vaulted over the wall and held out his arms to encourage Marguerite to do the same. 'The opening for the gate is another kilometre further west. If you prefer, we can drive there?' She shook her head and he leaned forward, swept her up over the stones and spun her with a whoosh. She weighed little more than a rag doll. As he did so, their faces brushed, almost touching, and he hesitated, holding on to her, longing to kiss her, but she broke the moment by turning away from him and he lowered her tenderly to earth.

He pointed, drawing her attention towards the sloping hillside, the valley beneath it and the rising hill opposite. 'This soil is rich. A great basin of fertility,' he boasted.

It was transformed: no longer a chaotic arrangement of wild flowers and green shrubbery. He had begun to stake out terraces, to create natural rectangular lengths of garden. Most of it was bare earth, reddish brown, but in some beds further over he had planted the first of the rose crops, and had staked and wired them. Row upon row of bright green shoots.

Marguerite was astonished. 'You've worked so hard. It's magnificent.'

'I want to have all the roses bedded before the end of October. They need to be well installed before the weather changes and any frosts take hold.'

'Have you done all this alone?' Pride and affection soared within her. A trio of seagulls were squawking overhead, agitating the graceful swallows, squabbling over invisible boundaries. In spite of the bickering sea birds, the atmosphere was peaceful, restorative. She sighed, releasing a long hiccup of breath, letting go, thawing the jagged shards of misery that had been building up in her for weeks.

'Where's your house going to be?' she asked him. The question came out strangled. Her throat was tight, so constricted she could barely speak.

'Come on, let's go. We'll drive there. You need different shoes. Can't walk from here in those.'

Moving along the country lanes, her body sliding back and forth alongside him with the roll of the old truck, whose springs creaked, she felt herself grow calmer, the knot within her easing. She felt less abandoned. Life seemed less complicated at this distance from the coast, and she envied Charlie the ability to fall into such a rhythm, such a lifestyle.

Climbing yet another boundary wall, they plunged and pitched down the steep slope – wood pigeons, blackbirds fluttering to flight in their wake – to a point where she could make out a rectangle of big stones. The foundations for Charlie's house.

'See how it's taking shape, growing up out of the ground, winging its way upwards like the birds, like a graceful Pegasus.' He was drawing with his fingers the imaginary structure of it, his vision. 'And over here, an open courtyard for dining during the summer months.' He had planted up a copse of almond trees to give shade and fresh creamy nuts for his breakfast. 'Let's go.' He sprinted on ahead of her, supple and springy.

As they descended, she slipped and slid, then fell lightly, diving and tumbling. Nothing was broken. No hurt done. She kicked off her sandals, hooking them through her fingers, carrying them, arms outstretched like an aeroplane, allowing her bare feet to be submerged within the tall grasses, which on close view delivered a treasure trove of small coloured flowers, wild orchids among them.

'I'll buy you a pair of espadrilles later. We'll stop in Grasse or one of the villages on the way back down and grab a late lunch.'

A cart laden with big blocks of limestone stood close by a stone *cabano* partially covered with ivy, an ancient construction with only a fraction of its roof remaining. 'It was used for sheep originally or a shepherd's overnight lodging when the winds were too harsh to sleep out beneath the stars.' She crept to the opening where a disintegrating wooden door hung loose. Charlie had swept it out and placed a mattress on the stone floor inside. A circle of semi-burned candles were lined up alongside it. A pile of books. She pictured him here, alone at night, reading by a flickering flame, open to the elements, listening to the owls and badgers and every other creature of the night.

She didn't know that he often dreamed of her and had called out her name.

Metres away, a series of wooden beams were stacked high, buried beneath, protected by, generous layers of straw. 'The beams of the house,' he said. 'I don't want the humidity to get into them . . .'

'See the view from here,' he cried, now way ahead of her. His voice rose like a shooting star towards the heavens. She paused, panting to catch her breath, not strong and fit like him, looking directly ahead of her across to the opposite hillside where they had first parked. The tract of land resembled a shallow cradle, but of epic proportions. It was not too deep, but from all directions it was protected. Paradisical. Some areas were naturally cushioned, buffered from the winds by old tree growth, while other aspects were wide open and would be heated by the sun. Sunk in the valley, the plants would grow silently, securely, safe from harm and ill weathers.

'It will be a business to harvest. Backbreaking with so much climbing. That was what helped me negotiate a fairer price, even though the earth is the finest in the region. Fecund and nutritious. Two donkeys will be my labourers and I'll buy a horse for some of the transportation, take some of the load off the Citroën. I'll stake the jasmine all across that section there, where the sun will hit the plants from mid-morning onwards till evening. If I can harvest twenty kilos of the jasmine blossoms a day, I'll be winning. That aside from the May roses. Obviously, I can't pick all that alone.' He was lost in his project, fabricating the future, his eyes dancing and calculating. 'But, hey, you know what's best of all?'

She shook her head. She had reached his side, out of breath.

'I've found a water source fed directly from the mountains. Clear, clean, trickling through from the snowmelt. I'll sink a well and invest in a pump. Once in place, it'll save me francs and backache.' He turned his attention to her. 'What do you think?'

'It's a bit of heaven on earth, Charlie.'

'Stay with me, Marguerite. Make this life with me.'

How could she? Even should her own delusional existence have been cast aside, how could she be with any man now? The proximity of any male after what she had suffered was an alarming, distressing prospect.

'No, Charlie, I can't.'

'I love you. *Je t'aime*, Marguerite.' Charlie moved close, attempting to envelop her, to wrap himself around her, but she broke away, rubbing at her eyes.

'Speck of dust. Excuse me. You've done wonders,' she said softly. 'I am pleased to have seen it. Can you drive me back now, please? I have to post my letter and I . . . I need . . .'

He took her hands in his, clasped them between his firm, broken-nailed fingers, the rough skin of his palms proof of his manual exertions. 'Don't refuse me.' He stepped closer to her and wrapped himself about her. She felt herself weaken within his bear-like embrace.

'Charlie, please understand. I've explained it to you before.' Mumbling into his chest, the denim of his overalls a blue expanse before her, blue as the sky. His body was warm and colossal. 'It's not that I don't love you. It's just that . . . that . . .' But her reasoning faded to nothing, dried up like crumbs in her mouth. Her forehead tipped and rested against him. How could she ever be worthy of a love as big as his? If he were ever to discover the truth . . .

'We'll talk more over the next few days. I'm determined to persuade you.'

He drove her to an adjacent village. There in the central square – the only square – Marguerite posted her letter to her mother and resolved that she would be on a train to the north as soon as she could honourably terminate her arrangement with Lady Jeffries. From the only shop in the village Charlie purchased a pair of green, red and black striped espadrilles. They sat at the café in the square while Marguerite took off her sandals and donned her new footwear. He ordered a plate of *ratatouille Niçoise,* which they ate with chunks of black bread, and followed it with a *daube de boeuf.* One plate only, she insisted to the waiter. She'd pick at Charlie's. To wash it all down, a carafe of rosé wine. It was the most she had consumed in weeks.

'I'm going to christen the house La Paix – Peace. Did I tell you that?'

She shook her head.

He sloshed the wine liberally into the two glasses and lifted his towards her face. 'What shall we drink to?' he asked her.

A blush appeared on her cheek, refracted through the beaker of rosé. A glow of happiness, he hoped.

When she didn't reply, he said, 'I'll drink to us, but the decision is yours, Maggie.'

Her ladyship had departed, with an army of suitcases, bound for Calais, then across to London, where she had accepted an invitation to attend a cocktail party in celebration of the recent independence of India. From London's Waterloo station, she was booked the following morning on another train steaming to Southampton docks where a luxury cabin on the Cunard White Star Company's transatlantic liner RMS *Mauretania*, making its first sailing out of Southampton to New York, awaited her.

Marguerite had assisted with the bookings, seen her off at the station, struggling with a kindly porter over the boarding and stacking of such an abundant amount of luggage. Lady Jeffries' words on departure to her, after a warm embrace, were: 'Marguerite, you are to feel assured that there is a bed for you at the villa if you require it. Don't go running headlong into anything you fear you may regret later. I hoped you might confide in me, that I might have found a way to help you, guide you through this – this disappointment, which has so undermined you, and . . . Charlie is at heart a good man. However, sometimes the ear of another woman who has seen a little of life can work wonders. I will see you in April when I return from my lecture tour.'

Marguerite's treasured room, where she was standing now, was to remain vacant until the spring. The appointment of her replacement would not be addressed until after April when Lady Jeffries had settled back into her daily routines on the coast. Marguerite could stay if she needed to, along with the kitchen girls, as a member of the permanent team.

'The choice is yours, Marguerite.' Lady Jeffries' valediction.

The decision is yours, Maggie. Charlie's proposal.

Marguerite clasped a jar of skin cream, pressing the curves of the cold opaque glass against her cheek, rolling it backwards and forwards. The long white muslin curtains were blowing, their hems circling in the breeze, a mere movement of air, dusting against the stone tiles.

This room had been her safe haven. For months, its cool whitewashed walls had enclosed her, embraced her, shared her aspirations and her calamities.

She replaced the jar of Ponds Vanishing Cream on the dressing-table and scooped up a long row of faceted, sapphire-blue glass beads inserted with tiny specks of black rondels. She twirled them between her fingers, listening to the clink and spin of the small cuts of glass. A parting gift from Lady Jeffries, which she would be taking with her. She threaded them over her head. Gazing at herself in the mirror she saw they hung to her navel. She bent her head and doubled them over. Next, a crimson half-empty nail varnish. To pack or abandon?

She was grateful for the safety net Lady Jeffries had offered her, for she knew that the path she had elected was not going to be an easy one. Her small bag, deposited on her neatly made bed, was bulging. After seeing Lady Jeffries off at the station, she had strolled through the streets of Antibes back to this room for possibly the last time. She spun away from the dressing-table and perched on the edge of the mattress in silence. As she did so, the beads round her neck clinked and chimed delicately against one another. Their blue glinted in the light and reflected against her fingers. The windows were wide open, letting in slabs of bronzed autumn sun and the musky scents of the changing season.

On her dressing-table there remained a regiment of bottles, tubes and jars, creams, tints, rouges. The sum total of her earnings. Her investment in a career that had died before it had taken off. Would she carry them with her or abandon them here? Of what use could they be to her in the fields, in a situation of simple rustic living? Would the kitchen girls be grateful for them or scorn her for her foolishness, deride her for her haughtiness and overblown dreams?

Marguerite would be boarding the train north herself, for a brief visit to her parents, assuming the current nationwide strikes did not delay her. Afterwards, back to the south. A return ticket. She had accepted Charlie's proposal of marriage, although in her secret heart she would have preferred to reside within a less formal arrangement. 'Why marry? We don't need to.'

Charlie had responded with a guffaw, a mock-scandalized expression on his face. His grey-green eyes were dancing with happiness at the prospect of their future together. 'If anything should happen to me, and we're legally bound, the land is yours.'

'Don't be foolish. What's going to happen to you?'

I'm a wanted man, Maggie.

But now was not the time for confessions. Later, one day, when they were securely settled, he would confide the truth to this delicate young woman who was soon to be his wife. For the present, he changed tack. 'Our neighbours, the Provençaux, the villagers and farming community, Catholics one and all, will not look kindly on us if we are a couple living in sin.'

She had laughed at his argument. 'No one need know, Charlie, but us. And for what could they possibly judge us?'

Their relationship was celibate. He was the brother and she the sister she had so often painted them as.

'I hope it won't always be so, my darling Maggie.' He

had been puzzled, wounded and confused by Marguerite's inability to consummate their love after her acceptance of his proposal. 'Did I hurt you the first time, frighten you?' he quizzed her.

She shook her head, her mouth shut tight. On this topic she would not be drawn. On occasions when he had pursued the subject, badgered her just a little too virulently in spite of himself, pressed himself too close, hard with longing and love, she had clammed up completely, barely uttering a word for hours, even days, on end. She curled up on his mattress, or metamorphosed into a curved shell, hands balled into fists pressed up under her chin. He watched her sleeping. For hours he would study her, every line and curve of her, as though he intended to paint or sculpt her, her tiny frame sunk within a trauma he was not equipped to mine.

He had urged her to go north for a few weeks while he readied the *cabano*, which he intended to prepare as a form of temporary habitation for them both. He never expressed what was in his own heart, that if he could have visited his own mother and given her peace of mind he would have done so. For him, it was an impossibility. He was a wanted man. A deserter. He never forgot it. Prison would await his first footfall back in England, but Maggie could bring some reassurance to her parents and he encouraged her to do that.

Charlie wanted children, a barn full of animals. He craved a family. He dreamed of his own brood running free on the land, wild and liberated, in his role of father piling them into the truck, driving them on outings to the seaside, their daily lives intertwined with the lives of the plants and animals, all together: indigenous wildlife and domesticated pets, interweaving with the rhythms of nature. He would work his backside off, happily, to build them a natural paradise, a haven for himself of equanimity, far removed from the mental horrors of war, which still tormented him. The war and the ghosts of friends that squatted in his brain still woke him up, sweating and beleaguered. It was a requisite, had become a physical urgency for him, to settle here with Marguerite. Here, the perfect pairing, here in a place they would grow fond of, alongside one another, more idyllic than anywhere else on earth. *La Paix*.

How could he know what was haunting her? She had no knowledge of what had driven him to seclusion in this rural idyll. He let her be for the moment, surmising it was connected to her brother, and a visit to her home might well ease that loss, but once the house was fully constructed, with its fine roof of terracotta *tuiles* in place and the flowers were offering their first season's delicate pink and white petals and an income was trickling their way, he would persuade her and they would be lovers, then parents. For the time being, he accepted his lot. Although it was a bitter pill to swallow, with Marguerite as his wife at his side, her daily presence close by, it sufficed. She brought him joy and reprieve from the horrors that still harangued him.

Dawn, Paris, 14 November 2015

Kurtiz was pouring coffee for herself and Marguerite, who was looking worn out.

This was her third cup in less than an hour. Her head was reeling with fatigue and unanswered questions. She was listening to Marguerite but all the while worrying about Oliver. Why had no one got in touch with them? And she was sick with concern about Lizzie, out there somewhere in this besieged city. Twenty years old. She had been fending for herself, as far as Kurtiz and Oliver were aware, since she was sixteen. Might she also have married? Might *she* have turned to a boy, someone as kindly as Charlie, who had treated her in a considerate manner, who had loved and protected her? The scenario of her daughter having married was one that had simply never crossed Kurtiz's mind. In her thoughts and all her imaginings of Lizzie's life beyond home, her daughter had remained her innocent teenage girl. It was ludicrous, of course, even when every year on Lizzie's birthday, she had sat alone on the single bed in her daughter's room, looking at her posters on the walls, rummaging through her possessions for the millionth time, burrowing for an answer to the only question that mattered: *where have you disappeared to?* Contemplating options, she had always attempted to picture her another year older. Had she cut her hair? Grown it, dyed it? What of her figure? Was she fuller-bosomed? Still obsessed with dieting? Was she taking drugs? No, no, not that, please, not fallen into bad company.

Kurtiz had never accepted for one moment the possibility, barely voiced, that her little girl might be dead. What had Lizzie lived through since she'd left home? Would they ever know the answer? Back in the post-war days when Marguerite had run away, what anguish had her poor mother suffered? In the days before the internet, before social media, when a telephone line in the home was a rare luxury, what hope had those parents had? To wait each day for the post, for news. And what rushes of joy, relief when Marguerite had sent a letter and then returned, at Charlie's bidding, to Reims to visit them.

Why had Lizzie never thought to do the same? If she was safe and alive – and Kurtiz remained convinced that she was – why had she never sent them a message?

Marguerite and Charlie, La Côte d'Azur, May 1953

Sweet was the scent that floated across the hillsides. This was the plant's odour, its ester, given out to attract pollinators; the bees, the bumbles and honeybees, would soon be buzzing and scooping greedily. The roses of May, *Rosa centiflora*, the rose of the hundred leaves, the same variety as those that had been growing on the Grassois hillsides since the sixteenth century. Charlie's roses were opening, coming into bloom, promising a magnificent crop.

It was early in the morning soon after first light. Five years married now, Charlie and Marguerite were outside, drinking their coffee on the tiled patio Charlie had laid for them the previous summer. Its semi-open roof was a railway line of wooden beams, and in summer those beams would be pendulous with sharp green foliage and the darkening skins of ripening grapes. Droplets of dew, miniature translucent globes, clung to the pale pink rose heads, accentuating their perfume. The temperature was chilly and would be till the sun rose above their hillsides and shone from high above them.

They sat in their working clothes, wrapped in jackets and boots, sipping coffee, sweetened with local honey for Charlie, and a simple black for Marguerite from *faience* bowls. When they spoke, their words few at this early hour, their breath came out of them like distilled smoke. They ate soft white cheeses and creamy Brie spread like butter on cuts of baguette, dishes of olives and fruit. *Confitures*, from the produce on their land: apricot, peach, citruses, fig, cherry, strawberries, almonds. Marguerite had learned the art of preserve-making from her mother, boiling up the sliced sugared fruits in a heavy pan, taking pleasure from the task. From the local wives she had learned Provençal plates and dishes. *Tapenade*, a black or green olive paste steeped with anchovies and capers; delicate canary-yellow courgette flowers plucked and fried in batter; the staple vegetable ratatouille; Mediterranean chicken roasted with lemons and garlic, sprinkled and stuffed with dried herbs that hung from the ceiling in the kitchen and fragranced the lower floor of their stone and wood home . . .

Cooking, time in the kitchen, pleased Marguerite greatly, more than the backbreaking land labour, except during harvest time. The two harvest months Marguerite loved with a passion, with a girl's enthusiasm. These were the periods in the year when she and Charlie worked in tandem, both out in the fresh air. He guided their pickers from one floral bed to the next; she delivered empty baskets for filling.

Exulting in the fragrant warm air, Marguerite recalled the first occasion he had shown her – his damp earth-coated hands covering hers – how to lift the petals from a rose. 'Press your fingers over the open flower,' he had instructed, standing close behind her, his arms wrapped about her as though they were hers. 'Tug gently on all the petals and, if it's ready, the rose will release them.'

The showering of soft pale petals, the discharge of the heady perfume, it had been a baptism. She had cried with joy. The happiness was washing her clean, erasing the bitter memories and shame. She found great joy, too, in listening to the Italians sing as they worked. Mountain songs of love and war, sometimes heartbreak. She could not follow the meaning, even though she had learned a few phrases of their language.

Five years in occupancy here, the first harvest of this year was upon them: the May rose. A pink spring beauty. This morning, she and Charlie were preparing the barn, making ready the makeshift beds for the pickers, who were en route from Italy and, with luck, should be there before sunset. They journeyed through the mountains, negotiating the Alpine passes, in a convoy of open-backed trucks. It was the same team, give or take one or two, every year, every season. Two lorries came to Charlie's farm, carrying twenty-three or -four pickers. Others were hired elsewhere. Along with them, they brought their picking baskets, usually lined with hessian, and the women were each clothed in a generous white fabric apron with great gaping pockets in which they stored the delicate blossoms before transferring them to baskets.

One or two of the older women, mothers, even a grandmother of the younger females or the farming lads, chose to assist Marguerite in the kitchen. They were getting too stiff in the limbs for the bending and rising, the hill climbing, and their hands, their fingers were less steady for the picking. Marguerite was glad of the extra help when she was preparing repasts for between twenty and thirty hungry mouths. Together, they would transport the steaming food from Charlie's house (she still thought of it as Charlie's house), traipsing through the grasses, singing, humming, along the dust paths to the shade of the twisted olive trees, gnarled and stunted by time and wind. Multicoloured cloths were spread on the ground and the great clay pots were carefully placed there, out of reach of the thieving dogs, the long-bodied wasps, ants or swooping greedy gulls. Many of the dishes they could eat with their fingers, but not the plates of grilled mullet or the vegetable stews for which they needed hunks of bread and spoons. The wine flowed as they laughed and ate, and Marguerite sat proudly, while husband Charlie presided over the proceedings.

She had news to confide to him, a favour to beg of him when this rose harvest was over. But now was not the moment to approach the subject.

Before their evening meal, at the end of their shift, which was mid-afternoon because they had begun work at dawn, came the climax of the day: each of the Italians stood in line outside the barn, rings of sweat under their arms, scarves damp and hair frizzed from exertion, exhausted, yet full of anticipation for the weighing of their petals. Each took his or her turn to pour their day's fragrant pink beauties on to Charlie's scales. A fierce sense of competition arose. Pride, sometimes tears and disappointment or even anger ensued when the weight was announced, spoken loudly and clearly by Charlie for all to hear. He had meticulously oiled and polished his scales, confirmed their accuracy, so that at the end of each afternoon every picker, man, woman and child, knew to a split-portion of a gram how much their nifty fingers had gathered and what they had earned. An experienced picker would deliver somewhere between five and eight kilos an hour. In a six- to seven-hour working day, those women, for it was usually the women whose fingers were most nimble and deft, delivered an average of fifty kilos of petals.

The figures were painstakingly noted down by Marguerite, with perfect neatness. Perched on a rush-seated chair directly alongside Charlie's scales, trousered legs crossed, exercise book in her lap, fingers pressed tight around her pencil, she repeated the figures to herself as she wrote them down. There must be no mistakes, or there would be arguments later. Each was paid in francs at the end of their stay, according to the total of their loads.

As the sun was setting, the lorry from the perfume factory would arrive, grinding to a halt at the roadside on the hill's rimmed apex. It was there to collect the many baskets of petals, to hurry them back to the factory where the oils were extracted overnight and the process of perfume-making got under way. While Charlie bargained and debated the weight of the day's total collection with mean-mannered Arnaud, the factory's agent, the pickers returned to the barn, to wash and change from their soiled work clothes and ready themselves for dinner. It was served outside beneath the stars on a long wooden table Charlie had constructed out of disused railway sleepers.

These were the hours of repose, of conviviality, and

the Italians knew well how to get the best out of their leisure before they fell onto their straw bedding to sleep deeply, some drunkenly, snoring until dawn. Marguerite silently envied them their easy-going ways. She watched as their children skipped freely to and fro, tumbling down the hillsides, chasing dogs, running amok. Some evenings, if he had dealt swiftly with Arnaud, she'd enjoy watching her husband play with the kids, tossing them into the air, kicking balls with them, laughing, relaxed, their dog panting and gambolling at his feet. She knew how Charlie longed for children of his own, their own. And she wanted to be ready to give them to him, but she wasn't. Not quite yet.

During the long warm months from the commence-ment of this first harvest to the completion of the second, Marguerite and Charlie slept with the windows open wide, drinking in the scents of the night, watching the fluttering of moths, the sweep and circling of bats, drugged by the beauty, rendered serene by all that they had created together. Downstairs in the kitchen, their dog, a black and white gun dog, a Brittany Spaniel, who answered to the name of Fetch, kept watch while the donkeys, the mule and their one horse rested in a makeshift paddock not far from the principal stone premises. Most nights Marguerite slept in Charlie's arms, protected by him, sure of him. Occasionally they made love. It was a tentative unpractised business, but it was becoming more frequent. He had learned to be gentle with her, fearing for her fragile state even when his loins burned for her and he feared his passion might explode within her and terrify her. *Passion* . . . It was a word she hated. She'd borne no children. No son, or daughter. Each month he prayed that his young wife would greet him with the news that she was expecting. Round of belly. He dreamed of it. She was less skinny now. She was healthy, stronger, if a little on the small side. The doctor had assured him, over a *pastis* shared man to man outside the village bar, that she was a normal twenty-four-year-old with all her organs and body parts functioning as they should.

'Might there be mental problems?' He had almost dared not broach the subject.

The doctor shook his head vigorously. 'I wouldn't say so. However, if you are in doubt there are tests, special centres . . .'

Charlie raised a finger and shook it, to put an end to a treacherous thought he should never have voiced.

'Give her time.' The man of medicine and fellow member of the local *boules* team advised his English comrade.

Charlie was thirty-three. No age for a young chap, but he worked himself to the bone. Up before the sun rose over the eastern reach of his hill, bending and lifting, weeding, planting, irrigating till the sun disappeared and he could no longer clearly define the lines and grooves of the earth. Then he returned home by hurricane lamp for supper. Later there were the accounts to do. Marguerite took charge of the books. She had learned these rudimentary skills during her time with Lady Jeffries.

They had nothing to complain about, Charlie was well

aware of that. He was mighty grateful, all things considered. He could be back in Britain forced to spend time at His Majesty's leave, although His Majesty was dead now and there was soon to be a queen crowned. Instead, he and Maggie, tucked away in Provence, had found a quiet happiness. A humble station where he was safe from discovery, and the flowers were bringing in sufficient income to keep them in all that they required or could wish for, as long as their desires remained humble. In fact, Charlie was deliberating about whether to buy a further tract of land to extend his business. Of course, if a child came along he might keep back a little of that extra cash . . . His thoughts were swimming along such a stream as he carried bales of straw back and forth, readying the barn for the approaching Italian workforce.

Marguerite was preparing to drive the truck to Grasse to the weekly market, to stock up on provisions. She was loading the van with empty *bidons*, to be refilled with wine for the workers. She'd make a detour to pick up a couple of pairs of gardening gloves at the farmers' store – the weeds in the vegetable patches were rioting – when she heard the boy's cry and the shocking news was delivered.

'Come quick! Come quick!' A strained high-pitched voice was chanting, beating flat-footed down the lane. Bayard was a local lad employed by a neighbouring farmer two valleys along from the Gilliards.

'There's been an accident,' the excited juvenile, filthy socks crumpled over his scuffed boots, was shouting to anyone who might hear him. He was wheezing and out of breath. Fetch, close by, barked and growled at the new arrival, then settled back to sleep.

Marguerite, thinking the accident concerned Charlie, whom she'd seen not fifteen minutes earlier, was puzzled by what could have happened to him. Still, she hurtled out of the back door as fast as a salmon leaped. *'Bonjour, Bayard, qu'est-ce qui se passe?'*

'One of the Italian lorries has turned over way up beyond Col de Tende in the mountains, two kilometres on the French side of the border, and another has slammed into its rear. Passengers are trapped. The route is partially blocked off. Only small vehicles can get through. Some are hurt.'

'How do you know all this?'

'The Italian pickers hailed a passing automobile and begged the driver to make a detour this way to pass on to us the news. They need help. Need a doctor, medical aid. There are serious injuries. Monsieur Rivard says he and a clutch of the others will be riding up there together to see what assistance they can offer. Wanted to know if Monsieur Gilliard chooses to go along with them. It might be the lorry of one of his hired teams that has tipped over. No one knows much for sure.'

Marguerite dropped her cardigan on a chair in the yard. 'He's in the barn. I'll go and fetch him.'

'Gather together all the ropes you can find, especially those for hauling the bales, the heavy stuff. We'll need a vehicle lift, no doubt. Bayard, has someone notified the local garage or are they sending out a rescue van from Grasse?'

The boy didn't have a clue: he was only there to deliver the message.

Charlie slapped him on the shoulder. 'Good lad, you get on your way and inform whoever is next on your list. Maggie, give the lad one of your fine lemon biscuits for his trouble.' When the boy had gone off, running and chewing, Charlie turned back to her. His face was lined with concern. 'This is not good news. I'll have to take the truck so you'll need to postpone the shopping. If we don't require it, I'll park it at the Rivards' and you can walk over to Gabriel's and collect it from there. I should take food. Pack a box up quickly for me, Maggie, and throw in a flask of cognac for their shock.'

'I'm coming with you.'

'No, you stay. We need you here, Maggie. Get the barn readied for when I return with the Italians, and take charge of the watering and the animals. I'll bring back the pickers myself, or at least a handful of them. If that's practical.'

But what of the casualties? How many had been hurt in the accident? Charlie surveyed his acres of fine pink roses. Neither he nor his wife voiced the perturbing prospect of an insufficient team to gather the petals. He swung on his heels and gave Marguerite a peck on the cheek and, almost as an afterthought, wrapped his arms around her, hugging her tightly. 'I'll be back tonight. If I can't be, I'll send a message somehow.'

'Come back safe, Charlie, for the Lord's sake. *Je t'aime.*'

There was a brief hesitation before he swept himself up into the truck. This was the first time in over five years he had ever left his wife alone overnight. 'Maggie, if you can't manage, walk up across the plateau. Gabriel's family will be there. Keep one of the guns by your bedside. I'll take the hunting rifle with me.'

He saw the horror cross her face. 'They haven't seen wolves this side of the Italian border for decades.' He laughed. 'You've nothing to fear.'

Three days Marguerite waited for Charlie's return from the mountains; three solitary days with only the dog and the snails or bugs she feared would eat the roses, the ants and birdlife to keep her company. The worry was not that some accident had befallen Charlie – she would have received news from one or other of the farmers if that had been so – but what could be delaying him when he was so urgently required at home? They had no telephone because the lines had not been rigged up so far inland from the coast. And even if they'd had one, there was no means of communication from up in those high mountain passes. Their mail was delivered intermittently. Once a week if they were lucky. On most occasions Marguerite collected any letters and bills that came for them from the *bureau de poste* in Grasse when she drove to town to the Thursday market.

During Charlie's absence she kept herself occupied, toiling on the land, following his instructions, feeding the four-legged stock. It was the first time she had ever been there without him for more than a few hours, and she felt the lack of his presence deeply. By evening, worn out, she sat and watched the sun go down behind the hills, gazing upon their fine fields of roses, drunk on their perfume. This was the culmination of their labours.

Hers and Charlie's. She knew, too, that any day now the blossoms would be at their peak. When that moment arrived, they had to be picked immediately or they would start to deteriorate. They were a day, two at maximum, from their supreme beauty. Marguerite was willing time to hold back while praying for Charlie's swift and safe return.

Arnaud Barbin, the agent from the perfume factory to which Charlie and Marguerite were contracted, dropped by unannounced to offer to lend 'the pretty young lady' a hand and to see how she was coping all alone, or so he claimed. He'd heard about the delayed trucks and the accident, of course. News travelled fast on the community gossip vine. He'd been informed that several of the flower growers had lost their picking crews and might be struggling. He had the advantage.

He stood on the patio, legs apart, feet firmly planted on the wooden slats, noisily slurping the big bowl of coffee Marguerite had served him. He was surveying their plot, and then his calibrating eyes turned to her. It brought back memories of Katsidis. She shivered. She took a step backwards beyond his reach. Her skin was crawling, as if ants were eating her, but more than that: something inside her hardened, and she felt a geyser of hot anger and hate rise up within her.

She was no longer eighteen, no longer so impressionable and naive. It wouldn't take more than one wrong move on his part, just one move, she was thinking silently, before she'd grab the kitchen knife lying on the table and plunge it into him.

He must have sensed the wall she was bricking up

against him. He sauntered in a theatrically casual fashion towards the outer edge of the patio and took a step down onto the grass, concentrating his attention towards the flowers, keeping his back to her, his thick neck pink and runkled over his collar. His left hand, the one not clasping the coffee, hung heavily at his side, fingers agitating.

'If this gets too much for you and Charlie, you tell that man to come and talk to me. I'm the fellow who can help you out of trouble. We're always looking to buy prime flower-growing land.'

'He's not selling,' Marguerite retorted. 'We're never selling. There's nothing here for you. Nothing of any sort, you hear me?' She marched towards him and snatched the bowl of coffee out of his hand. She registered his flash of anger.

'When can we expect your first delivery of blossoms in?'

'My husband will be in touch. Now, if you don't mind, I've work to do.'

'*Husband?* So where's the family, then?' He smirked as he picked up his trilby from the patio table, slapped it with the back of his hand, stuck it on his balding head and hiked up the winding slope of gravel drive that extended back out into the world, to where his gleaming expensive car was parked on the ridge. 'No spunk, those Englishmen.'

On the third afternoon, unable to stay put any longer, Marguerite strode up over the plateau with Fetch to keep her company and safe. It was a fine warm day and the dog was gambolling back and forth, long-haired black tail windmilling, high on the scent of rabbits and hares. Or it would have been a fine day if Marguerite's head had not been filled with worries and a nagging presentiment that all was not well in the mountains. She would have taken pleasure as she always did from the patchwork of wild flowers underfoot. May was possibly the loveliest of all months at these altitudes, these lower mountain slopes set a stone's throw back from the coast. The stark serrated hills of winter had been transformed from infertile limestone into a wondrous brocade of colours, yellows and purples and rich pinks, each plant with its own uniquely seductive scent. Marguerite felt as though she had never encountered such an exquisite bouquet of aromas until she had settled in this region, this back-of-beyond nowhere land nudging Grasse, to make her universe with Charlie.

Living in the midst of the world's perfume capital had sharpened her senses. She had always recognized the woodsy smell of damp ferns, or the warm, pungent whiff of cows in the byres near her family village in the north, the comforting or sometimes claustrophobic savours of pastry crisping in the bread oven. She delighted at the awakening whiff of brewing coffee, the synthetic cloying perfumes she had liberally sprayed all over herself while with Lady Jeffries, but all that paled in comparison to what her senses were learning to identify up here in these lower Alps. Underfoot an assortment of *garrigue* plants was springing up: wild lavender, rock roses, luxuriant broom, rosemary, sage, chrysanthemum daisies, convolvulus. Wild heady scents to accompany her steps across the plateau that afternoon. Air as pure and fresh as mountain milk and as fragrant as the results of the skills of the finest perfumeries working a few miles down the hill.

She paused to catch her breath. Fetch settled at her side, panting, tongue hanging loose, paws flattening grasses, delirious from the energy expended during this unexpected escapade. She scanned the views in every direction: a spin of 360 degrees with barely a construction in sight. To her left, in the near distance, the peaks of the lower Alps were covered with fresh green shoots from the new growth in the coniferous forests. Nowhere was more beautiful. She was happy. She was energized, shot through with a rush of joy as she had rarely known it before. She laughed out loud with no one to hear her and peace settled upon her like a satin stole.

She had made the best choice, yet – oh, yet – she still occasionally hankered for the world of cinema, for the glittering fantasies she had concocted in her adolescence. She was bursting to tell Charlie about a minor film role she had been offered and had, tentatively, said yes to. Bursting for him to agree to let her go. She still dreamed sometimes of being an actress, even if the emotional scar from her hateful encounter with Katsidis was taking its time to heal. She was safe and she was cared for where she was. Charlie was more than good to her; his love enveloped her and she had knuckled down and pulled her weight on the farm because she loved him too, more deeply every day. Still, it was only right that she should be allowed to pursue her own goals, wasn't it? This offer had come out of the blue – and soon she must confirm her acceptance of it. In return, if Charlie allowed her to go to Nice to perform in the film, she would do her damnedest to master her physical inhibitions and give him the first child of the family he so craved.

Heading for the Rivards' holding, keen to find out from Marithé Rivard whether she had heard news from the men – the silence was growing disturbing – she found Gabriel's wife in her kitchen whipping up a meal for their four babes, two older boys and recently born twin sons. The squabbling quartet was bunched up like a fist of fingers round a solid oak table. Bayard was out in the yard chopping wood. As Marguerite approached she gave him a wave, but there was no sign of Charlie's motor anywhere along the driveway that led into the courtyard.

She had been hoping to use it to go to Grasse.

'Charlie took it with him. They needed all the vehicles they could recruit to transport as many as they could of the Italian teams back here. They rounded up four or five spare trucks from a few willing farmers to give them the extra space, but nobody's returned yet.'

'Have you any idea what's delaying them up there?'

'I've seen no one, not heard a word.'

Like many of the smaller or larger holdings surrounding them, the Rivards' main crop was jasmine so the loss of the roses would not hurt them as badly as it was threatening to hurt the Gilliards. The delayed return was less urgent for the Rivard estate. For Charlie and Marguerite, it represented a fifty per cent share of their business. Two hectares' worth of fine roses just waiting for the plucking – or the dying.

'If we don't have hands on those rose heads by tomorrow,' Marguerite worried, 'the blooms will begin to wilt and the petals will fall. And Charlie knows it.'

Marithé handed her a homemade raspberry biscuit and a glass of fresh mountain water. 'Don't fret. If the men are not back tonight, I could come over with a band of women. I could probably muster four or five, even half a dozen, of the other wives. We won't pick as fast as the Italians but we can save a few tons of the best of your crop for you. That is, if the factory will still buy from you, given you're not delivering your contracted load. You'll have to square it with Arnaud and, as we all know, he can be a right pig when it suits him.'

'Let's pick,' responded Marguerite, with a hug. 'I'll square it with that lascivious bastard, or maybe I'll leave Charlie to deal with him when he gets back.'

And that was what they did. Instead of a team of two dozen, five robust women, heads protected by scarves or large straw hats, set to work with the determination of dogs on the trail of truffles. Women with flesh like goat hide, who had grown up in these parts, who knew the rigours of harvesting on sloping territory and possessed the skill and temperament for the job, which was punctilious, repetitive effort. They picked off the petals with fire in their fingers. Marguerite contributed her enthusiasm, her share of labour, but she lacked the nimbleness, the oil in her limbs. In the years since she and Charlie had been growing flowers she had mostly taken care of the provisions and the house chores, organizing the victuals, bed and board for the teams. Days out in the fields in the harsh sun were not kind to her soft complexion, even if the exercise was good for her figure, which, if she returned to the cinema, would be a vital asset.

By the end of the first afternoon the women had gathered sufficient for the factory to send out their transport for the weighing and collection of the tonnage. And by that night Charlie and Gabriel were back. What a rousing welcome the circle of females gave their husbands, even if the men were weary, down at heart and not accompanied by a single Italian. They shook their solemn heads; sorry to have returned without helpers. Charlie and Gabriel's only companions were the farming colleagues who had set off with them three long days before.

'I am the luckiest wife to have you home safe.' Marguerite kissed Charlie's ear in a snatched moment alone.

Over *bidons* of wine and loaves of bread spread thickly with olive paste and tomatoes, shaded by a broad-branched chestnut tree through which a golden evening sun glinted, the wives listened to the news.

The accident had metamorphosed into a tragedy. Four had lost their lives, another six had been brutally injured while one body, a sturdy man, a fine and solid worker, had been ejected, when his truck door was flung open, over the side of the mountain to plummet into the ravine. The women listened open-mouthed, crumbs on their pink lips. Luigi's body had still not been found. The survivors had turned back for home, grieving, shocked, in mourning, heads set, weeping, for Piemonte. Charlie, Gabriel and the other Frenchmen had accompanied them, which was the reason for the delay. Together, they had transported the corpses with the injured, the shocked pickers and damaged trucks back to their villages and broken-hearted families.

It was a tragedy that had far-reaching repercussions. Charlie lost the better half of his rose crop. Their Provençaux neighbours rallied round them, worked fast and skilfully, loyal dancing fingers, but the blooms had passed their best. They were browning at the edges. The factory refused a fair portion of the consignments and Arnaud negotiated hard, beating down Charlie's contracted price, justifying his unkindness by saying the flowers were not top notch and he'd never be able to sell them to Chanel. He paid the Gilliard couple poorly because he knew he could get away with it. Charlie, blood boiling, swore that Arnaud was hoping his tactic would send them under so that the massive Grassois perfume factory for which he acted as agent could step in and buy them out at a rock-bottom price.

'Never will I give up my plot to them, do you hear me, Maggie? It'll be over my dead body.'

Had it not been for the funds Charlie had put aside for what he hoped might be an investment in more land, they would have sunk there and then. He and Marguerite would have been forced to sell. As it was, they had a small reserve to keep them tied over till the jasmine flowered in September.

Paris, November 2015

'Leastways, that was how we counted it. But it didn't happen that way. Life had a far crueller trick hidden up its sleeve,' said Marguerite to Kurtiz.

Marguerite and Charlie, La Côte d'Azur, May 1953

Charlie was less than happy when Marguerite broached the subject by soft candlelight, her head nuzzling his shoulders, whispering to him that she had a role lined up for two weeks of shooting during the month of July, and she had 'provisionally' accepted it. Charlie, worn down by his losses, protested, slapped his hand against the table, causing the cutlery and his empty dinner plate to jump and rattle, declared that he had been living under the illusion that she had put all that nonsense behind her. He had believed that their existence together had quashed that demon within her, that she had let go of all such starry-eyed imaginings. Had she forgotten how unhappy those screen tests and whatever else had gone on had made her?

It's the past, she had claimed only the previous year, best forgotten. Charlie had never challenged her on that; indeed, he had been quietly satisfied. She had seemed so content that he had never doubted she had moved on from the pipe dreams of her youth.

Marguerite was silenced by his tirade but not cowed because she was ninety per cent certain that his love for her and her happiness would win him round. In any case she was determined to play in the film – they needed the salary she would be paid, and better to have two sources of income than just the one. At the first opportunity after the men had returned from Italy she had driven the truck to Grasse and, from the same café where, earlier in the year, they had watched the Oscar ceremony together, she had put the call through to the studio director to confirm her participation.

That night, while Marguerite slept, Charlie sat on the patio alone, drinking one too many bottles of locally made wine, squinting bleary-eyed out at the darkness, the strips of dotted lights from the stars overhead, trying to figure out what in God's name had brought this on. Out of the blue, it seemed to him. And then he remembered that, on his birthday that year, they had driven to Grasse to enjoy an evening out, to celebrate at a café in the main square. There, together, they had watched the Oscars – its twenty-fifth ceremony and the first ever broadcast on television – in coarse-grained black-and-white images on a set more cabinet than curved screen. They had squashed themselves along-side dozens of hatted farmers, perfume-makers and sales girls from the local community to enjoy a show hosted by a bloke called Bob Hope, whom Charlie remembered from the wireless. His mother used to listen to Hope's shows in the kitchen while roasting the Sunday joint.

Marguerite and Charlie had perched on stools, sipped beer, gorged on platefuls of *saucisson*, olives and local goat's cheese while socializing with fellow flower producers. The fuggy bar went silent, awestruck. Here before them was the United States of America. Hollywood, the land of Marguerite's dreams.

Once the ceremony was under way, Marguerite was glued to the screen, open-mouthed, barely a sound expressed. Leo Katsidis was nominated. There he was, larger than life. However, he failed to be crowned best director for his latest offering, which also missed out on the best picture category. His leading lady, Jean-Anne Peters, at his side – nudging his shoulder, a new face to Hollywood, wavy-haired, pretty, bubbly – was not taking home the prize for best actress either. Katsidis' face was flashed up on the screen at intervals. Little could be read from his marble-eyed, hawk-nosed inscrutability. The only award bestowed on his film was for the best supporting actor.

'He's not done so well tonight, your director friend, eh?' commented Charlie to Marguerite.

Schadenfreude. Marguerite could not deny her sense of satisfaction, of jubilation, but reawakening within her was the longing to be there, to be a participant in the glittering celebrations, to be in front of a camera again, rather than sitting in that smoky bar in boots and trousers with farmers and shop girls.

Later, they had ascended the hills, scented with almond blossom, to their home, La Paix, through darkness, in silence. Was that when the worm had resurrected itself? Charlie asked himself now, as he listened to the hooting of the owls, the shuffles of invisible paws traversing the gardens, tramping leaves down upon the earth, while pouring himself another glass of unsteadily aimed red wine. What he dreaded more than anything else was that Marguerite would be hurt again, that she would return in the damaged state he had found her in when he'd rescued her from Lady Jeffries' villa those six years back. Emotionally crippled, incapable of expressing tenderness. All the patience it had taken, the restraint he had been obliged to show, to open her up, loosen her, gain her trust and affection.

Yet he knew that Marguerite was not his to own, not his prisoner, his personal prize. If cinema was the environment she truly desired, where she would come alive . . . except those studios had meted out not happiness or wellbeing but a different response . . . No, he couldn't let her go. But he must leave her free to make her choices . . .

His befuddled thoughts wound in ever-decreasing circles and he grew more groggy with every glass he poured until eventually he fell asleep in his chair. A short while later Marguerite crept barefoot to his side to nudge him awake and lead him up the stairs to their bed.

In spite of his reservations, soft-hearted Charlie, after one or two obdurate, tight-lipped days, set his disillusion to one side and acquiesced. Marguerite, in response, swung her arms about his neck and kissed his cheek. 'And the money will be a godsend too, Charlie. It's not a fortune but it will pay our summer bills. Buy feed for the beasts.'

How could he refuse her? July was a quiet time on the farm. The most arduous challenge would be the summer watering and he could handle that alone. He nodded. And after this role, he asked himself silently, will there be others? Would they ever settle to the family he so fiercely craved?

Marguerite and Charlie, La Côte d'Azur, June 1953

Marguerite and Charlie were pressed tight, buttressed among an animated crowd stepping out of La Maison du Cinéma down along the Croisette in Cannes. Jostled by bodies exiting from a full house, arm in arm, they were giggling, laughing uproariously, shouting over each other, Marguerite squealing to verbally re-enact a moment, bending over with mirth, eyes watering, relishing the slapstick moments the film had afforded them. They had been to see *Les Vacances de Monsieur Hulot*, the latest offering from the actor-comedian, Jacques Tati, whose genius had that effect on them both.

Such an outing was a rare event for the couple, these days. They had decided upon it partly because they needed respite from the responsibilities up at the farm and partly because they had been invited to a party. Lady Jeffries was giving a dinner party, a *soirée*, in honour of Queen Elizabeth II's Coronation celebrated ten days earlier.

Lady Jeffries was back from London where she had attended several of the cocktail events honouring the twenty-five-year-old princess, who had succeeded to the throne. A party, and one that they had been looking forward to for several weeks, was the special occasion – the rare night out down at the coast. They both needed their spirits lifted following their recent challenges and Marguerite's upcoming absence.

After the cinema, all dolled up in their modest party clothes (originally purchased for their wedding), they were making their way along the coastal route in the jalopy, which reeked of oil from a leak that never seemed to get fixed. They were recollecting, reliving moments from the film.

'And what about when the boy sets fire to –'

'And then when the boat collapses –'

'And the coughing car!'

Chattering over one another. And, once again, both were reduced to gales of laughter. Only for a fleeting moment had it crossed Marguerite's mind that she could have auditioned for the role Nathalie Pascaud had played.

They drove on, curving and swaying towards the Cap d'Antibes where Charlie swung left off the coast road to cut inland. 'Penny for them?' Charlie, still smiling, nudged her shoulder.

'Mmm?'

'Why so serious all of a sudden? We're going to a party, Maggie.'

Her gaze was firmly on the still water beyond her window, dark as slate.

'Have you ever been on holiday, Charlie? I haven't. I'd never seen the sea until you woke me in Marseille. Remember that first morning?'

'Of course.'

'We never went away when I was a girl.'

He was turning in through the iron gates of Le Rêve, left wide open for the arrival of party guests. They were on dangerous territory. Not their arrival on Lady Jeffries' estate, but the land of reminiscences, their childhood worlds. They never ventured there.

'I don't suppose my parents could afford it, or there was no one to look after the flour and the bakery business. Rather like you and me with our flowers. How I would love a holiday.' She sighed, closing her eyes, dreaming of yachts and film stars.

Once, when he was a boy not much older than the rascal in Tati's film, his parents had taken him, Robert Lord – a decade and more before he had become Charlie Gilliard – along with his younger sister, Sylvia, on an excursion just a few miles from their apple farm to the Kentish coast, to Dungeness Beach. Even though it had been a summer's day, once they set foot on the immense stretch of shingly beach they had been almost blown away by the force of the wind. They had battled a route through it, like a quartet of broken parasols. He, his sister and their parents had sat on their coats, hair flying high, as though electrified, and eaten the cheese sandwiches his mother had made before they left home. His father had sipped at a beer and picked flying sand particles from between his teeth. What Charlie remembered from that outing was the birdlife – there had been so many birds, wheeling and dipping in the strong wind – and the fact that his parents, usually so consensual, had started to bicker. To avoid the row, Charlie had rolled up his trousers and gone paddling in the cold sea. The icy water stung his white feet, piercing them like arrows. The pebbles rolled and turned under his toes as though the earth was disappearing, as though a great hole was being washed open and he would be swallowed, sucked into its sandy gums, and no one would know where he had gone because they were too busy bickering.

More than a lifetime ago. Another man's life, Robert Lord's. Ironic to think that he had been swallowed – swallowed by the open bleeding wound of war – and had disappeared.

Robert Lord was no more.

'Have you, Charlie?'

'What?'

'Ever been on holiday.'

He shook his head. 'No,' he said firmly. To close the subject he stepped out of the car, slamming the door behind him.

They were greeted by a butler, not a face they knew. Extra staff had been employed for the party.

Lady Jeffries, arms outstretched, came to greet them. She drew Charlie to one side when she caught sight of him alone a little later and handed him a newspaper. A special Coronation edition of *The Times*. 'I thought you might enjoy it. How was the film? Come and get a glass of something chilled.'

The room was crammed with guests, most of them British expatriates who had taken up residence down there. Charlie, foolishly, had not expected that. He felt his spine tighten. Neither he nor Marguerite knew any of them, and he preferred not to make their acquaintance. Who the hell were they all? Being surrounded by British citizens put him on edge.

His good humour had soured, curdled by his childhood memories and the fear of being recognized, no matter how minimal the chance. Marguerite had meant no harm in bringing up the past but it was a boundary he never allowed himself to cross. It had unsettled him. He had spent years ridding himself of the plague of memories. He wished now they had popped into Cannes or Juan-les-Pins and ordered a meal, just for the two of them, then returned home. Any social skills he might once have possessed had long since disappeared. It was a lifetime since he, Pete and their fellow RAF buddies had passed convivial evenings together in British pubs.

Marguerite had disappeared to the cloakroom to do her face. Charlie accepted a *coupe* of champagne handed to him from a silver tray by one of the kitchen girls. Her name had slipped his mind. Under normal circumstances he would have recalled it. He exchanged a few sentences with her, then broke away.

Out in the corridor, the silence and marble floor mollified him. He placed his glass alongside the telephone on a half-moon side table against the wall and idly leafed through the newspaper Lady Jeffries had given him. He had read, of course, of the death of King George VI the previous year and young Elizabeth's succession, but he preferred not to take an interest. England was his history, France his present and future. He read French newspapers when he had time to read at all.

For want of something better to do now, and to delay his entrance into the dining room, he flipped through the pages and glanced at the photographs. It was more than a decade since he had set foot on English soil. London would have changed dramatically, pulling itself up by the bootstraps after the bombings. Ration books were still in use, he noted. Here was the young Elizabeth in her robe of gold. The Archbishop of Canterbury decked out in all his finery. Guns and drums and oaths. Elizabeth stepping into the gilded State Coach, eight Windsor greys to draw it. Charlie turned the page, taking it all in, thinking about all those clamouring citizens standing in the rain; some had waited overnight, hoping for a fleeting glimpse of their new monarch.

He wondered how his family had fared. Might they have been present, jostled and peeping, among the sodden springtime throng? Better off out in the country, he told himself, attempting to stem the ache that was opening up inside him. He was cursing his memories of that day on Dungeness Beach. How old would his sister be now? She would surely be married with kids. Kids. Were both his parents still alive? Curse it. He must drive these memories out now. He tossed *The Times* onto the table, took hold of the glass, downed its contents in one and made his way into the dining room where the table was laid with dozens of plates and candelabra blazing. The dinner guests, sixteen in total, were gathering. Marguerite was seated at the far end, a coupe of champagne to hand, with an elderly gentleman either side of her. She waved at Charlie as he settled into his allocated chair, two seats to the left of Lady Jeffries.

Conversation was in full flight. The subject appeared to have been born in the drawing room while the guests were enjoying an aperitif. It concerned the armed forces. Charlie paid it little attention. The places to his right and left were now occupied by well-heeled women, glinting with diamonds.

A salmon entrée with mayonnaise was served, accompanied by an excellent white wine. Light-hearted chit-chat floated like bubbles. Charlie exchanged niceties at his end of the oblong table, glancing to confirm that Marguerite was fine. She was laughing flirtatiously, sipping her Krug, eyelids fluttering, gorging on the nectar of flattery. She was without a shadow of doubt the prettiest, no, the most allur-ing female at the table. Pride swelled within him. His gawky mudlark was maturing into a swan-necked beauty. Before they had left home this evening, as he was dressing, he had paused to watch her leaning in to her mirror, spray-ing cologne on her neck, dabbing her cheeks with a powder puff. Two Maggies: her reflection and his flesh-and-blood wife. She had lifted her immaculately made-up eyes and in the glass caught sight of him appraising her. She had swung on her stool, tilted her head, beamed at him – 'How do I look, Charlie?' – and the room had lit up.

How he dreaded that the world of cinema would steal her from him. Or that his own past would come knock-ing and lock him away from her. If his life was to be without Maggie, he would rather not live it. That was the depth of his love for her.

His reflections were abruptly broken. 'Deserters? Shoot every yellow-belly one of them, I say,' spat a retired grey-haired chap seated across from him. The fellow had the air of ex-army about him.

'Sir Thomas, you are being harsh,' Lady Jeffries inter-rupted.

Charlie clenched his teeth, placed his fork with delib-eration back on his plate and took a slug of wine. He was not in the mood for this. The very mention of the sub-ject detonated a rush of opinions back and forth, swirling about the candlelit room.

'The Bill is a nonsense,' continued the knighted army chap. Others assented. Plates were removed. More wine poured. Charlie had no idea which Bill was being debated, but the mood was growing heated, argumentative. Sweat began to pimple his temples. He glanced again at Maggie. Could they reasonably make their escape? She was oblivious to the discussion in progress, lost to the honeyed compliments of her two admirers, whose attentions were hers alone.

Damn it. He needed air, a cigarette.

'And what is your opinion, sir?' Some fat woman, with arched brows and too many pearls seated alongside the blusterous colonel-type, quizzed him.

'On which subject is that?' he managed.

'Why, the deserters and the Freedom Bill, of course.'

'There is no discussion to be had. Hang, draw and quarter them. Miserable cowards,' her neighbour bellowed.

Charlie's views had been forgotten. The guests had moved on, clamouring to throw in their tuppence-worth. He was disregarded. Thank the Lord.

'And what of this fellow who speaks of reprieve, of damaged minds, of war trauma?' shouted one from the far end. 'Does he have a point, do you think?'

'Poppycock!'

A sweat bead dropped treacherously to Charlie's jaw. He lifted his napkin, dabbed his lips and discreetly wiped his face. Laying the napkin on his bread plate, he rose as unobtrusively as he was able. 'If you'll excuse me.' Nobody was listening. The debate was rising in volume, fired by copious servings of fine wine. He left the room swiftly, colliding in the hallway with the cork-nosed cook, carrying a steaming dish of new potatoes. She let out a cry. He made hasty apologies and headed on down the corridor towards the back of the house.

He'd sit outside on the porch for a while, rescue his self-control. Re-inhabit Charlie Gilliard, drive down the temporary resuscitation of Robert Lord. The whooping and loud voices diminished, then died away as he stepped out into the warm night air. The zizzing of a grasshopper drew his attention, a decidedly more amiable companion. He lowered himself into a rattan chair at the table where the cook used to shell peas. He should go and keep Maggie company. Or was she content for a short while with those aged admirers to entertain her?

He raised a hand to his face and rubbed at his mouth, dry and tight. Robert Lord was not a yellow-belly coward. He was just a man, barely more than a teenager, who could no longer stomach the decaying stench of death and killing. But he was gone. Gone. Robert Lord was no more. A tidal swell rolled up within him. Was he about to be rumbled, to lose everything for a second time?

He would like to take Maggie on holiday, whisk her away, to Greece perhaps, the ancient sites, the islands, just the pair of them, away from the responsibilities of flowers and farming, away from the clouds rising ominously above the perfume-making capital. Make love, read poetry, create babies. He would have had the resources to cook up such a plan a month and more back – *why* hadn't he? – but their funds were too tight now. His savings were spoken for. He and four other local farmers had clubbed together and sent a small pot of money to the Italian villagers who had lost lives and family. He was the most junior of the producers in his area. Handing over his donation had cost him dearer than his neighbours, who had few debts against their land and homes. Still, he could not have refused to contribute his share.

Was time closing in on him? What if someone should come looking for him in the light of this wretched Bill, if Maggie should ever learn the truth? If she should be publicly humiliated and judged for his ignominious past? Better to kill himself than bring her to shame . . . *Why* hadn't he confided in her?

'There you are. I wondered where you'd got to. What are you doing sitting out here alone?'

'Oh, listening to the night,' he said, brushing away a tear, conjuring up a phoney smile. Wasted. She couldn't detect it. She was standing behind him.

'I see you had a browse through the photographs. All that pomp and ceremony. It was quite marvellous, very moving. An event unlike any I have ever attended.'

'Yes,' he agreed, preferring not to be drawn further on thoughts of home and bloody England. He heard the creak of wicker, the swirl of a skirt as his companion sat down.

He and his erstwhile employer remained hushed, in stillness for a full minute or two, imbibing the perfection of the night.

'And one or two rather interesting developments have come out of all this, which you may not have heard about it.'

Charlie maintained his gaze towards the garden where, beyond sight, the sea pattered softly to the shore. 'Really?'

'The big debate in Parliament that has that bunch in there all heated concerns the "missing members of the armed forces". Our "lost men".'

'Lost?' He coughed.

'Men who went missing in the war . . .' She paused.

For dramatic effect or . . . ? Charlie's torso shifted. The cane chair released a squeaking sound, betraying his disquiet.

'It may have come as a surprise to you. I know you don't follow events back in England . . .'

'The farm keeps us busy. It's been a difficult year.' He cursed the reedy tone in his voice.

'I thought you might have heard of the men lost in the theatres of war?'

She waited. His lack of response hung in the air. 'Perhaps not. Well, a debate has been raging in the UK. Oh, for six years now. A chap called Austin triggered it. A decent individual, the Honourable Member for Stretford. He has been fighting for . . . those who . . . deserted, who found themselves as deserters. Austin was lobbying for their pardon.'

Charlie barely dared draw breath. Hand shaking, he pulled from his left-hand pocket a squashed packet of Gitanes, drew out a cigarette and dropped the packet on the table. His first fag in days, but he had no light, no match. He could not turn his head. Lady Jeffries was seated across the table from him. However, her chair was placed a foot or so further back. To face her, he would need to swing his body and that, at this moment, seemed a physical impossibility. He was frozen.

'The British government has finally agreed to an amnesty. Churchill announced it in February. An amnesty for wartime deserters from the forces as part of the Coronation celebrations. It's been getting a great deal of heated attention. There are as many as a hundred thousand men unaccounted for. Personally, I think it quite marvellous, don't you?'

Had she gleaned the truth? Had she always known it?

'It certainly has my vote. New opportunities for those disenfranchised boys to begin their lives again as honourable British citizens. A clean slate.'

Charlie lifted his hand, with its unlit cigarette, to his face, rubbing his thumb against his left cheek, feeling the hollow beneath his cheekbone, his fingertips against his right. He had shaved before they'd left home. His skin was smooth to the touch, smoother than usual. It was a rare event for him to shave any time after his morning wash.

Charlie Gilliard/Robert Lord was left-handed. His dead pal, Peter Lyndon, whom to this day he still missed with a deep-fisted grinding in his gut, had been right-handed. Was it even vaguely conceivable that, when the remains of Pete's body, lying in burned shreds and shot bone shards on the beach, had been gathered up and pieced together, it was evident the remains were from a right-handed corpse, and only one corpse at that? That there were insufficient body parts for two men? Whatever had he been thinking? What skewed, traumatized logic had driven him onwards? Might it have been written into the war records that, in spite of Robert Lord's brevet ditched on the shore alongside Lyndon's right-handed body, it was clear to all that Robert Lord was not there? Was it possible that Robert Lord had gone down in history as missing, not killed honourably in action? Missing, possibly deserted? Had he fooled nobody?

And if that were the scenario, what had they told his mum, his parents, and dear Doris Sprigley? His mum, his dear old mum, whom he would give the world to see again, to wrap her in his arms, lift her off the ground and swing her about as he used to do, escort her and his dad down the road to the Plough for a pint . . . But how could he ever look them in the eyes now? Doris, Dad and his mum . . . How could he admit the lengths to which he had gone to deceive everyone?

Tears were falling, dampening his unlit cigarette, the flesh on his hand, and he was grateful, damned grateful, for the lack of light out there. No overhead electric bulb glaring down upon him, only the starlight creeping in from outside, creating shadows, and the distant wash of the sea.

'You know, Charlie, many deserted to preserve their humanity, despising the cruelties they had witnessed and had been obliged to partake in, not because they were cowards. Lost men are returning to their families after years in hiding. No judgement, no charges against them. A free pass home to pick up their lives where they left off.'

Lady Jeffries rose. He winced at the jarring scrape of cane legs against flagstones as she pushed the chair backwards. She crossed a step to him and rested a hand on his shoulder. 'I suppose for those still in hiding abroad, who have attempted to build new lives, this must be an almost impossible choice.' She handed him a lighter, waited while he fumbled to ignite his cigarette.

'I had better be getting back to my party,' she said softly. 'A houseful of hungry and irate guests champing at the bit. Bigoted old buggers.' He heard her soft laugh. 'We'll see you inside for the main course. When you're ready. No hurry, Charlie.'

No hurry? No hurry? It was too damn late.

'It was around that time, after the evening at Lady J's, that I began to notice changes in Charlie's personality, his comportment. The signs were insignificant at first, but they grew more alarming over the weeks. His personality began to inch away from him, turning him sour. Yes, sour and moody are the adjectives I would use. Even with me he snapped, and he had always had a loving gesture for me. Girl that I was, I put his moods down to the financial pressures we were living through. It was partly accurate, I suppose. A general malaise was setting in, and its negativity was spreading. A greater number of the farmers were worrying that the glorious days of the perfume industry were numbered. Synthetic scents were the future, or essences pressed from plants grown in foreign countries where the labour was cheaper. Egypt for jasmine. Bulgaria for the roses. Up at the pressing plants in the centre of Grasse, concerns were mounting as to how long they could maintain their jealously guarded position as the perfume centre of the world. Those who sourced the blossoms that were transformed into natural aromatics and scents, which is to say the agents – Arnaud, in our case – and the factories that purchased the raw materials were starting to haggle over the prices they had previously agreed with the flower producers.

'Arnaud paid us an unannounced visit, well in advance of our jasmine harvest, a week or two after our evening at the cinema and dinner with Lady J. He was requesting, or rather demanding, we sign a newly drawn up contract. He wanted a guarantee of more flowers, a greater crop load, except he was offering the same money. For every kilo of jasmine delivered to him, he was offering us thirty *centimes* less than he had paid the previous year. Charlie argued with him, refused the deal, then lost his temper, which was so out of character that I was taken aback.

'It was a considerable cut and we were in no position to accept it, even for one season. Arnaud's riposte was that a greater harvest yield would bring us back up to the same figures. I thought Charlie would punch him. Charlie, whom I had never seen lift a finger even against the livestock. He tore up the written contract and flung it back at Arnaud. Then he stormed from the kitchen, hurled himself into the truck and sped off in a flurry of dust and stones. I told Arnaud to get out.' Marguerite shook her head wistfully at the memory. 'It was the second time that year I had ordered him off our farm.' She chuckled. 'Later, when it seemed I had lost everything, the mean bastard tried to grind me further into the ground. But he didn't win. Oh, no, even to this day, he didn't win.'

Marguerite and Charlie, La Côte d'Azur, late June 1953

When Charlie eventually returned home, Marguerite could see right away that he'd been on the booze. She was down in one of the pastures feeding barley straw to the donkeys. They had also acquired a few chickens and geese; the latter were honking for supper. She spotted Charlie's silhouette against the backdrop of an epic violet evening sky as he swayed, slipping and sliding, descending the track that led to the rear of their house. He was on foot. Where was the old bus? This excessive drinking was becoming a habit. She wished he would confide in her, open up about what was eating at him.

Marguerite let drop the buckets and picked her way hurriedly back up to the patio that led through into the kitchen. 'Charlie?'

There was no response.

She found him at the table, clothes damp and stained with petrol, head bent over his folded arms. He was exhaling great gulps of air. Marguerite, poised uncertainly at the open doorway, thought he was sobbing. She glanced about the room, taking in the state of the place. A photograph of their house when it was semiconstructed hanging on the wall had been knocked askew. He must have banged against it as he came in.

Otherwise, everything was as it had been. His jacket had been thrown across the back of another chair. 'What's happened to you?'

When he lifted his head, there were no tears, but puffiness, the whites of his eyes like a map with red roads, and his breath on fire. In all the time she'd known him, Marguerite had never seen her husband in such a condition. It frightened, panicked her. 'Charlie? Tell me what's happened.'

He had run his truck off the winding road into a ditch on the ascent out of Grasse. A man in a black beret driving a small white convenience van, a country plumber from somewhere not far off but not a face Charlie could have put a name to, had pulled over, given him a hand to get out of the truck and offered him a lift home. He'd deposited him up at the ridge. From there Charlie had called in at Gabriel's but none of the family had been at home, so he'd staggered on down the drive.

The following morning, cursing his hangover, Charlie trudged off with Gabriel and sets of pulley ropes to haul the Citroën out of the ditch. It needed to be towed to the garage on the outskirts of Plascassier for two new tyres, wheel hubs, a mudguard, but it wasn't a write-off, which was what Charlie had been anxious about when he'd woken with his throbbing head. In the past, he'd have taken the mishap in his stride. They would have dealt with it. But he appeared to be losing his grip – his head full of sorrow and shame – and they had little spare cash as things were, never mind laying out for another vehicle. Gabriel had driven over in his truck to tow Charlie's out of the ditch. Charlie sat behind the wheel of his vehicle. The bugger was jammed and wouldn't budge, wheels spinning, spitting up stones and roots. The air was charged with the smell of burning rubber. He yelled to Gabriel to hold off a minute, then go easy on the accelerator pedal: he'd get out to give his 'old tin can' a push from the rear. The bugger was bucking, jammed against a stone or a rock, as the rope dragged her.

'Take it slow, Gabriel, *mon ami*, or she might roll back on me, crush me beneath her weight.'

The dust and earth rose and rippled, sending grit whorls skywards. For a few moments, a slow-motion point in time, they blocked Charlie from Gabriel's sight. Gabriel was keeping a careful eye through his rear-view mirror, foot gently on the accelerator, backwards, forwards, easing and pulling, taking it steady. When the clouds settled Charlie, who had been bent over at the back, shoving and heaving, coaxing his beloved old truck upwards onto the road, was staggering backwards, flapping his arms and kicking to regain his balance.

Gabriel no longer had him in his line of vision. He called out of the open window. 'Charlie! Charlie?'

No response. He called again. Still nothing.

The world had gone silent.

'*Mon Dieu.*'

Gabriel slung his gearbox into neutral, switched off the engine and threw open his unoiled door. He jumped out, boots slapping hard against earth and pebbles, lizards scurrying for cover. He was rubbing sweat from his drenched face with the sleeve of his shirt, calling again to his neighbour and friend. 'For God's sake, Charlie, speak to me.'

The response was the wind blowing gently through the gorse and the birds overhead. Charlie was gone. No sign of the man. Gabriel circled the two vehicles and dropped down into the trench. There he found his dear friend, arms outstretched as though on a crucifix, dead in the ditch.

Dawn, Paris, 14 November 2015

'Later, it was confirmed that Charlie had suffered a fatal heart attack.'

'I'm so sorry.'

'His young heart had given up. Such a generous, forgiving heart.'

'You must have been distraught. So young to be on your own. What did you do?'

'I was lost on that hillside. I accepted the role in the film. Anything to keep my mind off my isolation. Lady Jeffries offered me work, but the film proved to be rather a success so I decided to return to Paris and study theatre. It took me years to come to terms with the loss of Charlie. I have a faded photograph of him somewhere. Let me see if I can find it. It must be in one of these drawers, tucked away beneath goodness knows what. I know when I downsized from our lovely house in Saint-Germain-en-Laye I gave away the greater part of my possessions, but I kept Charlie's photo. Nothing would have persuaded me to part with it.'

Marguerite was rummaging through drawers in a sideboard, wiping away an unexpected tear, when Kurtiz glanced at her damaged watch – 7:24. Neither of them had slept. They'd been up all night, talking. She should leave and let this dear soul get some rest. 'I must get on my way, Marguerite. Let you go to bed. Check into my hotel.'

'Here it is. Goodness, what a scruffy dog-eared souvenir it's become. I ought to have framed it, but I never did. A sense of respect for Henri, I suppose. Charlie and I were together for such a short time in the greater scheme of things that those brief, treasured years went into a separate box. Henri and I grew together over the decades. He was a good-hearted, patient chap, who worshipped me and gave me everything, and accepted with sanguinity that Charlie had been, for me, irreplaceable. Dear Charlie. What would he say if he could see me, an old lady, sitting here recounting our love story? Perhaps he can. And do you know, this photograph, taken on the day we were married in 1948, is the only one I ever possessed of him? He hated having his face in front of a camera. In fact, he was almost paranoid about it. I teased him sometimes, asking him if he had something to hide. I wondered from time to time whether there had been a dark secret in his past, but he always fobbed me off, ragged me for talking foolish nonsense. Lola! Lola! Oh, dear. Give me a moment, the dog is scratching at the cupboard doors again. It must be almost time for her breakfast. She's destroyed that kitchen. I seem unable to train her to stop. Just a moment, dear.' Marguerite placed the photograph on the sideboard and hurried into the kitchen, cooing and fussing.

Kurtiz stood, stretched her back and massaged her head. She glanced at her phone for the hundredth time, pleading with it to produce news from Lizzie. She shook her legs, kick-starting her circulation. Moving with no real purpose, she crossed the compact room to a well-polished walnut sideboard, displaying a cut-glass fruit bowl holding half a dozen apples, and picked up the snapshot, which had been placed face down. The landline in the sitting room began to ring. Kurtiz froze. It had to be the hospital or the police. She placed the photograph back on the sideboard without looking at it and stepped towards the phone.

Marguerite was picking up the receiver. '*Allô?* . . . Give me a moment to jot it down, please.

'They have traced your husband. He is in the intensive care unit at the Pitié-Salpêtrière Hospital. It's in the thirteenth. Come along, I'll drive you there.'

Back on the deserted streets in the Mercedes tank, dawn was breaking, a raw grey winter gauze unfolding. Violet lights were still flashing up and down the boulevards, giving the cityscape a burned-out, other-worldly aspect. Dying embers. A stillness. Everybody holed up in their homes. Locked in. Kurtiz peered up at the windows of passing blocks. Even at this hour, the blink and wink of television screens could be seen in dozens of darkened rooms. Had anybody slept? Had there been further attacks, or was Paris safe now?

She lifted her phone and typed a message: *Dear Alex, I am safe. Oliver has been hit. We haven't found Lizzie.*

He answered instantly. So, he, like every French citizen, must be watching the news. The dawn patrol. *Sorry to hear about Oliver. I am in Boston but could take a flight out tomorrow night if you need me. I will call you Monday. Don't leave town without talking. If there's anything I can do . . . A x*

She smiled to herself at his authoritarian tone. *I am coping. Thx for yr concern. Pls don't change plans for me. K.*

And his response. *Stubborn as always. I won't wait for u forever.*

She read his words, knowing them to be true. Decided not to reply, and then another message pinged. *Or perhaps I will. Be safe. A.x*

In the ring of streets that surrounded the hospital there was nowhere to park, every slot taken, vehicles clustered together bumper to bumper. They drove for a while in ever-widening circles until they found a space some half a kilometre distant and were obliged to walk. Kurtiz tried to persuade Marguerite to go home and get some sleep but the old woman, whose skin had grown translucent with fatigue, stubbornly refused. 'I am coming with you,' she insisted. 'At some point you will need a lift back. It's too far to walk and, as you know, there's no public transport.'

When they reached the hospital grounds, they found queues of residents and foreigners outside in the cold, patiently waiting to approach the main doors. Would they also have to stand in line? Kurtiz wasn't sure she could remain upright for any length of time.

One queue, which tailed beyond the hospital grounds to the street, was made up of men and women volunteering to give blood, to replenish the stocks used during the course of the night. Men, women, teenagers denying themselves sleep to make this gesture, to help save lives. Turn the destruction on its head. Give back to the city and its citizens its dignity. Paris for Paris.

Others, like Kurtiz, stricken-faced, were there for news. She and Marguerite made their way to Reception, and were greeted by a woman, ginger hair bunched on top of her head, like a scruffy nest, who looked as if she'd been there all her life.

'We received a call to come directly.' Marguerite was taking charge.

Oliver was in intensive care. Two bullet wounds; bullets fired from a Kalashnikov AK-47.

'May I see him?'

'You will need to enquire of the staff on duty. Take the lift to the second floor, on the left beyond the swing doors.'

The receptionist, who admitted she hadn't left her post since eight the previous evening, glanced at a screen, then scribbled down the ward and directions to Oliver's room, tore the page from a notebook and handed it across the desk.

'One quick question,' begged Kurtiz.

The woman wiped her nose and scratched at her bouffant with a biro.

'My daughter was also at the Bataclan. Lizzie Ross. Has she been admitted?' Obligingly, the member of staff ran through dozens of pages of files on the screen, lists in brilliant green lettering. She shook her head. 'No one here by that name. You'll have to telephone the central information number. They will have more up-to-date details.'

'We have. Several times. It's always engaged or there is no trace of her. Someone must have word of her.'

The receptionist let out a sigh. She was evidently at her wits' end, suffering the sharp end of every stranger's grief and anxiety.

'*Merci* for your efforts,' said Marguerite, covering for Kurtiz's visible disappointment.

The woman shrugged. 'Sorry, but I cannot assist you further. *Désolé*. Next.'

A Tunisian, or perhaps he was Algerian, Maghrebian for sure, wearing a small white *taqiyah* cap and black bomber jacket with sleeves too long, shuffled forward. He was carrying a plastic bag. 'Washing things and clean clothing for my daughter,' he muttered. 'She was injured at the concert.'

Kurtiz and Marguerite watched him while they waited for the lift, which they rode to the third floor. There, beyond sliding doors, they waited again, until an orderly, dressed from head to foot in Robin Hood green, appeared. He was carrying a clipboard. 'Ross?'

Kurtiz gave a cursory nod.

He looked from one woman to the other. 'Which of you is next of kin?'

Kurtiz raised her hand, barely capable of speech. The corridor reeked of cleaning liquids or vinegar and pickles. Disinfectant. Formaldehyde or a similar chemical. The aromas were unpleasant, almost asphyxiating. She feared that if she took a deep breath her lungs would be seared.

The medic pointed to a bank of connecting wooden seats where two men and a woman wearing a headscarf were in attendance, hunched over their knees, hands cupping faces. The female, about Kurtiz's age, early forties, glanced upwards. Her eyes were ringed dark and deep, and she was weeping. The orderly promised with little certainty that a doctor would be along shortly. Oliver was in the operating theatre. 'Please wait.'

Marguerite and Kurtiz joined the others. Kurtiz was feeling nauseous. She closed her eyes. How long before a doctor turned up? Did Oliver, with his battered liver, have the physical resources to pull through this? Later, as the minutes ticked by, one damn second after another, Marguerite left for home at Kurtiz's insistence. 'No sense in both of us falling apart.'

Kurtiz had been alone for almost two hours now, limbs aching, churning over her past, recollecting. Lives in fragments. Might Lizzie have found out about her father and Angela's mum? Had that been the trigger? Did any of it matter now?

A door opened and a male nurse, an African, appeared. He looked shattered, eyes bloodshot, barely able to keep upright. 'Mrs Ross?'

Kurtiz staggered to her feet.

Oliver had been returned to the ward. He had undergone an operation. This first procedure was to stem internal haemorrhaging. 'We still need to remove two bullets from his solar plexus.' His condition was stable but critical. The practice, she learned, in modern medicine is to take it in stages. Treat the most precarious issues first, allow the patient to gain strength, then return to pick up less threatening problems with further operations. Minimize the invasive aspect. Lessen the trauma.

It was too soon to give any prognosis. 'In theory, a patient could survive gunshot wounds such as Mr Ross has suffered . . .'

'But?'

'. . . but it will depend on the fighting strength of his organs and his heart. We need to make sure he loses no more blood and that no infections set in.'

'May I see him?' The nurse led her to a window, a great glass partition through which she saw one bed in the middle of a private room in which lay a man with his eyes closed. Oliver. He was connected to a dazzlingly complex array of drips, hoses and a catheter, each attached to a machine, flicking, flashing, digitally signalling information or recording numbers. His pallor was bleached, etiolated, whiter than the bedding in which he lay. She watched for his breath, which was slow, erratic, barely discernible.

'Is he unconscious or sleeping?'

'A bit of both. He was anaesthetized for the operation and now is being fed painkillers and a lighter sedation to keep him comfortable.'

'Is he going to live?'

'It's too soon to make any predictions but you can be assured we are doing all we can.'

She felt a tear the size of a golf ball heave up from within her, locking her throat, coasting treacherously down her cheek. How she had loved this man. How she had sometimes despised him for his weaknesses, his drinking. How they had allowed the loss of Lizzie to tear apart the skeletal bones that had remained of their marriage.

And for so much of it she blamed herself. If she had not been with Alex on that fateful night . . .

'You should try to get some sleep. He'll need your strength and confidence later when . . . at the next stages.'

'Has he regained consciousness at all, said anything?'

The nurse shook his head. A small bleeper the shape of a pen or thermometer began to sound and flash orange. He raised a hand to shut it off.

Kurtiz took a step, clearing distance between them. 'Please, don't –'

He was speaking over her: '– as soon as I can. Go home for a few hours. If anything changes we'll call you immediately. Leave your number at Reception. They'll organize a ride home for you. The city's on lock-down.'

She had no desire to leave and she had nowhere to go. What were her choices? The room she had booked? It was too late. Nor could she presume further on Marguerite's hospitality although it had been generously offered. Before she left Paris she would return to rue de Charonne to thank her. In fact, it now occurred to her, her bags were still there. She returned to the bank of chairs and settled herself uncomfortably across two, legs curled up under her buttocks. A creature battling the elements. She was safer, better off, here. She lifted her phone, tapped in her code, scrolled through the messages, looking for Lizzie. She found Alex: *Thinking of you. A.*

She glanced at the time this message had been sent. Friday evening at 7:14. She would have been disembarking the Eurostar, queuing for a taxi. Before the massacres and the night when her life had changed. She wondered what had caused its delay in reception. Further along, beyond dozens of *#porteouverte* messages brimming with support and offers of assistance, she found another, a two-liner, also from Alex: *Are you safe? Send me a message, some reassurance, for God's sake. Allow me to come to you, let me know where I can reach you. You're in my thoughts. A.*

Had network overload caused their delayed delivery? Might there be others from Lizzie waiting arrival? *Oh, Lizzie, Lizzie, Lizzie.*

Alex. My God, she craved his warmth, his level-headedness but Alex was in Boston and Oliver was here, fighting for his life . . . Oliver who had dedicated every day to searching for Lizzie.

London, September 2015

Alex had arrived ahead of her. He was at the table, sitting alone towards the rear wall of the Italian restaurant. It was an old-style establishment in the heart of Soho, which was filling up with lunchtime diners, many of whom worked in Wardour or Old Compton Street, diehards of the film industry. He was scribbling, taking notes in one of his *carnets*. Head bent in concentration, he had not yet spotted her. She paused momentarily by the door, shoulders brushed by others as they passed her stationary figure. She was using the activity of shrugging off her raincoat to catch her breath, calm her heart. It had been four years. Four difficult, lonely years since she had said goodbye to Alex at Tel Aviv airport.

Take the time you need, bring your daughter home and then come back to work. You hear me? I need you on the team.

Weeks later, after ignoring every one of his calls, texts, emails, she had written:

Dear Alex, I have so much to thank you for. A whole new world has opened up for me. I am working from London now, accepting only the commissions that allow me to stay home so that I am here for Lizzie, if she returns. When she returns. I won't be joining you all in Libya, or anywhere.

*Please, don't leave the post open for me. Please go ahead
and find yourself another photographer. Thank you for so
many moments. Yours, Kurtiz*

Alex had bombarded her with refusals to accept her
resignation, reasoned out in writing why the decision
she was making was a foolish one:

*You are under stress, hurt by the loss of Lizzie. I saw her
picture in the papers, a very lovely-looking kid, like her
mother. Let me know when you're ready, Kurtiz. There
will always be an opening for you. I WILL wait.*

She had not replied, not to any of these missives. It was
easier for her to cut him out, to put that episode of her
history behind her. If she had never taken the work . . . if
she had switched on her phone . . . It had gone clean out
of her mind to call home because she had been with Alex,
numbed by the death of a stranger, the Palestinian adolescent, while her own child was lost somewhere and possibly
in trouble. She blamed herself, and the reasons for her
guilt could not be shared, could not be offloaded.

Don't go, Mum, please.

Lizzie. The pain had never dulled, never stopped gnaw-
ing at her. The guilt was like a lead jacket but worse, far
worse, was the aching loss. A part of her had been ampu-
tated. And the not knowing. The not comprehending . . .
Where had she disappeared to? Into thin air.

'Signora! Signora?'

'Yes?'

'Do you need a glass of water? May I help you find
your table?'

Jolted back to the present, to Alex who had spotted her and had risen from his seat. His hair was tinged with grey but still that healthy strong physique, that open enquiring face, smiling now as he held out his arms across the crowded restaurant. She made her way slowly, a little unsteadily. For a woman of her age, forty-two, she had lost her spring. Her bounce. Living alone, living for her work. Visiting Oliver, cooking for him so he had a decent meal, caring for him in his despair.

'Good to see you.' Alex smiled, eyes roving over her, drinking in her lips, the crow's feet gathering round her eyes, the sadness embedded there. She took the seat opposite him, lightly gripping the table, an insurance against an accident, a wrong foot. She tended to be clumsier these days, less assured.

Once she was settled and he reinstated in his seat, he closed his Moleskine jotter, placed his pen on its black surface and lightly slid both to one side of the table. He leaned in. She dropped her gaze, partially lowering her head. Before she knew it, his hands were enveloping hers.

'Look at me,' he said, commanded.

He always had given the orders. She smiled to herself, then lifted her gaze towards him.

'It's good to see you,' he said.

'So, you're working in Paris?'

He slid his hands to the table and entwined his fingers, like a pastor. It was then she noticed that the slender band of gold was absent. The bond to the woman he had never spoken of. 'Editing there, yes.' The waiter was approaching. 'You want what? Wine, whisky?'

'Water, please.'

'Two large whiskies. Something decent, single malts, please, and bring some ice on the side. And a bottle of San Pel. Thanks.' His attention back to Kurtiz. 'I'm thinking of moving to Europe, setting up a post-production unit over here.'

She frowned, drew a breath, wondering where this might be leading. Was it connected to the missing wedding ring? She bit back a moment of elation at such a prospect. Alex free. Liberated. Available. But it was too late. Her life had careered off in another direction. There was Oliver to include in all equations. Oliver, more a child than a partner. Separated, in any case.

'My French is not a hundred per cent. This film has a semi-French subject. It makes sense.'

She must stay on track. She would not have agreed to meet Alex except that his email had intrigued her. 'You said there was something you wanted to show me.'

His eyes bored into hers and there was a pain in his regard, a hesitation.

'My film. We have a first assembly. It's still pretty rough and needs work, but that's not the point. I think you should see it.'

Her face was creased, puzzled. She attempted a laugh. 'You've never needed my approval, my input before,' she joshed, a little edgily.

'This is different.'

'In what way?'

'We'll grab a bite of lunch and then we can watch the film. I've hired an editing suite just up the street. How long have you got?'

All the time in the world, she thought. 'I cleared the afternoon,' she replied.

'Paul, this is Kurtiz. Kurtiz, Paul's our technician for this session.'

They were seating themselves in a chilly, air-conditioned studio about half the size of a one-car garage. A room with no windows and no natural light. In front of them and to their left was a complex wall of machinery and editing hardware, consisting of computers, a bank of screens, fitted shelving neatly stacked with hard drives, CDs, DVDs. The three of them were alongside one another. Alex was in the centre and to his left was Paul, a young man in horn-rimmed spectacles with dark hair tied in a knot on top of his head.

'Let's roll it from the top, the opening credits, and keep rolling till I say stop, okay?'

Paul began to flick at dozens of switches. Rewinding. A million images rushed before their eyes at a speed beyond recognition until they were back at the top of the film. The opening image was of Place de la République in Paris. It was jam-packed with people. The image was now frozen.

'Kurtiz, we have no credits laid on yet. This is just pictures and some commentary I recorded myself as a form of signposting. You with me?' She nodded, confused as to what all this was about.

'Occasionally I'll speak a few lines to give some time frame to the story.'

She nodded again, puzzled but lulled into a false sense of serenity at being back in his company. She forced herself not to lean her shoulder into him, close to him, longing to make physical contact with him. Instead she inched forward, elbows resting on the wooden deck.

'*Je suis Charlie*.' Alex spoke the words with a poor French accent. 'January six, 2015. Earlier this year in the eleventh *arrondissement* of Paris . . .'

Kurtiz watched the unfolding of the drama that had shaken Paris nine months earlier, swept through France and brought hundreds of thousands of French citizens out onto the streets to leave flowers, candles, messages of love and support, to stand in silence as a mark of respect for the artists, the cartoonists, the publishing team and the police officer who had lost their lives in the attack. In the aftermath, said Alex, there were many demonstrations, many rallies of subjects from all walks of life brought together to honour those who had died and, as importantly, to stand up for two of the corner-stones of French philosophy: freedom of opinion and freedom of speech.

'Who are these people who call themselves a state, who claim they speak for a religious faith? Who is funding them? Who is or are the intelligence behind them?'

The pictures on screen had moved from France and crossed from Europe to Syria.

Alex laid a hand on Kurtiz's left arm, which broke her concentration. 'Paul, you can fast forward through this, please. Take us to somewhere around nine minutes into the material, please, nine forty-three, somewhere there. Back to Paris to the demonstrations, the aftermath. And then I want you, please, to freeze the frame and zoom in. I'll tell you when.'

Paul pressed a button and the film began to roll forward.

'Watch carefully,' Alex whispered to Kurtiz, who had no idea what this exercise was all about. The screen returned to the crowded Place de la République. People squeezed together, like sardines in cans. In anguish, in peace. Tightly packed against each other, holding aloft French flags, candles, banners. The camera was roving over faces, some painted blue, white and red, the colours of the French flag. It hovered by groups. Faces blown full and large. Faces streaked with tears, contorted by shock and grief.

'Paul, hold it there, please, and now take the image in slow motion. One frame at a time.' The zoom was moving tighter, creeping towards a group of students, adolescents, teenagers. 'Stop. Hold it there.'

Seven faces on the screen with blurs of other figures encircling them and deeper in the shot. Young folk in duffel coats, clutching high above their heads the national flag. One or two in woollen hats. Paris in full winter. Paris in shock. Paris speaking out.

'Start to zoom the image in, please, Paul. No, to your left a tad. See the girl on the far left of the image?' Alex was pointing towards the bank of screens all transmitting the same image. 'There, with the short dark hair. Inch towards her, please. Stop. Yes, and now a millimetre above her head. Hold it. Continue to move the film forward like that as a tight shot. Frame by frame, nice and slow. Yeah, hold it there. See the young woman in the background there? Lifting her profiled head, turning her face towards the lens. Got it. Hold it. Freeze the frame, please, Paul, and go in a little tighter if you can. It'll get grainy, but . . .'

Alex held his hand over Kurtiz's bunched fist.

Kurtiz stared at the over-exposed image of a girl, a young woman with sandy hair turning her face from profile towards the camera, in slow motion. The girl's eyes on the screen were closed. It seemed to take a while for her to open them. Her large hazel eyes, full of pain, looked out directly towards where the camera was shooting.

Kurtiz stared at the screen. If she had not been leaning on the deck with one hand firmly held by Alex she might have fallen from her chair. She swung in her seat, tearing herself free, and staggered to her feet, trying to reach into the monitor. Paul the technician was confused, concerned for his expensive equipment. 'Would you mind, can I ask you not to put your fingers on the screens, please?'

'Paul, can you give us a moment, please?'

Paul rose, uncertain whether to stay or go.

'Two minutes, Paul, please. Just wait outside and I'll give you a shout.'

The young operator slouched from the room, leaving Kurtiz leaning over the deck, heaving, tears flooding down her cheeks.

Alex stood slowly, and hesitantly wrapped his arms around her. 'There are one or two close-ups, far better images of the same girl. Another day, a different demonstration. Always in Paris. I was alerted to the fact that it could be your daughter when I caught her in a less crowded sequence. We shot her, this same young woman, a day or two after the events, placing a biro in the hand of one of the figures on a frieze at the base of the monument. I recognized her from the photographs in the newspaper cuttings I kept after Lizzie went missing. I went back through all my rushes, the stock for this film, spent days looking for shots of her. I wanted to see whether any of it led me closer, to an address in Paris, a shot of her exiting an apartment, or ... before I contacted you. Can you handle watching these moments?'

She nodded, eyes closed tight, blind.

'It's Lizzie, right? I wished to God I'd noticed it was her when we were in situ shooting. We could have asked her to give us an interview. Played for time while I called you over.'

Kurtiz let out a sound. A strangled cry. Yes, she was certain of it. No, no, she couldn't be sure. The girl had grown, matured, was not little Lizzie. No longer little Lizzie. She had to call Oliver. But not yet. Not yet.

'You want a coffee, a break first, or shall I call Paul back in?'

Four years. She slumped back into the chair and let her head fall into her arms resting on the deck. More emotions than she would ever have been able to identify rushed through her. A floodgate. Immense relief that Lizzie was alive. Fear that it wasn't Lizzie. Just another twenty-year-old who resembled her daughter. A doppelgänger. A picture that told a lie. That promised false hope. Yet another fickle trail. How many times had she rushed full-on at some unsuspecting young woman, mistakenly believing it was Lizzie? Anger that her daughter could have lived on while she and Oliver had died inside, withered through loss, given up on so many areas of their lives, grieved and blamed and grown embittered, and had murdered whatever might have been saved of their marriage. Oliver's drinking and despair . . .

'I never accepted that she was dead,' she mumbled to herself. She had clutched to that sliver of hope against all odds. 'Prove it to me, prove she is dead,' she had screamed then at poor destroyed Oliver, at the DI who had informed them in their living room that the investigation was being closed, that they were calling off the search for Eliza Ross. 'There is no body. You have failed to find her. Nothing to say she is not still alive.'

And now here was Lizzie. In Paris. How old was this footage? Eight months?

'I want to see everything, Alex. Every frame of footage, all that has been edited out, anything that might include her.'

'The rushes, the full stock, are in Paris at my post-production base.'

'I have to go to Paris. We have to find her.'

'I'll take you back with me.'

'No.' She shook her head. 'Show me what you have in the cut film first.'

Oliver was foul when she broke the news to him that evening, raging with tears and hot blame. 'You have to stop this, KZ. Why do you torment us both with these imaginary sightings of her? It's not the first time. Let it be, for God's sake.' He had not touched a drop of alcohol for more than a year. Kurtiz had taken him to AA; after several attempts he had enlisted, and this time had not fallen off the wagon. His career was still in tatters but he hoped to be employed again at some point. He lived alone, hermit-like, in the downstairs rooms of their Tufnell Park family home, which had recently been put on the market. It was for sale because Kurtiz had moved out and because neither of them could bear to climb the stairs. Part of Kurtiz could not abide the reality of selling it, of letting it go, to strip it and tear herself away from the last vestiges of Lizzie and her overcrowded but now tidied room.

Alex was returning to Paris. He invited Kurtiz to stay that night with him at the Groucho Club, but she refused him even though it pained her to do so. Seeing him in the flesh again had revitalized love and longing. She was starved of love. Starved of her daughter's affection, starved of the caress of a man. Even so, her place was with Oliver, in spite of his ill-tempered reception of the news. Their challenge now – all over again – was to find Lizzie.

She spent that night in Tufnell Park in the spare room upstairs. The room Oliver had slept in during the later stages of their marriage. It had been closed for a couple of years and smelt mouldy. The sheets, the bedding had a dampness about them that seemed to seep into her organs. She lay awake listening to Oliver downstairs, shuffling to and fro from the living area, through the sliding doors, down two steps to the kitchen at the back of the house, rattling cups and saucers, with the television turned up too loud. Was he going deaf or was he trying to send a message upstairs to her?

She stayed because she feared this information might

set him back, send him to the off-licence. Tears fell in slow drops. Could those pictures from Paris really be Lizzie? Their vanished child? When, how, why had she gone to Paris? She had possessed her own passport, but it hadn't been found in her room. Hadn't it been handed to the police? Obviously not. It was all such a fractured jumble of memories she could no longer be sure of anything except that, for a decade and a half, Lizzie had been their joy and then she was no more.

The following morning Kurtiz took the tube with Oliver into town to the editing suites where Alex had left a copy of the unfinished film with Paul. She glanced at her watch. Alex would be boarding the Eurostar by now. She chose the same seat as the day before, and she and Oliver watched the film side by side in silence. Afterwards they thanked Paul for his time and left the building without a word. They chose a coffee bar in Old Compton Street. Over cups of frothy cappuccino decorated with hearts, Oliver apologized to his wife, which took her aback.

'What do you think?' she asked him.

He nodded. 'It's Lizzie. Yes. I think so. She's grown. Lovely, eh?'

'Lizzie in Paris. I wonder since when.'

Lizzie and Alex both in Paris.

'Of course,' continued Oliver, 'there's nothing to say she's still there now. Perhaps she travelled over in January with a group of demonstrators.'

'Why would she?'

'Why not?'

'Should we be talking to Interpol?'

'I'm going to Paris,' he said. Kurtiz hadn't seen that steely determination in his features for several years. 'You'll have to lend me the money, though.'

She more or less supported him as it was. He received unemployment benefit and a small amount of disability aid. How to explain the trauma he had suffered over the loss of his only child? Mental issues had been recorded on his medical file.

'Then we should both go.'

He was adamant. It was an opportunity for him to –

'To what?'

To make good. Prove himself. Find his daughter, re-unite the family. Explain to his girl that there was a future for the three of them if she agreed to come home. They'd make it up to her.

Kurtiz listened, feeling choked, as though her Adam's apple had turned to stone. Then she wrapped her hands gently over Oliver's, enveloping them, recalling how Alex had made the same gesture with her only the day before. 'Oliver,' she whispered, struggling against the roar of the espresso machine at the bar behind them. Like the rumbling of a steam engine, it promised to drown her words. Vital words. 'Oliver, even if we find Lizzie . . .'

'*When*. I will find her, KZ, if it's the last thing I do . . .'

She waited, dreading her own words. Softly she must step. 'It won't heal our marriage, Oliver. You cannot promise that to Lizzie.'

He broke his hands away from under hers, an explosion of raised fingers as his spoon went spinning to the tiled floor. He spread his hands wide, palms down, clutching at the table's edge. His face in profile now, eyes looking from right to left, fighting back tears. His pain knifed her in the gut, eviscerating her. This was her Oliver. Grey-haired, features striated by grief and booze and disappointment. 'Give me another chance,' he mumbled, through trembling lips, incapable of looking at her full on. 'I'm getting it back together, Kurtiz, you can see that I am. I'll be back at work before you know it, stepping into Oliver Reed's shoes . . .'

She smiled, lowered her eyes, frowned. What could she say?

'One brief affair. If you hadn't gone away . . .'

'Oliver. It's not about Jenny Fox.'

'Then what? What?'

She loved someone else. But even that was not it, for she had denied herself that love. Oliver and she . . . their time had been and gone. Circumstances had burned it out, trodden their love, the passion, into the ground, strangled the joy out of it.

'Don't just discard me, Kurtiz. I'm doing all I can.' He turned back to her. Bloodshot eyes from sleeplessness and hopelessness were pleading to her. Maps drawn with red-coloured crayons. His *cri de coeur.*

She felt a shot of anger. She had to defend herself or she would be sucked back into his self-pity. Why could he not accept the reality? Their marriage was over. Over.

He tightened, hardening, sensing that this was not going his way. They read each other intimately, every gesture, every flicker of the eye. 'Well, then, will you buy the ticket and fund me a hotel? Any fucking little hole will do – I don't give a shit. You think I like asking?

Begging you? But I will look for her. I won't stop till I find her. I'll walk every street, knock at every door. Ask your director friend to print me up some of those stills. They'll be the most recent pictures we have.'

Director friend? Did Oliver know? Impossible. There was nothing to know, except a profound sense of loss for a choice that had never been made, a direction not taken.

Cautiously she opened her mouth, measuring her words, stumbling, attempting not to tread on his volatility, his fragility. 'Oliver, it's a terrific idea . . .'

'But?'

'I think . . . it probably needs a professional team, a –'

'They never fucking found her the first time, remember? Two years dragging us through the papers, dredging our guts up along with shit from the riverbeds. Do you want to go through all that again? Remember it, KZ, remember? Journalists like hyenas at the gate. You couldn't piss without them flashing their cameras.'

She raised an index finger to her lips and bit at her nail, chewing deeper, touching skin, close to blood. Yes, she remembered. How could anyone bury that hell?

'I *need* you to let me do this, Kurtiz. On my own.' He buried his forefinger and thumb into the sockets of his eyes, as though attempting to gouge out the memories.

She was reluctant, hesitating, oscillating. Was Oliver sufficiently responsible for this? Was he up to such a tremendous responsibility? No, no. Of course he wasn't, but she couldn't drop everything and go. She was the financial pillar. One of them had to stay, work. But were they going to allow even a slim possibility of reconnecting with Lizzie slip like water through their fingers? If she rejigged her working programme she could spend weekends with him, or visit for short bursts of time. Might that work? 'What say we put it in the hands of the French police?'

'Oh, yeah?' He was tugging at a stray strand of cotton on the cuff of his shirtsleeve.

She wanted to tell him to leave it alone, to snip it with a pair of scissors later or he'd unravel it into a hole, but she forced herself not to mother him. Not to know best. 'Oliver, realistically, you don't speak more than a smattering of French. And who do you know in Paris? Who could you call on?'

'And who do *you* know?'

Alex, she thought silently.

'You have a career. Get back to work, KZ. Be the breadwinner, as you never stop reminding me. Bankroll me and leave me to find Lizzie. Buy me a ticket on a train for tomorrow and I'll be ready to go.'

Did she have the right to refuse him this chance of winning back his dignity, of restoration? Of a shot at success? If nothing came of it, what was the worst that could happen? She'd be poorer and Oliver, though disheartened, could be proud that he had given it his best shot.

And if he failed and, through despondency or loneliness in a foreign city, took to the bottle again? She blue-pencilled this immediately from her thoughts. Give the poor guy some credit, cut him some slack, a yard of freeway, she warned herself. You're too tough on him.

That afternoon Kurtiz requested Paul to blow up and print every still from the film that contained even a distant outline, a poor quality, rough-grain facsimile of Lizzie. These she slid into a large envelope. She then located an English-speaking Alcoholics Anonymous meeting house in Paris near the small hotel she had booked for Oliver, guaranteeing it for a month with a credit card. She drew out cash and changed it into euros, sufficient to keep him fed and accommodated for a month. Then she booked him on a late-morning Eurostar. They ate a light evening meal together at their erstwhile family home, during which she made him promise that if he found even the slightest trace or clue he would be in touch. 'Don't go silent on me, Oliver. Give me your word on that.'

The ticket was trembling between his fingers. He coughed and stared at it while digging in his jacket pocket for his passport.

'Got everything?' She bit her tongue for asking such a question. They were both skittishly nervous. Strangers bumping against one another. Strangers who knew everything about each other, every sinkhole, every hairline crack, yet nothing any more.

Kurtiz had accompanied Oliver on the tube to St Pancras, insisted upon it, to give him, she assured herself, a parting hug. Her guts were straining at the prospect of leaving him alone, of leaving him with the responsibility of locating their daughter, who was probably not even living in France. As an afterthought, she scribbled down on the back of an old receipt Alex's Paris studio number. Oliver stared at it as though it were a curse, then stuffed it into the back pocket of his jeans without a word. 'I'll call you,' he said, and stepped away from her, his rucksack bobbing against his spine.

She waited, watching his retreating figure, ready to wave, to give him a thumbs-up, until he was out of sight, but he didn't look back.

When he was through the barrier gates and out of sight, she wandered away, found a bar and bought herself a glass of wine.

Good luck, Oliver.

Because what if, just suppose . . . What if Oliver should chance upon that needle in the haystack? She almost choked contemplating such a far-fetched possibility.

To stand face to face with Lizzie, gazing into those troubled hazel eyes again after four interminable years. It was worth the gamble, worth every cent. Just as long as Oliver could hold himself together.

One text message to confirm that he had arrived safely was all the feedback Kurtiz received from him. Frustrated by his silence, towards the end of the first week she rang the *pension* where she had booked his room.

'He's absent at present,' the receptionist informed her. 'He spends most of his days out in the city, sightseeing, I suppose, rarely returning before late at night.'

At least he was still there. 'Is he . . . keeping well?'

There was a silence, a hesitation. '*Mais oui, pourquoi pas*? Is there a problem?'

'No, no, of course not. Please ask him to make contact with me when he has a moment. Kurtiz Ross, he has the number.'

*

Towards the final days of Oliver's month-long stay in Paris, there had been no sightings of Lizzie, not even a hope less slender than a butterfly's wing. Lizzie was not in Paris. Or if she was, how were they ever to make contact with her? Kurtiz had spent hours on Twitter and Facebook trying to track down variations of names their daughter might be using, but eventually she gave up: the possibilities were too vast. The net they were casting spread to all seas. The reality was that if Lizzie had managed to get herself to Paris, she could be anywhere by now. The venture was hopeless. It was time to recall Oliver, bring him home before his positive energy curdled and turned against him.

Until, out of the blue, he called her. Late one evening, she was sitting alone in her studio flat, feet up on the sofa, drinking tea after a long day on location. Earlier that evening, before boiling the kettle, Kurtiz had made a provisional booking date for the return half on Oliver's ticket. She dreaded being the one to call it off. To close the door on their hope.

'I might have located her.'

'What? Where? Is Lizzie in Paris?'

'If she's in Paris, or even close to the city, I know where I'll find her.'

Kurtiz paused, stalling her excitement. 'You mean you haven't located her. Or you have?'

'Eagles of Death Metal are playing a gig at the Bataclan concert hall in mid-November. There are still a few seats available.'

Both Oliver and Lizzie were huge fans. Kurtiz knew that. These American rock performers were one of the groups that had bonded father and teenage daughter.

They had made pilgrimages to concerts together in the past. The posters were still up on Lizzie's walls. Of course she might have grown out of the band. But it was possible, just possible, that this was the needle in the haystack they had been digging for.

'If she's still in Paris, Oliver.'

'We have no better options. I'm going online to buy a ticket.'

'Make it two, Oliver. I want to be there.'

'No.'

'What do you mean *no*?'

'Let me do this, KZ. If she sees two of us there, it will freak her. She knows that style of music is not your thing. Seeing me there wouldn't make her run. She could believe it's a coincidence. I can talk to her, gain her confidence –'

'Then I'll be nearby, waiting in a bistro for you both after the concert.'

Kurtiz booked Oliver's ticket to the concert and made a reservation for herself, a weekend train ticket from London to Paris. She checked her diary. She was booked for the whole of that November week. She'd have to travel over early on the Friday evening and back on Sunday night. Maybe – who knows, who knows? – they might all three travel back to London together on the Sunday . . .

How could she or he have predicted that it would end in bloodshed? That it could cost Oliver his life?

Paris, November 2015

Kurtiz was woken by the sound of a door opening. Oliver's room. She sat upright, bleary-eyed and woozy. The intern moved towards her and lifted his arm to stay her. 'There's no change.' He spoke softly, adept at causing no alarm.

'May I go in?' She rose to her feet.

'Not just yet. The surgeon will be along to see you as soon as he has an opportunity. It's been a hellish night.'

'What time is it?' Her words were slurred, like those of a stroke victim. Her head was beating as though a sledgehammer were trying to free itself from within.

'Almost nine.'

'Morning or evening?'

'Sunday morning.' He smiled kindly, his eyes crinkling. 'It's been a long night for everyone.'

Kurtiz nodded and stepped backwards, bumping clumsily into the chairs, keen to release the fellow, to allow him to get a break, a few hours' sleep, if that was possible. She rubbed vigorously at her back. It was aching, screaming at her to lie down, to get some decent sleep. Her head was swimming, giddy, almost incoherent with tiredness, but under no circumstances was she leaving here. Not until she knew what the future held for Oliver.

*

She was seated at his bedside. The intern had returned and had provided her with a travel pack similar to those handed out on planes. He pointed her to a public shower room so she had, thankfully, been able to clean her teeth and have a brisk wash. Fresh clothes would be a luxury but she wasn't ready to leave yet. A clock on the wall above the door in the clinically white room read ten minutes to eleven. Oliver's condition had marginally weakened but not drastically so. The surgeon, a tawny-skinned man in his fifties, had passed by but provided her with scarce new information. 'We are fighting for him,' was his consolation. The man looked as wrecked as she was. 'There are many dead,' he muttered, moving along. 'Many to heal.' She thought he might be a Muslim. Not a good moment to be a Muslim in Paris. The extremists would point the finger against all Muslims, use this as a call for border control, clampdown . . .

The door was ajar. The surgeon had left it so, whether on purpose or out of forgetfulness she did not know. But it was open when the shadow of a figure crossed the tiled floor, lit by the bleak sunlight that shone in from the wintry morning beyond the window. Church bells were ringing somewhere in the distance in a sombre, muted way. An appeal to God against all the vileness that had befallen the city overnight. She expected the arrival at the door to be the nurse, who had provided her with several cups of sweet tea, back to adjust the machines or generally make gestures of support and healing. But it was a woman in civvies. A young woman, sandy-hair cropped short, in jeans, pale blue Converse sneakers and navy duffel coat. She hovered by the door frame, neither in nor out. Her eyes were red and swollen. Her nose a ball of pink, reindeer-like.

Kurtiz lifted her head and stared at her, coltish, pretty. Her innards sank, seeming to implode. This wasn't a dream, was it? A delirium seeded by sleep deprivation? She choked on her breath. No words would form, except 'You've cut your hair . . .'

The girl raised a hand to her head as though to remind herself of the fact. She remained by the door.

'Lizzie? Lizzie.' Kurtiz staggered clumsily to her feet, almost disconnecting a pair of transparent plastic tubes bubbling with liquids, slung low from a machine about the size of a fridge. She balanced herself against the bed, trying not to disturb Oliver.

Lizzie took one step into the room, holding onto the door frame. 'I saw your tweet. I went to the Bataclan this morning,' she said. 'Dad's name was on a list. I've been to three other hospitals. I was beginning to fear he was dead.'

Kurtiz swung back towards the figure lying uncon- scious in the bed, as though to confirm that there was someone there. That 'Dad' was here with her. With *them*. Disbelieving, incredulous, stunned, she was at a loss. She wanted to run across the room and hug the almost unrec- ognizable and yet completely recognizable pretty young woman who had just crept back into their lives. This was her Lizzie, yet not her at all. Someone more formed, with features well defined, less plump, not that she had been plump. Never plump, but adolescent. Yes, adolescent. Freckles? Yes, still freckles all across her nose like fallen petals. Oh, Lizzie . . . She must not weep. Her daughter might leave, might run in horror at any expressions of emotion. Lizzie always hated the way she and Oliver had argued. 'Out-loud emotions', she had called them.

Kurtiz had now reached the foot of the bed. The iron bedstead at the base was her security, her support. She was overwhelmed, inadequate. The moment she had played in her mind over and over and over was here and she had no idea how to be, to behave, to respond. 'Lizzie,' she repeated. 'Thank God.'

Lizzie stepped into the room and moved towards her mother, who was now sobbing, unable to control herself. Overtired, a pathetic sight, she was wrung out. 'I'm just tired,' she bumbled. 'It's been a long . . .'

A long four years.

Lizzie lifted her arms and hooked them round her mother's neck.

The smell of her daughter. A floral scent. Fresh. Shampoo or cologne, or perhaps soap. Yes, it might be soap. Floris, perhaps. Mint? Lily? What did it matter? Was she beginning to hallucinate? Was there no Lizzie? A mirage born of exhaustion, trauma. But yes, yes. The strength, reality of those arms about her, of that soft flesh. The strap of a watch that scuffed her ear. Was it the elegant little Marc Jacobs Oliver had given to her for her thirteenth birthday, the one she had so loved that Kurtiz had to fight with her to take it off when she climbed into the bath? *I have celebrated every birthday since you left. Celebrated and mourned.* The wool of the duffel coat rubbed against her cheeks.

Kurtiz, whose arms had been hanging, dangling like becalmed flags, reached for Lizzie's waist with her fingertips, her hands, rediscovering the reality of her. Gingerly, she slid her arms round Lizzie's midriff. So slender. And they held one another, squeezing tight, tighter, tighter still, locked about one another, sinking into one another, faces hidden, bodies gently swaying, like twin trees in the breeze. Or Christmas baubles when Oliver had tapped gently at the tip of a needled branch with his finger, causing the golden glass balls to swing in little circles and the child Lizzie had pointed and chortled with glee. Remember? Remember, Lizzie, all those pine-scented Christmases? Remember us, Mum and Dad?

They held each other for a sustained, unbroken amount of time, a perfect amount of time. Drinking in the heat of the other. The heartbeat. Kurtiz felt warmth and then dampness on her neck. The tear-stained snout of Lizzie pressed into the curvature of her neck. And the cold fear within her that, over time, had frozen solid and closed down her heart began to dissolve, to dissipate. Some inner part of herself that had lived on the outer limit for four years – four years and five months and twelve days – was unfolding, uncoiling. An iceberg melting. A part of her that had stood rooted at the brink, wavering at the edge of the cliff, staring outwards towards a vast blank horizon, seeking, seeking, waiting, was being released. Never knowing where you were, whether you were in pain. That knife's edge, serrated uncertainty. The desperation and the impotence. The calling into an empty void with never a response. Lizzie, are you alive or dead?

And here you are, alive and in my arms.

'Lizzie,' she whispered, saliva bubbling about her lips. 'Sweet, sweet Lizzie.'

*

Kurtiz hauled a second chair to the right side of the bed where she had been seated and they settled together, holding hands.

'How bad is he?'

Kurtiz glanced towards her husband's immobile form and shook her head.

Lizzie rose from the chair frequently, restlessly, placing the back of her fingers against Oliver's forehead as though anointing him. He was so pale, his flesh so cool. It was the machines more than the man that confirmed to them he was still living. Staff came and went. Lizzie popped out to a bakery and returned with ham and cheese baguettes and steaming paper cups of milky coffee with oodles of sugar. The bread tasted like old socks in Kurtiz's mouth but the hot drink did her a power of good, restoring some lost energy. Her phone was out of battery again, but it hardly mattered. They were here together, the three of them. She asked no questions of her daughter. All that could, would, come later. It was Oliver who needed them now. They took turns to sit up close to him and talk to him, sing or hum to him – he had always proclaimed so proudly, his chest puffed out, what a fine singing voice Lizzie had – reminding him of their voices, the timbre, the cadence, attempting to penetrate the black depths of his coma.

They took it in turns to stretch their legs, to pace the sickly green lino-tiled corridors, eavesdropping, without wanting to, on the tears and distress of others: their shocked gasps, their paralysed silences. The hours of expectancy, hospital clocks ticking, sweet papers unfurling, noses being blown. The wheeling of gurneys. Rubber against lino. Footsteps against lino. Walking sticks against lino.

One of them stayed put while the other popped out for a pee, a breather, fresh cold air inhaled through an upstairs corridor window. One woman always at Oliver's side, stroking his arm, caressing his face, whispering to him in the hope that the words were connecting with him, deep and lost to them, wherever he was.

Lizzie disappeared around nine on the Sunday evening, promising to be back as soon as she had 'sorted out a couple of matters'.

'Where are you going?' It was the first question Kurtiz had asked her. 'Can't you stay?' The second. 'It won't be long now, I fear.' They both knew he was slipping away. The bank of ICU machines had been giving off bleeps and high-pitched warning signals since some time after the delivery rounds of the hospital dinners. An infection had set in. The visits of staff had become more frequent. An extra pipe and two cables were bled into his arm. A ventilator to assist his breathing was wheeled in and switched on. The surgeon had popped his head round the door, his thoughts clearly occupied with those whose lives he could save. 'These are critical hours,' he explained. 'If he can keep fighting on through the night . . . His liver is a little weak.'

Lizzie kissed her father on the upper bridge of his nose above the mask he had now been fitted with and hovered at his elbow for some time. She was battling tears, torn in different directions. 'I have to go,' she murmured, to her mother, eventually. 'I'll be back.'

Kurtiz clung to her hand. 'Promise me,' she begged. 'Don't disappear on me, Lizzie. I need you.' Lizzie nodded, stuffing her purse and car keys into her duffel-coat pocket. Lizzie, driving. Does she have her own car? Kurtiz was asking herself, as she watched her grown-up daughter disappear beyond the room. What could be so urgent that she must leave at this critical hour? She lifted her feet and rested them on the chair Lizzie had been sitting in. She was so tired there were no words left to describe her exhaustion.

She was desperately in need of a wash, to lie down, eat something warm and nourishing, although the thought of food made her queasy. Her bones were aching, her head sounding a relentless rhythm. This was her third all-nighter.

In spite of the discomfort, she eventually fell asleep. She was 'flumped', as Lizzie used to say.

A high-pitched unremitting warning bell woke her, but it was the arrest of the heart monitor that was the cold slap in the face. It had gone quiet. The machine had *stopped*. The incessant beep-beep-beep that had been present and continuous ever since and before her arrival was silent. She shot to her feet, brutally awake. 'Oliver!' Should she call someone? She took his limp hand. Oh, God, *no*. She made for the door but before she had reached it a nurse, a short podgy female in white, a member of the night staff she had not encountered before, was in the room. She shoved past Kurtiz and was at the bedside, flicking and monitoring, twisting and flicking. Until she let her arms fall to her sides and everything – this hive of mechanical activity – became inactive. All in one fell swoop, it seemed, although in reality probably not. The nurse was Polish. She spoke in ill-fitting French. The syllables, consonants, meaning a jumble, not quite as they should be. Lumpish. Clumsy. Kurtiz was considering her words and did not fully register the content of the sentence. 'I have to up bring the doctor. Is dead somehow your spouse.'

Is dead somehow?

Really dead? Or only partially gone, still in a coma with all external signs of one who is dead? The hardware, all appliances, had been closed down. Two further members of staff were sweeping through the doorway. The bed would need to be vacated, one explained to her, in a matter-of-fact fashion. It was urgently required. The capital was in a state of emergency. All of which Kurtiz had forgotten while cocooned here in the midst of a life-and-death scenario. Theirs was one couple's story among dozens and dozens. All across the City of Light, now shrouded in a flying grey cloak of mourning and grief and maximum-security issues, other couples, parents, lovers, brothers, sisters, best friends, single mothers, such as the woman she had bumped into outside the Bataclan who had been waiting for her only son who had saved hard to pay for his ticket, all were in the same boat. Praying for a miracle: a loved one's life.

What was the latest toll on the shootings and massacres?

She flopped back against the wall at the foot of the room, watching as an empty trolley was wheeled in. Bedding was peeled back. Hands slid beneath Oliver's legs and back and her husband was lifted, poised above it.

'Wait,' she called.

Three heads turned towards her.

'Could I have . . . Please, give me just a few moments with him before you take him away.'

His body was repositioned on the mattress. 'Of course.' The staff disappeared. A marching crocodile well trained in discretion. Kurtiz walked to Oliver's side. His eyes were closed, though his mouth was still open and slack. Already his flesh appeared to be yellowing, or was it the light? Already his cheeks were growing cold. So swiftly life turns its back. Nothing more to be done here. Move on. She stared at the body that had already begun to lose all traces of the stunningly handsome young Oliver, Oliver the Romantic. Instead, she looked upon a sad and haggard middle-aged man, a disappointed actor. Mid-forties. The man whose heart had broken and never repaired when he lost his only daughter. 'Lizzie's back, Oliver.'

What a waste. What a fucking waste. And what timing!

'I'm sorry for everything,' she said to him, confident that he was hearing her. 'You know you found her, don't you? *You* led our Lizzie back to us. *You* were spot on about coming here to Paris. And *you* were brave. In spite of everything, we loved one another and we had many good times together, didn't we? I'll always cherish them.' She bent and kissed his head. Cold as stone. '"Goodnight, sweet prince; And flights of angels sing thee to thy rest." Goodnight, Oliver, until we meet again.'

The trio of staff were standing in the corridor chatting softly, heads lowered, when she left the white room. She nodded her gratitude and made her way through the sliding doors. It could have been a lifetime ago she had first stepped that way, now moving in the opposite direction.

She took the lift down to Reception. There was nothing more to be done here. A receptionist, not the lady with the bird's-nest hair, another looking business-like with a rather grim expression, informed her that she would be required at some point later the following day, in fact today, Monday, to present herself at the mortuary to officially identify Oliver.

'Which one? Can you give me the address?'

'We will notify you later in the morning. There are so few vacancies at present.'

A queue for the mortuaries.

'Do we have your phone number?'

She nodded and signed a form, and after a short wait was handed a large envelope. Oliver's few possessions: his watch, telephone, wallet, driver's licence, passport. Did she want Mr Ross's clothes? She shook her head.

Could this be true, the reality? She was leaving here with an envelope, and that was it?

Now what?

She had still not checked into her hotel way across town in the eighth *arrondissement* but in any case the booking was two days old.

Was it too early for the Métro? No Métro. Although now that it was Monday the trains would be running again. As would the taxis.

The British press would be all over the story once Oliver's name was made public. Somehow she had to contact Lizzie but she had no idea where her daughter had slipped away to. It was as though her appearance had been of a phantom, which was nonsense, of course. Lizzie was here in Paris somewhere. Should she hang out here in the reception area and wait for her? She simply couldn't face it. No more hours waiting on an unrelenting bench. Or might . . . ? She swung back to the desk, clutching the brown envelope.

'Was there something else, Madame Ross?'

'My daughter. She came to visit her father before he – he passed away.'

'Yes?'

'Might she have shown you some identification? Given you an address, or . . . ?'

'Because she wasn't Mr Ross's next of kin, she would have been obliged to sign in, yes, and, due to the high alert, she would have been obliged to furnish identification. Yes.'

'Did she give you an address? Her name is Lizzie. Lizzie Ross.'

The woman drew a ledger towards her and turned back the pages. The number of visitors over the last twenty-four hours was staggering. 'Can you remember approximately what time it was when she arrived?'

Kurtiz puzzled. She wasn't entirely sure she could even identify the day of the week, let alone . . . 'Wait. I glanced at the clock. It was close to midday yesterday.' The doctor had been in. 'It could have been a few hours later, of course.'

The woman ran a finger down lists and lists of signatures. She was shaking her head. 'No one by that name presented herself here.'

'Might she have signed in elsewhere, at another entrance?'

'There is no other way through. Look there. We have rigged up emergency security machines, a directive from the Presidency yesterday.' Kurtiz glanced to her right where a scanner and two armed, beefy security men had appeared at some point since she and Marguerite had first turned up.

'She would have been obliged to pass by screening.'

'May I have a quick look myself?'

The woman lifted her arms, shocked, affronted. 'It's rather irregular.'

'I'll recognize her handwriting.' Would she?

The ledger was pushed towards her and Kurtiz riffled back and forth, attempting to find approximately the hour at which to begin her search. There was no one whose initials tallied with Lizzie's. At 2:21 p.m., she came across L. Dubois. There was a certain similarity in the handwriting, the squiggle of the 'L'. At a stretch. She traced a horizontal line to the address and read 32b, avenue Haute Seine in the sixteenth. Some distance across town in a very elegant suburb. Could this be Lizzie, living under a different name? Quick as she could before the receptionist lost patience, begging a sheet of paper, she jotted L. Dubois' details down. Then, before reluctantly handing back the ledger, she skipped back and forth one more time. And it caught her eye, the last name on a page that had curled over – someone perhaps had leaned on the paper and partially hidden this entrant: 3:44 p.m., *Lizzie Ross*, inhabiting a far less salubrious district on the edge of town. She turned her sheet of paper over and briskly copied down Lizzie's address. *'Merci. Merci.'* And she was at the door, then swinging full circle back to the desk for the last time. 'If my daughter returns, tell her, please, that I have gone to her home and will wait for her there.'

The flat was on the fourth floor. The lift was out of order. Kurtiz began to climb an echoing stairwell in a hastily constructed modern block situated beyond the city limits in a *banlieu*, the outer suburbs, which skirted Paris's southlands.

The fabric of the building was scruffy but moderately clean. She passed a woman descending as she was going up. The young woman was negotiating a pram, clunking one wheel onto a concrete step followed by another. Empty shopping baskets hung from the handles. Behind her, gripping her overcoat, was a second child, a small girl.

'*Bonjour.*'

'*Bonjour.*'

The premises lacked all adornment, were functional, little else. Coming at her from various directions as she huffed her way up the winding, solid flights was the echoing ring of raised voices and infants bawling. Was this really where her Lizzie lived? Was she unemployed, down on her luck? Desperate? It stung Kurtiz to think of her in dire straits. Three doors leading to separate apartments on the fourth-floor landing. The surroundings smelt of tomcat. Or nappies. Urine. Strong bitter coffee, ripe cheese and spices. Checking her sheet of paper, she pressed the bell that married with the address she had for Lizzie. There was no name. It sounded a high-pitched growl. No response. She rang again, tapping her booted foot. It was Monday. Was her daughter out at work? Or at a place of study? University? Should she leave a message? Tear off the scruffy edge of her sheet of paper?

Just as she was about to do that, having lowered herself to her haunches to dig through her bag, placed on the floor, for a pen, a neighbouring door opened. A woman put her head out. She was North African, holding a small child in her arms, a lighter-skinned child, who was possibly three or four. '*Bonjour.* Are you looking for Lizzie?' From behind her, the yelling and squabbling of a pack of infants. A dog elsewhere began to bark. Kurtiz winced. Tiredness made her nerves raw, on edge. She nodded. 'Does she live here?'

'She's gone to the hospital. Her father was caught up in that appalling attack at the Bataclan. I'm minding Laurence for her till she gets back.'

Kurtiz stared in incredulity. 'Is this Laurence?'

The woman nodded. 'Cute, eh? Very bright.'

'Shall I take him?'

The woman glared at her with dark suspicious eyes.

'I'm L-Lizzie's mother.'

It made no impact. If anything, the woman marginally retreated into her own nest, back beyond danger, clutching and protecting the light-haired boy, who was pulling and twisting at his carer's dark hair. He had the same smudge of freckles, like a miniature cluster of fallen leaves, across his nose and cheekbones, the same as Lizzie had displayed when she was small. The likeness, now Kurtiz focused on the child's features, was quite remarkable. Who was the father? Was he still present in their lives? Considering this address, Kurtiz guessed not. Her daughter must be surviving as a single parent. Unless she and Laurence's father were both struggling students. Had Lizzie run away because she was pregnant? Terrified of confronting her mother and father? How old was little Laurence? She recalled her own mother's reaction when she was carrying Lizzie. She wanted to be understanding, embracing.

'I'd like to wait, if I may. Unless you have a telephone number for her?' And then she cursed, remembering that her wretched phone had still not been charged.

Laurence's keeper lifted a dark hand, displaying elegant fingers with many slender silver rings set beneath pale, manicured nails. She made a gesture, common in Arab countries, which Kurtiz remembered from her travels with Alex: fingers upright, pushing the palm of her hand repeatedly at the air as if to say, 'Patience. Wait one moment.' She disappeared with Laurence and returned moments later without him, brandishing a key. 'Do you want to wait for her in her own flat?' She offered it to Kurtiz, who was confused as to whether Lizzie would object to this intrusion.

Tentatively, she stepped forward and accepted it. 'Shall I take Laurence too? Sit with him for a while?'

The neighbour seemed less concerned about the handing over of a key than the release of the child. 'I was about to prepare him a snack. He eats like a horse.' She grinned. 'Let yourself in, and when he's cleaned up, I'll knock. I'm Fatima, by the way.'

Lizzie's flat was a large studio, offering a sofa as pull-out bed. It smelt, surprisingly, of exotic plants like an aromatherapy clinic. The kitchen and bathroom were both off the main room. The plain cream walls were decorated with dozens of sketches of 'Mummy' with exceedingly large hands, cheesy smile and keyboard teeth. Lower down the cupboard a few others of a long-haired 'Daddy'. To her surprise, there were also several newspaper clippings of her own work. Most were from French newspapers such as *Le Monde*, but one or two were from British press. A method of staying in touch? Had Lizzie kept track of her parents from a distance? Had she missed them both? There were so many questions she was dying to ask. Kurtiz folded herself onto the sofa bed, shrugged off her boots and was overwhelmed by tiredness, by depression and, yet, here she was in Lizzie's little home. A part of her was being pieced back together. Atoms that had been split apart four years ago were reconnecting. Oliver lost, but Lizzie gained. Lizzie and Laurence. She would take them home, gather them up like a hen. Sweep them into her embrace. Care for them. Make sure the boy was given a decent education. Everything would be resolved . . .

And then she was asleep, twisted by sadness and grief and yet, in some curious fashion, safely berthed. A lonely odyssey reaching its final act. Or she prayed so.

When the key was slipped into the lock and the front door opened, the movements of people approaching did not rouse her. It was the plump hand with small fingers on her shoulder, shaking her rather too energetically that roused her.

'Hey, missus woman.'

Her eyes opened. Bleary. A headache as though she had been slugged. Grief washed through her, like a sharp-edged knife filleting her flesh. Something had been taken away from her. Where was she? Who was this pulling at her, chivvying her to get to her feet?

'What?'

A face beamed into hers. Lizzie. Little Lizzie. Big eyes, like a bumble bee's, penetrating hers. Their baby girl. Oliver must be in the kitchen making coffee. Yes, she could smell that comforting aroma. She lifted her head and faced the boy glaring at her. 'Mummy says you're her mummy.'

'What?' Kurtiz struggled to a sitting position. Where was Lizzie?

'I'm making coffee.' The response came as though her question had been telepathically received.

'Can I help?'

'No, sit still and make yourself acquainted with Laurence. Clever of you to track us down.'

Well, it has taken close to five years, thought Kurtiz, wryly, but she didn't say a word.

After the coffee, which was very necessary and very delicious, Lizzie pulled the sofa out into a bed and the three of them boarded it, making themselves intimate and comfortable. An island sanctuary for a trio of Ross family survivors.

'We're on a ship, we're sailing far away.' Laurence should have gone to playschool several hours ago but it was fine that he would give it a miss today. His grandfather had gone to Heaven and he had the right to stay at home and be with his mummy, Lizzie explained to him, to look after her and his grand-mummy because they were sad. The boy looked from one woman to the other and nodded gravely, awed by such responsibility. He was a good-natured child and easy of manner, even if Kurtiz could not quite take in that he was her own flesh and blood.

She was bursting with questions, with reproaches too, which she was biting back. They needed time. Time to get the feel of one another. Time for her to comprehend that Lizzie was a fully-functioning mother in her own right. A woman, even if twenty years old and Kurtiz would have preferred to relegate her to the character of little Lizzie, to give herself the opportunity to catch up on the lost years. She wept then for Oliver, who would never know the answers, would never journey with them into that lost past through the narrated tales from Lizzie's recent history. The gaps. For the first time in years, she longed for the touch of him, his gentleness. He, whom she had once loved so unconditionally.

'Who is Laurence's father?' Kurtiz allowed herself that one question.

Lizzie pouted, considering. 'His name's Pascal.' She pulled her legs out from under her and slid from the sofa, walking away from their mattress retreat and a potential inquisition.

'Pascal who? What does he do?' Kurtiz drilled into her daughter's back, rising, stalking as she quizzed.

'A French guy I met back in England.' They were in the cabin kitchen now, squashed alongside one another, bumping arms, treading on toes, an awkward jig, about to prepare a pasta lunch for the three of them. 'That boy has such an appetite.' Lizzie grinned, bright face full of pride and maternal affection.

Kurtiz remembered then the empty container for the Dutch cap she had discovered among the chaos in Lizzie's room. Sixteen years old. She bit her tongue, reining in the accusations. Had there been many lovers?

Lizzie opened the fridge and drew out a plastic container of shiny vegetables. 'There's wine, if you fancy a glass?'

Kurtiz shook her head. 'I'd keel over.' She was exploding with a hunger to understand, to fill in the harrowing years. She knew the moment was inappropriate – they were not yet ready to plumb the deep and murky waters: they needed to take it gently, coast, get to know one another again. Or so Oliver would have advised, but Oliver was gone, gone, and she could no longer contain herself. A tsunami was rising within her and she was too tired, too fraught and full of pain to contain it. Even if she knew as she opened her mouth that she was digging a wall.

'Why did you go, Lizzie? Why did you leave us?'

Lizzie was reaching for a pan. She paused a moment, then ran it under a tap. 'Mum . . .'

Kurtiz hovered expectantly. 'Why, Lizzie?'

'These are big questions, Mum. Can we just take it a step at a time, please?'

She rubbed at her head, scratched. 'What about Pascal? Is he from a good family? How did he manage to smuggle you out of England?'

Lizzie diced steadfastly: spring onions and roundish red onions, readying them for gently heating in a pan of olive oil and herbs. If there were tears, blame the onions.

'There was no trace of you anywhere. The police dragged the Thames. Did you know that? While the press camped outside our front door, they searched the parks. Areas of Hampstead Heath were cordoned off. They notified all the borders, gave orders to report your attempted exit if you were identified.'

Lizzie reached for a sprig of parsley sitting upright in a glass on the window ledge, beyond which was a grey skyline, brushing Kurtiz's shoulder as she did so. She returned to the small wooden board and began to chop fast, leaving a film of damp green on her fingertips. 'I didn't know all that. We didn't look at the news. I was too . . . I met Pascal at a rock concert.'

Kurtiz considered this. She wanted more. 'Did you

leave England immediately? Why didn't you write us a note? Even Marguerite eventually wrote home.'

'Who's Marguerite?'

Kurtiz shook her head. She was getting everything muddled. 'Why did you never call to let us know you were safe and that we could stop breaking our hearts, that we no longer needed to turn our guts inside out, we could sleep in peace? Oliver would've cut back on the booze. I could've returned to work. I could've . . .' She sighed at all the could-haves. Better not to go there. 'Did Pascal never express a desire to meet the parents of the girl he was about to abscond with?'

The oil splashed and sizzled noisily as Lizzie threw in two thinly sliced tomatoes, then wafered another, as though she was murdering it.

'Why, Lizzie? Please try to explain to me why you just disappeared and broke our hearts.'

'Mum, I'm really sorry for the pain I caused you both, honestly I am, but . . . please, can we leave all this for now and discuss it another time? Please?'

'I think you have no idea.'

Lizzie lifted a hand and took her mother's arm. There were smudges of black mascara beneath her eyes. 'Mum, we can talk about it, all of it, in minute detail if you really want to, I promise, but not now. Let's just . . . You know, Dad's dead.'

Kurtiz opened her mouth, like an expiring fish, then closed it. She nodded grudgingly, glancing about her, unlocking and shutting cupboard doors until she slid down a trio of plain white IKEA dinner plates from one of the shelves. 'Knives and forks?'

'In that top drawer there next to the fridge. No, the next one along. Yes, there. Mum?'

'Yes?'

'I'm glad you're here. And, more than anything in the world, I wish Dad was here too, that . . . that I'd had a chance to say goodbye to him. There were things he and I needed to clear up, but I can't talk about the past, not yet. It's like a knot inside me. Can you understand that?'

Could she understand it? She lifted forks and knives onto the plates. 'Not really, Lizzie, no, I can't, but I'll try not to ask. I just don't . . . no, I feel . . . lost. I'll get on with this.'

Kurtiz carried the cutlery and plates through to the main room, grabbing salt and pepper pots as she went, breathing deeply as she laid the small pine table for three. Laurence was still on the outstretched sofa. He was humming softly, deep in conversation with a lurid green crocodile. It had yellow eyes and immense off-white woollen teeth, dirtied by wear and tear. 'Are you hungry, Laurence?' Kurtiz tossed the question to him with a natural intimacy, as though she was in the habit of speaking regularly to her grandson. *Grandson.* She would get used to this. Yes, she was already relishing their future together.

'Of course,' he replied, without turning to her. 'Tick-Tock is hungry too, but he wants another chunk of Captain Hook.'

All at once, a flood of memories rushed at her and froze her to the spot. Young Oliver at the foot of Lizzie's bed only a short while after they had bought the house in Tufnell Park. Lizzie had been allocated her own room for the first time. Her own shelf of books to discover. Pop-up books, novels, illustrated compendiums of fairy tales.

Oliver, reading to her from *Peter Pan*, acting out the characters with booming melodramatic delight, the sword fights, Wendy's flight through the night skies to Neverland, the terrifying Captain Hook shadowed by Tick-Tock, both of whom had caused Lizzie to giggle and scream and wriggle dementedly beneath the bedclothes for fear the crocodile would come and snap off her fingers, begging Daddy to save her. Great bear hugs from Daddy. Laughter and happiness exuding from Mummy until Wendy and the boys had been safely tucked into their beds.

She would take the Tufnell Park house off the market. Lizzie, Laurence and she could decorate it, install themselves there, begin a new London life together. Her mind threw up an image of Alex, and for one moment she felt the familiar grab on her heart. She had learned to be without him for so long now . . . Lizzie and Laurence must take priority. She couldn't leave them here to struggle. She must help them. Or was she jumping the gun?

'Mum, are you laying the table or not? The pasta's almost ready.'

'When all this is over, Lizzie, when we've got Dad home and . . . and the funeral's behind us, I'll help you find an excellent school for Laurence. We can share Tufnell Park. I haven't been living there for a while, but we can do it up together, divide it into two flats. Or if you prefer I'll stay in my studio in Covent Garden and you can have the house . . .'

Lizzie was standing at the door to the kitchen, clutching a steaming bowl of spaghetti with two big wooden spoons sticking out of it. Her hair was damp and awry, her cheeks pink and glistening with perspiration. There were blotches of oil or cooking ingredients on her pale blue T-shirt. She looked shocked.

'What? What is it, Lizzie?'

'Mum, please don't start getting ideas.'

'Ideas?'

'I'm not coming *home*. This is my home.'

Kurtiz frowned. 'But, Lizzie, it's not very comfortable here. All those flights of stairs to manage with a small child . . . I want to give you the opportunity to –'

'This isn't about what *you* want. This is about Laurence and me and Pascal. Jesus, Mum.' Both women glanced surreptitiously towards the boy, who was tussling with the crocodile now wrapped in bedding. 'Laurence's dad is here, and I love him and France. I'm at home here. Okay, I'm not crazy about this flat, I know it's grotty, but when we can we'll sort something better out.'

'We'll sell the house and you can have –'

'Mum, we're fine and we're happy . . . and I don't have to listen to screaming rows every five minutes.'

'Oh, God, Lizzie, I'm so sorry.'

'Don't be. It's the past.'

'Is that why you left?'

'I've just asked that we don't discuss any of this now. There's too much to say and I cannot face a row. Not now. Let's eat. Laurence, *viens, mon petit.*' She had crossed to the table and laid the bowl down at its clothed centre and seated herself in front of it, spooning a giant helping onto her son's plate while Kurtiz, chastened, stood over her, mortified by how clumsy, how clodhopping and thoughtless, she had been.

*

After lunch, Lizzie at the wheel of a dull-silver VW Polo that surely would not pass its MOT in England, so shabby was it, they lurched away from the kerbside.

They drove on in silence to the mortuary. There, on her own while her daughter and grandson waited outside in the parked car, Kurtiz officially identified Oliver. Life had rarely felt bleaker. She would get the necessary paperwork behind her, organize the repatriation of Oliver's body to the UK and take the earliest available Eurostar to London. She needed time. Her entire life had been turned on its head over one weekend. But what was to be done about her daughter and grandson? She couldn't just abandon them to the life they were leading.

Resettled in the passenger seat, she begged one more favour of Lizzie. To stop at a florist, then drive her to rue de Charonne where her luggage was still stored with Marguerite, whose house number she could no longer recall. She would recognize the building and the doorbell when she arrived. Lizzie acquiesced, though the mood between them had grown sombre, monosyllabic. Laurence, oblivious to the darkening atmosphere, chuntered happily to himself on the rear seat or sat bolt upright and demanded answers to unlikely questions.

'Mummy, has your mummy arrived by stork like Auntie Fatima's two new babies? Or is she too big for the stork to carry in his mouth?'

He was the saving grace of the day, and Kurtiz could not deny that he gave every indication of being a well-balanced happy child and that Lizzie was a thoughtful, caring mother. She was trying so hard to refrain from begging Lizzie to return to London with her. She wanted more than anything in the world for them all to be together. Was this so unrealistic? Was she being selfish? Now that she had found Lizzie, the prospect of being so far from her, across the Channel, wrenched at her.

It cut her deeply to realize that she and Oliver had driven their daughter away. That she had not been present when Lizzie needed her. Was she being hard on herself? In the early years of her marriage she had been a devoted mother, had sacrificed her own career for Lizzie and Lizzie's upbringing. As she would do today, if she had the time over again.

If she had those years over again . . .

Rue de Charonne was, of course, closed off, its heart still in tatters, bits of debris not yet hauled away. She had almost forgotten where this hellish long weekend had begun. Lizzie pulled up in a narrow street off Bastille. 'You'll have to walk it from here, I'm afraid.'

'That's fine.' Kurtiz managed a smile but made no move to open the car door. The scarlet amaryllis she had bought for Marguerite was perched on her lap.

'Mummy, I want to wee.'

'We'll find you somewhere in a minute, Laurence.'

'Will I see you again before I leave?' Kurtiz asked, a catch in her throat.

'Sure, why wouldn't you?'

'That night when you asked me not to leave, not to . . .'

Lizzie lifted her hand off the steering wheel, pulled off her gloves, wiped her cheek, tears, and reached across to her mother's arm. 'We both have regrets, Mum. I'm sorry too, sorry I'll never make it up to Dad, never hold him tight again . . . The last time I saw him . . . you were gone, working somewhere or other . . . I begged you not to go. I was pregnant and getting pretty freaked and Dad was . . . was . . .'

'Was what?'

'I yelled at him that I hated him. I screamed and screamed at him. It was the morning of the day I left, the last time I ever saw him.' Lizzie slapped at the steering wheel with her gloves.

'Mummy, I need to wee now.'

'We're going, Laurence. Hold on tight for a few more minutes.'

'Why were you screaming at him? Because I wasn't there for you to vent your anger?'

'Partly that.'

'Because he was having an affair with Angie's mum?'

'You knew?'

'Not till later. Much later. I don't blame him.'

'I'd like you to meet Pascal.'

'Tick-Tock needs to wee too. He says he can't hold on a few more minutes.'

'Right, let's find a loo for Tick-Tock.'

Kurtiz began to smile. 'Why don't you come up? I'm sure the old lady won't mind. She's a sweet soul. Rather lonely, I think. I'd like to meet Pascal. Let's do that soon.'

'WEE, PLEASE.'

It was beginning to spit rain. Lizzie locked the car, pulled up the hood on Laurence's two-sizes-too-large duffel coat, which swamped his face.

'I can't see! Tick-Tock can't see.'

'Give me Tick-Tock.'

'No.'

The three of them set off together, walking side by side the short distance to 71 rue de Charonne. Laurence took Kurtiz's hand as though it were the most natural act in the world. The other arm was clutching his toy. Marguerite answered the intercom, which was a relief because Kurtiz had not taken a phone number from her and it had only now occurred to her that the guardian of her cases might be out.

'Second floor, remember?'

'I've got my daughter and – and my handsome grandson with me, if that's not a problem?'

'Your daughter! How splendid. I'll put the kettle on.'

When the lift reached the second floor, Marguerite was waiting at the open door, smiling her irresistible smile, all dolled up and looking as though she was about to step out on stage. She accepted the potted plant with the grace of a leading lady receiving an opening-night bouquet. Laurence, with his dog-eared woollen croc, bolted from between their legs and barged into the apartment, yelling, *'Pipi!'* Marguerite followed him swiftly and manoeuvred him, hopping, to the bathroom.

'Laurence, take your hood down and let's get your coat off.' Lizzie scooted fast on the tail of her son, closing the door behind them, leaving Kurtiz and Marguerite alone.

'You found her? I've very pleased. I've been concerned. How's your husband?' She placed the plant on the sideboard.

Kurtiz lowered her head and knocked her boot against the edge of a chair.

'I'm so . . .' Marguerite nodded gravely. 'I know the depth of that loss.'

'We'd been separated for a while . . . but still . . .'

'Oh, I see. I hadn't understood.'

'No, I . . . wasn't very forthcoming.'

Lizzie stepped from the bathroom, clutching Laurence's coat. 'Sorry about that.' She held out a hand to introduce herself to their hostess. 'I'm a great admirer of your work, Madame Courtenay,' she said.

Marguerite clasped both her hands in front of her and squeezed in her shoulders, like a child who had been awarded a top prize.

Kurtiz was taken aback at the discovery of Lizzie's acquaintance with the actress's work.

Lizzie sat in one of the chairs. A kettle in the kitchen was hissing. 'Oh, what have you seen?' begged Marguerite, ignoring the boiling water.

'When I first arrived in Paris about four years ago, you were playing at the Odéon Theatre. The Nurse in . . .'

'*Roméo et Juliette. Mais, oui*, that's right. You saw that?'

'I thought you were wonderful. I've been a fan ever since. Afterwards, I looked out for your earlier films. I found a couple on DVD and bought them. I particularly remember a cameo role from the fifties. You were awesome.'

'*Death in the City*?'

'Yes, that's the one. You played the wicked blonde.'

Marguerite swung triumphantly towards Kurtiz. 'That's the film I made just after Charlie died. It opened up many opportunities for me.'

'My father's also an . . . he was . . . an actor. I love the theatre.' The mention of Oliver broke the upbeat mood, reminding them why they were all there.

'And what do you do, Lizzie? Are you also connected to the arts?'

Lizzie shook her head. 'No, I work in a shop but I'm doing a course in aromatherapy.'

'How fascinating.'

'I love plants, nature.'

Already Marguerite had learned more than Kurtiz had.

Laurence had entered the room and slid himself coyly behind his grandmother, burying his face in the warm curve of her thighs. Tick-Tock was his camouflage. 'Shall I make the tea?' suggested Kurtiz.

'I would have bought a cake, had I known,' replied Marguerite, clearly delighted by the new arrivals.

Kurtiz swung about to release her grandson and present him to their hostess. 'Come on, Laurence, come and say hello. Don't be shy.'

Marguerite, whose attention was caught up with Lizzie, revelling in the compliments, held out a hand to the child. *'Bonjour, Laurence, comment vas-tu?'* then turned her head to take him in for the first time. She frowned. And fell silent.

Kurtiz looked from one to the other. 'Are you unwell, Marguerite?'

The old woman appeared to be in a daze, fixated on Laurence, who began wriggling with embarrassment. She was staring at him as though she was in the presence of a ghost.

Laurence watched her mistrustfully, quizzically.

She cupped both hands over her mouth. 'I need a large whisky,' she muttered.

Marguerite and Kurtiz had left the blue Mercedes in the *parking* beneath the old port in Cannes. It was just a few steps to the town hall.

'I still remember the way.' Marguerite giggled, striding with the vigour of one half her age. 'Here,' she called. Kurtiz, who had been at the wheel all the way from Paris, was bringing up the rear. Marguerite, arm outstretched, was pointing triumphantly. 'Here, right here, this is the spot where the photograph was taken. Oh, a lifetime ago.'

She lifted the picture and studied it. Kurtiz, at her side now, was peering over her shoulder. Two young people standing before the town hall in Cannes, flanked by towering palm trees and a couple of carelessly parked post-war Nimbus motorbikes. The man, much taller than his young bride, was laughing. His face was tanned, full of joy, of victory, of optimism. He was a man in love. His left arm was wrapped round the shoulders of the nineteen-year-old Marguerite, hugging her tightly towards him, pulling her into the bow of his torso while her body language suggested shyness, a certain reticence.

Charlie Gilliard, newly married man, was wearing a

striped suit with wide lapels and a tie with a large knot, shoes polished to a spit, smartly attired for this auspicious occasion. His hair was combed neat and flat with a side parting. It was an image of its time. Late forties. A black-and-white photograph, tightly posed for the camera. Kurtiz stared at it. 'May I?'

Her travelling companion handed it to her. She flipped it over and read: *Our wedding day, Cannes, March 1948.* Kurtiz's mother, Roberta, would have been a month off five years old when this photograph was taken in 1948, when this upbeat ceremony had taken place. Roberta, the daughter of Doris Sprigley and Robert Lord. Kurtiz recalled her dear nan's voice, and her kindness when she was pregnant with Lizzie. The fifty-pound gift, and 'bring her to see her great-grandma as soon as you can'.

'You can surely see why Laurence reminds me of him? He's Charlie's spitting image.' Marguerite was tottering, on heels, backwards, taking in the town, the changes, calling up a world of memories. 'Of course, you can't get a real sense of his profile from this angle, and the photograph lacks colour. Even so, you can see how the land had coloured his skin. The white of his teeth, the gleam in his eye. He was very handsome, was my Charlie.'

What were the chances? Kurtiz had been asking herself that question for months now, eyes fixed on the stranger caught in a moment of time, a moment in another's life. His life, long before hers had been conceived. The man whom Doris had never stopped loving, just as Marguerite had held him in her heart.

Marguerite leaned in and took hold of the photo,

repossessing it, gazing into it, studying it, as though her whole life had been captured in that moment.

'1953, he died. He was thirty-three years old.' She sighed. 'We had a blissful six years together, five of them as a married couple up on his hill near Plascassier. I say *his* hill, but it was ours. The theatre has been my universe for decades, but if I had to pick five years out of my life to live again, to cherish, it would be those rural days hidden in the hills with Charlie. I loved him deeply and felt safe and cared for by him. In spite of Leo Katsidis' treatment of me – well, today, if he behaved towards a budding young actress with such disrespect, she would bloody well take him to court. In spite of that frightful day, I still harboured dreams of working in the cinema. Katsidis humiliated me. He ground my confidence into the soles of my shoes and destroyed my ability to enjoy a healthy sexual relationship, but he never killed my vitality, my spirit. It took a beating, I'll admit, but my drive and zest for life were resurrected. Thanks to Charlie.

'When I married him, I fretted that I wouldn't be able to make marriage work, that I wouldn't be able to give myself to him, to trust any man again. But that perfumed hillside and Charlie's loyal gentle heart healed me. It was five years before I even thought of going back to the studios in Nice.'

'What was Charlie's reaction to the news?'

Marguerite Courtenay sighed, slipped off one of her shoes and scratched her leg with the sole of her foot. 'Well, he died before I played in another film. He wasn't so happy about the idea. He expressed his disappointment, begged me to be content with all that we were building together, but he didn't stop me. He never tried to stand in my way. After he was gone – what bleak, lonely days they were – I was incapable of farming the land alone. I hadn't the strength or skills. Acting was my only path forward. There, I could bury my grief in worlds of make-believe.'

They were walking slowly side by side towards the old port. Kurtiz was asking herself whether her dear old nan would have liked this part of the world.

'Did Charlie allude to his family life back in England?'

'Very little. He was cagey about his past. Well, most of us were back then. We were all hiding our scars of war. He did tell me that his father was an apple farmer from Kent.'

Kurtiz smiled, inexplicably warmed by the idea that her grandfather – could she genuinely think of this man with another name as her grandfather? – had been generous of spirit and not controlling. And it was a fact that Laurence, little Laurence, four generations later, was his identical twin. Or as alike as a small boy and a man can be. There was no doubting the bloodline.

Charlie Gilliard was Robert Lord. He had survived the war, somehow or other.

'It hasn't changed much, this town hall, certainly from the exterior. I can still remember the room, down a corridor to the left, where the registrar conducted the ceremony. It was all over in fifteen minutes.'

'Shall we grab a quick coffee and be on our way? It's close to midday. They'll be waiting.'

*

Kurtiz was at the wheel again. The old Mercedes chugged and spluttered as they ascended the winding lanes and made their way out of Cannes to Grasse, then followed the signs to Plascassier.

'All these roundabouts. They weren't here in my day. Good Lord, such construction. No wonder I have been inundated with letters from estate agents begging me to part with the land. In the early days I refused to sell to spite that horrid agent of ours from the perfume factory, Arnaud. And then I thought, why sell? My career rewarded me well. Dear Henri, my second husband, much older than I, was a very wealthy businessman. I didn't need the money and I enjoyed the idea of the land still being here, of Charlie's flowers growing wild, reseeding themselves year after year. Rather as if Charlie was being born again each spring. No ghastly housing estate erected over them. Wait! Turn right here and then first left. Good Lord, I remember it as though it were yesterday, and there should be a gate around five hundred metres on the left.' The car windows were wound down. A breeze was blowing, bringing with it fresh spring scents.

'Ah, smell it, this perfumed land. It's bringing it all back. After this bend, you'll spot the gate.'

As they rounded the corner, a display of balloons of every colour greeted them. A forest of happiness. Lined up along the wall, on lengths of string held fast to the surface with stones. Each balloon defying gravity, bobbing, dancing in the spring sunshine. Each sported a handwritten greeting.

'Welcome!'

'You are home again!'

'Bonjour, Marguerite!'

'Hello, Flower Lady!'

'Ha-ha! Look at this!' exclaimed the old woman, lifting her feet and clapping her hands.

Kurtiz smiled. Typical Lizzie to make Marguerite's homecoming into a party.

'They've done some serious work here. It must have been exceedingly overgrown.'

'Lizzie told me Pascal has bought a chainsaw and cutter.'

From the sale of Tufnell Park, Kurtiz had given them the money for the agricultural machinery. The gate was open, awaiting them. She hooted and pulled in, parking beneath an almond tree, which might have been planted by Charlie. Or not. She had still not finally decided whether she should think of the man whose land she was now walking across as her grandfather or someone she didn't know whose name had been Charlie and, like Oliver, hated violence and had died too young.

An arrow on a stick painted with pale purple letters read: 'Half a House Standing: This Way. Welcome.'

They strode in the direction indicated, stepping down a steep slope, looking out for Lizzie and little Laurence, but it was another who came into view first. Long dark hair so curled it looked like ringlets. Lean. There was something of the shepherd about him. *'Bonjour.'* He waved.

'Who's that?' whispered Marguerite, a little alarmed. 'I might need you to give me your arm. I'm not the girl I once was for these inclines. I need a pair of striped espadrilles,' she laughed, 'to negotiate the brambles and tree roots.'

Kurtiz was waving. 'It's Pascal. Laurence and . . .' Her sentence hung in the air. She'd leave them to reveal the surprise. 'He's Laurence's father.'

'Handsome,' cooed Marguerite.

They descended the hill slowly, taking care that Marguerite didn't twist an ankle. As they reached the shallow where the land bottomed out, Lizzie came striding into view. She was wearing a floral peasant dress. From beneath the bosom it hung loose, flowing like that of a young hippie from the sixties. A flower girl. How such an image suited her. Pascal took Marguerite by the hand, after introductions, hugs and kisses, and led her in a stately fashion to what remained of the house, to where, alongside it, there was the broken structure of a patio sheltered by strong stately almond trees in young fruit. Above, wooden beams, old railway sleepers, had been hollowed by woodworm and years of no protection against the weather. 'I'll soon fix these,' Pascal assured them.

Marguerite was turning in circles, her fingers pressed against her cheeks. 'Oh, we breakfasted here . . . We ate by candlelight just there. Charlie built this terrace. I handed him the nails!'

Laurence was hanging onto Marguerite's skirt, expressing a desire to dance with her. Pascal was arriving from the makeshift kitchen with chilled champagne. 'We invested in a mini fridge after I got the electricity reconnected.'

Lizzie was padding to and fro, placing dishes of crisps and olives on the table, securing paper napkins beneath them so they wouldn't be blown away in any wind. 'I need to sit down,' she panted, hands pressed against her extended belly. Each had been given a glass. Nothing as elegant as champagne flutes: a pack of half a dozen wine glasses from one of the supermarkets in Grasse. Pascal was pouring bubbly into them, moving from one woman to the next. Lizzie held her hand over her glass. 'I'll have juice.'

'Just a sip, *chérie,* to toast and welcome our very generous guests.'

She conceded with a grin. She'd caught the sun, Kurtiz noticed. It suited her. Freckles aplenty.

Pascal raised his glass into the space between them all. 'To Marguerite,' he said, 'for her gift to us. For offering us a future beyond our wildest dreams, and to my, erm, not quite mother-in-law, Kurtiz, for being, well, very cool.'

'And to Charlie,' butted in Lizzie.

'Charlie? Yes, my dear, dear Charlie, whose dream this was.'

'And the next Charlie. Charles Oliver. I know the name's a bit sentimental but it's what we want to do, isn't it, Pascal?'

'To Oliver and Charlie and Charles Oliver.' Kurtiz smiled.

'Congratulations,' whooped Marguerite.

The young man, more herdsman than urban suit, nodded and wrapped his arm round Lizzie's shoulders. 'To those who have passed this way and those still to make an entrance.'

'I have one request, if I may,' begged Marguerite. 'Have a large family. Don't stop at two. As many children as you can afford. I will help you. Keep livestock. Grow flowers. Fields and fields of flowers. And you will bless the memory of my Charlie, if you do.'

'Lizzie's going to turn this into an organic flower holding. Organic essences and essential oils. It's the new Grasse, Marguerite. And while she works, I'll rebuild the old property and bring up the children. We'll do you and Charlie proud, I promise.'

'Can I dance with you, please, Granny Marguerite — now, please?' Laurence was still tugging at her skirt.

Marguerite placed her champagne on the table and led the small boy beyond the patio, stepping down on to flat grassland. She began to sing. A song from long, long ago. 'La Mer' . . . '"The sea with summer clouds dancing . . ."' She took Laurence by the hand. Boy and octogenarian began to swing, to pirouette, twist and turn, giggling, swaying, while the others looked on, sipping their champagne and then, before long, they were all singing: *'La mer . . . la mer . . .'*

'We're at the sea, Charlie,' chanted the old woman, clapping and laughing with tears rolling down her face.

'Thanks for all this, Mum, from the bottom of my heart,' croaked Lizzie, raising her glass. 'It's Heaven, beyond dreams.'

'It's Marguerite you have to thank for signing this place over to you. My contribution is minor by comparison.'

'You'll come and spend heaps of time with us here, won't you?'

Kurtiz looked her daughter full in the face. What a truly lovely young woman she had blossomed into. 'Is that what you want, really?'

Lizzie, big-bellied, embraced her mother. 'I want us to get to know one another and be friends, women and mothers.'

Kurtiz, a little overwhelmed, turned her head and watched as the old woman and the small boy pranced and spun, twirling in ever-widening, giddying circles, heads thrown back with euphoric joy. She lifted her camera and took a series of shots. Then, the camera hanging loose on its strap, Kurtiz continued to gaze upon them. In her loose white silk blouse, with her arms outstretched and her white crinkly hair lifting in time to the movement of her body, Marguerite looked to Kurtiz like a bird taking flight. A dove of peace. Or perhaps she was an angel. Yes. Lizzie and Laurence's and, soon-to-be, Charles Oliver's very own guardian angel.

'Marguerite slipped into our lives on the very darkest of nights, and has never left us since.' Kurtiz's train of thought was broken by Pascal leaning into her and topping up her glass. '*Merci* for everything, *ma belle-mere*. I am so happy that you and Lizzie are reunited.'

Mother and daughter smiled. They raised and clinked glasses. 'Thank you, Pascal, and here's to absent friends.' At that moment, a message on Kurtiz's iPhone buzzed in her pocket.

Paris, May 2016

Kurtiz was outside at a table on the pavement. It faced across the busy street towards the Théâtre Marigny in the gardens of the Champs-Élysées. She was idly watching the philatelists, a gathering of old-timers in rimless spectacles and cardigans, shuffling to and fro on the park benches, huddled over thick, scruffy albums of stamps, discussing, assessing, exchanging. A curious passion, but each to his own. The restaurant where she was waiting was Le Berkeley. The chestnuts in the public park would soon be in full flower. The citizens of Paris were slowly venturing out from beneath the unthinkable to return to the cafés along the boulevards, to stroll or cycle the canals, congregating in public places after a winter of mourning behind closed doors. They were welcoming the season, warming to spring, its buds bursting with new life. The healing power of regeneration. The light of the sun, and the iron resolve that gave no one the right to scotch the way they chose to live. *La Liberté*.

She had flown north with Marguerite that morning after a magical and therapeutic week *en famille* in the south. Oliver would have enjoyed it too. He would have made a perfect grandfather. The powder blue Mercedes had remained with the youngsters on the farm. Marguerite had offered Kurtiz a bed in rue de Charonne for tonight, which she had declined. She had an appointment. But, first, she paid a visit, a pilgrimage to the Bataclan, closed for the foreseeable future, to lay flowers and a candle. She wept there for Oliver, who was at rest now in England, and for all those whose lives had been taken during that abominable night.

She was early. Impatient. She flicked her phone and read her messages. One, undeleted, from a week back: *I should have mentioned it when we met in London last year. Ann and I filed for divorce. It would be very fine to see you again when you are next in Paris. I miss you, Alex.*

Another, just in from Lizzie: *We love you, Ma. Come and spend some summer hols with us. Come for my twenty-first birthday. Stay for Bastille Day. We can go to the beach. Celebrate together. Be with us for the birth of Charles Oliver. Merci pour tout. L & P xx*

She typed her response. *Dearest L & P, Merci for the invitation. Would love to. Let's check dates soon. Love and peace to you both, Mum xx* As she was pressing *send*, a shadow came to rest above her, blocking out the late-afternoon light. 'You waiting for someone?'

She lifted her head, recognizing the voice, and beamed a smile. He was looking fit. 'No,' she replied, 'not any more.'

An Air France *pochette* landed on the table beside her elbow. She frowned. 'I seem to remember that, once upon a time, I promised you a visit to a vineyard. No war zones. Two tickets from Charles de Gaulle to San Francisco. Ten days in the Napa Valley. I thought we'd have dinner tonight across the road at Le Petit Palais – I booked for eight – and we'll leave bright and early in the morning for the airport from my place. What do you say?'

She dithered, delayed. Uncertain.

He sat opposite, cupped her hands. 'Time to begin to live again, Kurtiz. Because if you don't, they win. They'll have murdered you too.'

She nodded, loss surging, and then, slowly, her features relaxed, releasing hesitant laughter. Time to begin to live again? 'Is that an order, Alex?'

Je suis Charlie

In memory of all those innocents who lost
their lives or were injured in the Paris atrocities
of November 2015. Each had a family.
Every one of those families has stories to tell,
losses to learn to live with.

Nous sommes tous Charlie

Acknowledgements

I watched the unfolding of the November 2015 Paris atrocities on television with my mother. Rarely has any news coverage so affected me. To such an extent that I put aside the book I was just beginning to write and settled to this one, *The Lost Girl*. Three months later, my mother died. It was a grim and very challenging period for me. Through all that followed a group of friends stepped forward and held me up. In no particular order, Pat Lancaster, Rhona Wells, Chris Brown, Marie McCormack, Mae Garrod, Mary and Tom Alexander, Jane Bullock, Bridget Anderson and Liz Gruenstern. Thank you, each of you, profoundly. Your friendship has been healing.

My husband, Michel Noll, has proved yet again that he is a man in a million. I am very fortunate to have him at my side. *Mille mercis, mon cher.*

Frank Barrett and Wendy Driver at *Mail on Sunday Travel* for fine parties and professional support.

Jonathan Lloyd, my terrific agent and friend: you have been such a hugely supportive voice throughout the process of bringing this book to publication. Hugs and thank you, kind sir. At Curtis Brown literacy agency, I want to say a big thank you to the super girls Alice Lutyens, Lucia Walker and Melissa Pimental, and to Mark Williams and Katherine Andrews in accounts.

Lastly, top billing for the fine team at Michael Joseph,

Penguin, that has made the book possible. I want to thank my editor, publishing director Maxine Hitchcock, for her continuous support and editorial feedback that has helped make the difference. A big thank you, Maxine. Matilda McDonald and Nick Lowndes for allowing the everyday publishing details to be smooth and hassle-free. A big shout out to my meticulous copy-editor, Hazel Orme – it's great to work with you again – to Claire Bush for marketing magic; to Sarah Harwood, my new publicity gal; and to Cliona Lewis, Penguin Ireland.

Thank you.

Reading Group Discussion Points

1. Discuss the parallels between the present-day story and the storyline set in post-war France.

2. What do you think Marguerite's primary role in this story was? How do you think life changed her between her youth and the present day?

3. Discuss the theme of motherhood in the story. Do you think Kurtiz was a good mother to Lizzie – both in the past and when they reunite? And what do you think Charlie's one-time girl-friend Doris, as a single mother in the post-war era, would have had to cope with?

4. Do you think anyone was to blame for the end of Kurtiz and Oliver's relationship? What role did Alex and Lizzie each play?

5. How did Charlie's desertion shape your opinion of him? Did you sympathize, or not? Discuss whether he should have returned to his family after Churchill's amnesty was announced.

6. Why do you think Lizzie felt she had to leave her parents without warning? Do you think it was linked to Kurtiz's absence, or not?

7. Discuss the significance of the flower farm in Provence. What does it mean to the different women in the story?

8. Is there more than one 'lost girl' in this story? Who, besides Lizzie, could the title apply to?